BURI SECRETS

An absolutely gripping crime mystery with a massive twist

ADAM LYNDON

Detective Rutherford Barnes Mysteries Book 3

Joffe Books, London
www.joffebooks.com

First published in Great Britain in 2023

Cover art by The Brewster Project

ISBN: 978-1-80405-873-2

AUTHOR'S NOTE

This book is set in 2010, and uses a fictitious version of the direct entry recruitment programme — actually introduced in England and Wales in 2013 — as a notional plot device. In addition, the 2017 demolition of Eastbourne's Arndale Centre and many of the buildings in Gildredge Road has been brought forward several years, as has the closure of the police station in Grove Road. The author begs the reader's kind indulgence with these historical liberties.

PROLOGUE

January, 2010

"You don't have to do this, you know."

"I know."

"You don't have to hurt me."

Barnes frowned.

"Who said anything about hurting you?"

He looked down at the man sitting opposite him. The stone room was so large that the light from the weak overhead bulb failed to reach the corners, and the man was sitting on the only piece of furniture in it. If you could call a rotted kitchen chair a piece of furniture, that is.

Barnes looked at his watch.

"It won't be long now."

"Can I have a cigarette?"

Barnes obliged; then, without giving it too much thought, took one for himself. He was a lifelong non-smoker, but something told him he could do with it. It seemed apt somehow. He didn't cough, but the nicotine hit his bloodstream like a thousand espressos and made his vision swim.

Barnes looked at his watch again.

"They're coming."

Kevin Bridger hung his head. His breath jetted from his nostrils in heavy, frozen spurts. The cigarette had relaxed him, but not much.

"I know."

"We don't have long. All I need is a name. Just a name, and this will all be over."

"I . . . I can't."

Barnes exhaled smoke through his nose.

* * *

Outside, in the cut-glass moonlight, eleven men and one woman shuffled along the perimeter of the barn in formation, the only sound the chorus of their nervous breathing and their kit rattling against their bodies. They didn't bounce as they moved, but absorbed the weight at their hips so as to keep their weapons steady. Their breath vapours rose up in the freezing air as if from a herd of corralled, impatient cattle.

The firs looming up along the treeline were black against the cloudless sky; a wedge of moon burned against the opaque navy blanket.

The armed officers split in a "V" and spread out around the barn.

"All units, Team Leader. Confirm when in position." The voice crackled with static in the earpieces of the officers as they fanned out.

"Yankee-One, Team Leader. Confirm in position black side. No stimulus stronghold."

"Yankee-Two, confirm same."

"Yankee-Three, in position red side."

"Yankee-Four, confirm same."

"Yankee-Five, containment on, green side. No stimulus."

"Yankee-Six, same."

"Team Leader, all units, stand by, hold position." Team Leader spoke into his collar mic. "Silver, from Team Leader. Containment is on. No stimulus from the stronghold. Myself and Yankee-Seven are holding white side with FSD. Permission to move to limited entry."

"Silver, received. Permission granted. Proceed to limited entry."

The team leader and the two armed officers comprising call sign Yankee-Seven, with a firearms support dog behind them, moved quietly up to the door of the barn. Despite years of neglect, it was still reasonably solid, the wood cut in typical two-piece stable style. Team Leader didn't mind that. It meant the lower portion would offer another layer of protection, even if it wouldn't stop a bullet.

* * *

"They're here," Barnes said. "Apparently we were quite convincing."

Kevin didn't raise his head. For a moment, Barnes thought he was crying.

"Come on, Kevin."

"Do you have any idea what it's like, man? I'm in permanent exile. I don't do for you, I end up in prison for the rest of my life. I don't do for them, I end up buried in an allotment. What kind of life is that?"

"I've looked after you, haven't I? I haven't *tied* you to that chair. You've earned a living, like anybody else. It isn't my fault you chose to stick all that money in your arm."

"Maybe one of these days I'll OD. Then none of you fuckers can have me."

"That's no way to talk, is it?" Barnes said, dropping the foul-tasting cigarette on the cold stone ground. "All you have to give me is the name."

"They'll kill me."

"Two words. And I'm gone."

"I can't."

Barnes bent down and gently placed a finger under Kevin's chin, pushing his head up so their eyes met.

"Kevin. Tell me who killed my wife."

Kevin's face contorted in pain.

"I can't tell you. Why are you doing this to me?"

"Look at me, Kevin. We are in an abandoned farmhouse in the middle of nowhere ten miles north of Beachy Head. I'm pretty well off-grid here. I can't even get a phone signal. If you don't tell me, I'll cut you into fish bait long before your crew gets hold of you."

Kevin looked towards the door. It was the only way in or out.

"They'll shoot you."

Barnes straightened up.

"Let's see. I'll count to three."

"Barnes . . ."

"One."

There was the sound of shuffling and low voices on the other side of the barn door. *Not yet, not yet*, Barnes thought.

"Two."

"Come on, please."

"I won't say it came from you. Two and a half."

"Okay, okay. I . . ."

"Three."

"Okay, Jesus, I'll tell you! It was—"

There was an almighty crash, and a line of armed police officers appeared at the door behind a black ballistic shield wall, red laser lines beaming into the darkness, catching the cloud of masonry dust as it floated gently away from the ruined doorframe.

"Armed police! Don't move!"

Barrel-mounted flashlights penetrated the gloom, catching the freezing air and exhaled breath swirling around the doorway of the barn.

"You! In the suit! Standing up!" Team Leader yelled the command from the doorway some twenty feet away, with nothing between them but a spread of barely resilient floorboards.

"I guess that would be me," Barnes said to nobody in particular. He looked down at the trio of red laser dots circling on his chest like mad fireflies.

4

"Put your hands on your head and lace your fingers."

Barnes did as he was told.

"Give me the name, Kevin," Barnes said, looking down at the man in the chair.

"Stop talking! Don't talk to him," Team Leader shouted. "Turn around so your back is to me. Good. Now, nice and slow, walk back to the sound of my voice. Keep walking, keep walking, keep walking . . . No, don't look back. Don't look at me. Just keep walking towards my voice."

The walk felt interminable. Barnes knew there wasn't a single obstacle between him and the door — Kevin's kitchen chair being the only item in the farmhouse — and yet the slow walk felt disorienting. Which, he figured, was sort of the point.

Eventually he got close enough to hear heavy breathing and catch a whiff of aftershave.

"On your knees."

Barnes obeyed. Footsteps moved towards him. A gloved hand took his wrist and pulled it down off his head, then did the same with his other hand. Barnes heard the zip ties go *zzzzzppppptt* around his wrists, then a large boot pushed him between the shoulder blades and he fell forwards onto the dusty floor; without his hands to break the fall, his chest took the brunt of it, and an involuntary grunt escaped him.

"I don't think that was completely necessary," he said to the floorboards, inhaling a load of dust as he did so.

Several pairs of large hands moved up and down his body while he was prone. One shouted, "Clear!" and then another series of footsteps rushed past him in formation to where Kevin was sitting. Neutralise the threat, then deal with the casualty. Not that Kevin was injured, but that wasn't the point. Barnes knew he was just sitting there, head hanging down, contemplating his own personal exile and wondering how his life had arrived at such a binary set of distinctions.

The armed officers fanned out around the farmhouse to search it. It didn't take long. The ceiling had long since collapsed, while the internal partition walls had either fallen or been knocked down, creating one huge stone room with impenetrable dark corners and solid oak beams running across the centre of the structure. It smelled of damp and rotten wood.

Eventually they came back together in the centre of the room, and the tension dissipated a little as they established between them that the only threat was a greying detective inspector eating sawdust off the bone-dry floor.

A couple of paramedics rushed in and covered Kevin Bridger with a space blanket.

"He's not hurt," Barnes called, as two armed cops pulled him into a sitting position. One pulled off his helmet and goggles. He had a square jaw and was greying at the temples. He rubbed the sweat out of his eyes. Team Leader, Barnes presumed.

"What now?" Barnes said.

"Not my call," Team Leader said. "But I imagine PSD will want a word."

They got him to his feet and led him outside. The moon had spread a pale white sheet over the black countryside, and the ground crunched with size-ten boots breaking a film of frost. Barnes shuddered suddenly as they got outside and hit the cold air.

A thin patchwork of clouds overhead began to drift in, and shifted like tectonic plates. Beyond the treeline Barnes could see smudged streaks of rain falling like black ink onto the veil of orange light settled over Eastbourne. Behind him, the shape of the Seven Sisters undulated towards the horizon like a row of black knuckles.

A confederacy of emergency vehicles, parked with no particular care or coordination, surrounded the farmhouse. Two armed officers led him to a carrier and sat him on the metal step below the rear doors, a blue wash strobing off his face, and started milling about.

"Am I under arrest?" Barnes said.

Team Leader eyeballed him.

"These cuffs are biting into my wrist, that's all."

Team Leader sniffed and spat. Barnes watched as Kevin was shuttled out of the farmhouse by the paramedics and led up into the back of the ambulance. Barnes tried to catch his eye, but he was a good fifty feet away, and appeared to only be interested in his shoes anyway.

A bolt of tension suddenly shot through him. Close. He was so *close*. Closer than he'd ever been before. He tried to ignore it. What now? Kevin gets swanned off to a Premier Inn, tells the cops to piss off and ends up back in his bed-sit inside forty-eight hours. Barnes hoped he'd engineered enough of a ruse to give his quarry a bit of top cover. The question now was whether PSD would buy it.

But Barnes wasn't giving up. Not when he was this close to a name.

He just hoped he could get to Kevin before anyone else did.

PART ONE

CHAPTER ONE

February, 2010

The centre of Eastbourne is made up of many grid-like streets, long straight thoroughfares bisecting each other into squares like a lattice waffle, lined on either side by houses like vertebrae. Many of these houses have been converted into flats, with subterranean studios occupying space that might once have been a scullery or servants' quarters or a playroom for rich Victorian children.

This particular basement flat was in Ashford Road, just along from the mainline railway terminus. Two of his men were standing outside it, with — he knew — two more already inside.

Named — as far as he knew — by his Spanish mother after some eighteenth-century forebear or other stationed at a Pennsylvania military fort, Duquesne "Duke" Kenley walked past Junction Road, the square bulk of the abandoned NCP multistorey like a giant black tombstone against the cold indigo sky, and beyond it, patches of waste ground and the wide sprawl of the railway tracks. He passed the zebra crossing opposite the skeletal remnants of the Arndale Centre. There were a couple of Eastbourne & Country Octavias in the taxi rank. Their drivers leaned against them, smoking and talking.

The blade of the knife was as cold as the 3 a.m. morning against the inside of his wrist, his palm sweating slightly on the grip. Adrenaline was causing a feeling like butterflies' wings to beat inside his chest. He swallowed and breathed deeply. A cloud of icy vapour drifted from his mouth into the night.

At the flat, his two men — Blue Ray and Golden Wonder — stepped aside without making eye contact. They had read the knuckle-draggers' manual, of that there was no doubt — leather donkey jackets, tattooed knuckles, shaved heads on bull necks. In half a minute they could see to it that you would never walk normally again, and then go home, watch the darts and sleep soundly.

Kenley was glad they worked for him.

The concrete staircase was steep and narrow, and Kenley had to duck to shoehorn his six-one frame into the space required to descend. The stairs led down to a tiny landing about the size of a coffin, where no light seemed to reach. A window box full of dead weeds was the only concession to homeliness; otherwise, it just felt like being chucked into the bottom of a walled pit at feeding time.

The front door was right underneath the staircase. It was already open, a square of yellow light from inside just about allowing Kenley to pick his way over the step into the narrow hallway.

As he walked inside, he heard nervous chatter and smelled an odour like rancid feet, cigarette smoke and Red Bull.

The front room was to the right of the hallway. It was about the size of a snooker table, with a stolen TV in one corner and an orange sofa that Kevin must have rescued from a fly-tipped pile off the Marsh Road. There were Special Brew cans overflowing with fag ash and carrier bags everywhere containing random electrical accessories. Tubs of emollient cream were stacked in various locations, necessitated as they were by the occupant's rather unpleasant psoriatic condition.

The place was an utter shithole.

Kevin himself was sitting on a wooden chair that had been brought in from the kitchen. There had been no need to tie him to it — he was obviously terrified, and fear had paralysed him. He wore a yellowing vest and boxer shorts and was twisted in the chair as if to preserve his dignity. The red blotches on his shoulders and thighs were angry and bloody in places, and the rug — such as it was — was caked in dead white skin flakes.

He alternated between scratching his shoulders and biting his nails as he spoke — meaningless, gibbering chat, as if any pauses would give Kenley an opportunity to expedite what he had come for. Two more of his men — regulation donkey jackets again — were standing either side of Kevin, obviously getting progressively more fed up as he continued to babble.

All three turned to look at Kenley as he appeared in the doorway. Kevin's eyes widened and he made to stand.

"Kenley. Thank fuck you're here, man. Listen . . ." His voice was pure Merseyside, and sounded like it had been through a cheese grater.

There was a white fragment of fingernail stuck to his lower lip. One of Kenley's men gently but firmly shoved him back into the chair.

"All right, Kevin, take it easy," Kenley said. His voice was steady, outwardly betraying none of the anxiety he felt.

Kenley looked at the two knuckle-draggers. They were expectant, looking to him to control the operation that they — well, Kenley — had planned a week or so ago. Nothing in their faces suggested they thought he was a fraud.

Which was lucky, really. Out of the five of them, at thirty-one Kenley was the youngest by at least six years. Two of the men had killed before, but Kenley hadn't. They didn't know that, of course, but somehow he had ended up the leader.

Kenley sat down on the spongy end of the sofa, and got straight to the point.

"Kevin, you've been talking to the police."

His eyes widened.

"No, Kenley! Listen, you've got it wrong."

Kenley didn't say anything, just let Kevin use up all his protests. After a minute or so, he ran out of air, and all was silent again.

"Kevin, we're not here to hear the evidence, to hear your side of it, to decide your guilt or innocence. Balance of probabilities — you've been talking to the cops. Even if you haven't, I can't afford to take the chance."

Kevin's lower lip jutted out and started to wobble. His eyes screwed up as tears started to brim in his eyes like raindrops on a leaf.

Kenley moved forwards and knelt on the floor in front of Kevin. He slipped a hand around the back of Kevin's greasy neck and pulled him gently until their foreheads touched. Kevin smelled like a Gruyere fondue.

"Kevin, I don't *want* to do this, but it's the only way," Kenley said with a sincerity he almost felt. He didn't *want* to kill him, but he was going to have to.

"Kenley . . . I'll leave. Fucking Orkney or Shetland or somewhere. You won't ever hear from me again. No one will."

"Kev, you probably mean that now. I believe you do. But if I walk out of here, you'll wake up tomorrow and you'll have forgotten all the things you promised."

Kenley could *smell* the fear on Kevin, like a wet blanket of dog hair. It had turned his skin pale, and it turned Kenley's stomach.

Kenley stood up. The moment had come. He recognised the window of procrastination — and so did the others. If he didn't do it, he would lose his nerve, his credibility and possibly his life.

Although Kenley had not killed before, he had thought about it enough. Seen enough Cronenberg movies. The pre-match nerves were familiar — thudding heart, sweaty palms, flutterings of adrenaline in the sternum that felt like oxygen deprivation — but he felt fairly sure that he could do it and

13

not dwell on the consequences. Not suffer unduly. He felt fairly sure that he was cold enough to do the deed, bury it deep within him and move on.

One way to find out.

To the right of Kenley, there was the click of a switch-blade being made ready, as if his crew could sense hesitation. Kenley looked at him. He was a tank called Len Sterling — as in, you've done a sterling job — and saw the blade in his hand.

"Hang on a minute," Kenley said.

All eyes turned to him. Sterling's eyes widened slightly. He may have been experiencing a degree of reluctance in having to do Kevin *and* the boss because the boss didn't have the *cojones*, but Kenley felt sure he would probably get over it.

Kenley didn't say anything. Didn't explain himself. If you have an idea or a plan, he reasoned, it's always better to keep it to yourself. He moved closer to Kevin again and touched the material of his vest. He rubbed his fingers together and sniffed. They were greasy, and rank with the odour of a thousand layers of emollient cream.

"Kenley, what's . . ." Sterling began. Without looking at him, Kenley held up an index finger and silenced him.

He turned back to the sofa, where a brown pillow and thin tartan blanket suggested that this grotesque item of furniture also doubled up as Kevin's bed.

Kenley picked up the blanket and felt the material. Like Kevin's clothing, the blanket was stiff and practically damp with emollient residue.

Kenley passed Kevin a cigarette and lit it for him. He sucked on it gratefully, and Kenley lit one for himself.

"Kevin, you know what a burns victim is?"

His watering eyes widened in fear. He opened his mouth to speak, but only a dry, sucking noise came out.

Kenley stood up.

"Someone who's read too much Scottish poetry."

No one laughed.

There was no more talk.

"Kenley . . ." Kevin began.

Kenley flicked his cigarette onto the sofa. Even he was surprised at how quickly it went up, engulfing the sofa with a low *whomp* in seconds.

Unsurprisingly, Kevin leapt to his feet. As he did so, Kenley swung a fist in an arcing roundhouse at the right side of Kevin's neck. It connected perfectly. It slammed into his carotid artery, and he went down with an involuntary yelp like a sack of spuds. Out cold.

"Everybody out," Kenley said, as the fire ate up the horrible nylon throws held up with clothes pegs that passed for curtains.

Kenley's crew did not need to be told twice, but even in the flurry he could tell they were impressed. It was a useful trick they had apparently never had use for. Interrupt the flow of blood to the brain in a short, sharp stun and cause instant unconsciousness, leaving no discernible injury or anything else that might vex a pathologist. They often aren't out for long.

Just long enough.

Before Kenley pulled the door shut, he made the mistake of taking a last look at Kevin's feet. He was already twitching, and Kenley felt a pull of something in his insides. He hedged his bets that the fire would claim Kevin before he came round. He thought briefly about barricading the door, but that would rather defeat the object of this particular modus operandi. Kenley watched and waited for death to enter the flat to take the useless informant named Kevin Bridger.

The crew climbed the stairs and moved quickly away from the flat. As the fire rumbled and popped and the windows started to shatter, they disappeared down Junction Road, towards the railway tracks, and into darkness.

Kenley felt the battle with conscience and morals and horror begin to unravel inside him, but he fought it down. He set his jaw, narrowed his eyes, filled his veins with cold and told himself he felt nothing.

He wasn't surprised when it worked.

That's why he was the leader.

CHAPTER TWO

Although East Sussex Fire & Rescue extinguished the blaze — and reported the body — fairly quickly, it was morning before the blackened remnants of Kevin's flat were cool enough for CID and SOCO to get inside to look.

The control room caught Detective Sergeant Paul Gamble on a good day — or as close to a good day as he tended to have. It was a Sunday morning, so the CID early shift had gone out for the customary cooked breakfast at the Sunflower I in South Street with precious little in the way of interruptions, operational or otherwise. All five of his DCs had opted in, which meant it had cost him a little more than usual, but this was offset by the comparative novelty of having a full complement of staff. Best of all, however, was that there were no prisoners in the bin to deal with and no crimes overnight to warrant the immediate attention of CID. As such, Gamble was able to devote some thinking time to the pile of thick green files that made up his caseload. He found the physical act of clearing his desk immensely therapeutic, and was more than a little apprehensive about the advent of wholly digital files that seemed to be looming, both in the police station and courtroom. Maybe it wouldn't happen before he retired.

As it went, the novelty of being able to concentrate on enquiries and paperwork wore off after about half an hour, and so he was almost grateful when the phone rang. He would never have let on, however, and he greeted the duty inspector's instruction to attend the scene of an arson with the usual begrudging acquiescence.

"Grant," he said, hanging up the phone and putting on his jacket. "You fit?"

DC Chick Grant looked up from the desk, and then looked around, apparently realising that her colleagues had already gone out the door and that she had made something of a novice error in staying behind.

"Come on, you want to grab the car?" Gamble said.

"What have we got?"

"Scumbag toastie, by the sound of it."

"I had one of those already this morning."

"Very funny. Let's go."

Outside the main railway terminus, where the one-way system cut across the bus lanes, a frenetic level of activity was taking place. Grimy yellow machinery was in the process of razing every single building on the east side of Terminus Road, from the Gildredge right down to McDonalds. The poster of the artist's impression promised a light airy shopping complex with an awful lot of glass, but it was difficult to visualise from the acreage of metre-high rubble mounds behind the site fencing.

By contrast, the clamour around Kevin Bridger's flat was as wretched as a poorly attended funeral. Two yellow-jacketed PCSOs stood outside, one with his hands clasped in front of him, the other fiercely clutching the scene log. There was a press photographer — the gappy teeth and four-day beard leading Gamble to conclude he was freelance — and, quite literally, one man and his dog. It was an inauspicious end to an inauspicious life.

The detectives pulled on scene suits and booties while the larger of the PCSOs carefully detailed their arrival on the scene log before standing aside.

The inside of the flat was thick with residual heat, like the monochrome aftermath of a particularly vicious barbecue, with charred black walls and the white crumbling charcoal of incinerated wood. It was nevertheless a welcome change from the freezing air outside.

Gamble delicately covered his mouth with the back of his hand, edging towards the thing on the floor that resembled a log with teeth.

"Is there an SIO coming out to this?" Grant asked.

"Not yet. I put a courtesy call in, but the duty has to come from Guildford, so as you can imagine, she wanted a half-solid hypothesis before getting in the car."

"Guildford?"

"Brave new world."

Gamble squatted down next to the briquette that was once Kevin Bridger, and peered towards the general head area. He opened his mouth to speak, but was interrupted by the dull incessant bass thud of a particularly powerful car stereo pounding from the street above.

"What the hell's that?" Gamble said.

"Sounds like Rage Against the Machine, Sarge," offered Grant.

"I thought the bloody road was closed," Gamble said, standing up.

The music stopped. The sound of a car door closing. Some low chatter. Then the sound of footsteps descending carefully down the icy steps into Kevin Bridger's mausoleum, and the intrusion became an idle curiosity happening somewhere else to something right here demanding the ranking officer's attention.

Grant and Gamble turned at the same time as the figure appeared in the doorway to the tiny front room.

He didn't look more than about thirty, but the scrub of spiky blond punk hair, a red hoody poking out under the scene suit and his five-eight stature easily shaved another five years off this. There was a small metal stud in his chin, one in his nose, and a large black hoop inserted in his earlobe.

There were five angry pink triangles on his neck — the product, it seemed, of some recent laser surgery to remove the tips of a flame tattoo that ran from his wrist to his shoulder, and his hands, fingers and knuckles were swathed in abstract hieroglyphs.

"What . . . what in the hell are you doing here?" Gamble said. "Who let you in? This is a closed crime scene. Who are you?"

The man — kid — didn't say anything, but looked at Gamble with bright silvery-grey eyes that were almost white. They were large and piercing, and looked like shards of ice.

"Did you hear what I said?"

Slowly, the figure reached into the pocket of his scene suit. Both Gamble and Grant, trained to anticipate threat, instinctively took a step forward.

The figure produced a small trifold leather rectangle from his pocket. It fell open to show an ID badge and police crest, one that Gamble and Grant knew all too well.

"You have got . . . to be joking," Gamble said, taking another step forward. "Where did you get that? Did you steal it?"

The figure didn't move, and Gamble moved closer still, until their noses were practically touching.

"Samson Kane," said the figure. "Detective Superintendent."

Something jarred within Gamble, something that told him to change tack, but more words in support of his chosen stance were already out of his mouth.

"You're good, I must admit," Gamble said. "Doing that with a straight face. Totally deadpan. Proper Royal Shakespeare. Now get the *fuck* out of my crime scene."

Now their noses really were touching.

The man calling himself Kane tilted his head up slightly, so as to remove his nose from Gamble's, then backed slowly away towards the door. His expression remained impassive, however, and nothing in his gait or countenance suggested he was in the least bit intimidated.

19

Gamble was not satisfied with this, and he moved with Kane, scowling.

"Sarge . . ." Grant said, softly placing a hand on Gamble's upper arm.

Gamble didn't hear her, and he kept moving forwards, not allowing the shorter man any distance, an alpha cop ejecting the challenger from his territory.

Kane kept his eyes on Gamble, even ascending the stairs backwards, feeling for the handrail as he went.

At the top of the stairs a light-hearted conversation between the two PCSOs on scene guard began to evaporate, and they turned to watch the bizarre stand-off. The photographer, apparently sensing blood, began hauling his camera into position as well.

He wasn't far wrong. Gamble stopped at the top of the stairs and stood with his fists on his hips, watching the younger man walk to his car.

The car — some piece-of-crap Mitsubishi Lancer — seemed to be something else that cemented Gamble's theory.

Grant appeared behind Gamble, just as he started advancing again.

"Sarge," she tried again.

"Hold on a minute," Gamble said. "You're not going anywhere."

Kane turned to face him. Gamble walked over and poked Kane in the chest, just as he opened the driver's door. His foot twisted on the edge of the kerb and he fell on his backside in the road.

"*Paul!*" Grant screeched.

But Gamble was moving in for the kill. He reached down and pulled the warrant card from the pocket of the prone-and-unresisting Kane, reaching for his own mobile phone as he did so.

He scrutinised the warrant card as he dialled the control room, and something changed in his face as he did so. Like, the delay was allowing his brain to catch up with his mouth. He already knew the answer he was going to get.

"Comms, this is DS Paul Gamble. I'm at the scene of the fire. What fire? The one in Eastbourne. The one with the barbecued body on the end of it. Op Blackwater. Can you run a warrant number through SAP please? Charlie-Bravo-two-zero-two. Yeah . . . it does? Who does it . . . oh, I see. Does it say anything about . . . he's a new joiner. I see. What else can you . . . is his mobile number in front of you? Do us a favour, okay? Ring that number after I hang up . . . what's that? *I* don't know what you should say — say it's the control room testing the line or something. Just call it."

Gamble ended the call. After an interminable ten-second wait, Public Enemy's "Bring the Noise" began to emanate from Kane's jeans pocket as his mobile phone rang. He didn't answer it. He didn't need to.

Kane pulled himself to his feet and climbed into the car. He'd barely said anything throughout the entire interaction, and didn't start now — he simply started the engine and held his hand out through the open window.

To his credit, Gamble's expression remained neutral; he'd gone too far along this particular road for any acts of contrition to be tolerated by any of the embarrassed onlookers. However, his Adam's apple disappeared into his collar and then bobbed back up again as he swallowed, dropping the warrant card into the new superintendent's outstretched hand.

"There you are . . ." Gamble said, as the thrashing sound of "Renegades of Funk" marked Kane's departure from the scene, ". . . sir."

CHAPTER THREE

Unbeknownst to Paul Gamble, this was Samson Kane's first day. First day as a superintendent, first day on the streets as an operational cop. As a new joiner under a lateral entry scheme, at thirty-two he was the youngest superintendent the streets of Sussex had ever seen, and one without a jot of policing experience.

Someone had told him his duty time for his first command was 9 a.m. on Monday. Find the office, meet the team, that sort of thing. He had thought that seemed at odds with things. He may have been inexperienced, but Kane was not green. It didn't make sense to him that on a Monday morning you couldn't get a space in the staff car park for love nor money — well, possibly money — but on a Saturday night over a bank holiday weekend it was all too easy. He figured that insurance call centres kept business hours. Criminals didn't.

So, at 3 a.m., when he'd called the control room to find out if anything was going on and was told about Op Blackwater, the fire in Eastbourne town centre, he had thought that a crime scene with a body in it might be a better place to start than trying to read the agenda for the first meeting he was meant to chair. That line of thinking had landed him on his backside in the gutter — at the hands of another cop.

As it turned out, his joining instructions would have made him late anyway. The outer cordon had been put on either end of Ashford Road, so Kane drove against the run of the one-way street past the wrecking site for the new Arndale Centre and rejoined Terminus Road heading out of town. He went up Grove Road and paused before the town hall. He checked the papers on the seat beside him. His normal place of work was, apparently, the command suite at Eastbourne Police Station, Grove Road.

He looked out of the window. He knew where the police station was. He knew that the cell block stretched way out the back and that fighting prisoners were dragged through a side door from the garage's vehicle turntable straight into a cell. He knew that the smell of vomit and booze fumes and shit and blood had seeped into the cold concrete walls over so many years that no amount of bleach and scrubbing could ever get them clean. But he knew all this from a very long time ago.

Even without the benefit of this knowledge, the blue police lamp over the doorway indicated he was in the right place, but the heavy wooden doors to the police station were pointedly shut. Sellotaped to the wood was a faded hand-written poster — WE HAVE MOVED — with an arrow pointing the wrong way down the one-way street. Kane drove round the block to try this, but found only a council office that wasn't open yet.

He again called his new most useful contact — the control room — and established that the long-defunct police station had been moved lock, stock and barrel to an industrial estate on the outskirts of town some time ago. Kane slowly slipped the car into gear. His first morning was not going as he expected. But, somehow, that was Samson Kane all over.

* * *

As it turned out, there was actually no such thing as a police station in Eastbourne. It was more like a police village. The main site was a fenced compound opposite a plastics factory that ran alongside the Horsey Sewer.

Kane sat in front of the main gate, the engine idling. His finger hovered over the intercom button, but just as he was about to reluctantly press it, he saw the card reader, and was relieved when he held up his warrant card and the device chirped green. The enormous iron gate with its crown of razor wire and large blue "NOT OPEN TO THE PUBLIC" sign slid slowly open.

The site comprised a patrol base, a command building, a huge evidence warehouse and the Major Incident Suite. The custody and investigations centre, for no good reason that Kane could see, was a quarter of a mile down the road, at the very end of the Hammonds industrial estate and the last outpost before the golf course and the sprawling outer wilderness of Cross Levels.

The command building shared accommodation with the Major Incident Suite but, it being a Sunday, there was little activity besides the odd SOCO going to and from the evidence store. He'd called out to one of them — safe distance, no likelihood of being assaulted again — and asked her if she was going to the fire scene. The SOCO looked sideways at him — *who are you?* — then called back that she didn't know yet, but that she supposed there was a tasking on their work queue. Probably too hot to examine yet anyway.

Tap-tap-tap.

Kane sat in his ultra-modern, glass-partitioned office with its paper-thin monitors and metal-framed safety windows that afforded a view of the scrubland across the Levels, and tapped a pen across the heel of one of his Converse.

But for this, the silence smothered him like a blanket. He had a guided itinerary of sorts for his first official day — but that was twenty-four hours away yet, and he didn't really have a clue in hell what he was doing there, either on this particular day or, following the events of the morning, at all. The office was a fair size, featuring a sofa and wall-mounted flat-screen television, which Kane supposed was a reflection of the rank.

Tap-tap-tap.

A bunch of people at a national assessment centre had seen enough in him to decide that not only should he be a cop, but that he should be a senior cop, straight off the bat. Kane still couldn't quite see it himself, but suspected the standout points were the fact that he had run a small business and the fact that he had spent some time working for UNICEF in the Solomon Islands, building shelters and stuff. His feedback report had made comment about his own personal brand of diversity — for which, read tattoos and piercings — as being more representative of the community as a whole. The cynic in him had yet to decide whether or not they genuinely meant it.

Tap-tap-tap.

He figured a superintendent coming into the office on a Sunday would probably be catching up on paperwork, and so — after realising to his irritation that his imagined superintendent was six-one and had a short back and sides — he switched on the desktop computer and logged into his network account. To his surprise, he found that his system access had already been set up. This included an email account, and a quick scan of his inbox revealed that it was already full of messages from chief inspectors that began, "Sorry to bother you on your first day, but . . ." and then proceeded to complain about shoestring budgets, shrinking numbers and the general welfare state of the cops. It was like the simulated scenarios he'd had to undertake for his police recruitment assessments all over again.

He switched it off quickly.

A roar of leaf blowers firing up out on the golf course suddenly penetrated the Sunday morning silence. He got up, pulled the windows shut on the noise and thought he might walk over to the patrol base. It was a 24/7 operation, and so he figured he could say hello, introduce himself, meet some people. Halfway down the corridor, however, he faltered, replaying internally, for the nineteenth time, his encounter from earlier that morning.

Instead, he went into the gents' and looked at his reflection, suddenly feeling like an ant under a microscope. The pink edges of the lasered tattoo seemed to be glowing. The hands he could do nothing about, but after a moment's hesitation, he removed the piercing from his chin.

He walked back, shame and self-doubt weighing down his footsteps, and so was glad for the presence of another human being in his office.

The visitor was tall, with a slight stoop and a slim frame that might have just been starting to slide. He had watery eyes, and the dark hair that was greying at the temples was side-parted with a cut that was all kinds of ordinary.

Kane thought that if there was an advert for someone chewed up and spat out by the job, this man was it.

"Boss," the man said with a furrowed brow, sticking out a hand like an afterthought. "DI Barnes. Sorry for the ambush. And on a Sunday."

Although the man called Barnes didn't smile — in fact, if anything, there was a kind of tension radiating from him — Kane, despite his increasingly guarded countenance, took an instant liking to him, not least because his eyes remained fixed on Kane's and did not flick to the tattoos or hair as most of his introductions to date had done.

"DI? You duty?" Kane said, gesturing to a seat. It seemed like the kind of thing a senior officer would say.

"Not exactly. I'm from intel, but I'm shoring up the rota. It's about this fire. I gather you've been to the scene?"

They both sat down — Kane behind his desk, Barnes at a small round conference table the other side of it.

"I just got back. There's a dead body in there. CID are calling it accidental death."

"That's why I'm here."

Barnes drummed his fingers on the table and held Kane's gaze. He looked nervous.

"Yes?" Kane said, when Barnes was silent for another half a minute.

"I know we're too early for an ID, but the scene is the residence of one Kevin Bridger, and I'll bet a case of Merrydown that he's the deceased. The former Mr Bridger is — was — a registered informant."

Barnes paused for a moment, and swallowed.

"Given his, er, lifestyle choices, accidentally burning his own house down is not beyond the realms of possibility, but if he had been compromised then a fire is a good way to disguise a murder."

"How likely is that?"

"That he'd been compromised? Shooting their mouths off is the most common cause. Usually when they've had a skinful. Generally, it's a pretty tight ship, but that end is difficult to control."

"Was he any use? As an informant, I mean."

"I'd need to get the source unit to go back over the files, but nothing springs to mind. That doesn't necessarily mean anything, though. If word got out, *someone* would have put a price on his head, symbolically or otherwise. Why take the risk of waiting till he's got you locked up? And besides, it's possible he had information he didn't know the value of. They know that he knows but don't know that he doesn't know, you know?"

Kane's expression was neutral. Barnes cleared his throat.

"You say symbolic . . ."

"Yeah, you know — send a message to the criminal fraternity about what happens to informants. That kind of thing."

"Yes, I get it. I was going to say that if that were the case why go to the trouble of trying to disguise it with a fire? Why not just string him up from a lamp post?"

"Well, I don't know. It's all speculation until the PM."

"Now you will have to help me."

"Sorry. Post-mortem. In my experience if you treat it as murder and it turns out not to be, then all well and good."

"Until you get the bill."

Barnes gave a thin smile. "I thought you were new to this."

Kane made a grunting sound in the back of his throat.

"So, what now?" Kane said.

"Well, I need to get hold of the duty DI. It's her bag, really, but I'm going to put a call in to the Force SIO as well. Major Crime should know about this, even if they don't end up taking it. If the SIO approves a Home Office PM then we'll have a much better idea of what we're dealing with."

"Leave it. I'll call the SIO."

"I don't mind."

"It's fine. Control room will have the number, yes?" Kane picked up the desk phone and gave a thumbs-up as Barnes made to leave.

The DI called Barnes paused in the doorway of the glass partitioned office.

"My involvement is strictly top level," he said. "I'm telling you because you're the new boss. You're running things around here now. But this is sensitive information. There's no need for anyone else to know his status. Including the media. It needs to stay between you, me and the SIO — whoever that ends up being."

"You."

"I beg your pardon?" Barnes stiffened slightly, as if expecting a rebuke.

"I want you to take it."

The DI was momentarily speechless. Kane could see the various strands of logic as to why he *shouldn't* take on the case wrestling on his face.

"Why me?" he said eventually.

"You're the only one I've met so far that's offered to shake my hand."

"I can't. I can't take the case on."

"Why not?" Kane said. "Why can't you?"

"Look, I'm always happy to muck in. I'm not going to tell you *not my job*. Many would. But the deceased and I . . . well, we had a bit of history."

Kane put the receiver back on the cradle.

"What sort of history?"

"Look, we have to employ a few theatrics when we meet with these people, just to provide a bit of cover. You know, in case anyone's watching."

"Pretending to arrest them, that sort of thing?"

"Well, not specifically — fake arrests tend to be counter-productive — but that's the general idea. To make them look like they aren't complicit."

"And in your case?"

Barnes exhaled heavily.

"I staged a kidnap. Took him to a barn. Someone called it in. There was an armed raid. I was in custody for about forty-five minutes."

Kane didn't say anything. He looked flatly at Barnes, wondering if this was a wind-up. After the morning he'd had, nothing would surprise him.

"So, going back to your previous theory," Kane said slowly. "About a fire being a good way to disguise a murder. Does your . . . *history* tend to support that idea?"

Barnes chewed his lip.

"And what am I meant to do with this information?"

"Tell PSD. Professional Standards," Barnes added, by way of explanation. "They'll do the rest. IPCC will be very interested, I expect, subterfuge notwithstanding."

He looked slightly forlorn.

"I take it that's a bad thing?" Kane said.

Barnes shrugged.

"Good or bad is almost irrelevant. You can write off two years of your life waiting for an IPCC investigation. But the point is, it wouldn't be ethical for me to investigate it."

Kane picked up the phone again.

"Okay, I'll speak to PSD. But you're still taking this case."

"This *is* your first day, right?" Barnes said.

"Tomorrow," Kane said.

Barnes left without another word.

Kane watched him go, and in the ensuing silence recalled another entry in his feedback report:

Candidate Kane makes things happen.

Kane called him back.

You're running things around here now.

"Do you know a DS called Paul Gamble?" Kane said, one hand still on the receiver.

Barnes's expression became half scoff, half grimace, in a way that told Kane pretty much all he needed to know.

"Yes, I know Paul. He's not one of mine, but he's been around forever. Two years off retirement, I believe. And before you ask — I've already heard about this morning. So have most of the duty staff. That's something you'll learn pretty quickly — gossip spreads like wildfire. No pun intended."

"I need to make an example of him. Who can I call?"

CHAPTER FOUR

Kane gazed at his reflection, thinking that he'd spent a disproportionate amount of time in police station toilets in the last three days. Coming to work on a Sunday morning, when the nick was quiet, had been a good idea. Now, midweek, the place was humming, and it created a pit of anxiety in Kane's stomach that he hadn't previously felt.

He splashed water on his face, leaned on the sink and shrugged in the uncomfortable uniform. The so-called "operational uniform" he'd worn at the weekend had been a rather comfortable affair effectively comprising a black T-shirt and combats. Now, as a superintendent, the formal white shirt, tie and dress shoes seemed incongruous to the rest of him. The shirtsleeves were slightly too long and bunched at the wrists, and he suddenly felt ridiculous, like a child in the dressing-up box trying to persuade a bunch of grownups that he was the real deal.

He took a deep breath, stood up straight and, after a moment, put the stud back in his chin piercing as a sort of bejewelled comfort blanket.

As far as he could see, he had two options: run for the hills, or talk such a good game that no one would doubt him.

After all, how bad could it be?

* * *

As it turned out, it was worse.

The sharp smell of the new synthetic pile carpet hit him as he entered the boardroom. The conference table stretched down the middle, and was lined along each side by eleven grim-faced men and two women, most of whom were in the same uniform as Kane — with the exception of the decoration on their shoulders.

Kane sat down at the head of the table — the only spare seat — and took a moment to look beyond the heads of the assembled delegates through the windows at the line of orange-jacketed leaf blowers on the lip of the golf course that landlocked the patrol base footprint and stretched away over the Levels.

"Morning, sir," someone said.

Kane looked up. It was the DI he'd met on his first day. The troubled one, the one who liked to kidnap informants. Barnes.

Kane's eyes returned to the table. He made a point of looking each of them in the eye, before settling on the clutch of papers in front of him that, he felt, could end up being either a prop or a crutch.

"Morning," he said. All eyes turned to him, and his lines disappeared in a vacuum of stage fright. "Can I . . . shall we . . ."

"What about some introductions?" Barnes offered.

Kane looked down at the agenda clutched in his tattooed fingers. The first item was "Introductions and apologies". The last time he'd been in a room like this with the pressure of a structured institution bearing down on him, he'd been slowly flunking an A-Level English course. He'd thrown a chair at the tutor, flipped the bird at his classmates and walked out. He was feeling close to doing something similar again.

He thought he heard someone snicker. This wouldn't do. Being patiently indulged wouldn't last long, and he didn't want to be patronised. Whether they liked it or not, he was the boss.

"I'm Superintendent Samson Kane. I'm the Eastern Ops commander as of this week."

They went round the table. Kane navigated his way through the meeting using the agenda as his compass. He survived the resourcing update, the intelligence update and the finance update relatively unscathed. So far, so good, he thought.

The operations update was given by a bony man with bad teeth and a sandy comb-over.

"DCI Ed Shaw, East Downs crime manager. First up is Op Cassius. This is a stranger rape from last week. Victim woke up in an alleyway half-naked, doesn't remember anything. CCTV trawl likely to prove definitive, but no suspect yet. Op Sawgrass, high-value stately home burglary, no change from last week, searches continuing. Op Blackwater, straightforward enough. House fire, one fatality. Confirmed ID still awaiting dental, but if it's who we think it is, best guess is a spaced-out junkie leaving too many candles burning. Looking to write that one off as an accident within the week. Op Foxglove . . ."

"It's murder," Kane interrupted.

"Come again?" Shaw blinked.

"Murder. Op Blackwater."

Shaw looked round the table, then sort of uncurled himself, stretching his arms across the table.

"Now — sir — I know you want . . ."

"Want what?"

"There's absolutely no evidence to support a homicide hypothesis at present."

"Then go find some."

"Mr Kane, come on . . ."

"I don't want to hear it," Kane said. "It's a murder. Treat it as such until I tell you otherwise. Mr Barnes here has a running start. He'll report to you."

Shaw stood up, his body tensing. His eyes flicked to Barnes and back. A pink flap of untucked shirt hung over his belt.

"Don't take this the wrong way — due respect, and all that bollocks — but I've got twenty-five years' experience under my belt. Twenty-three as a detective, eleven as a crime manager, nine as an SIO. I consider myself pretty well qualified to conclude whether something is a murder or not."

Kane stood also.

"Then you won't have a problem doing your job, will you?" He swept his gaze around the remaining wide-eyed attendees, resting momentarily on Barnes. "Meeting adjourned."

* * *

Barnes eyeballed his mobile. It rested silently on the desk, taunting him with unfettered belligerence.

He willed it to ring. He knew it was going to. It hadn't stopped all day, so why should the evening be any different?

At thirty-seven, with eleven years' service under his belt, an outside observer might have thought that detective inspector wasn't a bad milestone at all, and that Barnes might even yet enjoy something resembling a *career*.

He knew differently, of course. As far as Barnes could see, he'd be lucky to make it that far. With barely a third of his full pensionable service served, Barnes had already seen colleagues slain on two separate occasions, which, he'd decided, was not a recipe for a wholesome relationship with your occupation. If that wasn't enough, his wife of nine years had been killed four years previously when a Mercedes flatbed carrying three burglars being pursued by a cavalcade of police vehicles had ploughed into Barnes's Orion. Wrong place, wrong time — that seemed to be Barnes all over.

His career had always been a team effort, so when she died, Barnes came to work because it was better than going home — and, he knew, because the three occupants of the truck had never been found. Detective inspector had happened in spite of him.

Barnes's office was at the far end of a disused room that couldn't decide if it was a conference room or an office or a canteen. At some point it had probably been all three. It had a narrow panelled dark oak door, part of the Georgian building's original features, covered as it was with scuffs and scars. There was no signage anywhere, and if not for the electronic keypad in place of the original brass doorknob, most people would have mistaken it for a cleaner's cupboard . . . which, it seemed, was the desired effect. The solitary window in the top corner of the back wall would have afforded a half-decent view of the Saffrons and the crumbling dome of the town hall next door, were it not the size of a chessboard and caked in Georgian grime.

Shrouded in a skeletal carcass of scaffolding, the police station abutted the town hall and was, on the surface of it, mothballed, but had found sufficient demand as an emergency shelter for Barnes and his team to just about keep it breathing.

The police station itself resembled little more than a crypt that had been opened to sunlight after a century of being sealed. As part of an inaugural history lesson, Barnes had told Kane that the station had actually been sold off some years previously, until some by-law buried deep in the council archives had thwarted its development for anything other than policing. And so, it had sat gathering dust, until someone got the idea that a police station that wasn't obviously a police station might be a handy thing indeed. Now, the exterior retained the facade of the non-operational, but the inside was very much alive and kicking.

Barnes, at 8 p.m. on this particular Tuesday, was glad to be able to retreat to an office whose location and purpose was not widely known. He had unwittingly found himself in charge of a murder investigation that nobody else thought was a murder investigation, and his phone had not stopped ringing all day. Which wasn't to say he had been productive. He just felt that all he'd done was manage the incoming demands from all the people that wanted a piece of him. The one person that hadn't called was Shaw, but he had apparently gone on strike in the last day or so. Barnes wasn't quite sure how it had all played out this way.

The answer, of course, was the new guy. Superintendent Kane. He was the only one throwing Kevin Bridger's death around as murder. So far, no one was having it. He clearly had quite a few trust issues, and so he had kept Barnes close and asked him to get the confidential files on Kevin scoured for anything that might jump out as a half-decent motive for offing him.

He had promised Barnes that this state of affairs would only last until the post-mortem, but unfortunately, this had got out, and Barnes had found himself fielding calls from a never-ending carousel of people who had a stake in the investigation. The house-to-house manager, the crime scene manager, the media officer. Some were on the ground, undertaking their own little piece of the puzzle and wanting to pass it back to Barnes in the hope it would form part of a coherent whole. And some were above him, calling with a demanding regularity to enquire about the progress, the politics, the potential fallout. None of them bothered to ask how he was doing — at least, not with anything approaching sincerity.

With the possible exception of the strange new superintendent with the tattoos and the piercings. Barnes took it all in his stride, but in the same way that a man has to contend with an iPhone when he's only just got used to a Nokia, Barnes could sort of understand Paul Gamble's reaction.

Kane was the reason Barnes was doing this. He knew plenty of other DIs who would have gone straight over Kane's head the minute a murder had been dropped in their lap. No way would they want to carry the can when *that* went wrong. No way a lot of them wanted to do anything approaching hard work.

But, in an intuitive way, Barnes trusted Kane, and as far as he could see, the guy had precious little in the way of allies. Barnes didn't envy him. Superintendent was a thankless enough rank even *with* the benefit of twenty years' policing behind you. He knew Kane had taken an instant dislike to his inbox and the meetings in his diary, instead preferring to get on the ground and learn about the business of policing, and maybe that was what the job needed.

There was another reason too, and it was the reason he was eyeballing the phone like a cat about to pounce.

It rang. He grabbed it.

"DI Barnes," he said as he answered, unable to keep the urgency from his voice.

"Barnes, it's Sharon Brooker. Can I just check the house-to-house parameters for Op Blackwater with you? We're stretching down as far as Susans Road, but I think we should extend to—"

"Whatever you think, Sharon. I trust your judgment," he said, ending the call abruptly.

He placed the phone back on the desk.

It rang again, almost immediately.

He picked it up. *MARLON CHOUDHURY* appeared on the display. Barnes felt a bolt of adrenaline flare in his system. This would be a normal reaction for any sane cop when Professional Standards came calling, but Barnes had been expecting it — and probably with good reason.

He and DCI Marlon Choudhury had history, and despite the most arcane of circumstances surrounding their last encounter, Barnes had nevertheless found him to be fair and reasonable, if more than a little eccentric. Barnes put this down to his size, his ubiquitous grin and the fact that his policing experience was almost double Barnes's age.

"DI Barnes," he said, slowly.

"Mr Barnes. Good evening. I'm sorry to trouble you." The voice was clipped, precise, and did not betray the autumnal age of its owner. Barnes couldn't help but picture him on a Chesterfield in a wood-panelled study, a light aria on the gramophone, his churchwarden's pipe clamped between his teeth.

"You always say that, Marlon. How can I help you?"

"I've had a rather odd referral from your new superintendent, Mr Kane."

37

"Oh?"

"He seems to think you might have kidnapped one of your own informants mere weeks before the same individual perished in a fire."

"It's better than that. I'm now leading the investigation into said fire."

"Do you feel up to sharing? This wasn't any old inform-ant, was it?"

"He knew, Marlon. He was going to give me the name."

"Mr Barnes . . ."

"The name of the man who killed her, Marlon."

"Does he know? Mr Kane?"

"He knows Kevin was probably killed for letting something slip. He knows he was one of my informants."

"Meaning he *doesn't* know of your personal reasons for wanting to cultivate a relationship with him?"

Barnes didn't answer. Choudhury sighed heavily, as if his patience with a recalcitrant child was wearing thin. So Barnes, expecting noises about conduct, ethics and the general *wrongness* of the whole thing, was surprised when Choudhury said:

"Just remember, Mr Barnes, it's not all about you. I'll be in touch."

He hung up. Barnes stared at his mobile.

As ever, the man had a point and, as ever, he had knocked Barnes's current thought trajectory off course.

It didn't matter how horrible you were, murder to silence someone was a big deal. Murder to send a warning to others just in case was an even bigger deal.

In any case, it had done the trick. Barnes's handlers were reporting that information was drying up. People were either running scared or, realising that the associated risk had increased the value of their commodity, were demanding greater reward. Or both.

Barnes believed his first theory — that Kevin had mouthed off while high, intentionally or otherwise — was the most likely reason word had got out. And as he had postulated to Kane, this in itself could have been enough to kill him. It didn't necessarily mean he was holding the secrets to the universe — what he knew, and what he might have let slip, were practically irrelevant.

Kevin had never been particularly indiscreet. He wasn't a pub bragger. His biggest problem had been staying off the gear, which tended to taint his reliability as he became more and more desperate for cash. He'd actually been inactive for the best part of the previous year after getting arrested for burglary, thus breaking the rules of engagement.

He had never provided anything that could be described as solid gold. Never given them the Hatton Garden robbers, or the Lord Lucan kidnapper, or the man behind the grassy knoll. His information had been rather less glamorous. He tended to provide snippets that needed work and development, and formed part of a larger bundle that made sense when it was verified and fitted to other pieces of corresponding information. It was unfair to say he had never provided information that led to a successful prosecution but, when weighed up against all the other bits, it took a fair bit of unravelling.

Barnes sighed and sat back, wondering if Kevin had a family out there of sorts — a line of thinking that wouldn't have been front and centre had it not been for Choudhury's call.

Barnes enjoyed intelligence. Enjoyed covert policing. You didn't, for instance, see many detectives from the intel unit chairing press conferences. Or being hung out to dry in community meetings. Or ripped up in the witness box. In fact, if it came to a choice between binning a prosecution or compromising a source, the former was invariably preferable. Security trumped justice in more than a few cases. Anything like public scrutiny and covert policing held the final trump card of pulling the plug in the name of anonymity.

He didn't suffer the same finger-pointing at the daily management meetings, the same urgency over operational demands, the same pressures of grunt work. That's not to say his work was less important or more comfortable. A lazy cop, couldn't, for instance, hide happily in intel. The pace was just . . . different. The hours were better. Gave him more time to indulge his hobbies.

Not that he had any. Tinkering with the Rover didn't really count.

It hadn't been his decision alone, of course. Somebody somewhere had worked out that Barnes's colourful career trajectory to date didn't lend itself particularly well to survival, and that a change of scene might do him good.

Barnes had a better relationship with main-office CID than many in his unit. As well as mucking in on the DI rota, they shared information, discussed theories and hedged career bets. He didn't have the same daily chaos that CID had — and he had no particular desire to change that.

All of which was Barnes kidding himself. Only Choudhury suspected his real motivation for wanting to point his career towards intelligence, for wanting to run informants — to get closer to the one person that could have maybe identified the person responsible for his wife's death.

And now that man was dead.

CHAPTER FIVE

The toilet bowl was cool against Kenley's damp brow. He rested for a moment, his weight on his knuckles. There was nothing left to bring up — and there had only really been whisky to start with — but he continued to dry-retch until he felt like he'd done a thousand sit-ups.

It wasn't Kevin's pleading face that he kept dreaming of — he was indifferent to, almost contemptuous of that — but it was the way his feet had twitched as he started to come round, and Kenley couldn't stop wondering how conscious he had been before the fire claimed him.

In one dream, Kevin walked through the flames, grabbed Kenley at the doorway and pulled him inside before locking the door shut. In another, Kevin screamed and bolted for the door, hammering on it from the inside before Kenley pulled it shut.

Kenley flushed the toilet and pulled himself to his feet. He blew his nose, brushed his teeth and tried to tell himself he felt a little better. Tried to tell himself that Kevin deserved it, that you can't have a morality tale where there's no morality.

Certainly, Kenley found it easier to think of his crew as animals, not men. Give up hope, he thought. Don't expect to look into their eyes and appeal to their human nature. Don't think of them as children, or as having parents, or as having any kind of normal life. Better to think they just materialised one day in a rain-soaked alley, already wearing donkey jackets and clutching baseball bats, with no other purpose in life than to break bones without a thought for the consequences. Kevin should have thought of them that way. Anybody should think of them that way. That would make it a fraction easier when they come to your house at 2 a.m. with bolt croppers and jump leads.

There are two reasons criminals get caught, Kenley reasoned. The vast majority are stupid, careless and impulsive. They care too much about getting laid or getting high. This lot make it easy for the cops. Leave evidence like a kid's treasure hunt. The ones who do it as a profession — well, they tend to get got when one of their own runs his mouth. This tends to happen for two reasons — they're either trying to save their own skin from ending up in custard, or there's a cash incentive. Sometimes it's a bit of both. Loved ones are often a bit of leverage.

But if you're careful, then you should be okay. At least for long enough to put a bit away. This includes keeping your car's MOT up to date, but also looking after and incentivising your people — and eliminating the weak links.

Kevin was a potential weak link. Kenley couldn't tolerate that.

Kenley had his suspicions, but he wasn't completely sure exactly how much Kevin knew that could actually hurt the Keber crew. Even if Kevin did know anything, he didn't know whether he was bright enough to realise its value. Kenley certainly didn't know if Kevin got around to sharing it with anyone — the cops, the vicar, his key worker.

But to an extent, that didn't matter.

Word had got out that he was a grass. And as a fringe member of Keber, anything other than a decisive move would have been disastrous for somebody in Kenley's position. Unfortunately for Kevin and others like him, the burden of proof did not particularly favour the suspect in such matters. Rumour and suspicion tended to be enough.

Kenley didn't feel a need to stick Kevin's head on a spike in front of the police station, or mail his fingers to the local rag. Far more effective to shroud the whole affair in mystery and speculation. *Did you hear about what happened to . . . Yeah but there was never any proof . . . But I heard that . . .* and so on. Before you know it, the thing has sprouted roots and you've got yourself a little piece of folklore.

From a more practical perspective, Kenley happened to know that the resources being chucked at the accidental death of an oxygen thief like Kevin Bridger would be scant indeed. One DC and his dog — and that's if he was unlucky. Throw the "M" word into the mix, however, then along come the homicide detectives with their never-ending toolkit of troublesome tactics — surveillance, phone tapping, prison informants, high-end forensics, big rewards, national intelligence. When Major Crime go shopping, there is no credit limit. And homicide investigations never, ever go away.

There wasn't even any point trying to find out what he'd shared — if anything — or with whom. Someone in Kevin's position, once they realised what was happening, would just babble and splutter and say anything they think you might want to hear — something that could reasonably be construed as an unreliable confession. And besides, guilty or innocent, who doesn't get defensive when the finger's being pointed?

Kenley splashed water on his face and looked at his reflection in the mirror, then left the house and drove to Newhaven. He drove a silver Vauxhall Insignia, registered — like all the Keber fleet — to a fictitious lease firm called UK Holdings. Very bland and uninteresting.

Kenley lived in a simple two-bedroom semi in a new estate happily called Park Meadow, one of several developments springing up in and around Sovereign Harbour. Kenley figured that new builds these days were like Japanese paper houses, but he kept himself to himself and was careful about his phone conversations, so the wafer-thin walls were of no particular consequence. He had a new three-piece suite, a modern kitchen and a large, neon-lit aquarium filled with tropical fish that he was rather fond of. Next door was a retired widow with whom he was on first-name terms, and she thought he was wonderful. He did her lawn occasionally and took in her parcels, but he didn't get too friendly. She respected his privacy, and it was a healthy set-up.

She thought he was a senior house officer. Working all kinds of hours in A&E. Bastard NHS grinding that nice young man into the ground. The other neighbours didn't talk to him, which suited Kenley. He made a point of avoiding eye contact, so eventually they stopped trying.

He knew they might come for him one day. They might walk up the driveway, warrant in hand, and when that happened, all the neighbours would be shocked beyond words that such an unassuming young man was a villain. But Kenley was not the sort of person to expedite his own demise by leaving a yellow 911 Carrera on the drive.

What happened to Kevin was harsh, but he knew the risks. He was on *this* side of the fence. Bulldog clips on the testicles were an occupational hazard for anyone in Kenley's game. Kenley didn't fleece old people. He might burgle — or cause to be burgled — the odd rich person's house, but he didn't rob the innocent or steal from people who couldn't afford it. And he certainly didn't use violence in public unless he really had to. Armed robbery was practically a thing of the past, anyway — you got twice the spoils and half the sentence from online fraud, and the banks bore the loss. Kenley felt he could live with that — felt, actually, that most people could.

The rain at the port felt like God was reaching into his bucket and flinging great handfuls of freezing, dirty water across the world. It blew across the car in haphazard sheets, by turns ferocious and quiet.

The car rocked, but Kenley stayed put. It wouldn't do to deviate from the arrangement. He squinted across the Ouse to where the ferry was crawling into port, a barely discernible movement against the smudge of grey that represented the crumbling principality being consumed by algae and scum. The steel and glass attempts at gentrification had stalled some years back, and the dream of dockside apartment living for families and young professionals had been beached like a trawler out on the sandbar.

The railway line was beyond the sandbar, an unguarded track leading out of the port and across the deserted flats following the coastal edge. It looked as precarious now as it did when it was operational, as if at any moment the shingle could surge and the water would claim it.

The car was stuffy, but Kenley resisted the urge to open the window. His heart began to drum as the ferry disappeared from view, unable to keep doomstruck fantasies from his mind — armies of blue lights scrambling towards where Stratton Pearce had finally been rumbled.

But, no, there he was, in glorious Technicolor. He came loping along the exposed railway line after about twenty minutes, hands thrust deep in his pockets, the hood of a grey top pulled so low over his face it brought the Reaper's cloak to mind.

Kenley didn't relax, however — and wouldn't until Pearce was back on the damn ferry. They were both as exposed as open wounds. Kenley reminded himself to mind his mouth; nerves tended to bring smart remarks to the surface which, in turn, tended to piss Pearce off.

Pearce opened the door and got in the back, letting a blast of soaking air into the car. He didn't say anything, just sat there, taking deep breaths, the hood still up. Kenley could only barely see his face under the hood.

"Good trip?" Kenley enquired.

"Cold," Pearce grunted.

"Any issues?"

"Some old guy in a hi-vis. He was asleep. Passport stayed in my pocket."

"Look, mate, don't take this the wrong way, but can you drop the hood? For all I know I've picked up Jimmy Hoffa."

He didn't drop the hood, but instead placed his right fist on the shoulder of Kenley's seat. "LENA" was tattooed across the knuckles, with "HECTOR" creeping up the back of his hand.

"Good enough for me," Kenley said, and started the car. "Where are we headed?"

"London," was all he said.

* * *

Kenley was a nervous wreck during the journey, but tried hard not to show it. He tried to gauge Pearce's mood by periodically checking him in the rear-view mirror, but he just stared out the window the whole time.

"You keep staring at me like that, we'll end up in a ditch," he said, not taking his eyes from the countryside as it raced by.

Kenley didn't answer.

The journey took them through the back roads of Sussex and Kent, a technically still functional but utterly mullered and seldom-used network through the Garden of England that stitched together London and the outposts of the south coast. Kenley worried excessively about cop cars appearing in his rear view, but didn't see any. In retrospect, he wasn't surprised. Rural policing was headed the way of the dodo.

They traversed west from Bromley and nosed into Croydon. Pearce gave directions and eventually told Kenley to stop outside a minimarket that abutted a cluster of high-rises. Kenley tucked into a bus stop and switched off the engine.

"Now what?" Kenley said.

Pearce sank into his seat and folded his arms. "We wait."

And they did. They sat for the best part of an hour, saying nothing, Kenley's inner tension increasing like an elastic band being pulled ever tighter.

Eventually, he broke the silence.

"What is this, Stratton? We're exposed here. Someone's gonna report a hostile reconnaissance before too long."

"Hostile reconnaissance of what? Sainsbury's?"

"You can't account for what these muppets are thinking."

Pearce said nothing for a minute or two, then: "What happened with our friend?"

"Friend?"

"Don't be thick. You know what I'm talking about."

Kenley shook his head. Career criminals were worse than management consultants for talking elliptically. Pearce was the kind of person who'd pat you down for a wire on your deathbed.

He was talking about Kevin, of course.

"It's fine. All behind us."

"Did he talk? To the cops? Did he give them my name?"

Kenley pulled a face. "Does it matter? We couldn't take the chance. It doesn't make you any less wanted, however."

Pearce grunted. "I had nothing to do with it. You know that."

"You were there, though. Right?"

"I was in the cab. I didn't know what they were going to do."

Kenley shook his head again. The truth was a bit like expensive credit where people like Pearce were concerned — if you are actually innocent, it's righteous, hard-earned cash; if you're not, then the truth is a high-interest loan that you can falsely lay claim to — even in the face of incontrovertible evidence. If you don't have it, don't spend it, et cetera.

"It was a cop's old lady, Stratton, whichever way you slice it. They have long memories. And there were other casualties."

"Collateral damage."

Kenley snorted.

"Fuck's *sake*," Pearce groaned, as if the thought had never occurred to him. They sat in silence for ten more minutes or so, then he sat up straight in his seat. "There she is."

A slim woman in her late twenties appeared from a wide parade that led between the high rises. She was clutching the hand of a young boy in school uniform who was holding a lunchbox and half walking, half skipping alongside his mother — for that was clearly what she was. They had the same dark eyes, and the same thick, shiny black hair. The boy's skin was paler than the woman's, however, and at that moment Pearce dropped his hood.

In the rear-view mirror he looked like a skull, his skin stretched taut over his bald head, the blue serpent tattoo creeping up from his neck onto his scalp. All the bones in his head seemed to be visible and, as he stared at the woman and the boy, a knot of muscle in his jaw flexed tightly, in rhythm, like a pulse. He said nothing, but his eyes glistened. There was a car door and fifty feet between him and Pearce's girlfriend and son, but they may as well have been on another planet.

They rounded the corner of the minimarket and disappeared from view.

"They look good. Happy," Kenley said, rather fatuously.

Pearce inhaled suddenly and wetly through his mouth, stifling a sob.

"You watching out for them, yeah?"

"They're fine, Stratton. Nothing to worry about."

"We're in the age of the fuckin' flying car and a mixed-race kid can't live on an estate like this without getting shit . . ."

"Stratton, they're not getting hassle. Your reputation still has legs around here. They're fine."

"Watch them, Duke. That's all I'm asking. Just watch them."

Kenley nodded, but said nothing. He felt a selfish wave of relief. It seemed like the outing was winding down. Two, maybe two and a half hours back to the port and Pearce could be back and through the Schengen zone in time for afternoon tea.

"Come on, then," he said. "I want to check in on some of the operations."

Kenley's heart sank.

"I'm not sure that's such a good idea."

"What?" His voice was low, and Kenley knew this conversation wasn't going to end well. He didn't back down, though. Well, not immediately.

"I said: that isn't a good idea."

"You telling me what to do?"

"No."

"So start the fucking car."

Kenley did so, but didn't let it drop.

"All I'm saying," he said, as they headed south out of Croydon, "is that it's dangerous. You're exposed enough as it is. Why take the risk? Everything's running fine, and if there was an issue, we'd get a message to you."

"I want to go to Telstar, Vadim and Girder. That way they're at least en route."

"You're not listening to me, are you? Time was you used to ask my advice."

"But then you became the leader, eh?" Pearce said, a note of malice in his voice.

"What's that supposed to mean?" Kenley said.

"You just keeping my seat warm, Duke? Or you planning on squatters' rights when the time comes for me to get back on it?"

"This is ridiculous. You *want* to get caught or something?"

"You know your worst habit, Kenley? It's talking to people like they're stupid."

"Look—"

"Or is there something you don't want me to see?"

"The operations are running fine. I'm just trying to keep you out of prison."

"This conversation is getting on my tits, Kenley. Now, drive me to fucking Telstar before I get upset."

Kenley took a breath.

"I'm taking you to the port."

It wasn't the kind of thing he'd counsel anyone else saying to Stratton Pearce. In his case, however, it would at least bring the conversation to an end.

One way or another.

There was silence from the back seat, then a low chuckle. Kenley heard the seatbelt buckle unclip, the springs in the seat creak; then, when he spoke again, his voice was only inches from Kenley's ear.

"You've got some balls, Kenley, I'll tell you. That title's gone right to your head, eh? Anyone else spoke to me like that, they'd never hear me coming."

Kenley felt something cold, sharp and hard against his neck.

"Eventually, you know, you lose track of exactly what you've served time for, and what's still on the Old Bill's to-do list. Stop the fucking car."

Kenley stamped on the anchors and wrenched the car into a bus stop, cutting across a lane of traffic. Pearce was flung across the back seat.

"Don't do this," Kenley said, as Pearce righted himself and opened the back door. "If you really want to visit the hives, we can arrange something. But let's get you away and safe."

Pearce stood on the pavement and faced Kenley, expressionless. He said nothing, but pulled his hood down low over his eyes. He stood there for a moment, breathing heavily, his eyes concealed, and then he turned and walked off back towards London.

As he walked, Kenley saw spots of blood dripping onto the ground, from where he'd stuck himself with his own blade during the emergency stop.

* * *

Kenley pulled up outside the small parade of shops that had been erected near his development to service the needs of the new residents. There was a small Co-op, a greasy spoon, a bookies, a pharmacy, a hairdressers and a fish-and-chip shop. What more could modern society want on its doorstep?

Kenley had limited patience for the car park, which seemed to him to be a ridiculous design — you had to practically drive around the back to park out the front, and the entrance was only big enough for one car. So, if Mrs Higgins took forever pulling out or Mr Jessup decided to wait because there was a space imminently available, the whole place ground to a halt. Far too often he'd been tempted just to drive over the kerb and shortcut all the nonsense.

He popped into the Co-op and grabbed a basket, the arctic blast of the air-conditioning an unnecessary distraction, and indiscernible from the outside air temperature in any case.

He'd collected tea, milk, bread and a bunch of bananas when he saw the headline of the local rag:

FIRE DEATH WAS MURDER, COPS SAY

And underneath, a glossy full spread photograph of Ashford Road that said everything and nothing. A black sky. An orange mushroom of flame. Police cordon tape. A grim-faced PCSO in a yellow jacket standing on point, hat pulled down low over the eyes. Kenley grabbed the paper and skim-read the story. It was scant in the way of detail, but that could yet change.

The first thing he thought was: why not crop the photograph? Half of it was of the night sky. How much ink must that have used?

The second thing he thought was: *Fucking bollocks shit.*

He then said aloud: "Fucking bollocks shit."

He dropped the basket where he stood and ran back to the car.

There was a powder-blue Fiat Punto crawling its way into the car park as he started the engine. It didn't seem to be in a hurry. Kenley didn't wait. He drove up onto the kerb and yowled his way out, nearly collecting the offside of the Punto as he went.

The driver — not unreasonably, in the circumstances — gave him an angry blast of the horn; Kenley gave a decisive middle finger in riposte. Part of him hoped that the driver might bite and want to tussle, and he could exorcise some of this anger.

But when he looked in the Punto's window, he saw only a pretty young woman behind the wheel, with a small child strapped in the back. They locked eyes for an instant, too brief for Kenley to even reholster his middle digit.

This didn't make him feel any better, and he carried on.

Halfway between the shops and Park Meadow, his mobile phone rang. He pulled over to answer it. Getting something like a ticket for using your mobile while driving was anathema in the Keber playbook.

"Yes?"

"Kenley, you seen the news?" It was Sterling.

"Yeah. They'll be all over it like ants now. Okay, listen, no more phone calls. We'll meet at the usual place to discuss. Just you, me, Thing One and Thing Two, okay? We need a plan before Head Office hears about it."

"All right. Anything else?"

"Burn your phone. We'll get new ones. I'll see you later. And speak to your mate, the DC. I can do without guess-work, okay?"

Sterling rang off and Kenley carried on home, his mind revving up to redline.

He was so preoccupied he didn't notice the removal vans until he pulled onto the driveway. By the time he got out and shut the door, he had already made eye contact with his new neighbour over the roof of his car.

Who also happened to make eye contact as she removed her young son from the back seat of her powder-blue Fiat Punto.

Oh, great.

CHAPTER SIX

Kenley wasn't one to blow his own trumpet, but until he got involved, his crew — a franchised local subsidiary of Keber proper — were not what you'd call professional. They risked serious time for no reward, and there was no organisation or coordination of their activities. The fact that their collective IQ only just about made double digits was an unshakeable part of this. Stratton Pearce was smart enough, but he was headstrong, and riddled with principles.

The crew had never, for instance, thought about fronting their activities with at least some semblance of legitimate business, both to give the cash a bit of a clean but also to occupy them with something other than hanging around outside the job centre trying to offload wraps of brown and white and serving no purpose other than to attract attention. They may as well have been driving one of those ice cream vans that have the signs on the back that say STOP ME AND BUY ONE! A crack dealer's ice cream van. *Actually*, Kenley thought, *that isn't a totally bad idea.* It might even work.

In Kenley's own humble opinion, he brought structure to their thinking. The crew now had a couple of technically legit operations on the go. One was a car park, the other a storage facility. Both involved the freehold ownership of large spreads of land — a no-brainer, in Kenley's view — and they were pretty steady, demand-wise. People always wanted somewhere to park and somewhere to put stuff. Kenley had read some stuff about driverless cars turning the roads into unused ghost highways, but decided he would eat meat if it happened in his lifetime. And as far as commodity went, even his crew couldn't cock it up. It hardly required specialist knowledge to run or maintain. All you were doing was selling space – something, based on their cranial capacity, his crew knew all about.

Kenley parked off the Courtlands industrial estate; a hi-vis vest and hard hat from the boot kept the thin veil of freezing drizzle off his head. He walked around to the storage unit, looking up at the building that housed it as he walked.

The four-floor block had, once upon a time, housed the local telephone exchange. Now it was partly a network of containers like cells bolted to the inside of the brick structure like a reinforced iron endoskeleton, partly urban decay. The left side of the building had been left to rot, with thick foliage punching through empty doorways and stairwells liberally sleeved in graffiti. Most of the window frames were covered in chipboard, while the few glass panes that did remain were peppered with spidery holes from where rocks or golf balls had been lobbed through them.

Kenley met Sterling and they huddled outside container #67. It was getting on for one in the morning, and the place was creepy even for Kenley's lot. Long criss-cross corridors of grey prefab steel containers in a vast warehouse that used to be an abattoir. Perhaps.

The dim yellow lighting was strictly functional, casting long black shadows into corners large enough to conceal clusters of the undead, and while they technically offered twenty-four-hour access to one's belongings, Kenley knew for a fact that this service was taken up on a very infrequent basis.

"This place freaks me the fuck out," Sterling said, stamping his feet.

"Where are Thing One and Thing Two?"

"They'll be here. They're probably just washing the blood off."

"Blood? Whose? What for?"

"You're a vegetarian, aren't you? Don't worry about it," Sterling shrugged.

Golden Wonder and Blue Ray arrived a few minutes later and, after echoing Sterling's earlier sentiments about the unwelcoming nature of the place, they settled in to listen.

"It's all over the papers, then," Sterling said, just as Kenley opened his mouth.

Kenley gave him a sideways glance. "A fire with a body is always going to make the local rags, especially when news is slow. Big, dramatic, they love it. I doubt it'll trouble the nationals, and even if it does, it'll be for less than a day on a spread the size of a postage stamp."

Nobody said anything.

"What worries me," Kenley continued, "is that the 'M' word has been used, far sooner than any of us were expecting. The expiry of a bottom feeder like Kevin should be pretty far down on the list of priorities for the boys in blue."

"Maybe they're sending a message. To us, through the media. Keep us on our toes," Sterling suggested.

"Well, it's fuckin' working, then, ain't it?" Blue Ray said. His eyes gleamed in his fat head.

"Maybe," Kenley said. "But calling something a murder when it isn't is a tough genie to put back in the bottle. There're elections coming up, promotions to think of. You don't want to be alarming the public any more than you have to. And I actually don't credit the cops with that much wit."

"What about your Karate Kid routine to his neck?" Sterling said. "Could that show up on an autopsy?"

"I take it that's not for the minutes?" Kenley said.

Sterling looked blank.

"I'm sure I haven't a clue what you're talking about," Kenley continued, just in case. "But, hypothetically, although it's possible, I doubt it. It certainly shouldn't do, and it's only been a couple of days. I'd be amazed if all those wheels had turned sufficiently for a line to be fed to the press already. No, this is purely a theory. Some bright spark who isn't afraid of spending a few quid or limiting their own prospects by creating a fanfare."

Kenley paused for a moment, to let Golden Wonder and Blue Ray catch up.

"What about the mother?" Sterling said. "Murder or not, they'll get around to the next of kin at some point. They always do."

"Not worried about her. She won't talk. We'll still go say hi, but she's solid. I'm more concerned about where the cops are going with this."

"She's holding, don't forget."

"Try not to worry, Len. I haven't forgotten," Kenley smiled broadly. "What about your guy? The DC with the hairpiece. Does he have anything to offer?"

Sterling shook his head.

"Nah. He's dead in the water. One of his mates just got suspended for looking up his ex's new fella on the computer, and it's shit him right up. He won't say anything, and even if he wanted to, they've moved him to some training job. He doesn't speak to anyone and can't access any of the systems."

"Goddammit," Kenley said. "Is he going to give us our retainer back, then? This isn't a temp agency. You don't just jack it in when you feel like it."

"Want me to give him a once over?" Sterling said.

Kenley tapped his tongue against his teeth as he mulled it over.

"No," he said, eventually. "We don't need the heat, and we don't have the time. Follow him home a few times, do his tyres and put an anonymous note in to the Professional Standards people. Just ruin his month a bit."

"You got it," Sterling said.

"Okay, let's play this out. There'll be no scene evidence — the fire took care of that. Autopsies give you how, not who. CCTV coverage in that particular corner is pretty limited, so we're looking at witnesses and intelligence."

Kenley looked around at them. *Not much of that here*, he thought.

"What about the taxi rank? Couple of cabbies there when we went round," Sterling said.

Kenley eyeballed him.

"Do it. ID them, then see what they're saying. If they're talking to the cops, then . . . well, you know the drill. Christ's sake, Sterling, this is where having someone on the inside helps."

He shrugged. "Plenty more fish in the sea."

"Well, start looking. The Christmas bills have not long landed on the doormats, so it's a good time to recruit."

Credit to Sterling, he didn't waste time. He stepped away into the shadows and started making calls on his mobile.

"If Kevin was a proper grass," Golden Wonder said, inserting a Vicks stick up each nostril and inhaling deeply. "I mean, if he was getting cash and stuff from the Old Bill, then he's not just a dead junkie to them, is he?"

"He'll always be a dead junkie. The fact he was running his mouth doesn't move him any further up the food chain in their eyes. But I take the point. They're more likely to err on the side of caution where his death is concerned. But I'm confident we left it covered enough to withstand any scrutiny."

It didn't sound particularly convincing, and Golden Wonder didn't look reassured. Kenley worried momentarily for his teeth, but was interrupted by his mobile ringing.

He swallowed.

"Hello?"

"Head Office," said the robotic machine voice, the one he had come to associate with bad news in the middle of the night. "A lot of bad press about the junkie."

"I'm dealing with it. It's just noise. Nothing to worry about."

Kenley deliberately avoided platitudes. Head Office wouldn't appreciate it, and he didn't want his crew to witness either defensiveness or some kind of arse-kissing routine.

"It doesn't look like that from where the board is sitting. You've put yourself forward as a rising star, young man. If your star is not rising, how else are you any good to us? Put it right."

The line went dead. Kenley used to cheer himself up by imagining that the senior Keber delegate that owned the robot voice was a crash-hot Victoria's Secret model who made the management calls in her underwear, but the image was not proving particularly comforting this time around.

"Head Office," Kenley said. "Just checking in."

Golden Wonder and Blue Ray looked at him. Kenley imagined his face said it all, but he didn't want to share. If Kenley didn't have the confidence of Head Office, then what confidence could they have in him?

Mercifully, Sterling stepped out of the shadows. He held up his phone and grinned.

"Got something?" Kenley said, perhaps a little too eagerly.

"You could say that," Sterling said. "This one is ripe for plucking."

Kenley stared at the screen.

POLICE OFFICER FACES MISCONDUCT INVESTIGATION FOR ASSAULTING SENIOR OFFICER AT CRIME SCENE

"You know something, Len?" he said. "I think you might be right."

CHAPTER SEVEN

Paul Gamble was not what you would call a forward-think-
ing cop. He was actually less old-school than people gave him
credit for, but fictional characters like Gene Hunt had given
him licence to wear his seniority like a medal.

You wouldn't, for instance, have been able to get Paul
Gamble to attend much in the way of diversity training. The
chief constable himself would have struggled to drag him to
a leadership away day. He was not front and centre when it
came to considering names for the promotion hat.

But he did recall a small portion of one of his CID training courses, which had featured an isolated segment on what
had been billed as "reflective learning". As he recalled, the
concept revolved around recalling and replaying a particular
event — kicking the arse out of it, as far as Gamble could
see — and documenting all the wisps and shreds of thoughts,
emotions and conclusions that swirled around your brain
after the fact.

The statement template you were meant to complete to
capture this rollercoaster of cognitive activity was pages and
pages long, and contained prompts and fields that amounted,
in Gamble's view, to "fuzzy bean bag bollocks". Sitting there
and thinking about the same thing for hours on end and

calling it work seemed to Gamble to be some academic chin-stroker's idea of making a living.

Now he wished he'd paid more attention.

Reflection, as it turned out, was pretty easy and, depending on the event, happened whether you liked it or not.

For instance, the episode in which he'd used a raft of curse words at his new superintendent before dumping the man on his backside in the gutter had a way of replaying itself in his brain in a manifestly persistent fashion.

In fact, he could think of nothing else. The recollection was stuck on a loop in his mind, and impossible to dislodge.

He sat at his desk in a trance, replaying the whole sorry tale over and over again. To the casual observer he was doing nothing — and Gene Hunt would have bawled him out for being a work-shy nancy — but the brain work was so intense it required his entire body. He certainly couldn't concentrate on anything else, much less the teetering stack of green files on his desk that required some form of input on his part.

Technically, the act — should the new boss wish to labour the point — amounted to violence in the workplace, which in turn amounted to gross misconduct and was thus a sackable offence.

He had reimagined the incident for the forty-seventh time — his face again contorting in an involuntary wince at the point where Kane slipped and fell in the road — when his reverie was interrupted by his desk extension ringing.

The thing was buried under an unsorted morass of paperwork, most of which went on the floor due to the shock of hearing it. The damn thing never rang. Most people just used mobile phones, mainly because people these days could seldom be found at their desks. Only washed-up detectives whose careers were staring down the barrel of a gun sat at their desks for any length of time.

It stopped ringing just as he found it. Chick Grant had answered it from across the office. Gamble picked up the indistinct murmur of introductory pleasantries.

"Sarge," she called. "It's for you."

"I guessed that, seeing as it was my phone that rang."

Grant went to transfer it, but instead she muted the call and pressed the receiver to her chest.

"They want to interview me, you know."

"Who do? And about what?"

"PSD. The fact that I'm a witness to you manhandling the new boss."

"What the hell is the matter with everyone? The new boss? He looks like he's on his way to a Green Day concert and forgot his skateboard. And he's a *superintendent*? Someone needs to explain that to me, because I still don't get it."

"Well, it's not for me to say," she said. "I just thought I should tell you."

"You are the only living breathing witness, I suppose."

"You not counting the two PCSOs and the press photographer, then?"

"This isn't making me feel any better. You going to put that call through or what?"

She muttered something and jabbed a couple of buttons on her phone. Gamble's own phone began to ring again, and he picked it up.

"Yeah."

"'Yeah?' Not 'DS Gamble, CID, can I help you?'"

"Who is this?"

"It's Craig." Craig Breen was a mortuary assistant at the hospital and had a closer working relationship with Gamble than most cops, mainly because of the disproportionate number of cadavers that Gamble seemed to bring in.

"Oh. I thought it was going to be HR."

"Waiting for the hammer to fall, eh?"

"If I'm lucky it might only be a posting out of the new guy's hair."

"Sounds optimistic. I heard you dumped the superintendent on his arse."

"What do you want, Craig?"

"I actually phoned to tell you something about the same boss, but if you don't want to know, that's fine."

"Spit it out."

"He wants to attend the post-mortem."

"He does? Why?"

"You tell me."

Gamble didn't immediately answer.

"Paul?"

"What?"

"Did you hear what—"

"Do us a favour, Craig. It's booked in for tomorrow afternoon, yes?"

"Yeah."

"Who's doing it?"

"Gillian."

"Even better. Move it up, okay? Let's do it in the morning."

"What? I can't—"

"Yes, you can. Just change the schedule and bring it forward. I'll phone Gill myself and pour some candy floss in her ear."

"I'm not sure this is a good idea."

"What did you phone for, then?"

"I just thought you would want a heads-up that the new superintendent will be coming to the PM with you."

"Craig, look. It's still my case until I'm formally removed or posted or suspended, so bring the fucker forward, okay? If I *don't* do anything on the investigation, they'll still probably try to hang me out for neglect of duty. So, let's get some wheels turning, eh?"

* * *

"I guess we're taking my car, then," Barnes said. "That's going to be pretty draughty."

Barnes and Kane looked down at the spiderweb crack in the driver's windscreen and deep gouge that ran the full length of Kane's Lancer.

Kane looked up and around, apparently scanning for CCTV cameras.

"They're not real," Barnes said, without looking up.

"Be too much to ask for Ed Shaw's fingerprint on one of these pieces of glass, I suppose," Kane said.

"It might not have been him," Barnes said.

Kane looked at him sideways. "Is the list of suspects that long?"

"Well, your car's safer outside a fortified police compound than in it. What does that tell you? For what it's worth, I think you've made the right decision by calling it as murder. Shaw probably does too, he just doesn't like it."

"I just figured that if you treat something as murder and it turns out not to be, that's better than the inverse."

"That's exactly right. It's not common for the coroner to send a body back from inquest with a third-party verdict and a *must do better* instruction, but it can happen. The coroner finding a homicide that the cops have missed tends to ruffle very senior feathers, so I'd keep the 'told you so' on ice if I were you."

"Couldn't they have smashed it in the summer?" Kane said.

Barnes took a few half-hearted photographs, found some cardboard to cover the hole and then they drove to the hospital in Barnes's Rover.

"I'm guessing you've not been to one of these before," Barnes said as they drove. It wasn't a question. Kane didn't say anything.

"They're not pretty."

"You can catch me if I fall," Kane said.

Barnes looked over at Kane as they slowed for a queue of traffic. Somehow his new boss didn't seem like the type to pass out or vomit. They arrived at the hospital. The bays outside the emergency unit designated for police cars were already occupied — the result of a pile-up earlier that morning — and so they drove slowly around, looking for a parking space. As it happened, the space they found was down in an overspill car park, which meant the most direct route to the mortuary was via the same service road that the undertakers took, rather than through the hospital proper.

The mortuary delivery entrance was situated in an undercroft, surrounded by industrial fans and laundry bins and smooth concrete ramps along which enormous bins of clinical waste were pushed towards the base of the incinerator. Above the undercroft, beyond the blue-tinted fluorescent lighting, the whirlwind of the hospital's daily operation continued apace, unseen and unheard from this dimly lit engine room.

The undercroft was perpetually dark, even on the brightest summer's day, with lighting that could just about be called functional. Other than an unwelcoming sign telling unauthorised persons they were not admitted, there were no immediate clues as to the mortuary's function. There was a red sliding concertina door that the ambulances backed onto, next to which was a service door for live humans.

It was this door that opened as Kane and Barnes approached. Paul Gamble stepped out, looking simultaneously furtive and like a man who had made good his escape. He turned straight into their path, and two pairs of eyes locked on his as he stopped. The undercroft was a dead end, with no other activity besides the humming of the fans, and no one else around. Even if he'd had a little more time, he still couldn't have avoided them. He'd obviously thought about it for a split second, though. There was a flash of shock and guilt in his face. He covered it up immediately, but Barnes caught it — and assumed his boss had too. The new guy didn't seem to miss much. A shrill bite of wind looped down through the undercroft.

"Morning," Barnes said with faux brightness. "Fancy seeing you here."

"Yes. Fancy," Gamble said, apparently opting for the surly teenager routine. As such, he didn't advance the conversation, instead — and perhaps unwisely — waiting for whatever was coming next.

So, Barnes didn't disappoint him.

"What brings you here?"

"PM," Gamble answered.

"I guessed that," Barnes said. "You wouldn't be coming out this door if you were getting a latte."

Gamble said nothing. He looked at his watch.

"*Which case?*" Barnes made it clear this wasn't just two detectives swapping case stories.

"I'm not sure what that's got to do with you—"

"Which case, Paul?"

"Op Blackwater is mine," Gamble said. "It's a house fire with a body in it. No cause. Unless and until Major Crime take it off me, CID keep it. That's main office CID, by the way. Real donkey work. Not your lot, dancing around the edges. Why intel needs detectives, I—"

"We're here for the same thing," Kane interrupted, taking a step forward. "The post-mortem is in half an hour. And yet you're coming out."

Gamble managed to look simultaneously guilty and smug.

"PM's done. McKinsey just finished up. No foul play."

"I rang yesterday to confirm the time. Two o'clock." Barnes's voice was dangerously low.

Gamble shrugged. "I guess they move the cases around. You know, manage the workload. You remember what that's like?"

"And you wouldn't have had anything to do with that, of course. A well-placed phone call, maybe."

"I resent the insinuation. But if I did, so what? It's my case to manage."

"Not any more, it isn't," Kane said quietly.

"Goddammit, Paul. I don't believe a word of this. I don't believe in a cut-price PM either. It's bloody sabotage," Barnes said.

"How dare you," Gamble said. There was no real conviction in his voice. "I don't know what the hell you're talking about."

"I want a Home Office pathologist to cut the bastard up," Barnes said. "You can consider that a lawful order. I may not be *your* DI, but I am a DI nonetheless."

"And I don't want you to touch it," Kane said. "Op Blackwater is not yours any longer."

"Whatever you say, sir," Gamble said, spitting the mode of address with poorly concealed contempt. "I look forward to written confirmation from HR, though. You bosses have a great afternoon."

He pushed past them and headed along the service road, hands in pockets, whistling a jaunty tune.

"I cannot believe the nerve of this prick," Barnes said, anger causing his voice to tremble. "I'd lay money that he got a sniff that we were coming and got the case moved up the list."

"One way to find out," Kane said, climbing the steps and knocking on the mortuary's red door.

* * *

The tune Paul Gamble whistled as he strolled back to the car may have been outwardly jaunty, but it was a facade contrived so as not to betray the adrenaline-charged tremble in his legs.

He had parked on a grass verge adjacent to the hospital's main entrance road. It was obviously not a designated parking space, nor was it regulated by any kind of obvious signage.

There were two large men standing around his car. One was peering into it. The car was far enough from anything else to mean they were interested in the car and the car alone. Gamble got an adrenaline burst for the second time in ten minutes, and he reached into his pocket for his warrant card.

"Bus stop's over there," he said, holding the tin aloft.

"Don't you have to park with all the rest of us, then, sir?" one of the men said, grinning as he did so.

They didn't look like parking attendants. They were mean looking and wore a donkey jacket and hoody respectively. Gamble thought he might even recognise one of them.

"What do you want?" he said, putting the warrant card away. They were obviously unimpressed. Maybe because they already knew he possessed one.

"Detective Sergeant Gamble, am I correct?" the first man said. "It's a pleasure."

"And you are?"

Both men grinned this time.

"Shall we go for a little drive?" the first man said.

"Do I look simple?" Gamble said. "You recognise the badge, yeah? You know what that means?"

"Relax, Sarge," said the man. "We're all friends here. We've got a little proposition for you."

Gamble said nothing.

"So, get your keys out and open the fucking door."

Gamble knew he had a handful of options. Run, fight, try to call 999 or make a lot of noise in the hope someone else would call 999 . . . or just go with it.

He opened the driver's door, then took a step back and held his phone to his ear.

"Yeah, control room? DS Gamble here. Don't ask questions, but if I don't phone you in ten minutes, I want you to GPS my phone and send the cavalry. Raise hell, okay?"

The man's grin didn't falter as he slid into the passenger seat.

"Clever," he said, his grin never wavering. "Although I'd hedge my bets there was no one on the end of that call."

"One way to find out," Gamble said as he started the engine. "Let's hope you're not as stupid as you look."

This time the grin did slip a little.

"That mouth ever get you into trouble?" the man said.

"Your girlfriend getting in or what?" Gamble said.

The man whistled, and the other goon crammed himself into the back seat. Gamble quietly thanked his untidy tendencies — he had earlier pushed the driver's seat right back in order to hold the mass of junk on the back seat in place. This meant the gorilla had to sit behind his colleague, not Gamble.

They moved off slowly, and pulled out into traffic.

"Seatbelts," Gamble said. "You never know when I might have to perform an emergency stop."

"Don't do anything silly, Sarge," said the man next to him.

"Best keep your eyes peeled for danger, then," Gamble said.

"Shall we dispense with the flirting?" the man said. "You're, what, three years off retirement?"

"Two."

"And how does that look? With a divorce and a couple of kids? She getting half the pension?"

"I'll manage," Gamble said, but some of the bravado had slipped from his tone.

"And, of course, that assumes you make it through the next two years without getting yourself into some kind of trouble."

The man reached into his pocket and pulled out a crumpled newspaper.

"Looking at this, it's a wonder you've made it this far."

Gamble glanced over. He'd already seen the headline.

"Some might even say you wanted to get knocked off your perch. I've seen naughty cops argue most things, but duffing up your boss is probably a difficult one to wriggle out of. And you think *I'm* stupid."

The man stretched in his seat and lit a cigarette. Gamble didn't say anything, and suddenly the status had shifted.

"So, what was it? Some jumped-up newly promoted young so-and-so push your buttons?"

"More or less," Gamble mumbled.

"That a problem for you?"

"It could be."

They headed into town, Gamble having some vague idea of burning up to Beachy Head and threatening to drive off the edge should it come to it.

"So, let's assume you get the boot. How'd you like to open a little, er, unemployment insurance policy? Maybe give the whippersnapper a little 'fuck you' into the bargain?"

"What do you want?"

"Information, Sarge, is the healthiest commodity in the market."

"You want me to feed you information? Are you insane? I'll lose my job."

"Looks to me like you're going to lose it anyway."

"And I'll go to prison. A disgraced ex-cop doing bird. Not exactly the way I want to spend my retirement."

"Be nice to go down fighting, no? Take down a few of them with you. Especially the pompous little fuckers."

"I am not and never have been bent. And I never will be."

"Sarge, Sarge," the man said, holding up his hands. "Calm down. We're not asking for your signature in blood. Just have a little think about it, eh?"

They were at the pier now, snarled up in traffic, Gamble having driven more or less in a straight line south.

The man opened the door, as did the gorilla in the back.

"Think about it," he said, tossing an item onto the passenger seat, where it landed with a soft thump.

Then they disappeared, between the cars, up past the back of the Queen's Hotel, probably into one of the less salubrious drinking pits that occupied this end of town.

Gamble picked up the item. It was a dirty bundle of twenty-pound notes, bound with an elastic band. He fingered it lightly, trying to estimate the value.

They already had him, he knew. It was like a ticking time bomb. Unless he picked up the phone right now and told someone, it was already too late. Game over.

He pulled into the car park of the Queen's Hotel. It was largely deserted, the winter sun like a dying flame on the horizon. He remembered when the entire top floor had gone up in a blaze during renovations, after a spark from a contractor's blowtorch had smouldered overnight in the rafters and then spread like a maniac when the midday sun warmed the building. Gamble had arrested some poor young bellboy for arson who had been acting suspiciously during the evacuation. They had scrapped like squaddies on the tarmac, right in front of the press. Kid only had a bogey of dope in his pocket, and the uniformed Gamble — who was only acting on the inspector's orders — had dusted him off and driven him home after the interview. The kid had been quietly grateful to Gamble for "not being a prick with me".

It seemed like a long time ago. What was it? Twenty-five years? The kid had been about nineteen. Gamble wondered what he was doing now. He suddenly felt like he was sliding down a long black chute, unable to get a handhold.

As it was, Gamble did pick up the phone. It rang as he did so. It was the control room, calling back as per his instruction. It took Gamble a moment to remember why they were calling.

He ended the call. And he did phone PSD. But he didn't tell them what had just happened. What he said was:

"DS Paul Gamble here. East Downs CID. How do you feel about running a few checks on our new superintendent?"

CHAPTER EIGHT

Kane stared at the screen. The email was terse, to say the least. Despite next to no time being a cop, Kane had already learned that, in most cases, emails appeared to be the preferred communications medium. Whether it was the presence of an audit trail, or the fact that you could make your point in a thirty-second email versus a ten-minute phone call, Kane was quickly discovering the tacit expectation that emails were there to be monitored — and responded to quickly.

Particularly if they were from the assistant chief constable.

It wasn't *his* assistant chief constable — there were three in force, each with their own command. The chain of command for uniform ascended the slippery totem pole up to ACC Damian Roy, while the CID equivalent slid alongside it up to ACC Gabriel Glover. (The third ACC looked after Ops, which gave him all the toys — dogs, firearms and traffic — but Kane hadn't made his acquaintance yet.)

In the space of about ten seconds Kane played out the most likely scenario — the disgruntled Shaw, needled at having his professional judgment upended by some tattooed upstart, had wasted no time bringing his complaint down onto the test-your-strength landing pad with enough force to ring the bell at the very top. Kane noted that it hadn't slid back down in quite so linear a way — in fact, Glover had abseiled off the roof and smashed through the window on Kane's floor.

Kane read *You'd better explain yourself* for the tenth time, then switched off the machine, grabbed his jacket and drove into town.

He headed along the seafront and drove a few aimless figure-eight circuits around Gildredge Park and the Saffrons, the large crack at the top of the windscreen a constant motif. *And probably not legal*, he thought. He drove up to the Wish Tower before heading back into the town centre and back down to the Ashford Road crime scene.

The cordon was still on, and a marginally effective diversion was in place around the already-makeshift one-way system that surrounded the still, activity-free demolition site of what would eventually be the new shopping centre.

Kane parked on the edge of the cordon and walked to where a string of blue-and-white scene tape stretched across the road from railing to lamp post, fluttering in the icy breeze. He looked back at the snarled-up traffic chain crawling past and wondered if someone was going to start making some calls soon about the impact of his crime scene on the town's economy.

He frowned as he approached the officer on scene guard. Yellow-jacketed officers were working in pairs, moving up and down the street, going from door to door. Kane, momentarily surprised by the amount of activity, scanned the street until he found someone he could zero in on.

She was standing inside the cordon, by the now-redundant Sainsbury's entrance doors, opposite the scene itself. She wore jeans and walking boots with a yellow hi-vis overcoat, and she was holding a clipboard with a pen between her teeth.

Something radiated off her that told Kane she was clearly in charge, and he walked over.

"Hello, boss," she said as he approached.

Kane frowned. He had a zip-up fleece on over his uniform, and his ID was still in his pocket.

She gave a half-grin and waggled a finger up and down at his throat.

"I think it's the tie and the piercing. Not a common combo. Plus, you know . . ."

"Word gets around?"

"Something like that. Shaz Brooker. I'm the house-to-house manager."

"I thought the house-to-house had been done?"

"It had. Now it's being done again, and then again. As a line of enquiry, it's a staple, but it's far from simple, and very easy to get wrong. You can miss so much if you take people's word for it when they say they didn't see anything."

"Or if you forget to ask if the lodger is down the shops."

She smiled. "Exactly."

"Mind if I tag along?"

"Help yourself." She gestured towards the pairs working the street like the hi-vis stalwarts of a particularly aggressive campaign trail.

Kane went over to the nearest pair, who were just descending the steps of a flat right next door to where Kevin Bridger had met his demise.

"Anything?" he asked as they passed on the bare concrete steps.

"Not much," came the answer. "She was asleep in bed with her kids. Spent two hours on the pavement with them after Trumpton evacuated the street."

"You mind?" he said, pointing at the front door with one hand while producing his warrant card with the other.

"Help yourself. Her English isn't great, though. Fair warning."

Kane nodded and climbed the steps to the flat door. There was a ravaged-looking rubber mat and a pair of yellow welly boots beside it. One of the boots was full of soil, with a Union Jack and a Filipino flag wedged into it and coiled around one another.

He thought about shrugging off the fleece and at least appearing to be a uniformed officer, but in the end thought better of it and instead clutched his warrant card as though it were the only thing keeping him from being cast headlong into a parallel dimension where he was neither a cop nor a criminal. Besides, he'd left his hat in the car.

He stamped his feet while he waited, and peered over the concrete balustrade to the shell of Kevin Bridger's house next door. It was little more than a scaffold skeleton now, the black-edged remnants of the wooden structure the only parts still visible underneath the metalwork. Despite almost a week of rain and now snow, the whole thing still had the stink of a washed-out barbecue.

A tiny woman, less than five feet tall, answered, letting a blast of warm cooking out into the cold air. Dark strands of damp black hair were stuck to her temples; her expression was tense, mirrored by the infant wrapped in her arms and wedged against her hip. Kane watched her eyes flick to his piercing, then the pink laser scar of his tattoo, and back to his eyes. Like so many others. Could set your watch by it.

"Hi there," Kane said, raising the warrant card. "Police. I'm sorry to bother you."

"I just saw police." Her accent was heavy.

"I know, I'm just . . ." He didn't want to say *I'm in charge* or *I desperately need to find evidence of a crime or the ACC will boot me out of the job inside a week.* "Can you tell me how you are?"

She frowned, not understanding.

"How I are?"

"How are you? Since the fire. How are you coping?"

She screwed up her face. Kane tried something else. He pointed at the infant and held up a finger.

"Just one? One baby?"

She shook her head and squawked back over her shoulder into the flat. With precise obedience two more children, maybe five and seven, appeared out of the gloom and hid behind her legs, peering up at the strange visitor.

"They okay? Are they sleeping?"

She seemed to understand. Her lips stretched back over her teeth in a frightened grimace, and her eyes widened.

"I wake up, I hear fire. I take children outside with blanket. Four hour we wait on street, till someone takes us to hotel."

"I didn't know about that. I'm sorry. I . . ."

"My husband, he work. Night shift. At the hospital. He come home, I not here. Now I read in paper. It is murder, police say. Murder." Her eyes widened even more, her face taut in a fixed grin of fear. "I am scared. Who would do this? Men came? Men came in the night to kill people, right where my children sleeping?" Her voice elevated to a screech, which prompted some wailing from down by her knees.

"Don't worry," Kane said. "We can protect you." But even as he said it, his mind was whirring with the insidious temptation of false promises. How could they protect her? With what? Give her a 24/7 armed guard and the whole street would want one, and Kane was already learning that there weren't enough cops to cover the basics, let alone anything more complex.

He started to mutter some more platitudes, then the whole thing fizzled out and he turned to go.

He'd got to the top step when he turned back.

"Did you say, 'men came'? How do you know men came? Did you see something?"

She stared at him. To the casual observer she was not understanding, but Kane could see the cogs whirring behind her eyes.

"Were there men? How many men? When was this?"

Her face started to contort in demonstrable anguish — contrived or otherwise, Kane couldn't tell, but it looked convincing. *Don't make me*, her expression said.

"If you saw something, you need to tell me."

"No English."

"Don't give me that. Come on. Please."

Her eyes narrowed.

"Dead man, bad man. They knock house down, my children sleep."

She glared at Kane, then slammed the door before he could say anything else.

Kane walked off down the steps two at a time. He called over Shaz Brooker and told her what he'd learned. Even as he spoke, he found himself losing the courage of his convictions, but Shaz held his gaze and the minute he'd finished, she was on her radio, calling the previous pair back up the street to try again. After that, she called Barnes on her mobile, told him they might have a *sigwit*, and suggested he might like to send a detective and an interpreter to the flat.

"Go easy on her," Kane said, quickly extrapolating "significant witness" from "sigwit". "She's no fool, and fragile at best."

"Leave it with us, boss," Shaz said. "Good job."

Kane met up with a couple more of the enquiry teams, but he was distracted, and most of the remaining houses were on-brand — apathetic at best, verging on hostile in other cases. Those that answered, in any case.

He found himself looking back along the street at the woman's flat. He hadn't got her name, and hoped the previous team had been a bit more thorough and professional than he had.

He chewed it over in his mind. In her broken English she'd said enough — Kevin Bridger deserved it, and now she might get some peace. If she'd seen something, prising it out of her would need some careful work, but Kane figured that was probably true of most witnesses. Most people sleep soundly in their beds, he thought, mostly untroubled, and most of the time. If the bad people come in the night, then they might pass on you, or they might knock on your door. You might pique their interest, or you might not, but, either way, you didn't have much of a say in it. And, if you did have the misfortune of getting in their crosshairs, there wasn't a great deal you could do about it.

Kane pictured, in his mind's eye, the unlikely coalition of circumstances that ended up with the tiny Filipino woman going to Crown Court as a key witness for the prosecution.

What would happen? Would she be firebombed out of her crappy flat? Something more insidious? More implicit? Having your tyres slashed and some crap sprayed across your front door might just be enough for most people, particularly when it became apparent to them that the police weren't going to be able to do a great deal to help. Most people just want a quiet life, and there didn't seem to be a whole heap of incentive to stick your head above the parapet by doing silly things like giving statements to the police.

On the run back to the station, the fear on the woman's face and her almost ungodly screech replayed themselves in Kane's mind. He parked up and then headed to the office.

He looked up the email from the ACC, got his mobile number from the signature footer and dialled it. The first couple of times it rang out and then cut to a very brusque voicemail greeting message.

On the third attempt, he picked up.

"ACC Glover."

"Sir, good afternoon. I apologise for the late call."

"Who is this?"

"This is Samson Kane. You asked me to call you. You sent me an email."

"That was hours ago."

"Forgive me. I've been out on patrol with my teams."

"That's not your job, Superintendent. We have bobbies for that. If you think this job is all fun and games . . ."

"Understood. Specifically, I was helping them with the house-to-house enquiries for Op Blackwater. The homicide enquiry," he added.

He heard Glover breathe deeply on the other end of the phone.

"You're killing me, Superintendent. This enquiry could have been done with one DC and an arson investigator. File for the coroner, misadventure, job done. You are rinsing my Major Ops budget — on the cusp of the new financial, by the way — for a dead junkie rat whom nobody is going to miss."

"Sir . . ."

"And who, precisely, has policied that the demise of this unfortunate gentleman was somehow the result of third-party involvement?"

"That would be me, sir."

"On what basis?"

"Initially, it was thought that strung-out heroin addicts could well accidentally set themselves on fire. But the deceased was an informant — I didn't like it."

"You didn't . . ."

"Plus, I figured that it's better to do it properly, and if it does turn out to be misadventure, no harm done."

"Tell that to the director of finance."

"Better that than suffer the ignominy of the coroner calling you up from Kevin Bridger's eventual inquest to say you've overlooked a homicide?"

Kane figured he owed Barnes for that one.

"I beg your pardon?"

"Anyway, as it happens, I may need you to weigh in for some witness protection."

"I . . . you what? You have a witness?"

"Potential witness. She doesn't speak English very well, and she's clamming up already."

Kane heard Glover sucking air through his teeth on the other end of the phone.

"Let me be candid, Mr Kane. And let's park the issue of whether this case is or isn't a murder. You'll have another ten dead bodies on your hands in a week, each with a family considerably more vocal than this one, and you'll quickly realise there's not enough hours in the day for your 'do the right thing' dogma.

"But you don't *ever* speak to one of my DCIs the way you did to Ed Shaw. Ever. I don't know who the hell you think you are, but most people with a crown on their shoulder *earned* it, through hours pounding a beat and years spent seeing the very worst of what people can do to each other, the kind of thing that eats up marriages and makes some cops throw a rope around a loft joist. Some beanbag academic at

Bramshill may have decided over a pain-relief joint that you could just be given that rank, but as far as I'm concerned, you're a fake."

"I understand, sir."

Glover's breathing suddenly became heavy in Kane's ear, like he'd pressed the receiver right up to his curled lips.

"People don't *want* cops with tattoos and piercings turning up when they've been burgled. Do you get that?"

"What about when people with tattoos and piercings get burgled?" Kane asked, and hung up the phone.

He got up and went to the window, looking at the perimeter fence and the Bridgemere allotments beyond it. The leaf blowers were not in view, but he could faintly hear them, buzzing through the Levels somewhere down by the golf course.

He stood for a moment, concentrating on taking deep breaths. In through the nose, out through the mouth. He felt strangely calm. Glover was just saying exactly what whoever had keyed his car had said, only in a way that was so unambiguous that Kane now knew exactly where he stood, from the top on down. It was an oddly steadying feeling.

All that said, Glover had, inadvertently or otherwise, zeroed Kane's mind in on one thing — Kevin Bridger's family. The person or persons that they were, technically, trying to get justice for. Barnes wasn't answering his phone, so Kane sent him a brief email asking him for a sitrep on the next-of-kin enquiries.

Kane flicked through the remainder of his emails without any conviction whatsoever, tried unsuccessfully to get hold of Shaz Brooker, and then browsed some brightly coloured job vacancy website, knowing full well that he wouldn't apply for anything.

He scratched his chin. He'd never been employed before. All his enterprising prior to becoming a cop had been vaguely entrepreneurial, whether it was setting up a business, left-field fundraising or playing out some fast and loose idea about selling that *amounted* to setting up a business. He'd always been in *control*, and now found it rather odd that his first foray into a steady paycheck involved the kind of disciplined hierarchy that was at complete odds with anything he'd done to date. Particularly if your face didn't fit.

But the bawling out from Glover wasn't occupying his mind as much the terrified face of the woman whose husband worked nights. In fact, he knew full well he wouldn't have had the balls to even call Glover back if he hadn't met her. Her contorted expression kept coming back to him. She was scared, and she'd either seen something or heard about it. Enough to have no trust in the cops.

No doubt his more seasoned colleagues would tell him he was being too soft, or investing too much of his own emotions in ten-a-penny witnesses, but he didn't particularly care. Even if he did develop a thicker skin over time, there had to be something about giving a shit. Didn't there?

Kane waited until the majority of the office-hours staff had cleared off home, then picked up his desk phone. He waited, the receiver to his ear, and listened hard for any other sounds in the building.

He dialled.

"Hello?"

"It's me."

"Ah! Samson. How goes the position?"

The tone was playful. Samson's mood soured immediately.

"Honestly? About as bad as it possibly can be. Worse, even. It's one hatchet job after another. One of the other detectives summed it up — he said my car's safer outside the police station car park than inside it. I'm on the verge of hanging up this bloody uniform, and it's not even the end of week one."

"Keep it to yourself. If they sense blood . . ."

"Thanks, that's reassuring. Besides, they already do. The fire investigation saw to that. I wanted it investigated as a homicide, and I practically had an insurrection on my hands."

"Stay pure. Even if they don't have confidence in you yet, they recognise the rank. No one is that work-shy they would risk outright insubordination for being asked to do their job. Cops are more likely to fight back if something threatens their way of life — particularly if that way of life includes a career built on cutting corners."

"Meaning?"

"The accidental fire that claimed the life of a drug addict is an easy theory. The theory where said drug addict is a registered informant who has been silenced is altogether more sinister — particularly as it is likely that at least a handful of cops are connected to it, and I don't mean in a good way."

"You mean dirty?"

"I'm afraid so. Where the handling of sources is concerned, there's always a risk of blowback on the inside. The lines can get awfully murky. Anyone with the wherewithal to murder an informant and make it look like an accident suggests to me they were above street level, which means they've undoubtedly got some cops in their pocket too."

"But you'll be looking at that, right?"

"Obviously."

"You think Gamble?"

"Actually, I'm not too sure. A thick-headed lout he may be, but I'm not yet persuaded that he's bent. Now, the other detective you mentioned. The one who gave you the car park analogy."

"Yes. Barnes, his name is."

"Rutherford Barnes."

"Yes. Why? Do you know him?"

"Indeed I do. It would be unkind to describe him as damaged goods, but . . . well. He's bright, and he cares. With two years' service, that can send you on all sorts of wonderful adventures. With eleven . . ."

"What?"

"Let's just say he wore his heart on his sleeve when he should have kept it in his pocket."

"I think you might be mixing your metaphors."

"Guilty as charged. Mr Barnes has, uh, been through the mill somewhat. He practically witnessed first-hand the murder of a colleague on two separate occasions, while the roads of Sussex claimed the life of his wife about five years ago during a police pursuit."

"My God."

"A terrible set of circumstances."

"Did they . . . did we catch who did it?"

"Regrettably not. A fact that Mr Barnes has become somewhat driven by, to say the least."

"I still trust him."

"Oh yes, no reason you shouldn't. In a circuitous way, he's one of the good ones. Which I think will always be his undoing. Is he involved in the fire investigation?"

"He's leading it, yes."

There was silence on the line.

"Are you there?"

"I'm here."

"Is that bad?"

"Is . . . ?"

"Barnes being involved in the arson enquiry. Is it a problem?"

"It could be. I don't know."

"Why?"

"Another time, dear boy."

Kane set his jaw. The man could be irritatingly elliptical when he wanted to be.

"Listen . . . why did you pick me?" Kane said after twenty seconds of silence.

"I'm sorry?"

"You must have known I'd be put through the wringer. Did you think I'd be assaulted by a colleague on day one?"

"Well . . ."

"There's any number of tattooed left-field fringe thinkers in my neck of the woods. Why me?"

The slightly playful tone of the voice on the other end disappeared.

"Listen to me. You are not like the others. You might like the same music, the same art, hold the same views on a capitalist society — but you are different. You have a certain something, my boy, and don't forget it. The storm you are currently being forced to weather is nothing we weren't expecting. You just can't see a way out of it right now. But when the clouds break, you'll do amazing things. Have you arrested anyone yet?"

"What? No."

"Go and see the duty sergeant. Use the rank. Tell them you want to go out on patrol with one of their team. Take some calls. Make an arrest. Say the words. Make sure you're the one to put the cuffs on. Preferably someone who's going to play up a bit, so the rest of the team respond to the call for backup. You'll feel better, and you'll earn instant respect. Once you have the patrol teams on your side, chinless DCIs in bad shirts who don't want to work for a living will seem easy in comparison."

Kane processed the idea in his head.

"Okay," he said eventually, when it seemed to make sense.

"Trust me. It will be okay. Don't quit."

Kane ended the call, left the office and drove north out of Eastbourne on the bypass, turning off after about ten miles onto back lanes and country roads until he came to the old railway line.

The Cuckoo Line had ceased operating as a mainline back in the sixties, and now formed a trail up from Polegate and into Waldron. Although it had long since ceased operating as such, having been converted into a family residence, the former Hellingly station still looked the part. The old car park was now a wide expanse of tarmac driveway, while the platform, separated as it was from the original line by a thick wedge of vegetation, still stretched out beyond the house under a canopy that, as far as Kane could tell, had kept the original intricate dagger board valancing.

Under the canopy today was an array of once-white linen pegged carelessly onto a nylon line. Concrete window plinths framed nothing but brick, and bright red doors to storage sheds that had once been waiting rooms and ticket offices and public toilets lined the former platform. The driveway was sizeable enough to hold a collection of vintage custom cars — but all Kane could see was a Ford Capri up on bricks and a windowless 1986 Bedford ambulance that had also once been white.

Kane followed the fence line parallel to the trail, passing under the concrete hangman arms of a long-disused signal. A metal frame hung off the cross-strut, suspended by two chain link lines, that had presumably once held signs saying STOP or SLOW or whatever. When Kane got to the platform he clambered over the driveway gate, pausing to see if Dooley decided to attack, but all was quiet.

The front door was also painted red, flanked by two boxwood planters that actually, Kane thought as he walked straight past, made it look surprisingly welcoming. He traversed the driveway and hopped over a gate into the adjoining field, which stretched parallel to the former railway.

The field was huge, and it took Kane a couple of minutes to walk right down to the corner, picking his way through still-thick snow that was slowly starting to turn to slush. Tucked under the treeline was a caravan that, from the foliage snaking up around the wheels, had clearly not moved in years, but still seemed to be in reasonably good condition.

There was an orange crate acting as a step outside the caravan's door. Kane hesitated. He didn't know what cops did off duty. He imagined the married ones went home to their families, while the single ones . . . well. He presumed they socialised with colleagues.

The DI, Barnes. He had the general countenance of a man who didn't have much else besides the job — even after just a few brief encounters, Kane knew that Barnes considered the notion of a career to be a moot point — but Kane didn't even have that. To be married to your job, or have a social life that revolved around it, necessitated not being completely ostracised in your first week.

And yet, Kane knew that his own family — such as it was — would have strung him up by the ankles from the hundred-year-old concrete signal strut outside Jimmy's railway station residence if they knew he'd joined the cops. So, what choice did he have?

The door opened just as he raised his fist to knock. Jimmy trotted out of the caravan, hot stuffy air coming with him.

His eyes, which carried the same silver-ice translucence as Kane's own, narrowed when he saw his nephew. Dooley stood by his master's heel and emitted a low throaty growl, but he stopped when he saw Kane. He trotted over and nuzzled Kane's hand.

"You have a house, you know," Kane said, trying, unsuccessfully, to give the man a smile. He bent down to make a fuss of the dog.

Jimmy shrugged.

"The cats like it more than me."

"Why don't you just sell it? Must be worth something."

He shrugged again.

"What brings you out this way?"

Kane shrugged. With a grunt, Jimmy indicated a couple of dirty plastic picnic chairs on the grass.

"Been a while since you've come around," Jimmy said, flopping into a chair and lifting a thin cigar. His belly strained against his vest, but his arms had clearly lost none of their power. A halo of silver hair spread across his shoulders and down over the backs of his triceps, then disappeared under a thick orange blanket that he pulled around his top half. "Last time I heard from you, you were, what? Opening an art gallery over Hastings way?"

"Sort of."

"How'd that pan out?"

Now it was Kane's turn to shrug.

"You see much of anybody? Ma?"

"Nope."

Kane hadn't expected much else. Jimmy was also ostracised from the family, but for his own reasons, and of his own volition. He wasn't exactly the sort of person to worry about

85

his no-claims bonus or his National Insurance contributions, but he didn't like the way the rest of the family stepped outside the law with frivolous regularity either. Living in the caravan in the corner of the garden while the house went to rack and ruin was just the physically imagined state of his own personal limbo.

Which was part of the reason Kane had gone to see him.

"I've got something to tell you," Kane said.

Jimmy gestured again to the empty chair opposite, then spluttered a phlegmy cough into the back of his hand. Kane stared across the field while Jimmy got himself together. The old man had arranged brightly coloured plastic tunnels, planks suspended between stepladders and kids' climbing frames around the field in a circuit.

"You training Dooley again?" Kane asked.

Jimmy hadn't finished coughing, but he nodded anyway. Kane looked back across the field, his eyes drawn again to the concrete crosspiece that had once held the signal arm for this stretch of railway; beyond that, the neat brick arch of Shawpits Bridge.

He closed his eyes and tried to imagine the train easing up from Polegate, clusters of men and women in Sunday best on the platform. Top hats and parasols, maybe. He tilted his head. What was further up the line that would necessitate that kind of wardrobe? Although, back then, they pulled on their three-piece suits for the school run, didn't they? And if the last train passed through here in the sixties, would it have been steam? Or was diesel already mainstreaming by then? He didn't know. He would have to find out. His idle daydream definitely featured a steam whistle. Mainstreaming on the mainline . . .

"You want a drink or something?" Jimmy asked. He seemed to have recovered.

Kane shook his head and sat back in the chair. The air was still and cold, but the appearance of winter sun was surprisingly warm.

"So, what was it you wanted to tell me?"

Kane didn't answer, but produced the small black leather wallet from his breast pocket and passed it over to Jimmy without making eye contact.

Jimmy eyed Kane for a moment, then flipped open the warrant card.

"Aye," he said, after a long time.

"That all you've got to say?"

"You tell anyone else about this?"

"Not yet. But look at my rank. Won't be long before I'm on some TV interview or something."

"Modest, aintcha?"

Kane shrugged.

"It's just a fact. Goes with the job."

Jimmy tossed the warrant card back. It landed in Kane's lap.

"I ain't seen you in, what? Got to be two years. What you bring this to me for?"

"I . . . I don't know. I guess, I thought . . . I'm not having a very good time of it."

Jimmy snorted.

"Doesn't surprise me. How they take people like you anyway?" He waggled a finger at Kane's tattoos and piercings.

"Well, I guess they figured people like me are victims of crime too. They want someone they can relate to turning up."

Jimmy frowned.

"You remember that time you got in that fight? Lost a tooth. Right on the bridge there."

Kane didn't answer.

"Cops turned up to that one. You'd have felt better if there'd been some tattooed punkster riding the jam sandwich?"

It was an honest question. Kane thought about it, and realised he wouldn't have done.

"They'd have still dragged you in, whatever they happened to be decorated with. Kicking and screaming. You remember that?"

Kane didn't say anything. He'd wanted to descend on Jimmy's doorstep and bare his soul, seeking some sort of solace, or counsel, from the only person that would listen — despised by colleagues one week into a new job, but with no prospect of going back. If the family knew what he'd done . . .

"Let me ask you something," Jimmy said. "If as many as half of the cops looked like you, do you think the other half would treat the people on the street better?"

Kane didn't answer.

"Honest question," Jimmy said. He stretched his legs out, then sat forward and lit a small camping stove on the grass in front of him. "You going to tell your mother?"

"That I'm a cop? Are you serious?"

"I don't know what you want from me, son."

Kane stared over at the tracks again. He wasn't sure either.

CHAPTER NINE

Kenley knocked on the black, gloss door and looked down at the embossed planter cubes either side of it, ladled with sprawling lavender. As new builds went, it had quite a lot of charm.

He saw the bob of blonde through the frosted glass. She paused there for a moment on the other side of the door, before reaching out for the latch.

The door opened.

"Yes?"

She was wearing a camel-coloured sweater hanging off one shoulder, and the right side of her face was partially obscured by the long, smooth sweep of hair. It didn't do much to conceal the look of suspicion — and possibly repugnance — that she wore. Kenley couldn't entirely swear she recognised him, but was willing to take a punt.

"Peace offering?" he said, proffering a bottle of Monbazillac and an enormous bunch of flowers.

She didn't immediately answer. She was thrown, he could tell. She'd set her stance for war, and hadn't expected concession.

"For what?" she said, eventually.

Kenley grimaced.

"You know."

"Let's assume I don't."

"We crossed paths in the car park. I was very rude and out of order. I came to apologise."

"Because you realised we're neighbours?"

"Pretty much. Come on, my arm's getting tired."

She slowly took the flowers and laid them carefully on the hall table, then turned back to him.

"Thank you," she said, unsmiling. "Was there anything else?"

He wanted to grin.

"How are you liking it? The neighbourhood, I mean?"

She shrugged. "It's okay."

"Just you?"

She frowned at the fairly bald question — he may as well have asked: *Are you single?* — but a small boy in a Spider-Man costume bounded up behind her and grabbed her legs, answering Kenley's question for him.

"Hey there, Spidey," he said, bending down to offer a high-five. He wasn't a shy boy, and he reciprocated with glee. Kenley could almost feel her roll her eyes. "You keeping the neighbourhood safe?"

He nodded emphatically.

"How do you like your new house?"

"It's good. My room is way bigger. And we have a garden!"

"We were in a flat before," she mumbled.

Kenley looked at her, then back at Spidey.

"I'm Kenley," he said. "Which means you must be Peter Parker."

He grinned.

"My name's Max. I'm five. My mum's called Natalie."

"Don't worry, your secret identity is safe with me. That goes for both of you," he added.

The small boy shot Kenley with imaginary web slinging; Kenley reacted accordingly, and Max bounded back into the house. Kenley straightened up and looked Natalie in the eye again. For a moment he thought something had softened there; he could have imagined it, but he thought he was about to get invited in.

He was interrupted, however, by the phone ringing in his pocket.

"Enjoy the wine. Goes nicely with cheesecake," he said, retreating back down the path. "And sorry again for being a dick. I'm crap behind the wheel, but I'm a pretty good neighbour. Hello?"

He put the phone to his ear as he crossed onto his own driveway.

"You free, boss?" Sterling said. Kenley was starting to feel like the guy was becoming a little needy.

"Always for you, Len," he said, getting in the car. "What can I do you for?"

"They've tracked down the mother."

"Okay. Hold your nerve. We'll see what she says, then go take her some flowers."

"Okay."

"What about those two cabbies?"

"Nothing to worry about. Only one of them was of any concern. That's been sorted."

"Okay. Good."

Kenley was about to end the call and head off to Croydon when a thought occurred to him.

"Len? You there?"

"Boss?"

"This info about the mum. It come from your new guy? The DS?"

"No, just from the usual. Not heard from him yet."

"I don't like that. Pay him a little visit, eh?"

CHAPTER TEN

For reasons Barnes couldn't quite explain, the new housing development made him think of a nuclear blast. It could have been the fact that half of the plots were occupied, while the remainder were just concrete shells in a bog the other side of a chain-link fence decorated with all sorts of menacing signage, or it could have been the deserted, brightly coloured playparks with swings sitting silent and static.

The houses were tan-brick cubes with white timber cladding. Impossibly smooth pavements led around the estate, dotted with evenly spaced shrubs. But the unfinished road was spotted with dangerously protruding iron drain covers at intervals, while nearly every intersection was a dead end leading into nothing but fenced-off churned mud mounds littered with saplings in white polymer sleeves that made Barnes think of a world war graveyard.

Eventually, he decided it was the dust. When the machinery had finished for the day and the convoy trundled off the site, a film of yellow dust caked brand new cars, freshly glazed front-room windows and rows of evergreen planters.

He walked around a fenced-off plot with a gully four feet deep running behind it. The dugout mud was baked and hard, and an ill-timed step would result in a turned ankle, minimum.

Barnes presumed the gully was going to be filled in at some point — a network of exposed cables and black corrugated drainage piping was a reminder of the unseen underground infrastructure that kept lives afloat.

From the outside, the house was, like all the others, in good order — new windows and door, a clean, weeded path and even a wind chime on the porch. When the woman answered, however, it was clear the interior was not keeping step. A thick wave of dog, damp and cigarettes oozed out, suggesting to Barnes that, even in the morning sunshine, there were no windows open.

"Yes?" She was instantly suspicious, a large woman in a tracksuit.

"Police," Barnes said, holding up his warrant card. "Detective Inspector Barnes. Sorry to bother you. I'm looking for Debbie Bridger."

"What's it about?"

Answering cop questions with questions. A seasoned veteran, Barnes thought, wondering if it was unfair to assume that she had him pegged as a cop, a debt collector or a social worker before she'd even answered the door.

"It's about her son, Kevin. Kevin Bridger."

Nothing changed in the woman's face. "What about him?"

"Are you Debbie?"

"I am."

"Can I come in?"

She pursed her lips and expelled air through her nose. "It's not a good time."

"I need to talk to you. I don't really want to do it on the doorstep."

"Is he dead?"

Barnes eyed her for a moment. "I'm afraid he is."

She stared back at him. Nothing changed in her face. Barnes figured she was processing it. "When?"

"A little over a week ago," Barnes said. The fact she'd asked "when" and not "how" told him a good deal about how close they were. "Obviously we'd have been here sooner, but it's taken a little while to track you down, I'm afraid."

"What was it, overdose?"

"No. Fire."

"Different. What do you need me for?"

Barnes felt a little surge of anger in his chest, but he tried to keep his tone light. He had learned long ago that moralising over people's basic caring capabilities was a fool's errand. Gather the evidence, make the referral, protect those you can. Besides, he just wasn't good at telling people off. He always got the tone wrong, and it inevitably ended up in a complaint. Some of his colleagues had a genuine knack for it, but not him.

"Well, you're his next of kin. We're investigating his death. Trying to get you some answers. On the surface of it, the circumstances point to an accident, but we're treating it as homicide."

That did raise an eyebrow. Maybe she was thinking about compensation. Or a bit of attention from the local rag.

He stepped a little closer. Her nose was red, and despite her weight, the skin on her face had a papery, slightly translucent look. Barnes had seen enough 10 a.m. vodka drinkers to recognise one off the bat.

"So, what next?"

"Well, I'm sorry it's taken so long, first of all."

"I don't have to identify him, do I?"

"That won't be necessary, I'm sorry to say. His body was quite badly damaged by the fire." This last part wasn't an essential disclosure, but *something* surely had to make a dent in the woman's rhino-like hide.

He was disappointed. If anything, she looked relieved that she wouldn't have to leave the house.

"When did you last speak to Kevin?"

She shrugged. "Weeks ago. Maybe months."

"Had he upset anyone? Made any enemies?"

She shrugged again. "He was a junkie thief. He pissed nearly everyone off at one time or another."

"I see. And how about you?"

"What do you mean?" Her eyes narrowed.

"Any odd visitors to the house? Strange calls? Suspicious cars hanging about?"

"No more than usual. Is this going to take long?"

Barnes inched closer still. He tried to sneak a glance past her shoulder into the house, but she cottoned on immediately and placed an arm across the doorway.

"Mrs Bridger, your son died a very unpleasant death. The smoke probably got him before the flames did, but in any case, it was not a nice way to go. Someone went to great trouble to make it look like an accident, with a view to scaring everybody silent. Not only that, but even if his existence was not exactly glamorous . . ."

"Junkie thief," she repeated.

". . . it seems a trifle Victorian to put him in the ground with absolutely nobody giving a flying hoot about how and why he died."

She sniffed.

"What I am saying is, I want to catch those responsible, and I want to do that for Kevin. And for you," he added.

She yawned. "Is that all?"

He felt his shoulders sag a little. "Yes, that's all. For now."

The door was shut in his face.

He walked back to the car, wondering how long it would be before the lack of care of the inside of the houses would translate to the outside. How long before the new-build sheen wore off and the whole thing resembled another housing estate peopled with people who just didn't give a shit about anything.

He thought again about his passivity at her apathy, and the very small handful of colleagues he'd had that could dish out a truly memorable telling-off. The kind of telling-off that, in a handful of cases, might result in giving someone the kind of wake-up call they needed to reset the machine. Break the cycle. Change their life.

They were never going to get that from Barnes, even if he wanted to try. Barnes would do enough to put them away, but nothing to stop them doing it all over again when they got out. Some might say that wasn't his job, that social workers, probation officers, counsellors were better placed. But cops saw you in the immediate aftermath, when you were at your most vulnerable. Your most susceptible. Before the lawyers got to you, when you were still thinking seriously about spilling your guts.

Harriet. Harriet had been good at that. As the children were taken off under police protection, she would say to the wasted mother: *Is this really how you want them to grow up?*

He stopped on the pavement and pinched his nose. God, Harriet. He hadn't thought about her in so long. And he thought, for the first time, there were not that many that had seen a colleague slain close at hand. That kind of thing didn't let you leave the job at the front door when you got home at night.

He made himself start walking again. His phone rang when he got to his car.

"DI Barnes."

"Barnes, it's Shaz."

"Shaz. The witness? The Filipino lady?"

"So, she's been debriefed. Turns out she didn't actually see anything."

"What do you mean?"

"It seems that when she was on the pavement at three in the morning with her kids, having been evacuated, there were a couple of other rubberneckers there. One of them, a man, told her he'd seen some men approaching the deceased's house. That's where she got it from. It's hearsay."

Barnes sighed.

"Dammit. What man?"

"We have a description of him and his car, but nothing distinct. That's it."

"Shit. Okay, thanks, Shaz."

"Good work by your new boss, though. Found a witness where others didn't."

"Yeah, he's a sharp one, it seems."

"Left me with egg on my face, but, yeah, I think you are right."

"Don't be daft. Thanks, Shaz."

He hung up and drove back to the station, where he convened a small huddle comprising himself, Shaz Brooker and the DC who had interviewed the witness, Monty Beck. Monty was a tall, well-built officer with eyes the colour of slate. With the regular churn of detectives through the CID, Barnes considered him part of the furniture, and was glad for his steadiness.

While Monty and Shaz made small talk, Barnes called Kane, figuring he might want to be part of this, but also figuring he was probably in a meeting. A superintendent's diary didn't usually allow for spontaneous gatherings.

He glanced over at Monty while he made the call, noting a slightly pensive edge to the Irishman's smile, and remembered that, like himself, Monty had also been through the mental wringer of witnessing a colleague fall at the hands of another.

He shook his head as he got Kane's voicemail. An office peopled by damaged goods. It was a wonder somebody hadn't put them all out to pasture.

The difference, as far as Barnes could see, was that Monty had moved on. He'd found himself a nice girlfriend, moved in with her, and now they were talking about children. It seemed pretty easy from the outside looking in.

He realised the empty voicemail recording was waiting for him to speak, so he left a garbled message and went over to Shaz and Monty, wondering what had triggered the almost debilitating bouts of reflection in the last few days.

Monty fired up a video screen as Barnes approached.

"The lady next door is Madeleine Veloso, thirty-two years old. She goes by Maddy. Husband is Ruben, works as a porter at the DGH. Originally from the Philippines; they've been in the UK about seven years. Three children — seven, four and six months.

"The house is divided into two flats — the main body of the house and then a basement flat which is accessed from the street. The basement is unoccupied; the Velosos have the main property and, obviously, heat rises, so even if there was someone in the basement flat, the Velosos would still have known about the fire pretty quickly.

"She and the kids were evacuated by Trumpton. Husband was on nights. It was a bit of a Fred Karno's, as you can imagine — complete chaos, so all they could really do was put her on the pavement initially.

"Now, Kevin Bridger's flat was at the end of the row. The flat above his was also unoccupied, thankfully, or we might have had more dead. I spoke to Trumpton, and the Velosos were the only ones displaced. But Madeleine — Maddy — says she stood on the pavement, watching the fireworks, with her kids wrapped in a duvet, with three, maybe four other people."

"We're going back along the houses opposite the scene to re-question the occupants about whether they went out on the street to watch, or stayed indoors. That question wasn't on the first round of enquiries," Shaz said.

"So, who were these other people with Maddy?" Barnes said.

"We can't discount passers-by but, that time of the morning, it's a little unlikely," Monty said. "Maddy says one of the men stood with her said he'd seen a group of three men approaching Kevin's house shortly before the fire. She doesn't know who he was, but described him as dark-skinned, in his thirties, heavily built with thinning hair. He was in dark clothing, and he was smoking."

"That it?" Barnes said.

"That, and she described his car. Black saloon. Not old, not new. Nothing distinctive."

"Could be anybody," Shaz said.

"CCTV gives us the bottom end of Susans Road. That's time lapse. Random rotation. Nothing real time until after the fire started and the operator started to monitor."

Barnes tried to think. He stepped away from them and shut his eyes. How were they going to track this person?

"Boss, she's a sigwit. Needs a cognitive," Monty said. "We might get something more."

Barnes opened his eyes and came back to them. "How did she know it was his car?"

"She saw him go back to it," Monty said.

"So, we need to add another question to the house-to-house pro forma," Barnes said to Shaz. "Did anyone leave their house to watch the light show, then go to their car rather than back indoors? Early start at work, airport trip, whatever."

"Roger," Shaz said.

"And that section of town is a one-way street, right?" Barnes said. "And nearly the whole thing is shut down to one lane because of all the demolition work. The place looks like a bomb site. You can't park, you can't do anything. There's a makeshift bus stop, a small section for residents' parking . . ."

"And a taxi rank."

They looked around. Shaz tilted her head. Kane, the new boss, the strange, tattooed superintendent with almost translucent eyes, stood in the doorway.

"He's a taxi driver."

Barnes knew he'd have arrived at a taxi driver theory pretty quickly — just, maybe, not that quickly.

"I think you're right," Barnes said. "Monty . . ."

"Already on it," Monty said, and left the office. No one said it, but this wasn't an action you took away and reported on in a week, at the next meeting. This was to be done while you wait.

Kane came over and stood with Barnes and Shaz.

"She's not an eyewitness," Barnes said. "But this other man may well have been."

"Why would he not have come forward?" Kane said. "We've got media appeals, scene boards, and Shaz has done more canvassing than the local Lib Dems."

Barnes shrugged. "Any number of reasons. Axe to grind with the cops. One too many speeding tickets. Or maybe he just figures we should go to him on principle. Why should he do our job for us, et cetera. I've encountered a fair few taxi drivers in my time. More than a few shop stewards in that crowd."

There was a moment's pause. Barnes and Kane locked stares.

"Or some other reason," Kane said.

"Oh, God," Barnes said, pinching his nose.

"We went through the CCTV, right?" Kane said.

"Nothing covering the scene," Barnes said. "We've backtracked through town for the deceased, but he'd been indoors for at least a few hours."

"She was on the street for about ten minutes before the man spoke to her," Monty called over from the corner of the room. "Trumpton reckons the fire had been going for anything up to fifteen minutes before they got everyone out."

"That's not a big window," Kane said. "We should be able to find something."

"Except — besides three men — we don't know what we're looking for," Barnes said. "Not only that, but we're assuming that Kevin's killers started the fire as soon as they arrived. For all we know they squeezed in a cup of tea and an episode of *Desperate Housewives* before they set him alight. So even if we get half a description off this taxi driver, that would be a start."

"Gives us something to do while we wait for Monty," Kane said.

Barnes said nothing, but with the sliver of extra second-hand information from Maddy Veloso, they went back to the CCTV trawl. Three big men, all white. They approached Kevin's flat and left less than fifteen minutes later. The rest was a matter of record.

No information about direction of approach. Nothing about a vehicle. Nothing on height, weapons or distinguishing marks. No information about their witness's eyesight, or how far away he was when saw them. No information about whether he'd made it up, or if he was a plant sowed to spread disinformation by the perpetrators themselves.

It was a pretty wide scope. The only thing going for them was the time of night — despite Kevin Bridger's flat being just around the corner from the main nightclub footprint, footfall thinned out pretty quickly after about three in the morning.

Barnes folded his arms and stood behind Shaz as she ploughed through the jerky time lapse footage, held in an archive of tapes in the CCTV control room. It was a time-consuming, arduous task, with no guarantees of success — in fact, quite the opposite. Not only did they not know if the information was reliable or not, but it would not be beyond the realms of imagination for a moderately well-organised outfit to conjure up a faux witness to keep the cops looking the other way.

Stranger things had happened, Barnes mused.

"How far back are we going?" Kane asked.

Barnes shrugged. "Working hypothesis is they drove in, parked nearby and drove out again. It's unlikely they'll have gone for a pint around the corner afterwards, but we can't rule it out. We go back an hour before the fire started, then two, then three."

"Then four?"

"Maybe."

"Much more of this and I'd be up for waterboarding the taxi driver," Shaz said.

After an hour or so of this, Barnes noticed Shaz's eyes beginning to glaze over, and he rotated her out, co-opting a DC from the late turn to take over to give her a break.

To Barnes's dismay, the late-turn duty DS was Paul Gamble, who cheerfully grumbled at the request, complaining about there being a five-hander in the bin for a drugs warrant — and subsequently being on the losing end of a pursuit — but Barnes told him he needed a DC to trawl all town centre cameras between one and four in the morning, and that he could go back to his prisoners after that.

"You're all heart, boss," Gamble had said.

Kane sat down with the DC, who looked slightly uncomfortable — at the rank or the piercings, Barnes wasn't sure. Barnes tapped his watch impatiently and paced, suddenly aware of the tension in the room.

"I'm going to find Monty," he said eventually. "But call me if you find anything."

"Anything like this?" the DC said, pointing at one of the monitors. "Not a definite, by any stretch. But it's three men."

Barnes rubbed the grit out of his eyes and peered at the screen.

It was a distorted, monochrome image with a pale pixelated wash from a nearby streetlight. The time display put the shot at eighty-seven minutes before Kevin Bridger expired.

"Where is this?" Barnes said.

"Seafront," the DC said. "A good fifteen-minute walk from the scene."

Barnes rubbed his eyes again. Only two of the men were visible; the third was just a shoulder and a massive arm. The guy on the end was huge — even through the poor-quality image he was clearly a knuckle-dragging ape in what looked like a donkey jacket.

The man in the middle was slightly taller than the two lugs that were flanking him, and even though the picture was grainy — made worse by the freeze frame — there was something about him. Barnes couldn't put his finger on it, but the gait exuded a kind of confidence. Or it could have been the face — there were shadows at the cheek and jaw that would be generally regarded as good-looking features, and what looked to be a head of thick dark curls. He was slim, with an upright posture and bespectacled young face that could mean . . . well, any number of things.

He tapped the screen with the back of his finger. It *dinked* on the glass.

"Excellent work. We need to get this image enhanced."

"I can do that," Monty said as he rejoined them.

"How did you get on?" Barnes said, noting the grave look on Monty's face.

"I didn't start with the ring round," Monty said. "First port of call was to look for any missing taxi drivers. Got a result on the first try."

Barnes felt something sink in his gullet.

"Go on."

"Brian Rose, fifty-three. Reported missing by a very grumpy wife whose favoured theory is that he's over the side with the receptionist. Last seen a couple of nights ago when he went in for a night shift. Didn't come home, didn't book in for any more shifts. The investigation is still with uniform. He's vanished off the face of the earth, but everyone seems to think he's eloped."

"I don't like the sound of that at all. What about mobile phone, credit cards, ANPR?"

"His taxi is still on the driveway, but he's pegged as low risk on the basis of the affair theory, so those other enquiries are still in the 'pending' tray."

"Oh, shit."

Kane folded his arms and stared at Barnes.

"Now tell me this isn't a bloody murder."

CHAPTER ELEVEN

Paul Gamble was not having a good day. His overnight remand prisoner — a serial creeper-burglar — had been bailed by the court with the merest scraping of bail conditions, while a conspiracy case he'd been expecting to go to trial had turned in an eleventh-hour guilty plea. While, on the surface, this meant less work and less time for him, the tactical pleading together with time served meant they hadn't even landed a custodial sentence.

The office was hot. The station's ancient heating system had two settings — "off" and "furnace" — and in the winter it was programmed to come on whether you liked it or not. The fabric of his cheap yellow shirt was sticking to his skin.

The stack of files in his in-tray was next on his list, but when the four Local Support Team officers burst through the door wearing big smiles and made a beeline for him, his heart sank.

They formed horns around his desk and plopped a green file down in front of him. He looked at it. It appeared worryingly thin.

"What's that?" he asked. It seemed a fatuous question.

The grins grew wider. "MDA warrant, Sarge. Five in the bin . . . after a short fail-to-stop. Good little conspiracy there, plus two grand in cash, some deal ledgers, phones . . ."

"Any actual drugs?"

The grins didn't falter. "Shake the tree. They'll come."

Gamble sighed. "Who exactly do you want me to give this to, boys? I've got a DC and a half on this evening and they've already got a robbery prisoner each."

The LST exchanged glances. One even tittered. *Not our problem*, it seemed to say. They turned to go.

"Next time can you please let CID *know* before you go kicking doors in? We might even be able to help."

Without turning around, the LST waved in acknowledgement as they filed out.

"Not to mention show you how to actually bag and tag before you go swanning off into the sunset leaving me to hold the baby," he muttered.

Their job was to be proactive and disrupt drug dealers. His job was to investigate whatever they turned up — including dealing with a cell block of prisoners. *They* got to cut and run. He had to make a silk purse out of a sow's ear, as far as building a case went.

It just wasn't right.

He had a disinterested flick through the file. Mother, boyfriend and son all in custody. One juvenile. Mother had mental health problems. Boyfriend was a psycho, and suicidal to boot. They'd already been in the bin five hours before the file had even been presented to him. He'd be chasing his tail from the off — and that was even *before* he'd looked at all the weak links in the evidential chain.

A wave of anger curled over his chest in the hot office.

A new message icon appeared in the corner of his screen. Ordinarily he wouldn't have paid it much attention, but he was glad for the distraction — and besides, the subject title — HR NOTIFICATION: POSTING INFORMATION — piqued his interest.

He read the email. It was a terse pro forma template, which somehow made it worse. Apparently, he was being posted to Hastings custody. The letter referred to it as an exigency of duty, which meant he wasn't subject to the usual ninety-day grace-and-good-manners period that would usually govern a forced posting. Effective immediately, in other words.

Hastings custody was a subterranean dungeon where madness often reigned. Career-wise, it was dead man's shoes. You could retire and die in the same week down there and no one would remember you. It was clearly the new boss, Kane, having a bit of fun with his chess set.

But, Gamble thought, effective immediately was effective immediately, and so he stood up, tossed the prisoner file on the desk, grabbed his jacket off the back of the chair and walked out.

He drove home. The phone rang in his pocket as he pulled onto the driveway. He ignored it. When it rang for a second time, he figured it was someone important wanting to know why he'd abandoned his post.

He got out and checked the display. Not work. Only Caroline.

He rang her back once he got indoors.

"Caroline. I'm at work."

"You're late with the maintenance," she said. No introduction.

"No, I'm not. Tomorrow it'll be late. Technically I've got the rest of the day to get it to you."

"You're saying I'll get it today? Matthew needs new school shoes."

"Already?"

"He's having a growth spurt."

"Okay, okay. I'll get it to you. Just to be forewarned, though, I'm being posted to Hastings."

"You are?"

"That's another thirty miles a day on top of my current commute, and petrol isn't getting any cheaper. It's nearly one-twenty a litre these days."

"Get it from ASDA. It's cheaper there."

"I'm just saying . . ."

"What about the overtime? Paul . . . why are you being posted to Hastings?"

"It's a long story. It's custody, though. No detective work. Probably no overtime either."

"Why?"

"Not sure. Enemies in high places." He chuckled to himself. "I'll get it to you, Caroline, okay? I promise. Sorry."

"Okay, thanks." He imagined her frowning on the other end of the phone. It wasn't like him to let his guard down. "Paul . . . are you okay?"

"Ask me again in a month," he said, and hung up.

He'd transacted the entire conversation in the hallway. He put the phone on the hall table and stood for a moment, hands on hips, looking at his shoes.

The flat was quiet. It was always quiet. He'd only moved in six months or so previously, deliberately taking a pre-furnished piece-of-shit place with floral print wallpaper and a green velour three-piece suite that he barely used. There was a faint smell of damp that reminded him of charity shops.

In the immediate aftermath of separation, the priority was just for shelter, somewhere to lay his head. He wasn't thinking about starting a new life or any crap like that, but Gamble's instinct was that there was an insidiousness about a stopgap residence — six months could become six years in a heartbeat, and so his selection of a piece-of-shit residence with vulgar decor had been deliberate, almost defiant. As if to say, *This is not me.*

Most of his stuff was in storage, Caroline having lost patience with having his crap everywhere about a month or so previously. That alone was costing him a hundred quid a month. With the new commuting bill looming, he'd have to haul it all out once and for all and get settled, but the thought brought with it a prospect of permanence that he didn't think he was quite ready to face just yet. He'd much rather spend a few more months in a chintz-riddled purgatory.

He walked into the lounge and regarded it for a moment. Maybe he *should* start a new life. Maybe the posting to Hastings could be the start of it. Move a bit closer to the station, out to rural Rother or somewhere with a view of the sea. Even if summoning the effort did seem, at that moment, to be rather unassailable. In fact, as he took in the surroundings, a thought flash-framed through his mind, so fast as to only barely break the surface of his consciousness, but it promised *exit* so completely that it was suddenly appealing.

The appeal was broken by a heavy, slow knock at the door. He opened it to be greeted by a solid-looking man in a hi-vis Parcelforce vest who was holding a clipboard.

"I'm not expecting a—"

"Hello, Sarge." The man looked up from his clipboard and grinned. The Old Spice came off him in thick waves. There was a St Christopher nestled between the red folds of his thick neck.

Recognition and fear caused the adrenaline to burn through Gamble like liquid nitrogen. This was not like a public ambush. His flat was not his first choice of home but it was still his sanctuary, and the thin layer of ice between private and professional life had been shattered with a clever, if unsophisticated, disguise. If no one ever saw Paul Gamble again, no one was ever going to remember a delivery driver.

"How did you find me?"

"Well, you made it easy. I'd settled down with the paper outside your nick, thinking I'd be there for a good few hours, but apparently you decided to come home for dinner. Early bath today?"

"Something like that."

"Anyone know you left early?"

"Of course, I . . . I told my DI."

The man grinned even wider.

"Of course you did. You not going to invite me in?"

"Be a bit weird, wouldn't it? Inviting in the courier? Blow your cover."

"No flies on you, Sarge, that's for sure. I told the boss we were onto a good thing with you."

"What do you want?"

"Just a sitrep, Sarge. A progress report."

"On what?"

The man screwed up his face: *come on.*

"On our little proposal. We left you a sweetener, and you took it, so now we are wanting something in return."

"As it happens, I do have something. They've spoken to the mother, and they're rechecking CCTV with a fine tooth . . ."

"Ssh. Not now, Sarge. Later."

Gamble swallowed.

"Later?"

"Yeah. Neutral ground and all that. We'll come for you."

"When?"

The man grinned again and scribbled something on his clipboard. He held it up. It said:

SOON

He stuck the pencil behind his ear, turned on his heel and trotted off down the path.

Gamble held it together just long enough for the man to disappear from view, then he gripped the doorframe tight and pushed his back against it as the strength went out of his legs. He got over it after a moment or two, then shut the door and wondered if he'd have been better off just picking up the prisoners.

CHAPTER TWELVE

Kenley now had Lena and Hector's routine pretty well down. The first couple of times, his attempts at static surveillance had led to some very long waits in the parked car, which in turn had resulted in his natural impatience being sorely tested. A couple of times he'd wanted to march up to the flat and bang on the door, just so he could say he'd seen her and she was all right. He'd even thought about acquiring a Domino's delivery driver uniform to assist with the subterfuge.

But, after a few deployments, he was only having to park up for a few minutes at a time. Half an hour, tops. School run, shopping on a Saturday, football on a Tuesday. Lena also went out a couple of evenings a week in gym gear with a yoga mat tucked under her arm. She got the bus and returned a couple of hours later, swapping places with a young woman that must have been the babysitter.

Kenley had no means of getting a message to Pearce to let him know they were all right. Well, strictly speaking, he could have done, but it was far too risky. Early on in his surveillance, Kenley had thought about taking the risk, but then, as time passed, he was glad he hadn't attempted it. He'd have swung from the vicarious pleasure of bearing good news to negotiating a shooting-the-messenger situation in a heartbeat.

School attendance, for instance, seemed to be a little patchy. There was a guy in a tracksuit who seemed to visit one or two evenings a week. He didn't stay long, but the mere fact of his existence would have been enough for Pearce to demand that he be strung up by his balls from the top of the Shard. Kenley hadn't presumed to follow Lena to her twice-weekly yoga classes, but if it was a cover they should think about hiring her. Besides, any woman with the wit and the cojones to go to those lengths in the interests of elaborate subterfuge was not what Kenley would describe as a keeper.

For a moment, as he gazed up at the hard, grey concrete block, he caught a glimpse of himself in the rear-view, thought about the Domino's uniform and pushed the mirror away.

Annoyed with himself for allowing his stakeout to drift into a moment's uncharacteristic soul-searching, he put the car in gear and headed out of Croydon.

The drive was relatively painless, with a low winter sun filtering through the trees as he took back roads into the countryside, and his mood was light when he arrived home.

When he rang Natalie's front doorbell, palm sweating over the box of Lego and the cellophane wrapped around the cake he was holding, he realised, like an idiot, that he was nervous. Despite the facade of suburban living, he was under no illusion that there was a whole world between passing the time of day with your neighbour on the driveway and actually inviting them in. It would have been a step up even if he'd been eighty-five and the neighbourhood busybody; as it was, they were both single and the right side of forty. Kenley figured it was simple social economics.

As the latch clicked, Kenley thought about bolting. Then, for some unknown reason, the image of Kevin Bridger's legs twitching as Kenley closed the door on him appeared in his mind, and he realised he had no business being nervous about anything.

The door opened. She smiled.

"Hi."

Boom.

"Hi," he said. "I'm sorry to bother you . . ."

"It's fine," she said. "I'm only hanging washing. Come in."

Like it was no big thing at all. Didn't even ask him what was up. Or maybe she simply didn't want a spontaneous interruption to muck up her plans for the day.

"Kettle's just boiled," she called as she retreated into the kitchen with her laundry basket.

Kenley thought he might have preferred a shot of something stronger, but it was still only late afternoon. Besides which, kettles made the world go round, so a brew was all right by him.

"No little man today?" Kenley called from the hallway. He debated kicking his shoes off — he didn't want to appear like he was planning to stay long but, equally, those carpets looked new. Plus, he figured if someone pegged you as having poor manners from day one, it was a reputational dent that was tough to bounce back from.

"He's at school."

Of course he was. Kenley wasn't sure where to go. Follow her into the kitchen, or wait in the hallway?

"I won't be a sec."

He opted for the front room, and sat down carefully on a sofa that looked almost as new as the carpets.

He gazed out of the bay window, noting that, unless he started pulling nose-in onto the driveway when he got home, anyone sitting here would have a clear view of him getting into or out of his car, and then looked at the television cabinet in front of him.

When he looked up he nearly choked, nearly bolted for the second time in as many minutes.

On top of the cabinet was an array of photographs. Most of them were of her and her son in various states of parent–child bliss — swimming, on holiday, at the beach, cycling and so on. The grins were so broad Kenley wondered if it was a deliberate two fingers to the father figure so conspicuously absent from all but one of the pictures.

In the middle of the photographs was a formal portrait of Natalie, a solemn but kind look on her face, aged maybe twenty. She was in full ceremonial dress, with the dice band bowler tucked under her arm. Above that, hanging on the wall, was another shot of her in full tunic, only this time wearing a shit-eating grin as she accepted a medal and a handshake from John Major. Next to that one was a formal group shot of her and her cohort as she passed out from Grosvenor Hall, October 1995.

She was a goddamn cop.

"No tea?"

She appeared in the doorway, smiling. Despite himself, Kenley felt himself flush. He jumped up, just about able to maintain the pretence.

"Sorry, I'll do it now. How do you take it?"

"Is that coffee and walnut?" She pointed at the cake.

He managed a smile and held it out, along with the Lego dinosaur. "I got little man something too."

"Oh, that's . . . lovely. You didn't have to."

They went to the kitchen, Kenley's mind racing. Natalie reboiled the kettle.

"I just . . . are you settling in okay?" he heard himself say.

The first and most obvious theory was that she'd been manoeuvred in next door to him to stake him out. But that made no sense. They wouldn't advertise the fact that she was a police officer, for God's sake, even if they *had* anticipated him setting foot in her house.

"Yes, very nicely, thank you. Met most of the neighbours. Most of them seem very nice."

"Well, I didn't want to overstep my bounds," Kenley said, pointing at the cake. "But I figured better to be friendly than avoid eye contact every time you go out onto the driveway."

"Is that something you're given to?" she asked, still smiling.

He smiled back. "I've seen it done."

So, she clearly wasn't undercover. Even the most cretinous covert command wouldn't openly advertise the fact that their UC was a cop. Which meant she'd been deliberately moved in next to him for no other reason than getting kicks out of how much he was sweating right now — a little *yoo hoo, we're watching you*, like the Christmas card Sterling had received one year when he'd had about six outstanding warrants — or it was a coincidence.

If the former, then he might be able to verify it. Unless it was a pukka covert deployment, then Land Registry and all that other civic information might hold a clue as to the purchaser. If it was a deliberate tactic, then it troubled him greatly. It meant there was an aspiring Nipper Read somewhere in the mix with Kenley in his crosshairs. Kenley didn't exactly put himself in the same league as the Kray twins but, in any case, nothing disturbed him more than a cop with a sense of humour.

"Sorry, what did you say?"

"Are you okay?" Natalie asked. "You seem distracted. I asked: do you know when the recycling gets collected?"

"Alternate Thursdays," Kenley said. "And, sorry. I must admit: your being a police officer threw me a bit, that's all. I saw the photographs." He figured fronting up was the most straightforward way of returning to the present.

"It happens," she said. "At least you didn't make a crap joke about outstanding speeding tickets and offer up your wrists."

"Do people actually do that?"

"You'd be surprised."

When the school run necessitated throwing him out forty minutes later, he was troubled by the fact that his eyes stung from laughing and that he practically skipped over the small bonsai hedge separating his own driveway from Natalie's. He was troubled by the fact that he seemed not to care that, had Head Office or any of his own crew borne witness to the last half-hour, he'd have been stuffed into a barrel and rolled off the edge of Beachy Head without a second thought. He was troubled by the fact that he was grinning like an idiot as he opened his front door.

He tried to get a handle on it by chalking it up to a physiological reaction of various chemicals racing around his body and intermittently firing darts into his hypothalamus, and that with some concentrated breathing and guided meditation, he could probably purge his system of it — whatever *it* was.

But what troubled him most was the fact that lie after lie had tripped off his tongue. She'd asked him what he did for a living — his cover for the rest of the neighbours was that he was a senior house officer, but that cover was contingent on keeping the entire street at arm's length or, ideally, further. Trying to persuade a police officer — a detective, no less — that he was a junior doctor would very quickly be found out, and so he'd come up with some fudge whereby he worked for the NHS but in some meaningless back-office middle-management role. Project manager or something.

He tried to rationalise it. Having a cop close could be useful for business, long-term — particularly if she was suggestible. *Persuadable*, even. Many were, and Sterling's attempts to date to recruit DS Paul Gamble into the Keber information loop had proved tepid at best. Another, slightly brighter ally within the inner sanctum of the police service could be extraordinarily helpful — and it could also prove a useful defence for his own ends should Head Office take exception to his willingness to get to know his new neighbour.

But they were a way off that yet. She was no fool, and no shrinking violet either. She was fun. He had seen too many of his counterparts gaslight and browbeat their women into conditioned submissiveness, which he'd never understood. It attracted unnecessary attention, for one, and created these cowering scullery maids who were frightened of their own shadow. Kenley had never seen the appeal. He liked confident women, and he liked helping to grow their confidence by treating them with respect and making them feel good.

It was a simple enough equation to conceptualise, but he seemed to be a lone voice. He'd mentioned this to Sterling once, who'd replied, matter-of-factly: "It helps that you're good-looking. But mainly it's because you're the only one I know who doesn't have mummy issues."

But, either way, attracting unnecessary attention was bad for business.

People in glass houses and all that.

As if to labour the point, his phone trilled in his pocket. He pulled it out. Sterling again, wanting to meet.

Kenley typed a reply:

C U THERE

Kenley fed the fish and then drove to the storage unit. By the time he got there, the last dregs of warmth from the winter sun had vanished, and the prefab metal walls of the unit were ice cold to touch. Sterling was alone in the usual loading bay, huddled under a weak lamp with a Styrofoam cup of coffee.

"I'll keep it brief," Sterling said. "They're going back over the CCTV. Fine-tooth comb."

Kenley shrugged.

"Standard."

"And they've been to see the mother."

"Also not a surprise."

"Mothers talk, boss."

"She'll be all right," Kenley said.

"They've been to see her at the house."

Kenley frowned.

"That's a good point. It's not just any old house, is it?"

"Indeed not."

Kenley raised his eyebrows.

"We'd better go say hi. Tell Golden Wonder to polish his shoes."

CHAPTER THIRTEEN

Kane was out on patrol with the early turn when Barnes called him up to co-opt him into a follow-up visit to Debbie Bridger's house.

"How was it?" Barnes asked.

Kane shrugged. "I was hoping for a foot chase or something. I went from one nervous breakdown to another."

"That's the job."

"So people keep telling me."

They pulled up to Debbie's house and parked outside.

"Not a bad area," Kane remarked.

"Everything looks new in the first six months," Barnes said. "Then it all goes to shit, or it doesn't. Just depends on how well you look after it."

Barnes frowned as the pair of them approached the house. Something was not quite right.

There was a smell like a barbecue that had been doused with stagnant water. One of the front room windows was wide open, and a net curtain was fluttering in the breeze. There was no front garden to speak of at all, and the window fronted directly onto the pavement. To the right of the open window were two spiderweb cracks, which looked like they'd been caused by some kind of blunt force, like a rock being lobbed at them, or a baseball bat swung in anger.

Barnes took all this in — noting that the windows had been broken from inside — and then poked at the front door. It was off the latch, but on the chain. Barnes stuck his nose in the gap and sniffed.

He pulled his baton out of his chest rig and racked it. He indicated for Kane to go down one side of the house while he took the other.

Kane looked blank, and Barnes remembered that he'd never been an operational cop.

"Go down the side of the house. I'll meet you at the back. If anyone jumps out at you, smack them in the head and shout like hell, okay? Got a stick? Or spray?"

"I've got a radio," Kane said.

"That'll do. See you in thirty seconds."

To his credit, Kane went off without quibbling, and Barnes slid down his side of the house, whispering into his radio as he went for a patrol car to back them up.

He reached the rear of the house without incident, and found himself at a tiny patio decorated with at least thirty terracotta pots of varying sizes, each with a healthy-looking plant of one description or another. Barnes felt a moment's sadness. It was well tended.

Kane joined him ten seconds later.

"Anything?" Barnes said.

Kane shook his head.

"Another open window."

They both turned to face the rear of the house. The patio led onto a conservatory of sorts, with a white uPVC door in the middle.

Barnes turned the handle. It popped open. He pushed it wide with his shoe.

"Police," he called. "Anyone home?"

No answer. He sniffed again. Cigarette smoke.

"Someone's here," he muttered to Kane. "Mrs Bridger? It's DI Barnes. We met before. Are you all right?"

The conservatory space appeared to be in use as a breakfast room, which was partitioned off from the kitchen by a white countertop.

Both had been trashed. Crockery and cutlery had been spilled across the various surfaces, with smashed glass spread across the floor. The washing machine had been yanked out of its recess, and it featured — along with the oven and cupboard doors — more of those spiderweb cracks, as if someone had gone on a spree with a lump hammer. The fridge had been upended and lay on its side, old food spilling out onto the lino.

"Somebody looking for something?" Kane said.

"Most definitely," Barnes said, pointing.

There was a hole in the floor under the counter where the washing machine had previously sat. The lino had been cut away to reveal an empty space deep enough for four two-by-two stacked shoeboxes. A square wooden board was propped up against the counter.

"What's that?" Kane said.

Barnes shrugged.

"Trap house, maybe," Barnes said. "My gut tells me it's probably more a shot across the bows."

They found Debbie Bridger in the lounge, sitting in an armchair, surrounded by more carnage. The armchair was the only thing still the right way up. She had a can of beer in one hand and a roll-up in the other. Her eyes were swollen shut, and her face was pinched into a scowl; her chin and lower lip had contorted into a sort of instinctively protective fold that made her look like an old man gurning. The blood down the front of her dressing gown was dark brown, almost black.

"Holy shit," Barnes said.

"I'll call an ambulance," Kane said, and moved into the hallway with his phone out.

Barnes squatted down in front of her. The faint tang of urine rose up in front of him. Her chest was rising and falling — shallow and raspy, but she was at least breathing.

"Debbie? Are you okay? Can you hear me?"

He gently reached out to touch her hand. The skin was cold. If she hadn't been breathing — just about — he'd have thrown her on the floor and started CPR.

"Do you need some water?"

"Cigarette," she growled.

Barnes looked around and saw a pack among a spatter of stuff that had probably all been on the same coffee table.

"Where does it hurt?" Barnes said.

"Everywhere."

He tried to scan her body for any obvious blood loss. The blood down her front was dry; there didn't seem to be anything wet or leaking.

"What happened?" Barnes said, lighting the cigarette for her.

She sucked at the cigarette, then flinched as a bout of coughing took over. Another plume of dark blood spurted from her mouth down her front. Barnes tried not to flinch.

"Think a couple of ribs have gone," she muttered.

And more besides, Barnes thought, looking at the blood.

"Was this intimidation?" he said.

"This was 'keep your mouth shut'," she said.

"Who? Who did this, Debbie?"

"Ambulance is on its way," Kane said, reappearing in the front room.

"Who took the gear from the kitchen? What was it? Were you safekeeping it?"

Debbie Bridger stuttered a bitter hiss that Barnes presumed was laughter of sorts.

"Look around you," she said. "If I wasn't going to talk before, you really think I'm going to now?"

Barnes straightened up, his knee suddenly cramping. A way off forty, but old and embattled, he thought. His probationer self had believed it could never happen to him, although, admittedly, the injury that had sidelined a lot of things in his life hadn't even happened on duty.

Kane moved in.

"Do you feel sufficiently dissuaded?" he said. "You know that if they think you've talked, they'll do worse? And they only need to *think* you have talked — the fact that you might not have actually done so doesn't even matter."

"That's exactly what happened to your son," Barnes murmured.

"So, you two plod turning up on my doorstep has probably done for me, then, yeah?" she said. "Especially if they're watching."

"Come with us," Kane said. "We'll protect you."

Barnes looked sideways at his boss. That was a lot of paperwork, and a whole heap of budget.

"You can save it," she said. "They put my boy in the ground. I never said a word, and this is the thanks I get. I'm already pissing blood."

Barnes felt a surge of something. Excitement, he realised.

"Talk to us, Debbie," he said.

"There were two of them," she said. Barnes moved a little closer. "Came over about midnight. One was a meathead. The other one was tall. Dark-haired. Glasses. Good-looking prick."

Her voice wobbled.

"The tall one stood right where you are now, while the other one wrecked the house right in front of me."

"And?"

"And the tall one said: 'Complaints hold the world to account. Mothers make things happen. We can't have that.' His exact words."

Her chest began to hitch and sobs began to escape her, punctuated by squeals of pain. Blood dripped down her chin. Barnes came closer. Kane moved out of the way.

"Debbie. I don't disbelieve you. But those are pretty specific words to remember."

She hissed something at him. He leaned in so his ear was near her mouth. He smelled cigarettes and something that reminded him of rotten onions.

"Four . . . eight . . . seven . . . four . . ." The hissing seemed to take tremendous effort.

A lemon-and-lime ambulance pulled up outside. Barnes opened the door and two green-suited paramedics raced in.

"Good timing," Barnes said. "I think she may have just lost consciousness. She's got internal bleeding."

The paramedics nodded and began tending to her. Barnes stayed in the hallway and called the office. He asked for a sketch artist to be called out and for a couple of DCs to meet them at the hospital.

The paramedics, after administering oxygen and checking vitals, looked at Barnes and Kane.

"She needs to go to hospital," one said. They'd only been at the house five minutes. "As in, now."

"Lead on," Barnes replied.

The paramedics loaded Debbie into the ambulance and took off with the full light show. Barnes followed.

"Can you keep up?" Kane said.

"Do my best," Barnes said. "One of these days they'll put blue lights in CID cars. I'll buy you a pint if it happens in my lifetime, though."

Kane looked at the houses as they raced out of the neat, new development.

"No one called 999?" Kane asked. "The noise?"

"Well, quite a few of them are empty, but would you? You've bought your little slice of new-build paradise, you've been in there five minutes, then something comes along to remind you that reality still exists. I imagine most were in denial."

Kane shook his head.

"I know people don't trust the police, but even so. I must be naive."

"For someone who's only been a cop five minutes, you're clearly not naive. But don't kid yourself. People seeing or hearing something is one thing. People picking up the phone is something else. People willing to *testify* about what they've seen or heard is something else again. Most people don't call the police — not because they don't trust them, but because it messes up their Friday nights."

"She's going to talk," Kane said. "Despite what they've done to her."

"They obviously overdid it," Barnes said. "I met her once before. She's tough. Instead of frightening her into silence, she obviously thought 'fuck you'."

"What was the number she gave you?"

"Lord only knows. A date of birth, maybe?"

They had lost the ambulance, but saw the blue lights in the distance as they got onto the bypass.

"They're not hanging around," Kane said.

Barnes didn't answer, but gently applied pressure to the accelerator.

They kept the ambulance in view until they came off the bypass. Their fellow road users' obliging deference to the Highway Code did not extend to Barnes and Kane, and it took them another ten minutes to arrive at the hospital.

They found the ambulance backed up to the doors of the resus area, next to a fleet of others, all silently awaiting their next call. Their two paramedics were nowhere to be seen.

Barnes and Kane walked in, immediately sensing the tension of a rush of activity. There were raised voices, chittering machinery, scuffling footsteps. Barnes tried to peer through the glass. He couldn't see much, but he saw enough.

"What is it?" Kane said.

"They're doing CPR," Barnes said. "Shit."

A stern woman in civilian clothes marched over and issued a challenge. Barnes held up his warrant card, and she drifted away again.

The vestibule they were in was an airlock to nowhere, Barnes figured. Whitewashed and stinking of bleach, he imagined — despite lifelong agnosticism — you took one door back to recovery, or you got wheeled down to the basement. Whether it was a gateway to heaven or hell sort of seemed like a moot point.

They hung round for about twenty minutes, before a gaggle of medical professionals streamed out of the unit, looking decidedly matter-of-fact, Barnes thought. A couple threw disinterested looks at the two men, but for the most part they were ignored.

The two paramedics were last.

"We lost her," one said, snapping off a glove. "Arrested in the ambulance. Sorry, guys. We tried."

"Goddammit!" Barnes said, staring at the ceiling, his hands on his hips. He looked at Kane. "Sorry, boss. Looks like that's another murder on your books."

CHAPTER FOURTEEN

Badged as Operation Cavalier, the major crime management structure settled lightly over Debbie Bridger's death with neatness and precision. Barnes, prior to the Force SIO taking over and grilling him on his initial actions, put a forensic strategy in place for the body in consultation with the senior Scenes-of-Crime officer and the Home Office pathologist, drafting in two uniformed officers to guard the body and two more DCs to start doing some house-to-house.

Barnes walked into the resus bay while he waited for the SIO to call. A sideways career move to intelligence had apparently resulted in him becoming embroiled in more homicide investigations than when he'd worked main office. Maybe the universe was trying to tell him something, even if in this one he was more a key witness than lead investigator.

A couple of machines were still whining in a monotone. Debbie's body was exactly as the resus team had left it — she was lying practically naked, her pale legs and arms at an awkward angle, as if she'd fallen from a great height. Her dressing gown had been cut off to make room for the defibrillator pads, and her head was arched back, her white jaw frozen in a silent, anguished plea. The front of her body had a cold, bluish tint, while her back was starting to turn the angry, red stain of post-mortem lividity.

Scattered around the trolley, lying among various items of discarded medical paraphernalia, were her few belongings which, for the most part, looked like they'd fallen out of her pockets.

Kane, having stepped outside, retrieved a blanket from another trolley and went to cover what remained of her dignity.

Barnes stopped him with a gentle, gloved finger.

"Nice thought," he said. "But we can't."

From the floor, Barnes collected her cigarette lighter, pills, pack of tissues, television remote, front door key and mobile phone, and shoved them all into an evidence bag.

They headed for the exit, Barnes stopping long enough to upset the two paramedics by telling them that their ambulance, now a crime scene, was shortly about to be lifted onto the back of a low-loader, and that they would need to surrender their uniforms and kit too.

"You should know you'll likely get a phone call from the IPCC after this," Barnes said as they walked back to the car, having left two uniformed patrol cops under strict instruction to guard Debbie Bridger's body like the Crown Jewels.

"What for?" Kane asked.

"Death following police contact. Other than the two paramedics, we were the last ones to see her alive. You'll have about eighteen months of discomfort, then they'll tell you there's no case to answer."

"Sounds great."

"Well, I can't imagine they serve papers on many supers, so it could be plus or minus. Rank can sometimes be a mixed blessing in these things."

"You'd know, I take it?"

"That's one for a cold beer or two. Suffice to say I'm practically on speed dial."

I can't tell you.

They drove back to the scene. Sharon Brooker, the neighbourhood sergeant and very competent house-to-house manager, met them outside the house with DC Monty Beck.

She looked unusually upset.

"Someone said this was the mother of the Op Blackwater victim? Some kind of intimidation gone wrong?" she said.

"I'm afraid so, Shaz," Barnes said.

"What's happening to this country, Barnes?"

"Hopefully nothing that a good bit of house-to-house can't redress. Am I being unreasonably optimistic?"

"As it happens, no. I might have something."

"Go on."

"So, two of the houses opposite are empty. Not sold yet. Not technically finished yet, either. Next door to your left heard some noises, thought it was the TV, didn't get up. I'm afraid I may have made her cry."

"It happens. And the other side?" Barnes looked at Kane as he spoke. The superintendent had moved away from them slightly and was flicking through his notebook.

"This is Mrs Soames. She's seventy-nine. Wouldn't normally have been up, but she had to use the toilet in the night. Heard some bangs and shouting, and looked out of the bedroom window to see two men walking out of the house and down the street. One of them looked around before they left. She seems to think she got a half-decent look at his face under the street light."

"Get a cognitive into her," Barnes said to Monty. "And a decent sketch likeness. Now."

"On it, boss." Monty disappeared off.

"Good work, Shaz," Barnes said.

"What did I miss?" Kane said, rejoining the huddle.

"We might have a witness from house-to-house. It's fragile, but it might be something."

"I might have something, too," Kane said.

"Oh?"

"Four-eight-seven-four."

"What about it?"

"It's Kevin Bridger's birthday."

Barnes frowned, and turned up his collar against a sudden bite of February wind.

"You're right. It is. Good spot. But why would her last words be to furnish us with her own son's date of birth?"

"I have no idea. A message, maybe?"

Barnes shook his head, frustrated.

"What is this, *The Da Vinci Code*? Can't people just say what they mean?"

"Does she want us to look again at Kevin? Will his date of birth give us something on his killer?"

They stood in the street, comparing notes, while construction machinery continued to rumble on the sites around them, and PCSOs went dutifully from door to door while others wrapped Debbie Bridger's house up in a swathe of crime scene tape.

"It could be anything. A postcode, a combination to a safe, a PIN number . . . or a set of coordinates to the foothills of Asgard — you name it."

"You might be overthinking it," Kane said. "What would the relevance of . . . hang on, what did you say?"

"When?"

"You said: a PIN number."

"Right."

"For a bank card, right?"

"I guess."

"People commonly use their relatives' date of birth for PIN numbers, yes? The banks routinely tell them not to, but most people do."

"So? You're saying her dying wish was for us to withdraw some cash?"

"No. What else do people use their families' birthdays for? Besides PIN numbers?"

Barnes expelled air.

"I don't know — everything. Anything."

"How about a code to unlock a mobile phone?"

* * *

They left the scene and drove back to the station. Barnes let them into the evidence store and they found the evidence bag with Debbie Bridger's mobile phone in it.

Barnes pulled on his third pair of latex gloves that day and held up the bag. "It's just a screen."

"It's a new one," Kane said. "An iPhone."

"A what?"

"Come on, where have you been living? A smartphone."

"Which is it? A smart-phone or an eye-phone?"

"Both. It's smart because it's basically a tiny computer. It's got a million more functions on it than an ordinary phone. Emails, messages, banking, camera, music, stocks and shares, weather forecast, you name it. You can do everything on it."

Barnes held the bag lightly between a thumb and forefinger.

"Are we having a look?" Kane said.

Barnes held up a hand. "No way. That's a good way to put this case in the bin before we've even got started. Not to mention your empty pension pot. This is one for the lab."

Barnes thought his boss looked a little disappointed.

"I'll get it fast-tracked. It won't be cheap, even for a homicide, but if I can throw the superintendent's weight behind it . . ."

"Do it."

"Just to forewarn you, 'fast' might be relative."

"How will they know what to look for? We only have the passcode."

"They'll look at whatever we tell them to look at, but your guess is as good as mine. She's got emails, text messages, photos, a notepad, social networking — you name it."

"One at a time, I suppose," Kane said.

"Let's think about this," Barnes said, slipping the bag back into the box of belongings and resealing the whole lot. "Here. You need to countersign. It's likely that our two superstars made an unannounced visit, right?"

Kane shrugged. He took out a pen and signed the label next to Barnes's own signature.

"Makes sense," he said.

"So, it's midnight. You hear an unfriendly knock. You can't run, so you let them in. You half know what it's about. They've been before. Maybe you're thinking they will do their usual: a bit of posturing and they'll be gone. You don't have a lot of time, so you're thinking on your feet as you walk to the front door. What are your options?"

Kane shrugged again.

"Well, we know she didn't raise hell and run to a neighbour. So . . ." He shut his eyes. "Your phone is in your dressing gown pocket, so you can — what? Dial 999 and leave an open line?"

"Right. And we know that didn't happen."

"You could send a quick message or post something on Facebook."

"And that — you would like to think — would have led to someone *else* calling 999," Barnes said. "And don't forget, she'd entertained them before. She wasn't expecting them to turn it up a notch. She was expecting to weather the storm."

"A hell of a storm."

"Indeed. So, maybe, instead of thinking your life is in danger, maybe all you're doing is creating a bit of an 'in the event of my death'-type insurance policy."

Kane's eyes widened.

"She recorded it. Recorded the visit."

CHAPTER FIFTEEN

"I did what you said," Kane said. "I went out on patrol."

"And?"

"I spent half a shift on Beachy Head trying to talk someone off the edge, and the other half in A&E with some thirteen-year-old that nobody wanted."

"Better than your board meetings, though, am I right?"

"Other than a shoplifting report, I don't think I went anywhere near a crime. People call us for all kinds of shit. I had no idea. I felt like a bloody social worker half the time."

"Welcome to the job."

"That's what Barnes said."

"Ah yes, the redoubtable Rutherford Barnes. He's become something of a mentor, no?"

"Not intentionally, but, yes, I guess so. He's a good man, Marlon."

"I don't doubt you, Samson. It's more the route he takes to get there."

"Well, maybe. Anyway, that's not why I'm calling. One crime I did happen to get involved in is the murder of Kevin Bridger's mother, likely by the same people that killed her son. It's going to come your way."

"My way? For why?"

"She just died right in front of us, Marlon. Death following police contact, according to Barnes. Right there in front of us."

"Are you all right?" His voice was quiet.

"I . . . I don't know. It just happened."

"These things germinate, Samson. Make sure you talk to someone. You've had a busy week."

DCI Marlon Choudhury ended the call. He stared at the phone for a moment, then slipped it back into his pocket and looked out of the window, where the land rose up towards the chalk hills of the Malling Down Nature Reserve from where Police HQ nestled in the bosom of the valley.

He sat back down, the office chair creaking under his weight, and turned back to the woman sitting on the other side of his desk. She looked ready for court in a smart, three-piece suit, and seemed to be trying to resist chewing her fingernails.

"DC Morgan. Natalie, if I may."

She nodded. He flicked through a two-page report in front of him.

"While I commend your diligence, most police wouldn't ordinarily come directly to me to get themselves re-vetted. New house, second job, money worries, new relationship — all of these things trigger a suitability check, but I have administrators for that."

"It's . . . it's not a new relationship, strictly speaking," she said.

He raised an eyebrow. Her eyes flicked briefly to the padlocked filing cabinets that lined the wall opposite the office window.

"But . . . but it could be. He's my neighbour . . ." She suddenly caught herself, and stared at the ceiling. "Shit, I'm talking to Professional Standards about going out with this guy before I've even discussed it with him."

Choudhury raised a hand.

"Your private life is your private life."

"Which is why I don't want your administrators poking around it. I trust you, boss. There aren't many PSD detectives I would say that about."

"Well, nuance aside about where exactly your, ah, burgeoning dalliance might be on the racetrack, there is no trace of the individual on our systems."

"Really?" Natalie said.

She didn't look particularly relieved, Choudhury thought. Surprised, maybe, but not relieved.

"You're not happy about this?"

"Well . . . I don't know. I mean, of course I am, but . . ."

"Do you have suspicions about him? If you do, I suggest that prevention is better than cure."

"Not suspicions, just . . . I don't know. Something about him. Not bad, exactly, but . . ."

"I should say that there is no trace of him, but we don't have a confirmed ID, of course. You gave us a name, description and an approximate year of birth. That was it. We'd need a little more than that."

"What about the voters' register? On the address?"

Choudhury shrugged. "Nothing on there. It's a new development. Another slice of administration that takes a while to catch up."

"The car?"

Choudhury shrugged again. "A lease. No name on the paperwork." He paused. "Does he know you are a police officer?"

"He does."

"And his reaction . . . ?"

"Nothing out of the ordinary."

"That's encouraging."

"I've been burned before, sir. I have a young son. I'm not going into anything without my eyes wide open."

"I admire your resolve, DC Morgan."

Choudhury stood, belly straining against his shirt, and extended a hand.

"Get me a confirmed ID, and we can do business. A copy of his driving licence, maybe. A passport. Even something with his DNA, if the situation presents itself. A toothbrush, maybe."

She flushed, and dropped her gaze.

"I'll see what I can do," she said.

* * *

After Barnes scared up an express courier service and Kane raised hell on the phone, there was nothing to do but wait. Kane couldn't concentrate, so he went to Jimmy's house — wanting to tell him that maybe hating cops on principle was a frivolous ethos, that maybe, sometimes, they did help — but the old man wasn't answering. There was a new pile on the driveway — rusty appliances, car parts and a tubular mess of steel office furniture that appeared to have been tossed out in whatever new clear-out Jimmy was working his way through.

Kane took the train to Hastings, wanting to sit idle and gaze out at the coast passing him by. As he rocked gently from side to side in the mercifully quiet carriage, he took in the dry marshland and Lego-brick caravan parks of Normans Bay and the wild shingle of Cooden — and mentally composed his resignation letter.

Despite the unfamiliar knot of tension in his sternum about what might be on Debbie Bridger's phone, he knew this role wasn't for him. He also knew that quitting, after only a couple of weeks, would mean a bunch of big fat told-you-sos from certain quarters. But he didn't care. The stuff he was meant to be doing — budgets, planning, meetings, performance — didn't interest him at all and seemed to be predicated on best guesses and who had the shiniest shoes.

By the same token, the real-cop stuff, the stuff he'd seen happen on his patch, was more than he'd been expecting. Barnes had said he'd just had an unlucky streak of serious crimes on the bounce, but being front and centre for Debbie Bridger's slow death was enough for him. He wanted to throw it all in the bin and go and live in a tent in a Scottish forest. Fish himself to death, maybe.

The club was called the Mausoleum; it was underground in all senses of the word. He walked down out of the cold into the stuffy basement and allowed the buzz-saw guitar and pounding kick drum swallow him whole. The lights strobed intermittently between blinding white spots and total darkness.

He descended some narrow stairs to where a metal three-piece were playing. By the time he'd reached the pit he'd been offered chemical enhancement by three different people; for a second, he'd been tempted.

There were so many familiar faces, he thought. Some pleased to see him, some who eyeballed him as if they couldn't quite place him, and some who turned their backs for reasons he couldn't begin to speculate on.

He stood still and shut his eyes and let the wall of music envelop him like a tidal wave, as frenzied bodies jumped and moved around him. The lights penetrated his eyelids, turning the inside of his head blood red, and images of the battered body of Kevin Bridger's mother spun in a kaleidoscope around him.

He opened his eyes, faintly aware of a commotion by the doors. He turned and saw frenetic movement at the top of the stairs, accompanied by just-audible shouts.

His first instinct — to ignore it — was somehow suppressed by an urge to walk towards it. He moved steadily towards the fracas, climbing the stairs to the main entrance, where he found a man in a tracksuit shouting obscenities at the two door supervisors, who held an arm each. On a counter next to them was a clear baggie full of various yellow pills.

"You okay?" Kane asked, holding up his warrant card.

The closest doorman squinted at the warrant card, his eyes flicking from the photo to Kane and back again, as if he didn't quite believe it. Kane just held the card steady. At least this time he hadn't ended up on his backside.

"You police?" the doorman said, after a moment. "Just pulled this idiot out of the line for a random search. Got half a pharmacy on him."

The idiot had obviously felt the door supervisors' grip loosen, for he attempted to bolt, but was quickly bundled to the floor amid howls of protest.

"You call 999?" Kane said, taking over one of the restraints and pinning the hapless street dealer to the cold, worn carpet.

"About ten minutes ago."

"Try again. Tell them Superintendent Kane is here, but off duty. I've got no kit or anything."

The two doormen looked at each other.

"Superintendent?" one said, before hurrying off, presumably to find a phone.

Kane kept his restraint on the man, while murmuring vague noises about calming down and taking it easy.

A police van pulled up two minutes later, and four yellow-jacketed town centre cops piled in to extract the street dealer in what was, Kane had to admit, a very neat operation.

Once the prisoner was safely ensconced in the back of the van, two of the cops came back to statement the doormen and seize the ton of tablets.

"Good little collar, boss," one said.

"Need me for anything?" Kane said, trying to conceal his surprise.

"Well, your statement would be handy, just to make sure that he doesn't get bail, but we've got it from here otherwise. Interested to know what else we might find in his bedroom."

The cops took off, and Kane followed them out onto the street, the blast of cold air feeling like every kind of reality. He watched the van disappear into the distance, blue lights ablaze as it headed along the seafront, a daisy chain of promenade lights like dots of white ink against the sharp, freezing, navy-blue sky.

He knew, then, that he was unlikely to ever come back to the Mausoleum — off duty, anyway. He also knew — whether he liked it or not — that his resignation letter would not, for now at least, be seeing the light of day.

He finished up his statement in the reports room at Hastings nick — attracting curious stares and comments alike from the patrol traffic passing through — and was driving back past Jimmy's when he got the call.

"It's in." Barnes was breathless.

"Already?"

"I don't know what you said to them, but it worked."

"Money talks. Just don't tell the finance people."

"You coming in?"

"Be there in ten. Already in the car."

"When this is all over, I'll remind you to sleep now and then. But that can wait."

Barnes was waiting in the conference room at the Major Incident Suite when Kane arrived. He was shifting from foot to foot at the head of the table. Shaz Brooker and Monty Beck were also there.

On the tabletop was a series of A3 images, neatly arranged in a straight line.

A still of the seafront CCTV on the night Kevin Bridger was killed, enhanced to zero in on the grainy face of the tall, dark-haired one flanked by the two big lugs.

An enhanced sketch likeness of a man in profile, leaving Debbie Bridger's house at some ungodly hour of the morning.

And a voice on a recording.

Kane looked at Barnes. "Well?"

"Lab found a twenty-minute recording. Timed at ten past one in the morning, thirty-four hours before we rocked up."

"She was sitting in that chair for over a day?" Kane said.

Barnes nodded. He pointed to the speakers next to a large video screen on the wall, which were connected to a laptop sitting next to the images on the tabletop. "I've rigged it up."

"Have you listened to it?"

"Not yet," Barnes said, holding up a white CD-ROM in a plastic envelope.

Kane stepped forward. "Well, let's hear it."

Barnes handed Kane the disc. "Want to do the honours?"

Kane took the disc and inserted it into the laptop. "Have we got an ID?"

"Not yet," Barnes said. "But we're close, boss. We're bloody close." He put a hand on Kane's arm. "And I should warn you — the lab said it's pretty tough to listen to."

Kane looked at Barnes for a moment — and then he pressed PLAY.

PART TWO

CHAPTER SIXTEEN

With his bird's nest beard, scrub of greasy hair, just-about-so-cially-acceptable odour and surfeit of exaggerated helpfulness, it was plain to even the meanest intelligence that Kenneth Rix had a couple of nervous breakdowns under his belt. He may even have had another one brewing.

"I can see you're paying with a card there, madam. Just slip it in the machine, double-check the amount and enter your PIN. Do you have a loyalty card? You may find it worthwhile. Let me write down the number of the member-ship team for you. They're extremely helpful. Thank you so very much, you have a good evening now."

He had the careful — if excessively loud — diction and thick glasses of a library intellectual. In a past life, he could have been a laboratory researcher, or a technical analyst, or maybe even a lecturer. But now, the wrong side of fifty, he was swiping goods through the till at the newly opened con-venience store at the Wallsend service station in Pevensey, one of only a handful of staff that were content to work night shifts on a regular basis.

While the existence of this latest branch was no doubt convenient, on this particularly cold Thursday it was not exactly being subjected to heavy footfall. A curtain of snow had started to fall, and the few customers that were in the store were limited to people dashing out to buy milk and bread and nappies and, by contrast, weekly shoppers who did everything according to a careful timetable and who probably would have got on famously with Kenneth in different circumstances.

Kenneth spent a lot of this particular shift — and indeed many — diligently stocking shelves, labelling reduced items and generally keeping the place looking presentable. He was not a supervisor, but who knew where he might be in a year? Kenneth may have been many things, but he was not idle. Continued effort equals reward, sooner or later. He could always find something to be doing, and through a sense of personal pride and duty would only properly relax if he were on an official break.

So, it was pure coincidence that he happened to be staring idly at the snowfall outside when the unkempt, bone-thin, screaming girl crashed against the window.

* * *

Kenneth was frozen with fear for almost half a minute. The woman crashed into the window with such a terrific bang he was amazed she hadn't gone right through it. She was screaming in terror, smacking her tiny fists against the glass as she begged for help.

His first steps forward from behind the till were tentative, and then when he noticed that the other customers in the shop were also frozen and staring at the woman, he felt his sense of duty swell in his chest. This was *his* store, and he had a responsibility to the people both within and without.

He rushed outside into a thick wall of falling snow and was relieved to see that whatever grim pursuer she was fleeing from was not in immediate sight. She was still banging on the window, however, and when he touched her lightly on the arm she jumped two feet into the air and spun round to face him, her face contorted in rigid fear. Then she appeared to register his uniform, and her brain must have taken this as proof enough that Kenneth was not a threat, and she collapsed into his arms.

Kenneth carried her back into the store, by now assisted by a couple of other members of the public — whom, he noticed, were quite content to defer to him. *You* call the ambulance, *you* find a first-aid kit, *you* fetch some water. By the time they got to the tiny staffroom, Kenneth was already entertaining fantasies about hero awards ceremonies and the flashing bulbs of photographers. It was only the periodic shrieking of the still-scared woman that brought him back to the present. She was like a newly hatched bird, shivering uncontrollably on the torn vinyl seat as she sipped, wide-eyed, from a paper cup of tepid water, her chest heaving as she struggled to get her rapid breathing under control. Kenneth put a coat around her ice-cold body and dragged an electric heater over from the corner of the room.

"Okay, okay, that's it. Take it easy. You're all okay now. All okay." Kenneth's soothing tones were designed for a distressed toddler, to the extent that the two men that had come in with him exchanged glances.

"Are you hurt anywhere?" he asked her. "Is it okay if I check you over for injuries?"

"Maybe we should wait for the ambulance to do that," said one of the men behind him. "She doesn't seem to be bleeding."

"I'm a first-aider," Kenneth said, not looking around. And then, to the woman: "What's your name?"

It was quickly becoming apparent that the woman spoke very little English. Kenneth pointed at his own name badge.

"Me Kenneth," he said, loudly and slowly. "Ken-neth."

"She Jane?" one of the men wondered aloud.

The other man snickered. Kenneth ignored them.

The woman's eyes were focused on her cup, and seemed to be flicking from side to side. It suddenly occurred to Kenneth that there were three men crowded around her in a relatively confined space, waiting for her to say something.

"Guys, I think we might be crowding her," Kenneth said. "Do you want to step outside the door a minute? One of you can keep an eye out for the emergency services," he added, just as one looked like he was about to protest.

They both stepped out. One of them went back into the store, apparently to do as instructed and flag down the cops, while the other hovered around outside the office.

"It's okay," Kenneth repeated to the woman when the men had left. "You're okay. You're safe. What's your name?"

He squatted down so he was not looming over her, and tried to catch her eye. The office was not particularly inviting — it had no windows, a battered filing cabinet, a CCTV monitor and a morass of paperwork strewn across the desk, just about held in check by a heavy glass ashtray that was in dire need of emptying. The only light came from a harsh fluorescent tube, and Kenneth could see marks and blemishes all over the woman's face and body.

Gradually her breathing started to slow down, and the change in her as calm began to settle was pronounced. She sat up a little straighter, and appeared to take in her surroundings. Then her eyes settled on Kenneth with a stare so intense that he nearly took a step back.

"Rocks . . . Pet rescue," she said.

Kenneth didn't understand, but he didn't want to ask her to repeat it, so he just stared at her stupidly for a moment.

"Pardon?" he said.

"Rocks. Pet rescue," she said again, pointing at herself.

"Pets? What about your pets? They need rocks?" he said.

Outside the door, the other man snickered again.

"Do your pets need help?"

She shook her head.

"Can you write it down?" he said, offering her a pen.

She took the pen, but shook her head again.

Kenneth straightened up, his mind racing during the silent impasse. *There must be a way.* Though he would never admit it, it was important to Kenneth that he make some form of progress with this woman before the police arrived.

He was essentially the first responder, and he wanted to impress the professionals when they arrived.

His eyes darted around the office, and settled on a dirty yellow Post-it on a noticeboard above the desk. It displayed a user ID and password.

Of course! Eastbourne, like many seaside towns, was a significant draw to overseas students in the holiday months, and they formed a significant proportion of the store's customer base. The store manager — after a suggestion from Kenneth, it had to be said — had agreed to sign up to a trial summer contract with a 24/7 telephone interpreting service. For a fixed subscription fee you could access the service as often as you liked. Unfortunately, most students either spoke enough English to get by or were happy to muddle through, and so the trial had been something of a damp squib.

Until now.

Kenneth dialled the number and got through to a central call centre, who asked him for his ID and password, and then asked him what language he wanted.

He didn't know the answer to that one.

Where are you from?

She stared at him.

He looked down. She had been doodling on a piece of paper while he was on the phone. It looked like a flag.

"Is this where you're from?" he asked. "Italy? France?"

No, it couldn't have been those. The left-hand bar was too dark.

"Belgium?"

She shook her head — *no, no and no.*

"Romania?"

She nodded emphatically.

"*România.*"

Kenneth felt a surge of excitement, just as he heard sirens in the distance. His bladder contracted. He had to do this.

He tapped his foot while the call centre connected him to a Romanian interpreter. It seemed to take an age. The sirens got louder.

The call was connected. The interpreter asked him what he wanted to know. Kenneth spoke in a rush, barely pausing for breath.

"Okay, ask her name, if she's injured, where she's come from and what's happened to her. Ask her why she's scared."

The interpreter repeated it slowly, presumably writing it all down, and then asked Kenneth to pass the phone over.

The girl spoke in soft, breathless tones, a stream of words that couldn't have made less sense to Kenneth. She seemed to be talking for hours. She waved her free hand as she spoke.

The sirens were very loud now, then they cut off suddenly and there was a short screech of tyres as the police cars and ambulance pulled up outside.

"Old bill are here," said the man outside the office door. Kenneth had forgotten he was there.

When Kenneth looked back to the woman, she was holding the receiver out to him, an expectant look on her face.

He took the phone from her.

"Okay, I have asked her those things you wanted to know," the interpreter said in an emotionless voice.

Kenneth listened intently. He stared as the police and paramedics began to arrive in one big rush.

"Her name is Roxana Petrescu. She prefers 'Roxy'. She is from a fishing village on the Danube, one hundred miles northeast of Bucharest. She was brought to the UK several weeks ago in a lorry. She has been held prisoner in a house since then. She isn't sure how long. A long time. She lived in the dark. Tonight she escaped. She does not know where it is, but she ran for thirty minutes, she thinks, before she saw lights. She ran to your shop. She does not know where this place is. But there were many men there, she says. Men coming and going. Men with guns."

The interpreter paused. Kenneth swallowed.

"And many more like her."

CHAPTER SEVENTEEN

Barnes dropped his keys in the dish. They clanged in the empty hallway. He pulled his tie loose and, for a moment, thought he could hear the waves of the Channel hissing onto the shingle half a mile east.

The new place was a Victorian apartment in Blackwater Road, with cavernous ten-foot ceilings and upholstered bay windows you could hide a cricket team in. The flat was opposite Eastbourne College, a vast construction that, at night, was bathed in a ground-lit amber glow that shrouded the place in Gothic shadow like Hogwarts.

He wasn't sure quite what had pulled him into the town — well, Lower Meads. He could count at least six serious crime scenes within spitting distance that he'd worked over the years. And it wasn't the sea. He'd used to enjoy running past the breakers, but now the size and wildness of the thing was all just too existential.

He went outside and fiddled around under the bonnet of the Rover for half an hour, then reheated some food and parked in front of the television. This couldn't go on. He was going to end up either dying alone of a stroke on his sofa or throwing a rope over the banister. Total immersion in your work was fine, except it wasn't. How much holiday time had he let slide, just because he didn't need it? How often was a good, complex case the thing that kept your mind from drifting idly into contemplation and regret?

He put down the half-eaten plate of food and, in an act of uncharacteristic decisiveness, opened his laptop. Within half an hour he'd booked an autumn week in the Lake District, a taster session with a personal trainer and an appointment with a counsellor. He even browsed some night classes for motor mechanics. Add a certificate or something to his amateur tinkering. He felt a little better after doing so, and stretched out on the sofa. If he wasn't on call, he might even have gone to the movies.

He hated being on call. Always had done. He'd rather work a night shift. Everything was exacerbated, of course, by the increasingly large gaps on the on-call rota, where it didn't matter what department you worked in — if you caught it, you bought it. This was his third on-call stint this month already. Apparently, someone was kidnapping all the DIs.

And while the on-call DI had the relative autonomy to decide whether to come out or not, and might decide to provide telephone oversight from the comfort of their own lounge, when Barnes got the call about the escaped kidnap victim Roxana Petrescu, he got in his car and went straight to the scene.

* * *

Well, as straight as conditions would allow. When he'd opened his front door he'd been surprised to step into a blanket of snow up to his knee, and he'd skidded, slid and spun from his house to Pevensey. It took him four times longer than he'd been expecting.

Cops standing around, Barnes thought as he turned off the Wallsend roundabout and pulled up on the forecourt outside the convenience store. The iconic image of our time. And it didn't matter however you tried to get the look right, it was always the one of them grinning inanely outside a murder scene, or with arms folded and a leave-me-alone expression that found its way into the paper.

It was funny — you send a couple of cops to deal with some wicked new problem on their own and the depths of innovation and problem-solving they could come up with knew no limits. Stick a command structure onto an incident, however, and they became unable to do anything other than exactly what they were told.

One of the cops outside the store was somehow a combination of all these. Barnes knew him — Adrian Willow and he had worked patrol together almost ten years ago, having joined the police only weeks apart. They had been good times, yet to be jaded by near-constant exposure to the more disturbing examples of human nature and the feeling that you were loathed by both customers and masters alike. They had been keen, hungry and felt some great collars as a result. Collars where the secondary investigation — by CID or Major Crime or whoever — had been made considerably easier by the tenacity of that first response and early arrest.

"Inspector Barnes, as I live and breathe," Willow said, striding forward and extending a yellow-jacketed arm as Barnes got out of his car. His nose and ears were pinched with cold, but he was grinning all the same. "You did well to get here. We seem to have copped a Siberian front all of a sudden."

"You haven't done too badly either." Barnes stamped his feet and buried his hands in his pockets.

Willow indicated a Land Rover Freelander behind him.

"Swapped out the patrol cars for four-by-fours. Only way we can deliver a service to our rural communities."

"I might have to get one."

Barnes and Willow hurried into the store and stood just inside the automatic doors, under a blast of heat from a ceiling fan.

"So, what's a DI from sneaky-beaky world doing out on the mean streets of Pevensey? Is there more to this little caper than a lowly PC like me needs to know about?"

"Nothing so exciting, I'm afraid. Just a shortage of Divisional DIs means everyone has to muck in on the rota."

"What, and you've actually copped a call-out? That was careless of you."

"Third one this month."

"I thought they just made up names for the spreadsheet."

Barnes smiled without teeth. "So, what's the story here?"

Willow took on a more serious expression. "Funny one, this. The short version is that we have a foreign girl who, it seems, has been held captive at a nearby-but-as-yet-unknown location for some time. Tonight, she's escaped and run to the first friendly place she could find."

"Foreign? Are we communicating with her okay?"

"Romanian, we think. The store manager had the presence of mind to use a telephone interpreter to do first aid."

"Clever. And you say 'girl'. Do we think she's a juvenile?"

"Pardon my relaxed turn of phrase — I would say she's early- to mid-twenties, but you'd be forgiven for thinking she's younger."

"Okay. Injuries?"

"Cold and a bit battered, but nothing major. Paramedics have been and gone. She could do with a KFC or two, mind."

"And she seems credible?"

"Well, just in terms of how she looks and how she presented to the manager, there's no reason to disbelieve her story."

"Okay."

"Two things that add some spice: first, she says that there were armed men guarding this place. Second, she says there are other captives."

Barnes stared at him. "That adds considerable urgency. Do we have any containment on this place?"

"We don't know where it is. And neither does she, by the sounds of it. She can describe it, and she says it took about thirty minutes running to get here, which gives us a search radius of about three miles, give or take."

"Thirty minutes running in this? She's lucky not to have hypothermia."

"Indeed."

"My concern is that if they've realised she's missing, the armed men and the prisoners could both be long gone by the time we locate them."

"I agree. That's why you're here, though, right? You're paid the big bucks for that kind of responsibility."

Barnes gave another sour smile.

"I'd better get a cognitive into her asap. Who's the DS with oversight?"

"McAllister, I believe. Which means he's put a shopping list of actions on the incident log and not done much else. You can call that oversight if you want. But I don't."

"Welcome to Divisional CID. All right, I'd better come and have a word with the manager."

They started to move towards the back office.

"His name's Kenneth. He's a bit intense, but he seems pretty switched on."

Barnes didn't say anything. In a way, he was envious of Willow. Cynical and gruff maybe, but he could be sensitive when he needed to be and certainly didn't have the countenance of a man held to ransom by the notion of a career. Barnes wondered if that feeling of liberation was worth the lower pay. Although, throw in a few PSU deployments and the odd major enquiry, and the end-of-year P60s probably weren't that different. Unlike Barnes, Willow still got paid for his overtime.

They walked through the store to the staffroom at the back. Barnes was expecting to see more of a police presence in the store. Willow's oppo was checking CCTV in an adjoining office, but they were the only patrol on scene.

Willow took Barnes into the tiny staff office. Barnes turned to stare at the other PC, his hands on his hips, and didn't take much comfort from Willow's befuddled expression.

"I thought you said she didn't go to hospital."

"She didn't."

"So where is she?"

"I'm sorry to say, boss, that's an extremely good fucking question."

CHAPTER EIGHTEEN

Kenneth sat in the car, trying to control his breathing. The excitement was building in his chest like a small rodent trying to chew its way out. The police would be so thoroughly impressed. There would surely be some kind of civic award. They might even find some kind of job for him.

Realising that, once Roxy's escape was discovered, time was of the essence where both her captors and fellow captives were concerned, he had driven Roxy back in the direction she had run from. His intention was to try to identify the location, conduct some kind of discreet reconnaissance, and then contact the police to brief them.

He had the interpreter on his mobile phone's loudspeaker and, as he had driven, things had come back to Roxy. A spread of snow-covered marshland stretching back from the main road into the darkness, peppered with her tottering footprints. A large oak blotting out the streetlights that made her think she was deeper in the country than she was. A red telephone box at the end of a lane.

And now they were sitting outside a large, gated house. Beyond the gate was a gravel driveway big enough for four cars, with a six-foot wall encircling the whole perimeter.

"How did you get out?" Kenneth said.

In the seat beside him, Roxy babbled an answer.

"At the back of the house is a tree. It has thick roots and the stumps of broken branches. She says she used it to help her climb," said the tinny voice from the mobile phone.

Kenneth squinted in the gloom. He couldn't tell much about the house itself, other than the grounds belied its size. It did not look especially large, but its secluded location would have put the price tag way beyond anything Kenneth could ever hope to afford. You could raise a bunch of kids here and let them roam safely. Or keep alpacas. Or retire quietly and let the garden keep you busy. Or run a clandestine and lucrative human-trafficking operation.

Kenneth saw movement. A dark figure appeared from around the side of the house and walked slowly around the front. It paused near the garage, seemed to stare out towards the road, and then continued its journey back around the house.

A sentry, Kenneth thought. As he thought this, another one appeared from the general area of the garden. This one was much closer to the gate and made Kenneth jump. Beside him, Roxy clutched his arm in fright, and his sense of protective duty neutralised his own alarm.

"It's all right, dear. You're quite safe."

The mobile phone piped up with a translation.

The figure was close enough for Kenneth to make out a baseball cap, pulled low on its head, and a thick jacket. Bomber style. And, Kenneth thought, something strapped across its front. A gun?

That was enough for Kenneth. He knew when to call in the professionals. He felt pretty sure what he had seen more than corroborated Roxy's account of events. Not only that, but the apparent lack of urgency in the movements of the two patrols he had seen suggested it was entirely possible her escape had not yet been discovered. Given the hour, it was possible that it might remain that way until the morning.

Kenneth told the interpreter he had to go. He had to make an urgent call. The interpreter ended the call in the same business-like way in which he had conducted it.

Kenneth wasn't sure exactly who to call. There were cops at the store, but he didn't have their direct numbers. Carelessly, he hadn't made a note of the incident number either. Would calling 999 cause needless delays? Would he have to tell the whole story again?

A security light flicked on, casting a brilliant white light across the driveway, the road outside — and Kenneth's car. They were lit up like lab rats under a microscope's halogen.

"Don't worry," he said to Roxy. "Probably just a fox. Must happen all the time out this way."

But she no longer understood him. And the headlights behind him and rumble of tyres on the country lane suggested otherwise.

Decision made: 999 it is.

CHAPTER NINETEEN

Barnes spread an Ordnance Survey map over the bonnet of the car; but for the petrol station's protective canopy and the bright arc lights therein, he wouldn't have bothered. Snow and darkness would have quickly rendered it a pointless exercise.

"We're here," he said. Willow peered over his shoulder.

Barnes was pointing at a small triangle that represented the petrol station. It sat alongside a thick green line denoting the main road, either side of which was a lot of white, carved up into irregular shapes by a series of pink lines.

"How long did you say she was running?" Barnes said.

"*She* said thirty minutes. Approximately," Willow said.

"Let's say very approximately. Let's assume she's not been particularly well looked after — poor nourishment, low energy, possible injury. Add to that hostile terrain and freezing conditions . . ."

"And it's bloody dark out there," Willow said.

"Indeed. I'd be surprised if we are looking at more than a one-mile radius."

"Against that I'd say you've got a very desperate woman in fear for her life," Willow said. "She says she was planning to hide, but when she realised she hadn't been discovered immediately, she didn't stop."

Barnes eyed him.

"It's a good point," he said. "Call it a mile and a half. If we come up empty-handed we'll widen it out."

He examined the corner of the map until he found the scale and measured out a mile and a half using his fingers. Not exact, but it would do for now.

"Control room'll probably do that for you, boss," Willow said. "Put a bit of science behind it."

"I need to be able to see it."

He pulled out a pen and drew an uneven circle on the map around the petrol station.

Barnes felt his phone vibrate in his pocket. He let it ring out; there was a pause, and then it began again. People — senior people — were starting to wake up to the fact that an escaped captive was now missing again, along with her erstwhile rescuer.

He ignored both the phone and the sudden clench in his bowels. The thought that the IPCC must have a file like a doorstep with his name on was momentarily inescapable.

"Not much in there," Willow remarked.

He was right. Nothing built up or residential. Marshes, wetlands, fields, large patches of water and a thread-vein network of river courses and waterways that were no doubt picture-postcard perfect by day, but potentially lethal in the darkness.

"What are you thinking?" Willow said.

Barnes shrugged. "Well, it's going to take far more than you and me to comb it. I need a PolSA and a proper search team. Lowland dogs, search-and-rescue . . ."

"What about the stronghold?"

"Well, the catchment is remote, but there are residences."

"Posh ones too. People pay good money to be out in the country, away from the riff-raff."

"Exactly. Big, expensive houses. Gated complexes, out-buildings, cellars. Perfect for the kind of operation she's describing."

"Want me to ask for the chopper?"

"Air support, most definitely. I need some intel done on this store assistant too. What was his name?"

"Kenneth."

"I'm assuming he's taken his car — ANPR might help narrow down the area."

Willow straightened up and, hands on hips, looked back over at the inviting glow of the glass storefront. "Why on earth would he have nicked off with the hostage? Under the noses of a bunch of cops?"

Barnes shut his eyes momentarily. His phone buzzed again in his pocket. "Is he in on it, maybe? He'll be lucky not to get himself nicked for kidnap."

Willow turned back to Barnes. "You thinking *Daily Mail* headline?"

"Not yet," Barnes said.

Barnes called the duty inspector and briefed her. Given the time of night, most of the Division's patrol resources were mercifully available. They were low on numbers, but that wasn't anything new. Most of the patrol teams had been carrying at least twenty-per-cent vacancies for the best part of a year. She started dotting them around the perimeter of Barnes's catchment — but no closer, on his say-so. Barnes didn't want marked assets showing out until they had a better idea of where they were going and what might lie in store.

The next call was to Ops-One, the control room inspector. Barnes was unsurprised to learn that he wouldn't get a search team until daylight hours, but a PolSA was roped in from Brighton & Hove and Hotel-900, the police helicopter, was asked to lift and maintain a discreet distance.

Barnes asked the control room inspector to start looking at Kenneth Rix — home address, ANPR, phone number. The inspector said he would get it done.

Barnes ended the call and bent down again to scrutinise the map. His phone rang again less than two minutes later.

"DI Barnes? Phil Toynbee, Ops-One. We just spoke."

"That was quick." Barnes continued examining the map.

"Well, your man, Mr Rix. We got his number from the 999 call he first made when your hostage appeared in his shop. We've been running off that log as the master. Just after you hung up a linked call popped up."

"A link?"

"Yes. Same number. Looks like he's just called 999 again. Well, that number has, at least."

"Not him?"

"Possibly, but it was a dropped call. No request."

"When was this?" Barnes forgot the map and straightened up.

"About a minute ago."

CHAPTER TWENTY

Despite never having seen one before, Kenneth instinctively knew the cold metal pressed behind his ear was the barrel of a gun.

"What the fucking hell are you doing here?" The voice was an angry buzz. Kenneth smelled cigarettes and cheap aftershave.

Kenneth didn't answer. He couldn't. He had spread his hands and placed them both on the steering wheel in another instinctive act of pre-emptive obedience; beyond that, however, all of his concentration was focused on maintaining control of his bladder.

The gun was shoved harder into his jawbone.

"Please . . ." Kenneth said in a rasp, his eyes screwed shut. "Please be careful."

"What? What? *What did you say?* I asked you a question."

"I . . ."

"What the fuck are you . . ." the voice stopped.

Kenneth wanted to turn his head, but couldn't. He was completely paralysed.

"Who's that in the car with you?"

The aftershave was suddenly amplified tenfold as the man stuck his head in the car. Kenneth felt the abrasive stubble of the man's zero-grade cut brush against his nose, then it scraped against his top lip as the man craned his neck further in; the aftershave stink was now so strong Kenneth could taste it on the back of his throat.

Kenneth felt the release of pressure as the gun was removed from behind his ear, and he managed to open his eyes a fraction. All he could see was white skin and the blue tail of a serpent tattoo that curled upwards from the man's neck, past his ear and around onto his scalp.

The man was peering into the back of the car, training his pistol on whatever he might find there — which, Kenneth knew, would amount to no more of a threat than several days' worth of discarded fast-food packaging, a pile of old motoring magazines he hadn't got round to recycling, his hi-vis and a torch.

Despite himself, Kenneth was embarrassed.

The man withdrew from the car.

"Just you two?"

Kenneth nodded. The gun made a reappearance behind his ear; Kenneth shut his eyes again.

"What are you doing out here? I ain't going to ask you again."

Kenneth's mind worked furiously. It was beyond his faculties to come up with even a vaguely persuasive lie, but he wasn't about to drop Roxy in it by telling the truth, either — notwithstanding the fact that he had done just that by bringing her back here in the first place.

In the end, he opted for a fudge by avoiding the question in favour of terrified pleas for mercy — which, as it happened, was not difficult to pull off.

"Please . . . please don't hurt us," Kenneth mewed. "We just . . . we were . . . oh my God, please don't do anything. I'm sorry. I'm so sorry."

The gun disappeared again. Kenneth opened his eyes and watched the man walk around the front of the car. The man paused long enough to read the number plate, then appeared at the passenger window and peered at Roxy.

He didn't speak, but scrutinised her as if she were an obscure celebrity whom he couldn't quite place.

"Where do I know you from?" the man asked.

Roxy didn't answer, but stared straight ahead, her hands balled in her lap. She didn't look scared, Kenneth thought; in fact, if anything, she looked a little defiant.

With a bit of distance between them, Kenneth was able to take in the man's appearance a little more. The neck tattoo sprawling onto his scalp was distinctive enough — the man was about thirty, with eyes like grey ice and an angular jaw that suggested the rest of him was little more than sinew and anger.

Roxy muttered something in her native tongue that sounded to Kenneth like a curse word.

"What? What d'you say?" the man said. He was getting vexed, Kenneth could tell. "Speak English, you fucking bitch."

The man made a sudden thrusting movement with the gun, as if to strike Roxy across the face with it, but she didn't flinch, didn't react at all. His face remained impassive as he slowly withdrew the gun, and Kenneth could tell she had impressed him.

As the man walked across the front of the car again, Roxy reached over and momentarily squeezed Kenneth's hand with hers. Kenneth looked down in surprise, then over at Roxy with a puzzled look of wonder on his face, as if she somehow knew what was coming next.

Kenneth didn't see the butt of the pistol, but he felt it smash across his nose like a small, cold brick. The pain was like a white light that radiated out from the centre of his face up into his brain. His eyes streamed and a warm curtain of blood flowed freely down his beard and onto his shirt front.

Even as he covered his broken mess of a nose with his hands and began to sob uncontrollably, he heard the car door being opened and that shaven head brushing past him again as his seatbelt was unclipped and he was dragged bodily out of the car.

Kenneth's yowling went up a notch, bordering on full-blown, childlike panic as he was hauled onto the damp grass verge and dropped like a fly-tipped Christmas tree. He couldn't see Roxy, and would have been mildly embarrassed to note that he had pretty much stopped caring about what happened to her. Blood was still dripping down his face and into his mouth, and he stopped crying only because he was sure that to do otherwise would mean he would only suffocate himself.

A second strike, this time on the top of his head, laid him out prone. He was still conscious, but the blow to the head had dulled the edges of his fear, and he was able to observe that fear was a survival function. Fear kept you alert, kept you alive. The second blow detached him from the moment, and he was momentarily convinced that he was about to be beaten to death in a snowy country lane in the middle of the night for no reason that he could possibly discern.

He kept his eyes shut and waited to die, but no further blows came. All was quiet, and he was suddenly cold, suddenly able to feel the wet of the grass soaking through his clothes from head to foot. As full consciousness began to creep back to him, he kept his eyes screwed shut and played dead — instinctively as much as anything.

There was a murmur of voices, and Kenneth was able to discern that the man was speaking on the phone, a little distance away from the car. He chanced the opening of one eye.

The man was standing about six feet in front of the car, lit up by the headlights and a misty sheen of moon that was battling cloud cover. In some vaguely satisfying fantasy that he knew would never come to pass, Kenneth thought about flinging himself back into the car and running the man over, but instead he focused on the man's conversation. It was difficult to discern much — the man spoke in low tones but, to Kenneth's ear, he sounded rational, even reasonable, and Kenneth found himself wanting desperately to latch onto this and use logic and sense to try to get to the bottom of whatever unspoken code he'd breached by driving out here in the dead of night with a recaptured escapee: *We're all adults here, I'm sure we can sort this out like gentlemen.*

Kenneth didn't properly remember the change of scene, only pieces of it that came back to him in fragments — several pairs of hands on his body, the change of atmosphere from the cold chill of the outside air to a dank chill of an indoor room, moving from a lying position to a sitting position.

Then a torrent of freezing water deluged him from somewhere in front of him; the cold encased him like a shroud, and he woke properly, gasping and spluttering for air.

The pain in his face, the pain in his head and a feeling of disorientation all competed for his attention, laced with a general sense of shock at the unreality of the situation. He tried to rationalise what was happening, but the effort was too great. It must surely all just be a nightmare.

Kenneth lifted his head and a swimming feeling like a cyclone in his brain nearly caused him to vomit. He was sitting in a chair, with cold bracelets biting into his wrists — handcuffs, he realised as he tried to stand up. The water dripped off him onto a concrete floor, and the cold and pain held him in a vicious embrace.

Eventually, his vision returned to some sort of focus. He was in a breeze block room that, judging by the narrow windows near the ceiling and the abundance of gloom, was a basement of some sort. Two yellow sodium wall lights cast a weak glow that was token at best, but did enough to cast silhouettes around the three figures that stood in front of him, and Kenneth realised that it was a near-perfect room to die in.

One of them — the man with the serpent tattoo on his head — stepped forward; Kenneth turned away from him, and in so doing realised that Roxy was handcuffed to the chair next to him. She was conscious, her chin raised, her eyes clear even in the darkness. Kenneth wanted to reason that she was in better shape because she hadn't been beaten senseless, but he was mature enough to quickly realise that, had he been untouched physically, he still would have been cowering in supplication. He parked the unspoken reflection this had on his own sense of masculinity, instead opting to draw some steel from the tiny woman's own resolve.

He turned his gaze back to the man, who, it seemed, was holding a soldering iron. The tip glowed red. Kenneth's resolve quickly vanished, and he hung his head in shame and fear.

"Why are you doing this?" he sobbed, shaking his head until he gagged. "I haven't done anything to you."

"That's not quite right, though, is it?" the man said. It was the same man from outside. The other two remained silent silhouettes in the gloom. They could have been mannequins. "You're parked outside my gaff in the middle of the night with one of my employees."

"I wasn't doing anything."

"Shall I tell you what you look like to me? You look like an interfering little prick. Nosing around in my business."

"I was . . . I was just bringing her home. We'd been out, and . . ."

The attempt at subterfuge left his lips before he'd had time to think about it. The ensuing silence was like a thick, accusing fog.

The man inched forwards, holding up a square, black object. It flapped open in his grasp.

"Kenneth Rix, twenty-fifth of the ninth, nineteen-fifty-eight. Flat 2B, 104 Seaside Road, Eastbourne. Born Reading. NHS organ donor — type A-positive. Blockbuster video member. Three points on your driving licence. Hospice lottery member . . . Shall I go on?"

Kenneth wondered how the man could read all that in the gloom, then realised in dismay that he had committed it to memory.

The man flung the wallet at Kenneth. It hit his chest and the various membership cards tumbled out onto the floor. Some landed in the puddle of urine at Kenneth's feet.

"Now, I know that's bullshit. You didn't take anyone out on any date. Reason I know that is because none of my employees get to leave the fucking compound. Ever."

The man took another step forward.

"So, I know you're lying to me. Which means, despite the convincing shit-your-pants-scared routine, you're capable of telling more."

He held the soldering iron out in front of him and advanced. Beside Kenneth, Roxy started to lurch in her chair in protest, cursing something in her native tongue.

"You can fucking shut up. I'll deal with you in a minute."

The man's other hand came out. In it was a white rag of some kind. He shoved it roughly into Kenneth's mouth and wedged it there — Kenneth cared not for the accuracy of his own guess, but decided the item was a tennis sock soaked in vinegar. It balled in his mouth and made his eyes stream, distracting him long enough for the man to launch forward, tear Kenneth's shirt front open and press the soldering iron against his chest.

CHAPTER TWENTY-ONE

"Phil, what are the coordinates of that 999 call?"

"Eastings 50.84220, Northings 0.33686. It's the middle of nowhere, somewhere north of the service station between the Coast Road and the Rickney Sewer."

"You try to call it back?"

"Couple of times. It just rings out."

"Okay, I'd pause on that now if I were you. There's a good chance the witness is compromised, possibly under duress. From what we know, there's a stronghold in that area, and if the information is good, there are armed subjects on the plot and possibly multiple hostages."

"Do we know how many?"

"Not a clue, I'm afraid. We only got the first cut of the debrief, before — and this is the bit I'm struggling with — our witness decided to disappear with our escaped hostage. From the location you've described, my inexplicably likely hypothesis is that he's taken her back to the stronghold."

"Is he one of them?" Toynbee asked.

"You're the second person to ask me that in half an hour. My instinct says no, but I am struggling to come up with a better explanation."

"Okay, understood. I'm going to put ARVs towards, with an authority, so I suggest you stay put. Where are you exactly?

"Still at the petrol station. It's a crime scene now, but it will make do as an RVP too. It's under cover, well lit, good routes east and west. We certainly won't get anywhere any better this close."

"Okay. Switch your radio on if you haven't already. We'll do some more work on this phone of his and see if we can get a better fix on the location. The coordinates should be pretty good, but they won't take you to the front door. Hopefully it's that remote that you won't have too many premises to choose from. ARV team leader, Ops-One . . ."

"My radio . . . is always on," Barnes muttered into the phone, but Toynbee had cut the call as he turned his attention to the team leader of the armed response vehicles and began to brief the crews over the air. Toynbee had the rank and the training to issue an emergency authority to the ARV officers to start arming up, which meant, for now, it was a firearms operation and Barnes was temporarily forgotten.

"What's happening?" Willow said as he ambled over from the forecourt shop clutching a Twix, a marshmallow plait and a huge bag of crisps.

"Technically, the shop is a crime scene," Barnes said, without looking up from the map.

"And its integrity is being carefully preserved by a motivated, well-fed officer," Willow said, his satisfied grin not faltering an inch. "Where are we up to?"

"Well, Ops-One has put guns to it, but they don't have an exact target premises, only the coordinates of the 999 call, which could have been made inside the stronghold or — for all we know — two miles away from it. He took his car, after all." He poked the map. "If you assume the call was made from nearby, then the stronghold could be one — or all — of a cluster of four or five farmhouses all roughly within a mile of each other."

"Chopper up? They might be able to get some heat signatures."

Barnes eyed him. "Yeah, they're looking. This time of night, we might get lucky."

A few minutes later, three ARVs pulled onto the fore-court in convoy. Barnes was relieved to note that, rather than heading directly into the wilderness, they'd come to see him first.

Barnes briefed the team leader — not anyone he rec-ognised, thankfully — and between them they decided that the line of enquiry most likely to bear fruit was going to be Kenneth Rix's car. Two of the ARVs were marked with the regulation blue-and-yellow Battenberg, but the third was plain black, and could conduct a quick-and-dirty reconnais-sance in the middle of the night without too much difficulty.

The team leader wasn't happy that they didn't know how many armed subjects they might be facing, nor how many hostages might need a welcoming committee, and he made a few calls for reinforcements before the three cars raced off into the night.

Barnes watched them go. Little more he could do now but wait. Wait, and make damn sure that any change in the information was relayed as a matter of urgency.

CHAPTER TWENTY-TWO

Kenneth had screamed himself hoarse. He was fairly sure that a soldering iron was small potatoes in the grand scheme of medieval torture methods, but right now this was cold comfort. The red-hot implement had been bad enough when pressed against his breastbone — and the stink of burning hair a torture all on its own — but when it was touched to his nipple and then up his nose it awoke his senses to a measure of pain he had never believed possible.

"I'm going to ask you again, Kenneth," the man with the soldering iron said. "Why the fuck are you out at my place in the middle of the night with one of my employees?"

Kenneth babbled an incomprehensible answer. His mind had ceased functioning on any kind of rational plane. He had soiled himself twice, then at one stage had panicked and started thrashing in the chair and, as a consequence, could not conceive of what the possible endgame might be. He had no idea what sort of information they wanted from him nor, if he gave it, whether the words that came out of his mouth would be any kind of truth. Right then, he wasn't even sure what truth was.

The only thing he was sure of was that Roxy was unharmed. Later, this would seem important but, right then, he didn't care a jot about what happened to her — which made his initial white-knight fantasies something of a moot point.

"Who else knows you're here?" the man asked.

Kenneth said nothing. He wasn't sure of the answer.

"Have you called the cops? What did you tell them?"

"Get his phone," one of the others said in the darkness.

"He ain't got one," said the man with the soldering iron. "You search the car?"

"Yeah. Nothing."

"Go and do it again. Take your lamps. Make sure you check the verges. There was a field opposite. Make sure you search that too. I want to know if the fucking cavalry is coming down on us."

Kenneth's sweat-drenched brow scrunched into a frown. Much as he would have liked to take the credit for hurling his phone into the darkness to throw them off the trail, the reality was that it had probably just fallen out of his pocket and disappeared into a McDonald's sack nestled in the mountain of crap in his rear footwells, and that the claimed search hadn't actually been particularly thorough.

The two unseen silhouettes disappeared off into a dark corner. Kenneth heard a heavy wooden door open and close, and then the man with the soldering iron came again — only this time he veered off on his approach and made a beeline for Roxy.

Surprising himself, Kenneth bellowed in protest, a despairing, primal groan. The man with the soldering iron stopped, and turned back to Kenneth.

"I'm impressed. Most people in your position would thank their lottery numbers that the attention was off them for a moment."

He moved back towards Kenneth, and leaned down slightly to undo the button and zip of Kenneth's fly.

Kenneth panicked again. This time, he convulsed and thrashed so violently that he almost persuaded himself it was involuntary. Certainly, when the wooden spindle connecting the chair legs that his ankles were bound to snapped, he wasted no time in flinging himself to his feet and charging off into the gloom towards what he thought was the door.

At the last moment he turned his back, and the chair shattered against the breeze block wall.

Stunned by his sudden liberation, he froze to the spot, facing the man with the soldering iron who, for the first time that evening, looked faintly amused.

There was a moment's stand-off — the man with the soldering iron simply watched and waited, while Kenneth, having wrestled a small vestige of control back into the equation, channelled a million different possible actions through his brain. One decision leads to another, and if the next one wasn't the right one, he might end up in a worse position than before.

"Whatcha gonna do now, Kenneth?" the man asked, as if reading the inertia writ large on Kenneth's face. "How far you think you're gonna get? Do you even know where you are?"

Kenneth hesitated.

"Even if you get through the door — even if you *find* the door — you're in the middle of a purpose-built compound with six armed guards. You've got to get past them in the dark — they've got night vision, by the way — one word from me and they'll empty a clip into you. You've then got to get past a secure perimeter designed to keep people in, and then follow a bunch of country lanes in the snow back to civilisation — on foot, because I've got your car keys. Oh, and there's the dogs, of course."

Kenneth's shoulder sagged a little.

"So why don't you take a seat?"

Kenneth looked at the man with the soldering iron, then at the door, then to Roxy, and then back again.

Then he bowed his head, bellowed like a rutting bull and charged.

CHAPTER TWENTY-THREE

"Found the car in a lay-by."

Barnes snatched the radio off the bonnet of the Rover and held it to his ear to listen to the team leader updating Toynbee. "No one with it. No keys. Bonnet's warm. There's a farmhouse about fifty yards south of the car, on the opposite side of the road."

"Any sign of a struggle, Team Leader?" Toynbee asked over the air.

"Negative. Stronghold is a walled compound with a large double gate. Looks pretty big, with a couple of outbuildings. I'm going to push the plain car past white side to get a better idea of the layout. I don't think I'm going to have enough to put a proper containment on. I need to leave at least one with the car."

"Roger that, Team Leader. I'll get 900 to fly over to help with that, and I'll ask Kent to start floating a couple of their ARVs over our way."

"Roger, Ops-One. Standing by."

Barnes set the radio back on the bonnet.

"The suspense is killing me," Willow said.

"And no new information," Barnes said. "No update from anyone. I need to ring Gold, get some work done on this phone."

He eyeballed Willow. "You might end up going to guard this car."

"Your wish is my command, boss."

"Ops-One, Team Leader." The radio chattered again.

"He sounds excited," Willow said.

"Team Leader, go ahead," Toynbee said over the air.

"I've got two subjects in custody. They pitched up at the witness's car just as we were about to move up. Both armed with carbines."

"Any injuries, Team Leader?"

"Negative. Instant compliance. Think they got a shock."

"Jesus," Willow whistled. "They're lucky they didn't get shot."

"I'm going to need some more troops here to get them out. I don't have enough people as it is."

"I'll take a van," Willow muttered, and disappeared off.

"Are they saying anything?" Toynbee said.

"One is pretty chatty. Reckons there's four more armed subjects, plus another without a gun, and as many as ten hostages. The unarmed subject appears to be in charge."

"Okay, that's helpful. Just remember he could be full of it," Toynbee said.

"Roger. He seemed very interested in the car, so we've had a quick poke about and found the witness's phone on the floor."

"Roger, Team Leader, good work. At least we know we're in the right place. I've got the downlink from 900, Team Leader. Your assessment is correct. Large walled farmhouse with two outbuildings to the north and two more to the east. They look like purpose-built sheds of some description. The perimeter wall covers a large garden to the south and a spread of what looks like a courtyard-cum-driveway. Outside the wall the north side runs parallel to the road, the east and west has woods either side and there's a lake to the south."

"I could do with a picture," muttered Team Leader. "That's going to be a bitch to contain with seven bods."

"And there's two roving heat signatures in the open. Possibly patrols of some kind."

A cold feeling welled up inside Barnes. This could end badly, on a number of levels. The odds weren't right, but in the middle of the night, nothing changed quickly.

"Any kind of stimulus from the stronghold, Team Leader?" Toynbee said.

"Not a thing," Team Leader answered. "All in darkness."

"What do you want to do, Ops-One?" he asked then. "We can contain and observe but I don't have enough options for decisive action with the numbers I've got. I need another five, minimum, and ideally some specialist capability in among that."

"That's going to take a long time, Team Leader," Toynbee said. "We've got hostages in that building."

"We've got to breach the compound and then slow search to contact. If we find any, we'll be stepping over hostages until we've neutralised the threat."

Silence on the radio. Barnes imagined Team Leader cursing to himself.

"I'm going to ring Gold, Team Leader. Stand by," Toynbee said.

Barnes drummed his hands on the bonnet. The radio was silent. The wind in the trees on the edge of the forecourt sounded like somebody whispering.

"Team Leader, come in?" Toynbee's voice crackled on the handset. "Gold wants Silver ground assigned for tactical command. I'm going to call her out now to the RVP. Stand by for transfer of command. I'm relieved. This is above my pay grade."

"Roger, understood," Team Leader answered.

"Thank you and good night," Barnes said to himself, imagining Team Leader gritting his teeth. He turned to make a remark to Willow, but his uniformed colleague had already gone.

"Diligent to the last." Barnes said. He was alone on the forecourt.

The radio crackled to life on the bonnet.

"Shots fired! Shots fired!"

Barnes grabbed his car keys and ran.

CHAPTER TWENTY-FOUR

Kenneth charged like a bull and collided with his captor, who lost his balance and tumbled, narrowly missing Roxy. The soldering iron clattered across the cold concrete floor as the man crashed into a row of wooden boxes and, winded from Kenneth's solid head drumming into his midriff, lay still.

Kenneth stood up straight, his shirt torn and soaked, panting great exhilarated breaths like he'd never breathed before, trying to get a handle on the — frankly unbelievable — feeling of being scared beyond his wits, utterly passive and close to an inevitable, painful death, to turning the tables against significant odds.

His wide eyes roamed the room, unsure of where to look. Eventually they settled on Roxy, who was staring at him with not, it had to be said, unconditional hero worship, but more a quizzical expression suggesting he might like to find the keys to her handcuffs, pronto, and preferably before the bald psycho woke up.

Kenneth read this and moved over to the groaning man, his steps becoming more tentative as he approached. He was down but not out, and Kenneth suddenly lost his superhero confidence as he realised he probably didn't have the will or the skills to do what it took to put this person out of commission permanently.

He gingerly patted down the man's body looking for keys. There was no resistance, only a dull groaning as he rolled from side to side, clutching his gut.

Kenneth froze momentarily. He had to put him to sleep. He couldn't kill him, knew he didn't have it in him, but maybe he could choke him out? Or tie him up before he came round properly? Or . . .

Too late.

The man sat up with a snarl, and chopped at Kenneth's windpipe with the flat of his hand as a blade.

Kenneth's eyes bulged as the air was forced out of him, and his hands flew to his throat. He began to cough uncontrollably.

The man pulled himself up and launched a kick into the stomach of the now doubled-over Kenneth, who was still coughing. The man looked around, grabbed a clay flowerpot from a recessed stone window ledge with no window, and brought it down onto Kenneth's head.

The pot shattered.

Roxy screamed.

Kenneth sprawled on the floor like he'd been hit by a truck and groaned. Thick, dark blood oozed from a gash on his scalp.

Roxy began to cry — the cry of someone whose faint embers of hope had just been snuffed out forever.

The man grabbed Kenneth by the tatters of his shirt and, with considerable effort, hauled him over to some pipework set against the wall. There were no chairs left, and the man fumbled for keys to handcuff Kenneth to the pipes.

It took him some time to drag Kenneth the ten or so feet to the pipework, and he stumbled several times trying to keep his balance with a throbbing midriff, sore head and Kenneth's not-inconsiderable bulk.

He paused several times, looking expectantly around him each time.

"Where the fuck are those two dickheads?" he said to no one. "How long does it take to search a car?"

He finally secured one of Kenneth's wrists on one of the pipes. The clang of metal on metal reverberated around the cellar. Kenneth groaned, more unconscious than not, and earned a vicious kick in the ribs for his trouble.

He stalked over to the door.

"*Du-te dracului,*" Roxy spat.

The man stopped and turned, hate in his grey eyes.

"I know you," Roxy said, in heavily accented English. "I know you."

The man's lips curled in a snarl. He moved towards Roxy, pausing long enough to collect a sugar cutlass from a shelf. The blade was rusty, and shrouded in cobwebs.

Roxy stuck her chin out.

The man advanced.

Then stopped.

A sound from outside.

A staccato thudding that lasted less than a second.

It was deadened by the stone walls of the cellar and several rooms between them and the outside. Down here, the untrained ear might even have mistaken it for a drumbeat, or a series of doors slamming shut, but everybody in the room knew what it was.

Gunfire.

Automatic gunfire.

The man eyeballed Roxy, then moved to the door. He pressed his ear against it.

Kenneth groaned, lifted his head and vomited. His head felt like porridge, but even he could register the new expression of his captor.

Fear.

The sound stopped. There was nothing.

Then unmistakable thudding of heavily booted footsteps. Moving quickly. At least three sets, maybe more, going from room to room.

More guards?

Or salvation?

Kenneth heard a faint, muffled voice issue a challenge: "*Armed police!*" and his spirits lifted. He tried to haul himself up, his breath coming in hoarse gasps.

Gradually, the footsteps got louder. Doors opened and closed. Someone shouted "*Clear!*"

Their captor backed away from the door and moved slowly towards Roxy. He was still scared, but Kenneth did not see unconditional surrender on his face.

The footsteps again.

Much closer now.

The door handle turned, and held.

A heavy knock at the door with the bottom of a fist. *Bam-bam-bam.*

"Armed police!"

The man moved like a gymnast over to Roxy and stood behind her, drawing the cutlass across her throat.

She froze.

Kenneth, the porridge in his brain causing his natural inhibitions to go haywire, lashed out with a kick at the man. He missed by a country mile, but Roxy, turning her head ever so slightly, saw what he was doing.

Distracted, the man turned back to Kenneth with a snarl.

And Roxy screamed. She screamed like the Rapture had descended directly on her head.

An almighty crashing noise — one, two, three strikes — and the cellar door banged open in a cloud of dust and ejected hinge fixings.

Kenneth registered that they were not bad guys. They took up position in the doorway — two with heavy-looking black shields, and a third training his carbine over the shields at the only threat in the room that they could see — and it was the man holding a cutlass to Roxy's neck.

A red laser circle settled on the man's chest.

"Armed police! Drop the weapons!"

"Fuck you," the man snarled.

"Last chance, buddy. Drop the weapon."

"Race ya," the man said, and lifted the blade.

He lost. Kenneth saw the muzzle flash, then watched the man drop to the floor like someone had just taken his batteries out.

The armed cops filed in, checking left and right, then rushed over to the man. They kicked the cutlass away, searched him and then set about trying to save his life. One started chest compressions, another tried to get a line into him, while another barked updates into his radio and demanded an ambulance, quick time.

Roxy dropped her defiant chin and began to cry. Kenneth slid back down the wall and allowed a cold wave of relief to wash over him, while the police officers continued trying to save the life of Stratton Pearce.

CHAPTER TWENTY-FIVE

Barnes called up on air and asked for the location of the strike. He couldn't get hold of Toynbee who, Barnes figured, having heard the *shots fired* update, was now frantically trying to put the genie back in the bottle and keep his pension intact.

One of the KB controllers obliged, however, and Barnes headed onto the Marsh Road and then turned towards Rickney. He had to pull over en route to make way for two ambulances thundering past, their blue lights creating a tunnel down the narrow country lanes. He caught segments of radio transmissions as he drove — *two subjects down, believed G5 . . . one shot, still breathing . . . two hostages recovered . . . no officers injured —* and found himself trying to work out when he last ate or had a cup of tea. It was going to be a long night. The snow had stopped falling, and it lay on branches, hedgerows and rooftops like a thick layer of Christmas icing. In the still, clear air the night seemed frozen in time.

It turned out the ambos knew the way, and so Barnes just followed the corridor of blue lights. A left turn, a right turn, left again, the lane getting narrower each time, and Barnes thought, *We really are in the middle of sodding nowhere.*

After driving for another couple of minutes the ambulances stopped. Two ARVs were blocking the road, parked in a snowplough formation next to a car that Barnes presumed belonged to Kenneth.

Barnes could see exactly what was going to happen next, and so he reversed the two hundred yards or so back up the lane to the last junction. It was a triangular spread of roughshod tarmac with a patch of grass in the centre and a massive oak looming over it. As holding areas went, it was makeshift at best, but Barnes knew if he didn't start filtering the inevitable influx of additional resources now, then those ambulances would never get back out of the lane again — and nor would anyone else.

It was a canny move, as it turned out. Willow, driving a Mercedes carrier, wasn't far behind Barnes, and nearly collided with the DI as he hared up the lane.

He skidded to a halt and wound down the window. Barnes stopped waving his arms and walked over.

"I nearly bloody hit you, boss. You need a hi-vis or something?"

"Over my dead body," Barnes said.

"It very nearly was. What's happening?"

"Well, if you're racing here for prisoner transport, I wouldn't rush. I think most of them are dead."

Even in the gloom, Willow's battle-hardened face blanched.

"I said most, not all. But the carrier will be useful in case we need to whisk the armed boys off for all the post-incident stuff. Could do with Golf-99 here for that, really."

"Want me to call her?"

"No, I'll do it. Should be me that ruins her night. You wait here and stop any more bodies from coming down the lane, or we'll have a traffic jam we'll never unjam — especially if someone loses their car keys."

Willow backed the van up and parked it on the verge, the fingers of an overhanging willow scraping the metal roof in a horror movie parody screech.

Barnes called Golf-99, the duty inspector, and told her she was going to have to coordinate the armed officers getting to the post-incident suite, and then, leaving Willow directing traffic, walked back down the lane to the scene.

He pressed himself into a hedge as the two ambulances flew back past him in a bubble of blue lights. Maybe Willow had been right about the hi-vis after all.

It took longer than he thought and, once the ambulances had passed, it was just him and a wide expanse of white, desolate countryside. White-fingered trees were silhouetted against a now-clear sky like a navy-blue canvas, and his own breathing seemed loud in the silence.

Eventually he saw Kenneth Rix's car as he approached the farmhouse. There was a surprising lack of activity, then he saw two armed cops milling around by their car.

The team leader, clearly hyper-aware, flicked his gaze towards Barnes and levelled his weapon.

"Whoa, whoa," Barnes said, holding up his warrant card. "Duty DI. Name's Barnes."

The team leader didn't immediately lower the weapon, but eyeballed Barnes. "You walked?"

"Left my car at the end of the lane with the cavalry. Too many vehicles down here and we'll never get out again."

The team leader slowly lowered his carbine.

"What happened?" Barnes said.

"We arrested two coming back to this car," he said, indicating Kenneth's car with the barrel of his carbine. "They left the gate open, so I made the decision to go in. We shot one, arrested a third, then heard screaming and searched the place. Shot one more, rescued two hostages."

"Two injured? Both bad guys?"

"Yes."

"And the hostages?"

"Safe. One's in the car. The other's gone off in the ambo. Looks like he's been tortured."

"Jesus," Barnes whistled. "And the second ambulance?"

"One of the injured subjects."

"You said you shot two."

"Other one didn't make it. Paramedics called it just before they left."

The team leader toed the dirt. Barnes didn't say anything. They both knew that likely meant a world of pain for the armed guys, if for no other reason than they'd breached the stronghold without Toynbee's say-so.

"Scene clear now?"

"It's clear of threats, but needs a proper search," the team leader said.

"I'll sort that. Anyone with the casualties?"

"Couple of mine."

Barnes held his radio to his lips. "Adrian, stop those ambulances. Get the armed guys out of there and swap them with a couple of yours."

"Roger that, boss." Willow's voice was tinny in the handset.

"And unless that bearded nutter from the petrol station is bleeding out, I want him to wait at the RVP. Leave a paramedic with him if you must. I want a word."

There was a pause.

"Er, righto," Willow eventually answered.

The team leader raised an eyebrow.

"Better you're kept all together. Your job is done now, I think. Golf-99 is going to bus you up and get you off to the post-incident suite. Good job, fellas."

Barnes pushed past them and walked through the huge steel gate into the compound proper.

He stood for a moment, feet crunching on the pristine gravel driveway framed by a neat brick border and a large overhanging oak that *shushed* in the night breeze and shed fresh snow onto the ground. Rhododendrons in snow-covered soil beds stood at intervals, lining the perimeter wall, which itself was six feet of solid brick crowned with spears.

Barnes turned as the huge gate automatically swung shut behind him. The team leader hadn't been kidding. Given the size of the location, the team leader would have needed four times the cops and double the skills to deal with this place properly. But there's always a reason to wait, and if he heard screaming . . .

He moved over to the red-brick kerb and kept away from the main spread of the driveway. At least two spent shell casings caught the light from the dull moon; beyond those was the twisted form of a dead guard lying in a halo of blood, dark against the snow. His head was mashed face-first into the ground, his arm twisted awkwardly underneath him. He'd fallen onto his weapon, and the barrel was pushing into his chest, practically propping his head up.

Barnes kicked himself for not bringing any scene markers, and made a mental note to point out the casings to the crime scene manager, but didn't think they'd struggle to find them — chances were, they'd find far more than Barnes could.

He pushed on along the edge of the drive, deliberately dragging his feet to indent the gravel and demarcate a common approach pathway to maintain the integrity of the scene. The main house could have come from some glossy waiting-room magazine — the previous features of the barn it had once been were still intact, but the reinforced timber, arc halogens and smartly framed floor-to-ceiling windows gave the whole thing a sheen of luxury. There had to be worse places to be held captive, Barnes thought.

Before entering through a side door, Barnes took another look around the main approach to the house. There were four outbuildings that he could see, in clusters of two. They were too small for much — maybe good for parking a quad bike or housing some machinery, but not much else.

He peered around the corner of the house. The rear fell away into a landscaped garden, at the bottom of which was a small lake framed by a brick patio and a huge willow. The focal point, Barnes thought. Very nice.

He stepped inside, passed through a small vestibule that contained little more than muddy boots, parkas and a few torches, and into a master kitchen.

It was glorious. Expensive, copper-bottomed pots and pans were carefully arranged around the island block, with a circumference of polished oak units around the edge of the room. There was room for a snooker table and a bar.

The whole place looked like it should have been in some window-licking property renovation show. Barnes hated those kinds of programmes, but they were popular. Who owned this? Was it some deliberate custom purchase that heinous villains could just scoop up with cash and a winning smile?

A cold feeling spread across his back as he wondered about the alternative means of securing such a property. Far easier than trying to purchase something of this size and value with dirty money would be to march into the luxury country dwelling of a law-abiding family, claim squatters' rights at gunpoint and then use it as their own. It would be tough to pull off, especially if the householders were missed, but perhaps not as tough as trying to conceal criminal assets. Barnes wondered if he was going to find the skeletons of a couple of retired barristers manacled in the basement.

He shut his eyes, forcing himself to remain objective and ignore the enormous silence in the place. Three arrested, two shot, one dead, one injured. Two hostages recovered, one injured, one — their original captive, Roxy, thank goodness — seemingly unharmed. All accounted for. The place cleared of threats.

So where were the other captives Roxy had spoken of?

Barnes opened his eyes.

He moved slowly through the kitchen, wishing — for no good reason — that he had a gun.

There were three exits off the kitchen — one opened out into a spacious living area with an oak mezzanine that led off to the bedrooms, one led down a corridor to more bedrooms and a guest bathroom, and the third . . .

Barnes opened it.

He flicked on the light. It seemed to be a utility room of sorts — there was a counter with various appliances tucked underneath and on top of it; facing that was a large rack bolted to the wall that held clothing.

Lots of clothing.

Different shapes, sizes and colours. Different ages.

The tiled floor was messy — dirty clothes, cleaning gear, buckets, washing baskets. Barnes had to pick his way through it, and steadied himself on the wall with the rack in so doing.

The wall was thickly coated in cool, dull, grey emulsion, and it absorbed Barnes's touch with a dull silence. He tapped it — underneath the paint was solid stone, or similar. There was a spread of cobwebs behind the rack, and the whole thing had the look of an original wall, one that had stood the test of time, with the *Homes & Gardens* fixtures and fittings growing up around it.

He looked over at the wall behind the counter. Similar, with air vents and an extractor fan built into it. But still old, and solid, and going nowhere.

Barnes moved into the room. The wall facing him was also white emulsion, but it had no signs of age, no cobwebs . . .

Barnes touched it with a finger, then tapped it. It made an echoing, hollow thud.

He swallowed. This was a plaster partition wall, at best. He pushed it. One good strike and it would go.

He turned his head and pressed his ear flat to the wall. For a moment all he could hear was the blood rumbling in his ears and the deafening swish of his own skin rubbing against the wall as he moved.

He screwed his eyes shut and forced himself to concentrate, forced himself to ignore the thunder from inside his own head.

There.

Faint, but definitely there.

A sound.

Barnes didn't want to put a name to it — even as a grown man he'd been continually surprised by the cavalcade of bizarre sounds that a nocturnal scene could produce, most of which had entirely uninteresting explanations — cats arguing, or foxes mating, or . . .

There.

Again.

It sounded like . . .

Say it.

It sounded like crying.

No, not crying.

More like mewing.

The pained, wretched protest of . . .

Of whom?

Barnes fumbled for the torch on his belt and looked around the room. Mounted on the wall — incongruously, unless it was another original fixture left for effect — was a Victorian flat iron.

He pulled it down, flicked the torch on and took a breath. He shut his eyes for a moment, then swung the iron.

The plaster yielded without any resistance at all, and fragments of plasterboard crumbled around the force of the iron.

Barnes swung the iron — twice, three times — and created a hole large enough for him to stick his head into.

He moved to the hole, grimacing at the warm stink that bathed his face, escaping the recess behind the wall.

He poked his torch in, realised he couldn't see anything unless he got in there too, plunged his head into the hole.

And recoiled in horror.

CHAPTER TWENTY-SIX

SOCOs, cops, UKBA officers and a team of six from a human-trafficking charity milled about the house, which had been roped off and lit up with spotlights provided by, among a bunch of other kit, Ops and Logistics.

Most of the crime scenes Barnes had been to featured dead bodies, not live ones, and he had reacted more violently to the latter. The torchlight had swept across the faces of seven or eight semi-naked adults behind the partition wall; fixed on the torch beam, their wide, gleaming eyes betrayed fear and panic. Then the cloying warm-body stink had hit him, and he ran outside into the darkness to vomit.

He called up and got Toynbee — well, Toynbee's relief — to start calling people out, and then had gone back, aiming for a slightly more forensic survey on the second attempt.

Now lit by powerful halogens, he could see that the dark space behind the partition wall was about the size of the back of a Transit. It had contained six men, two women and two very scared boys aged about ten. The floor was a rotting lino — another original feature, this one less well preserved — covered in urine and faeces from where the occupants had — perhaps not unreasonably, in the pitch darkness — been unable to find the carelessly issued buckets.

The wall itself was a relatively light plasterboard construction that sat in a custom-made cradle in the floor and ceiling. Niches at the edges acted as grip handles — it needed two people to lift the wall clear, but it was easy enough to do. Bashing a hole in the centre of what amounted to the fourth wall of the crime scene had been, as it turned out, unnecessary.

The men were manacled to makeshift iron rings cemented into the plaster, and all of them were partially clothed. On a third inspection, Barnes realised there was precious little ventilation, and that the ten people were lucky to be alive. Then he found the small space, no bigger than a cat flap, in a lower corner of the plasterboard, and theorised that this was how Roxana Petrescu had escaped. They were all malnourished, but not too badly, and Barnes could only speculate that they couldn't have been here that long, in the scheme of things. It probably felt like a lifetime to these poor bastards.

"Ambos will call a major incident when they see this lot," a SOCO said, hurrying past Barnes.

"That's nothing new," someone else said.

We might be doing the same, Barnes thought. Processing and documenting this lot would need two cops per hostage for the rest of the night at a minimum.

As it turned out, the team from the human-trafficking charity — all women, as it happened — were worth their weight in gold. They knew about evidential continuity, they had access to interpreters and they realised that, actually, talking to cops might not be the best thing off the bat for these wretched souls who, at the very least, probably had burgeoning PTSD, Stockholm syndrome and agoraphobia.

Barnes conceded the point, but when a minibus turned up and the woman in charge wouldn't disclose the exact location of the purpose-built facility they were supposedly about to be whisked off to, he held up the party and conducted a second round of slightly more rigorous checks. After several phone calls and a steep education in Home Office sub-departments that he had no idea existed, he was eventually convinced that the outfit was bona fide, but he was still unable to quell the odd sense of unease in the pit of his stomach as he watched the minibus trundle off into the countryside's midnight oblivion.

With the living suitably tended to and the dead subject to a strict sequence of documenting, Barnes left the compound in the trustworthy hands of the CSM and walked back down the lane to the holding area. It was less than a ten-minute walk, even in the darkness, but he was glad for a short period of reflection just to let his mind unwind a bit and think a little wider than the immediate scene. Fatal police shooting notwithstanding, the discovery of the slave farm was a headline grabber, no doubt about it — he would need to get someone from Corporate Communications out of bed. The local neighbourhood teams would have some reassurance work to sort out, while the whole thing needed an intelligence cell stood up to work out whether this was part of a wider network. And that was without the army of detectives he was going to need to start questioning these poor wretches, interviewing the living suspects and pulling some form of case file together.

For just a second, he was completely unsure of where to start, but then he arrived at the country lane junction doubled up as a holding area and felt better — the jumble there was far less than the one in his mind.

He weaved among the erratically parked police vehicles and headed for the single ambulance. He rapped on the door and an irritable-looking paramedic opened it. Barnes flashed his warrant card and the paramedic lowered the small, hinged steps from the back of the ambulance onto the road.

The man called Kenneth Rix was sitting on a trolley, head hanging down, a foil blanket around his shoulders and a patchwork of dressings on his chest, nose and ribs.

"He's been tortured," the paramedic said, just as Barnes opened his mouth.

He turned to the paramedic, whose intention to protect her vulnerable patient from stroppy cops was palpable. She was about thirty, with a battle-hardened but kind face and an obviously low tolerance for nonsense.

Barnes wanted to say, *Well, it's not like this idiot re-kidnapped an escaped hostage and put her back in mortal danger twice in as many hours*, but eventually he took the hint and softened himself up.

"Kenneth, right?" he said, sitting on the empty trolley opposite.

Kenneth didn't answer, but after an inordinately long pause, during which he didn't seem to realise Barnes was there, he lifted his head a little.

"I'm a police officer, Kenneth. What happened?"

A grunt.

Barnes turned to the paramedic. He thought about telling her that he couldn't *completely* discount Kenneth as part of the gang, or a suspect in his own right, but didn't think she'd take too kindly to that.

"Does he need to go to hospital?" he asked.

"Ideally," she said, writing on a clipboard. "But the cop out there said the officer in charge wanted us to stick around. I guess that's you." She didn't look up.

"You can go in just a second," Barnes said.

"If he needed to go immediately, I'd take him," she said, finally looking up.

Barnes held her gaze for a moment, then turned back to Kenneth.

Instinctively, he wanted to turn up the dial, but Kenneth's eyes were glazed, and something — maybe one of the limited theories behind the man's inexplicable actions in whisking Roxy away from under the gaze of the cops — told him to try a different tack.

"You did good, you know." Barnes's voice was almost a whisper.

Kenneth's head lifted a little.

"She trusts you. You got the information out of her *fast*. The telephone interpreter — amazing idea. You brought her back to the right place. We found it. We've saved all those people. Thanks to you."

Kenneth's dry lips parted. They made a cracking sound. The left side of his nose was swollen and purple from where his torturer had rooted around with the soldering iron.

"Is . . . is everyone all right?" he croaked.

"They've had a rough ride, but they'll be okay. Two bad guys shot. One dead, one will pull through. Personally, I think he's a bit of a drama queen." Barnes chattered laughter through his teeth, encouraging Kenneth to join him with his eyes.

Kenneth managed a grimace.

"How's the pain?" Barnes asked.

Kenneth bunched his hairy cheeks and screwed his eyes shut, like he was squeezing in tears.

"Not too bad," he said, his voice hitching.

You bloody hero, Barnes thought.

"How's . . . Roxy?" Kenneth asked.

"She's doing okay. Shock, mainly. But no real injuries. You saved her life, Kenneth."

Barnes heard the paramedic's pen stop moving. He felt her gaze, and tried not to look at her.

"Can I see her?" Kenneth asked.

"Not right now. She's been taken to a safe place. We can arrange something, I'm sure."

"Okay."

"So, Kenneth, tell me what happened. How did you come to take Roxana away from the first safe place she'd found after what must have been a terrifying thirty-minute run through the freezing darkness and foot-deep snow?"

"I . . . I thought I would try to help her find the scene."

"The scene. I see. There were two uniformed cops stationed right outside your staff room, Kenneth. Did it not occur to you to run your idea by them first?"

"Yes . . . yes. I should have done. But she was scared. She wanted to go. There were all those customers standing around, and the policemen, and the radio and the blue lights on the cars. She just grabbed my hand and told me to take her away."

And I bet you loved that.

"So, I did. The police here aren't like the police where she's from."

"And where's that?"

"Romania. She doesn't trust the police. She was scared."

"You live alone, Kenneth?"

"Yes. Why?"

"No wife? Husband? Kids? Parents?"

"Just me," he mumbled.

"And . . . your spare time? Movies? Walks? Video games?" Barnes said, trying not to feel like a hypocrite.

"This and that." The mumble was practically unintelligible.

"Is this relevant?" the paramedic asked.

Barnes shot her a look. She returned her attention to her clipboard. Barnes turned back to Kenneth. Aspiring defence lawyer, maybe.

"Okay, that will do for now," Barnes said. "Get yourself stitched up. Get some rest. We'll be around in the next day or two to interview you properly. Good job, Kenneth."

Barnes got up, clapping Kenneth's knee heartily as he did so. Kenneth flinched like he'd been stuck with a cattle prod.

"Oh, by the way. You've upset the operations of a mid-size criminal group — practically single-handed, no less. I'm going to send a couple of cops to keep an eye on you."

Kenneth's one good eye widened. Barnes nodded to the paramedic and trotted down the steps back onto the road.

"Hey."

He turned. The paramedic pulled the door shut behind her.

"What was all that about?" Her dark eyes gleamed.

"He put that woman in mortal danger. He brought her back to the place she had just escaped from without a word to the two police officers that were right outside his office."

"Maybe he didn't trust them to do a good job."

"He wouldn't be the first."

"You just scared the shit out of him."

"Top of my list was trying to establish whether or not he might have been part of the gang she'd just escaped from. It isn't beyond the realms of imagination for properly organised criminals with a setup like this to put sentinels in the radius of their operations. Working nights at a petrol station, or delivering milk, or driving a taxi — all give them a decent roving cover. A safety net. Eyes and ears in the community."

"The police ought to try that some time."

"You may be right."

"And what did you arrive at, after all that?"

"He's definitely not part of it. Best guess is some kind of armchair hero complex. White knight. Lone ranger. Et cetera."

She opened her mouth, then looked back at the closed rear door of the ambulance, and shut it again. Barnes couldn't help but notice that the half-light caught her cheekbones better than any photographer could.

"If you're done, a question for you."

"Yes?" There was suspicion in her voice.

"What's with all the questions? You an aspiring cop?"

"My ex-husband was a police officer. He was a serial cheat and a gaslighter. Probably worse than that, but ignorance is bliss."

"Forgive me, but that explains an awful lot."

The smile broke across her face before she could control it.

"And I have a duty of care to my patient."

"I'm Barnes," he said.

"Tamsin," she said.

"I'm going now, Tamsin. Thanks for looking after Kenneth. I'm going to send a bobby over to accompany him to hospital."

He walked off into the night. It was a good half a minute before he heard her climb the steps and open the rear door to the ambulance again.

Well, he thought, *time to write up this mess.*

CHAPTER TWENTY-SEVEN

"*Godfather Two*?"

"Nah."

"*Goodfellas*?"

"Not feeling it."

"What about this one?" Kenley held up the disc. "*Layer Cake*. Got the new Bond in it, before he got famous."

"Saw it last week."

"Well, what do you suggest?"

Kenley was kneeling on the carpet in Natalie's front room, surrounded by an assortment of DVDs. There was a bottle of wine chilling in the fridge and a steaming hot takeaway from the funky, neon-lit Indian restaurant that had just opened in the harbour and seemed to be a bit more interesting in terms of options for the discerning vegetarian. He didn't particularly want to dwell on the DVD choice; by the same token, it wasn't something you just rushed into. Movies and other popular media could sometimes bring questions and observations to the forefront of one's mind that would otherwise have been kept nicely at bay. He'd disregarded *Taxi Driver* for that very reason.

"Go check the post," she said. "There's a new one on the hall table. I'll dish up."

She got off the sofa and went to the kitchen, while Kenley did as he was told. He found the disc in a jiffy bag among an assortment of other letters, and resisted a powerful urge to scan through them. Everything would backfire drastically if he got caught, and there was a wonderful scent of promise in the air tonight. The boy was at his nan's, she'd turned off her work mobile, and they'd gone from road rage to frosty to a shared takeaway with a film in her front room in the space of four weeks.

"You get your DVDs sent to you?" he called.

"Yeah, it's a rental thing. You choose the one you want online, they send it to you, you send it back when you're done, they send you another one."

"Clever."

"What's there? I can't remember." Kenley heard the chink of plates on the worktop, the pop of a cork followed by wine glugging into one glass, then another.

"Looks like you've got a computer-animated thing about big blue aliens . . ."

"*Avatar*. Looks amazing."

". . . or Brad Pitt as a World War Two Nazi hunter."

She appeared in the doorway with two glasses of wine.

"Brad Pitt, naturally," she smiled, holding out a glass.

Kenley sorted the movie while Natalie brought the food through. The movie was violent, and after they'd eaten and Kenley had refilled their glasses, they gradually moved closer and closer to one another on the sofa, until they were pressed against each other, with Natalie periodically hiding her face in his top, her perfume and the smell of her hair conditioner the most glorious thing Kenley thought he'd ever encountered.

Kenley was on a cloud about eight miles above the earth when his phone started to vibrate gently on the arm of the sofa. He was slumped so far down on the enormous cushions that he couldn't see the display, but he knew perfectly well who it was.

It stopped vibrating, and then started again. After a third time, he sat up to look.

"Persistent," she said, sipping her wine and eyeing him over the rim of her glass.

"Work," he mumbled.

"They need a project manager at ten on a Friday night?" Her tone was light, not accusing.

"It's . . . it's a deadline for Monday. There's a bunch of figures to finalise for a presentation to the directors' board. Our budget could go ten shades of tits up if the sums are wonky."

She gave him a teasing smile. As if she knew full well it was bullshit — well, most of it was — but was too self-assured to lower herself to engage in any kind of challenge. It made him like her all the more.

He stood up.

"What, you don't ever bring your work home with you?"

"I did when I worked main office, Christ. But I'm in Child Protection now. It can be long days, but I'm basically Monday to Friday. Have to be, to get in step with all the meetings with social services. I'm on a call-out rota, but it's only once a month."

Finally, she'd let something out about work — and it was good news. The Keber gang had no interest whatsoever in Child Protection; by the same token, he was unlikely to ever be facing her in a police station interview on that basis.

Kenley's momentary sense of triumph was well and truly punctured when his phone rang for a fourth time.

"I'm going to have to take it," he said. "Sorry."

"Want me to . . ."

"No, no. Watch the film. I'll step outside."

Without thinking, he bent down and kissed her on the cheek, hating himself for every second of it. She was a little bemused, but said she would turn off the film and they could finish it — and the wine — another night.

She stood and gathered the wine glasses while Kenley opened the front door and went outside into the cool evening air.

His phone rang again. Bloody Sterling.

"Don't give up, do you?" Kenley said when he finally answered it.

"Worried about you, boss. For all I know you could be lying in a ditch somewhere."

"You sound beside yourself with worry. What do you want?"

"No need for the abrupt tone, boss. Sorry if I've interrupted date night."

Kenley wanted to say, *How did you know that?* But he clamped his mouth shut. The guy was fishing, and Kenley wished to neither confirm nor deny anything that amounted to an incursion into his private life.

"Anyway, we've got a bad situation," Sterling said.

"Hang on a minute, let me get in the house." He hopped over the line of bonsai separating his drive from Natalie's, jogged up the path and shut the front door behind him. He walked over to the aquarium.

"What is it?" he said, dispensing eyedropper-sized amounts of lunch into the tank.

"The hive was raided."

"*What?* Which one?" His arm froze over the tank.

"Telstar. Last night."

"How in shit's name did that happen?"

"One of the worker bees escaped. Ran to a store. They called the cops."

"Oh, Christ. What sort of numbers are we talking?"

"The bees weren't due for collection until the morning, so they'll have all of them. They've made four arrests. Including Stratton."

Kenley felt himself go pale, and he dropped rather more food into the aquarium than he'd intended.

"Stratton? Stratton's in *custody*?"

"That's what I'm being told."

"That's extremely fucking bad news. He wasn't meant to be stopping, just checking in. An hour, max."

"I'm just telling you what I know."

"Shit, I bloody *knew* this would happen. I *told* him it would happen. But would he listen?"

Kenley spun the phone round in his hand. This was not good. He was already on Head Office's radar for the Kevin Bridger saga, and this was considerably worse. Attention from the police was one thing, but losing a hive put a serious dent in the revenue forecasts.

He stood up. If the cops had linked up the two events, there'd be trouble, even if he didn't really think they had it in them.

Then again, he hadn't expected them to treat Kevin's death as anything other than an accident. Fool me once, et cetera.

He sat down again.

This was no good. Somehow, the police had upped their game. In Kenley's experience, that usually meant a single individual. Someone who, either through not having enough work to do or being brand new out of the box, was looking a bit closer at things than Kenley was comfortable with. Thankfully, if it was just one individual, they could be identified, rooted out, dealt with. That being the case, it would be equally straightforward to dissuade them. The vast majority of cops cannot stand it when their work spills over into their home life, and a few parlour tricks — a break-in or two, doing over the car, some crude threats — and this clever dick would calm right down and think more carefully about their pension.

"Boss? You there?" Sterling was still harping on. Kenley put the phone back to his ear.

"I'm here. What's their case like? Witnesses?"

"Maybe we shouldn't speak . . ."

"Answer me, dammit."

"Got nothing on that." Sterling had turned unusually sullen.

"Where's this bloody sergeant of yours. Has he given anything?"

"Nothing yet."

"Well, fucking get into him. Kidnap him if you have to. And what about the worker bee? The one that escaped," Kenley said.

"In the wind. Got whisked away to some safe house, I guess."

"That's not good, Len. We need to fucking find her."

CHAPTER TWENTY-EIGHT

A week or so later, Barnes bribed Kane with breakfast and a semi-decent latte, and the two of them headed off into Kent in Barnes's Rover.

"Where is this place?" Kane asked.

"Somewhere between Kent and Essex, I think. They were a little vague on the details."

"I hope this thing makes it. No offence," he added.

"This thing is about as finely tuned as you can get."

"You handy with cars?"

"'Handy' might be a stretch. I get by."

"Hobby of yours?"

Barnes looked over at him. "I guess."

"Cool."

Barnes faced the road again. "They want me to phone when I'm close, and then they'll talk me in."

"Pretty secretive."

"It's a purpose-built facility for victims of human trafficking. From the tone of the woman on the phone, they don't trust cops, much less like them. I would have liked to visit sooner, but I did well to persuade them to let us see her this soon."

The journey was arduous — it was a fight to get onto the M23, the M25 was down to a two-lane contraflow and the Dartford Crossing was something just the wrong side of carnage. And it was starting to snow again.

Barnes often thought that out-of-county enquiries, away from the office, away from meetings, were a good way to connect with whoever was in the passenger seat — no way was Barnes going to let anybody else drive — but for the majority of this particular journey all he could think about was that the woman on the phone would likely not tolerate any form of tardiness.

Eventually, they broke the back of the journey, and once they were well into Essex, Barnes pulled off the motorway and began to double back towards London. Barnes called the facility while Kane braved the sleet long enough to jump out and grab two foul-smelling coffees in Styrofoam cups from a lay-by tea wagon. Barnes watched him through the windscreen as he waited under an awning of sorts.

The directions from the caseworker took them another forty minutes of driving and practically to the Suffolk border. A-roads became B-roads became country lanes, and eventually they turned down a farm track that appeared to take them towards an abandoned barn.

"Wrong turn?" Kane wondered aloud.

But they continued down the track and then, to Barnes's surprise, as they rounded the barn, the track opened out onto a service road with a new layer of tarmac. This driveway was lined with neatly planted shrubs and well-tended borders and, after a quarter of a mile or so, rounded in a loop outside a building that looked, from the outside, like a brand-new office block on four storeys.

They shut the car doors and stood for a moment.

"You don't realise how much you miss silence until you hear it," Kane said, stretching.

"We could learn a thing or two from their design," Barnes said.

They were greeted at the door by a security guard who looked pleased to see somebody, gave their names to the receptionist, and then waited on two large green armchairs in the glass-fronted lobby.

"He must be bored to death," Kane said to Barnes, nodding at the security guard. Kane's voice echoed up into the atrium.

They didn't have to wait long. A tall, serious-looking woman appeared from a door by the reception.

"Officers?" she said from the doorway.

They went over and made their introductions.

"My name is Magda. I'm the operations manager. You're here to see Roxy?"

"That's correct," Barnes said. "We'd like to see how she is, give her an update on the case and ask her a few questions. If that's in order," he added.

"Well, ultimately that will be the decision of the nursing manager, but I am sure it will be fine. This way, please," she said.

She led them into a corridor that smelled of new wood and carpet, and offered them the stairs or the lift, then jabbed at the lift call button without waiting for an answer.

"As you can imagine, she is still fairly affected by what happened," Magda said as they ascended. "Being here has helped her adjust, but there has also been a residual displacement shock. It being only a temporary placement doesn't help, of course."

"What is this place, exactly?" Barnes said. "It's very impressive."

"Well, as I said to you on the phone, it's purpose-built, and somewhere between being a convalescent home and rehabilitation centre. It's also intended to give them the reassurance of safety and protection."

"It certainly does that," Barnes said. "No one's going to find them out here."

"That's why we don't give you the address. And at the end of the visit I will ask you to sign some NDAs. The nature and location of this facility must not appear on any police records."

Barnes and Kane exchanged glances as they stepped out of the lift.

"Who pays for it all?" Kane asked.

"Technically, it's run by our charity, but it's been helped along by a large dose of Home Office grant funding, recognising the insidious nature of human trafficking and modern slavery. In Roxy's case, of course, there is the additional risk that she was captive in this country and is an eyewitness against her captors — some of whom may wish to try to find her, I am sure. This is one of the accommodation wings."

They turned onto a long corridor with a line of pale wooden doors on either side, stretching away in front of them. There was a pale blue-and-pink carpet in a supposedly neutral design, with framed, individually lit watercolours of rivers and mountains lining the walls. Soft halogens dotted the ceiling like a runway leading away from them.

It was utterly silent. Barnes wondered what collective traumas hid behind the doors.

They took silent footsteps along the corridor; about halfway down was an open area with a workstation. A lone nurse sat at the deck writing up notes under a dull lamp. She didn't look up. The barely audible strains of a gentle string quartet piped from speakers recessed in the ceiling.

Magda knocked lightly on a door behind the nurses' station and spoke to a woman in a smart-looking suit, who got up as Magda walked in. They exchanged a quiet handover, then Magda took her leave and left them with the nursing manager, who introduced herself as Corinne.

If Barnes had thought that Magda didn't exactly exude warmth, then she had nothing on Corinne, who had a kind of cartoon-villain prickliness about her. She had very pale, almost ghostly skin, with dark red fingernails and masses of curls that had been just about tamed on the top of her head. She trotted off down the corridor; Barnes and Kane had to work to keep up.

"Do you get many police visiting you?" Barnes asked, hoping a bit of conversation might slow her down a little.

It worked; Corinne stopped suddenly outside one of the rooms and turned to face him.

"Considering the type of work we do, surprisingly few. Most police officers are content to leave us to it, provided we make sure the patients turn up to their appointments."

"Appointments?"

"Court, examinations, interviews. Et cetera."

"Sounds like you'd have preferred to come to us."

"From both a clinical and business perspective, that is generally preferable. The location of the facility is not secret, in the official government classification sense of the word, but we don't like to advertise it."

"Like a refuge," Kane said.

Corinne eyed him briefly, then turned her gaze back to Barnes.

"But some patients — your young lady included — don't like to leave the setting. After their experiences, navigating the outside world can require faculties that, in some cases, they have no wish to find out whether or not they still possess."

"Well, I appreciate—"

"Let's go over the ground rules. If at any point I think your questioning is going to affect her recovery, I will end the session."

"Okay. I—"

"Aside from the physical symptoms, including malnourishment and pressure damage, she isn't sleeping well. She is also prone to nightmares and flashbacks, as well as being generally anxious about most things."

"Fairly classic PTSD symptoms, no?" Barnes said.

"Indeed. And I have no idea how she will react to two large men in suits entering her room. I take it gender representation hasn't improved well enough in the police for you to have sent a couple of female detectives?"

Barnes and Kane exchanged glances again.

"We will treat her with the utmost sensitivity," Barnes said slowly.

"Did you bring an interpreter?" Corinne asked.

"End of a phone," Kane said, holding up his mobile. "How have you been communicating with her?"

Corinne eyeballed him. "Quite often it's not what we say, it's how we say it. But, as it is, hardly any of our patients are native English speakers, and so we also use interpreters. Several of the staff are multilingual too — albeit nobody that could help you specifically."

"Has she started any kind of therapy?" Kane asked.

"Not yet. And I don't want to hear anything about how disclosures made in therapy are disclosable to the defence. That is absolutely confidential."

"We wouldn't dream—"

Corinne held up a finger. "So you say. But the last two policemen that darkened my door tried exactly that."

"Met, were they?" Barnes said.

"You're dealing with an extremely traumatised young lady," Corinne said, ignoring the question. "I also gather that, having managed to escape, she was recaptured less than two hours later."

"Yes, we had a rather overzealous citizen trying to help the investigation," Barnes said, unable to suppress the instinct to respond with a form of explanation. "Unfortunately, he didn't choose to share his intentions with us before doing so."

"This would be the shopkeeper?"

Barnes raised an eyebrow. "You know about him?"

"Only because Roxy mentioned him with a degree of . . . well, fondness might be a bit strong. She spoke gently of him."

"You've had the interpreters on speed dial, by the sounds of it," Kane remarked.

"In any case, and as you can imagine, she considers herself lucky to be alive, if not doubly traumatised," Corinne said, ignoring him. "Are we clear on the ground rules?"

"Yes indeed," Barnes said, just about stopping himself from adding *ma'am*. "She is expecting us, yes?"

"We're here," she said, pointing to the digits on the door they were standing outside.

Barnes tilted his head. Had she wanted her patient to hear this?

Corinne tapped gently on the door. A nervous-sounding voice said, "*Yes?*"

She pushed the door open and ushered Barnes and Kane inside.

It was a decent-sized bedroom by any hotel's standards and, like the rest of the facility, the furniture, carpets and woodwork all smelled brand new. There was a floor-to-ceiling safety window that offered a view of the landscaped grounds, and a flat-screen television perched on a dressing table next to a sprig of lavender in a vase. Leftovers from breakfast sat on a tray with a silver coffee pot and, Indeed, the only concession to treatment and rehabilitation was the bed, which, although clearly expensive, quite obviously belonged in a hospital.

Roxana Petrescu was sitting on the bed, her knees up, a magazine draped across them.

She looked from Barnes to Kane nervously, then to Corinne for help.

"Yes?"

"Roxy, my lovely, these men are with the police." Corinne walked over with a tone as light as fairy dust, and gently held Roxy's hand. It didn't seem to matter that Roxy couldn't understand her. "They've come to see if they can help you."

Her manner towards Roxy was a million miles from how she'd greeted the detectives, and Barnes felt momentarily impressed by her protective instincts. Her patients were onto a good thing here, and she'd clearly be buggered if she was going to let two clodhopping cops muck all that up.

Roxy's long hair was wet, and she was barefoot on the bed in leggings and a T-shirt, as if she'd just got back from a swim. *She was probably quite relaxed until we turned up*, Barnes thought. Her arms were bare, the rings of mauve bruises like sleeves. She was tiny; Barnes wondered if she'd put any weight on since the rescue and, as his warrant card came out, he realised he hadn't actually met her in person before.

Kane took the lead, as if sensing Barnes's momentary hesitation. His tone was gentle, but there was no escaping the fact that — as Corinne had said — they were two men in suits flanking a terrified woman. Her nervous eyes flicked from one cop to the other.

"How you doing there, Roxy?" Kane said, in what sounded like a brave attempt to adopt Corinne's non-threatening tones while Barnes tried to scare up an interpreter. "We're the police. We're really sorry to disturb you. We just wanted to see how you are."

Barnes retreated a few paces to make the atmosphere a little less oppressive, and sat on a chair — upholstered, very comfortable — by the door. He busied himself with getting the interpreter on the phone.

After a moment's hiatus, Barnes finally reached a Romanian speaker. He activated the loudspeaker and stepped forward to place the phone on the mattress. Roxy eyed it, and unfroze long enough to finally put down her magazine. On the other side of the bed, Corinne folded her arms and stepped back until she was wedged against the windowsill.

"First of all, Roxy, we want you to know that you're safe," Kane said, perching with one hip on the conference table. "This visit doesn't change that."

There was a tense pause as the tinny voice from the phone converted Kane's words. Roxy watched the device as the interpreter spoke, then looked back at Kane and nodded.

"We've locked up the men that kept you in that place, but that only takes us up to trial. We found them there, so our case is strong, but to put them away for years rather than months, we need—"

"I'm sorry — 'put them away'?'" said the interpreter.

"Terminology, boss," Barnes said quietly from the corner of the room. Kane looked back at him momentarily.

"I'm sorry. For them to be sentenced for their crimes, we need your evidence. We need you to be a witness."

Corinne uncrossed her arms and straightened up. Barnes sensed an intervention brewing. He raised two placatory hands.

"You don't need to be in the court," Barnes said. "We can video record you and play it to the court as your evidence-in-chief."

"Evidence in . . . ?" said the interpreter.

"Your testimony." Kane said, taking over again. "We will ask you a series of questions about what happened. We will record that interview on video, and then play it to the court so you don't have to go in the witness box. We can record it here, in your room, or elsewhere in the building, or—" here he eyed Corinne momentarily — "you can come to one of our buildings."

"A police station?" Corinne asked.

"Not a police station," Kane said, "but a separate building that we use especially for video interviews. It's called a witness suite."

"It doesn't look like a police station at all," Barnes added.

All eyes went to the phone while the interpreter rattled it off.

"*Când?*" Roxy asked, in her native Romanian.

"Whenever you feel able to," Kane said, without waiting for the translation. "There's no hurry."

He looked back over at Barnes.

"Look, our case is strong. There's even a chance that the video won't be used. That there won't be a trial. If the case is strong enough, the suspects — the bad men — might plead guilty."

"Does that mean they will spend less time in prison?" Roxy asked, via the interpreter.

Kane nodded. "It might."

"How long?"

"I couldn't say. But, whether they plead guilty or not guilty, they are facing some serious charges. Kidnapping, false imprisonment, grievous bodily harm . . ."

Corinne raised a palm. Kane stopped talking, and nodded.

"How long?" Roxy asked.

"Until a trial? Again, I couldn't say. Inside a year, I'd be surprised."

Roxy pondered this for a moment, then looked out of the window. *She probably has no idea where she will be in a year,* Barnes thought.

"The others I was with," Roxy said. "Are they well?"

Barnes stood up. "To varying degrees, yes. One has some quite serious health problems that he isn't going to recover from overnight, but he should get there."

Roxy took this in. Her eyes glistened.

"Roxy, there are just a couple of things we need to iron out now, please. It won't take long, then we'll leave you alone. But it will help the case."

She stared at him as the interpreter spoke. Her eyes seemed to say, *Is that all I am to you?* Barnes hoped he was imagining it.

He moved over to the bed and flipped his notebook open.

"We arrested four defendants. Killed one," Barnes said, standing up. "That's five. How many are we missing?"

Roxy stared at him.

"You were there, what, four weeks? Six?" Barnes said. "Can you give us any idea about how many there were?"

Roxy shook her head and looked out of the window again — attempting, Barnes presumed, to recall the number of brutal faces that passed through. He hoped they weren't causing any painful memories to become unsuppressed — but, judging from the look Corinne was giving him, that hope was probably fairly forlorn.

"I know it's hard," he said. "But anything you can remember will help."

"There were so many that came and went," she said. "Some wore masks."

"Came and went? Like temporary workers? Hired help?"

"I don't know," she said. "But there were four men who I saw a lot. Regularly. Over time, I picked up their names. Krist, Vernon, Don and Karl."

"That's good," Barnes said. "That's really good. We can check that against the names of those that we have in custody."

"Krist was sometimes kind to me," she said.

Barnes looked at the phone, then to Kane, and back again. "The men in the compound, they're only a small piece

209

of the operation. There will be men at the port, men in other cities, men still in Europe. A network of people working together to take people from their families and send them to the places like the one you ended up in."

"I could not know all these people," Roxy said.

"No, of course not. I wouldn't expect you to. I'm just pointing out that we have some men in custody, but there are far more that we don't. It's a large operation. We have some of their phones and computers, which will be the best way to track them all down. But if you can remember any conversations you overheard, or names, or places — that would help us triangulate."

"You think . . . you think these other men — the men in Europe — will come for me?" Roxy's eyes widened.

Corinne pushed herself off the windowsill and opened her mouth. Without looking at her, Barnes held up a finger, and sensed anger starting to radiate from her. He was on borrowed time here.

"No, I think you are very safe. This location is secret. Roxy — how exactly did you escape? The room you were in couldn't be opened from the outside."

"Yes, it could. It took many weeks. I worked through the plaster with a nail until there was enough movement to open the false wall. That was difficult."

"In true *Shawshank Redemption* style," Kane remarked.

"And then what?" Barnes said.

"The work they made us do, it changed. Sometimes we were in the fields. Sometimes we were in the factory out-house. Sometimes we worked in the stables. I came to learn the grounds and where the walls were. Knowing the movements of the patrols — how fast they walked, when they took their breaks, when they were most bored — I learned this over many months. Once I was free of the wall, the rest was much easier."

"Was that the first time you tried to escape?"

She nodded.

"What kind of work did they have you doing?" Barnes asked. "This is an organised group. They have business in mind. What was it? Washing cash? Cutting drugs?"

Roxy shrugged: *Everything.*

"Was there anything you remember about what they might have had planned? Anything at all about what they might do next?"

"I . . . I don't think so."

"Did they ever hurt you?"

She wrapped her arms around herself. "Not in the way you are thinking. As you say, they are businessmen."

"Detectives, we are done." Corinne's voice was cold. "Please make your video interview appointment as you suggested. Roxy will attend, with her caseworker and her lawyer. I would be obliged if you send your questions ahead of time."

Barnes said nothing. He'd known Corinne would want the last word.

"Roxy, thank you for your time. I'm glad you are safe. We look forward to speaking again."

Barnes and Kane headed for the door.

"*Aştepta*," she called. "Wait."

Both officers turned.

"There was something," she said.

They edged back into the room, but she was looking at Kane; Barnes hung back.

"What is it?" Kane said. He moved around the bed and squatted down opposite Roxy. "What do you remember?"

Barnes surreptitiously pushed the phone with the interpreter still on the open line across the bed.

"They did not talk much about their work. They spoke little to us. But sometimes Krist would talk to me. And Vernon and Don liked to joke among themselves. And I hear things."

"And?"

"They are always careful. But I know they move products. They move guns. They plan robberies. They move people."

"Go on."

"They . . . they spoke of an event."

"What sort of event?"

"A popular event. Sport, I think."

Barnes frowned, and stepped forwards. "Sport? Do you remember what kind of sport?" He couldn't help himself.

Her eyes widened, and she shook her head in jerky, staccato movements. Kane cut Barnes off, holding up a finger without looking round.

"What else, Roxy? Anything else you remember?"

"I . . . I . . ."

"It's okay. Take your time."

Her eyes roamed the room, hands pressed into her lap.

"Do you remember when? Or where?"

"They talk about sunshine and heat. I think maybe summer. I know it is not far from here."

"From here?"

A strange smile crossed her face as she realised her mistake. "No, I mean . . . not here. Where . . . the farm."

"Not far from the farm? From where we found you?"

"Yes . . . Yes."

"Do you know what they plan to do at the event?"

"They rob it, maybe. I am not sure."

Kane gave her a huge smile. She reciprocated, nervously. Barnes had to admit he was impressed.

"Well done. You've done really well. We'll be in touch."

Kane squeezed her hands and stood up. Barnes ended the call with the interpreter and put away his notebook.

They headed for the door.

"*E dus cu pluta*," Roxy said in Romanian.

Both men looked back at her.

"Want me to get the interpreter back on the phone?" Barnes asked.

"No," Kane said. "I think I got it."

CHAPTER TWENTY-NINE

Barnes skim-read the two complaint files and made some notes on the most expedient route to getting rid of them. He was man enough to admit to himself that one of the advantages of working in intelligence was the fact that there was precious little call to interact with the public on even a sporadic basis. As a trade-off, he'd agreed to take these two hairy, fossilised complaint files with him when he crossed over from main office CID. He'd been going round in circles on both of them for about three years. One was from a man who was convinced — along with his two daughters — that there was a conspiracy to kill him at the local hospital trust, spanning nearly three decades. The complainant was just the wrong side of ninety, and Barnes's main hope with that one was that he just had to outlive the guy, then the coroner could decide if he wanted to summon the entire NHS executive board to the inquest.

The second one was a double nightmare — a wealthy couple out in the depths of the countryside with a nice house on a decent bit of land had taken exception to a planning application submitted by their equally wealthy neighbours. She was a parish councillor, he was a retired superintendent — actually, make that a triple nightmare — and they had complained, via their MP and the chief constable, about the police's failure to deal with said planning application. When it had been pointed out that this was purely a matter for the district council to resolve, all manner of murky allegations of a campaign of neighbourly harassment had mysteriously surfaced, including loud music, deliberate sheep worrying, reckless shooting and antisocial tractor-driving. The case was thinner than a gnat's wing, and yet the lack of a successful prosecution had caused outrage in all the wrong circles of power. At one stage Barnes had even considered taking the case to the CPS so *they* could be the bad guys, but his conscience had been pricked by the advising lawyer, who had said: "Don't you dare."

When the neighbours made an inverse, but otherwise identical, complaint about the councillor and the retired cop — simply not wanting to *hear* that wilful obstruction of a planning application was not a crime — Barnes got to do it all over again.

Generally, he noted, once you'd taken out the more insidious stuff, the majority of complaints about the police tended to be about customer service — the length of time it took to answer the phone, the fact that no one told me what was happening, the fact that it took you a week to turn up, by which time the gobby oiks were long gone. Failure to catch the offender didn't seem to feature much. People always wanted something *done* — they just seldom seemed to know what.

Much of it had to do with expectation versus reality, Barnes thought. On more than one occasion he'd sat down with a distraught and disgruntled family and explained exactly how many detectives he had at his disposal to deal with hundreds of live cases just like theirs. It nearly always caused surprise, even in badly wronged people who — often not unreasonably — thought their case should be top of the priority pile. Barnes had thought once or twice about taking a straw poll and then going public with the results.

And it seemed to matter not who was at the helm — be it a staunch right-leaning tough-on-crime home secretary or someone with a more centrist socially liberal worldview — there were always tough times coming down the pipe. Spendthrift centralisation seemed to happen in five-year-cycles — closing police stations, co-locating control rooms, outsourcing administrative functions or brutal quick-fire redundancies just to balance the books — and once you've departed a federated model, Barnes mused, you don't ever go back.

The bottom line was: nobody wanted to hear that the emperor was naked, and anyone daring to push the responsibility for a corporate failure to protect back upstream would find themselves eminently replaceable. Those chief constables with half a century's service and their pensions locked down might mount a devil-may-care assault on the lack of proper funding for policing services, but they were few and far between. You had to plan, they said. There were always tough times ahead, they said. Incisive budgeting was a big chunk of the job description, they said.

To an extent, it was a self-fulfilling prophecy. Overworked staff either quit or go on the sick, which puts an additional burden on those remaining, who then either quit or go on the sick. Eventually you end up with vacancies you can't fill, and anybody vaguely normal with half a brain avoiding a career in policing at all costs. Throw in a few adverse headlines, and the snake always ended up eating its own tail.

The nurse he'd briefly dated a year or two back — Annie — had told him it was already happening in nursing. Great chunks of unfilled vacancies that neither the government nor the popular media, for whatever reason, wanted to acknowledge.

She'd been a sweet, strong woman — perhaps unsurprisingly, for an ITU nurse — with an adventurous streak and a raucous sense of humour, and he'd found her both attractive and exciting. It didn't last, though — *couldn't* last. He worried he was too boring for her, and the ghosts of his unseen baggage seemed to loom in the air on the few quiet nights they spent together.

She was a few years older, and had been at pains to reassure him — *nobody* our age is without baggage, she'd said, which made him worry even more that a ten-year forecast of his being needy and in constant need of reassurance beckoned. Her rejoinder to *that* was: let's just have some fun and see where it goes.

He went along with that for a while but, in the end, his determination to find the trio that had ended his wife's life with a two-ton truck became like an iceberg between himself and Annie. Not only that, but he'd met Annie through work. She was a *witness*, for God's sake; with a slightly different set of circumstances that could have been a job-loser, and Barnes had already sailed too close to the sun far more often in his career than he was comfortable with.

It wasn't that he was consciously putting his dead wife above his burgeoning relationship — and although that's how it came out, she had been pretty decent about it — it was more that policing would chew you up whole and spit you out if you didn't keep one foot outside it: relationships, financial prospects, mental health. He'd known policing would be a tough profession, but one of the reasons he'd felt able to face it was because he'd met and married Eve *before* he joined up. Date a colleague, your life was practically public property. Date a witness, you'd be lucky to avoid the sack. Either way, policing had you by the balls.

To his surprise, he found himself thinking about the paramedic he'd met when debriefing Kenneth Rix — Tamsin, her name was. Maybe it was time to take his own advice and get back in the game. He needed to do *something*. The session he'd booked with the counsellor was looming, and he was already thinking about cancelling it — all of a sudden, he didn't feel ready. Kevin Bridger had been about to give him the name of the man who had driven his van into Eve, and until that particular wound had healed, he wouldn't be able to let go of anything. No amount of salsa classes would change that, he thought grimly.

He threw the complaint files back onto the desk, and reached into a desk drawer for the CD-ROM with Debbie Bridger's phone recording on it.

He slipped it into the player, lining up the CCTV image from the seafront and the sketch likeness from her neighbour on the desk in front of him.

He'd heard the recording a few times, but he still pinched the bridge of his nose and shut his eyes and winced his way through it.

Only one of them had been doing the talking. He spoke in slow, calm, almost jovial tones. His monologue was punctuated every so often by the sounds of crashing, or the low dull thud and then soft whimper or ratchety scream of Debbie Bridger being struck.

She didn't take it lying down, though. The mouth on the woman was fierce, and she gave as good as she got — verbally, anyway.

The noise had been horrendous. How the hell had anyone thought that was the television?

Barnes looked down at the two images on the desktop and imagined the tall, good-looking one holding court in the middle of the room, front and centre to where Debbie had been pinned into her armchair, while the other one roamed around, trashing the place.

Eventually her protests and fuck-yous had begun to dwindle, as the injuries began to mount up and the pain started to give way to unconsciousness.

The recording actually gave them nothing. They had a sliver of CCTV, a sketch likeness in profile and an audio recording. The three things might add up to a cogent whole, but they still had no ID — no confirmation, even, that it wasn't three different people.

"How's it going?"

Barnes turned to see Kane in the doorway. He gestured for the boss to sit.

"Still here?" Barnes asked.

"I guess," Kane said. "Though I'm figuring out pretty quickly there's a big glass wall between those that have to and those that want to. You don't have a family to go home to?"

Barnes just shrugged, but the words were like a branding iron on his skin — either because he'd never heard them before or, more likely, no one else had ever given enough of a shit to ask.

"Even if I did, that doesn't necessarily mean it's healthy to stay in the office just for the sake of it. What about you?"

"Just me and my cat."

"Then you're sending all the wrong sorts of messages, boss."

"It wasn't a pleasantry," Kane said, nodding at the paperwork on Barnes's desk. "How are we doing?"

"My cases?"

"You still working the murder? Kevin Bridger?"

"Well, as you can imagine, if the murderer's intention was to silence all potential informants, then it's worked. We've got a lot of smoke and mirrors, but no named suspects and nothing concrete in terms of evidence. Debbie Bridger got us close, but no further. That particular case is all but cold."

"Okay. And your other cases?"

Barnes gave a thin smile. "In the nicest possible way, boss, I've got a DCI somewhere around here to show an interest in my caseload. Having said that, I've only got a few crime cases on the go, and I only picked them up because I was helping out on the rota. In any other circumstances I'd hand them back. But . . ."

"But what?"

"I don't know, I . . . I guess I'd like to finish what I've started." He shut his eyes and squeezed his temples with the thumb and forefinger of his right hand. "Jesus, how cheesy does that sound?"

Kane didn't say anything.

"Anyway," Barnes continued, pointing to a green metal filing cabinet adorned with padlocks, "the point is that everything else is intelligence only, and above your security clearance, I'm afraid."

He smiled. Kane didn't return it. He nodded towards the towers of paperwork.

"What else you got?"

"You don't want to know."

"What about the farm?"

Barnes picked up a random sheaf of papers, flicked through them and then carelessly dropped them again onto the desk. "Well, purely in terms of logistics, it's a bloody nightmare. We've got ten very scared victims who don't speak English, two of whom are children, and, of our defendants — current tally stands at four — only one has any clout in terms of the food chain."

"Who's that?"

Barnes dropped a printout of an intelligence dump on the desk in front of Kane. "The one that got shot and survived. His name's Stratton Pearce. He's a delight, not to mention a classic case. Thirty-one years old, born Dover. Absent father, alcoholic mother, spent most of his youth in various children's homes. Took to drinking about the same time he discovered boxing. By all accounts, a natural talent, but his A-line angry streak saw him barred from the ring for life. Not many convictions, but he's got a couple of impressive Section 18 woundings in there. Last stint in prison was for robbery, came out in 2003. Not much since, other than some intelligence to say he's at least a middle manager in our disturbed little enterprise, plus what we think are some periods of time spent abroad."

"Abroad? Where?" Kane picked up the printout and peered at Pearce's front sheet.

"Don't know for sure. Europe — Spain maybe — possibly North Africa too."

"And the rest?"

"The rest are single-celled foot soldiers who are worth very little in terms of a conviction. I'm no lawyer, but some good advice where they're concerned would be to keep quiet and plead guilty — best possible sentence plus their reputations, in terms of loyalty, remain relatively intact."

"And what about our girl? Roxana?"

"She's certainly got something about her, wouldn't you agree? To have attempted escape in the first place. If she goes the distance, you can add courageous to tenacious. She's likely to be the glue that holds the prosecution witnesses together."

"When's her interview?"

"Next couple of days. Took some arranging, I can tell you. Chaperones, doubling down on verifying phone messages, the works. That whole unit's locked down like the Federal Reserve. But that's good. Reassuring. At least you know nobody posing as a cop is likely to get through their defences."

"Is that something they've seen before?"

"Not that they've said. But silencing witnesses is the best way to keep your case from getting in front of a judge."

Kane pondered this for a moment. "What about this information she provided? She talked about a sporting event. You have any thoughts on that?"

Barnes shrugged. "Could be anything. Although I will admit it stands out. Everything else she's told us has been about their ongoing enterprises. This sounded a little more specific."

"You think?"

"Well, specific might be pushing it."

"She said it was something in the summer. Near the farm."

Barnes frowned. "'Near' is relative. She could be talking about any number of things. Could be the cricket down at Hove. Could be the tennis. Could be the new stadium in Falmer. The London-to-Brighton bike ride. Or it could be any number of under-fifteen county league Sunday games."

"What could they be planning? Rob the takings, maybe?"

"Maybe. A robbery is as plausible as anything, but I have no idea how easy it would be, nor how cash-rich these events are, if at all. And how do we know they weren't planning anything more than an evening out on the beer?"

"We don't," Kane said. "Listen, they're not connected, are they? Kevin's death and the slave farm?"

Barnes raised an eyebrow. "What makes you say that?"

Kane shrugged. "Not sure."

Barnes thought about this for a moment. "Listen, I need to tell you something. Not now, but when I can."

"Something to do with that call you asked me to make to PSD?"

"Yes," Barnes said. "It . . . it's to do with my wife. My late wife," he added.

Kane was silent.

"It could look bad," Barnes said. "From a certain viewpoint. I would just rather you heard it from me."

"The way I see it, people become cops for different reasons," Kane said, eventually. "Someone who's driven by something that's happened to them personally, that could be a bad thing. But it's more likely to be a good thing."

Kane stood. "Let's go and see Roxana again. Arrange it."

"You're the boss."

"And the other one you mentioned. The one that got shot. The middle manager."

"Pearce? That'll be fun. We'd need to navigate the streams of protest his legal team will undoubtedly mount but, yes, we can arrange it."

Kane nodded. Barnes looked past Kane's shoulder and out of the window. Dusk had fallen over the patrol base, and the arc lights over the site were beginning to flick on, umbrellas of white with sheets of drizzle blowing through them. Barnes wondered where they all were, right now, this very moment. All the thieves, junkies, burglars, fraudsters, exploiters, abusers and organisers. All the people that gave him a reason to come to work every day. What were they all doing?

This time of the day, he almost missed the leaf blowers.

Kevin Bridger's voice in a barn in the middle of nowhere.

I can't tell you.

CHAPTER THIRTY

Kenneth Rix was suffering. His physical injuries had healed relatively quickly, just not quickly enough to stop him falling behind with his rent. The convenience store job had precious little in the way of sick pay and, when he did actually go back to work, the limp and the headaches kept him at around a quarter of the productivity he'd managed before the attack. And because he was not really of any use to the company, they'd both agreed it would be better if he just went. (The termination letter would later state that the contract had been nullified by mutual agreement; a decent employment lawyer might have described it as "constructive dismissal", but Kenneth had never thought to ask.)

But the physical injuries were offset considerably by the other trauma. Kenneth frequently found himself waking in the night, tangled in bedsheets and soaked in sweat. He would wake, wondering if the horrendous high-pitched screech he could hear was coming from foxes mating in the garden, before realising that, first, he didn't have a garden and, second, that the noise was, in fact, his own screaming. As he woke, it would take a good twenty minutes or so for the smell of the basement and the feel of the cold stone on his face and the exploding-watermelon sound of being struck across the head to fade. Once he even woke to find he had lost control of his bladder.

It wasn't just the nightmares either. Once or twice he'd been waiting at the checkout in broad daylight, when the mundane scene in his field of vision would be replaced by the dark basement where he sat bound next to Roxy. For a split second he could literally see nothing else, and then he would be back at the checkout. It was like the most horrific kind of total immersion time warp.

Stretched over all of this was the wounded pride of failing Roxy. Kenneth was hardly an alpha, and didn't model himself on some outdated hunter-gatherer, top-of-the-food-chain notion of what a man should be. Despite that, however, even he couldn't fail to recognise that his efforts to help Roxy reflected quite poorly on his own rather crude sense of masculinity. He'd come to her aid, only to get them both captured, and had then screamed like a pregnant albatross while she had remained stoic and impassive. That detective had been right. The rude one. Barnes, was it? He'd been right when he told the paramedic that Kenneth was an armchair hero. Detective Barnes hadn't realised Kenneth could hear him from inside the ambulance, but he was right.

The net effect of all this was that Kenneth, who was hardly resilient to begin with, was once again jobless, with an eight-week lead time before jobseekers' allowance and other benefits kicked in. Most of this time was spent applying for other jobs, with Blockbuster and the U-Shuttle Rent-A-Car trainee business manager scheme the only two that looked like they might amount to anything. (Kenneth found the constant popcorn aroma and cinematic ambience of the former quite appealing; the latter, as far as he could make out, was simply going to be spending a lot of time washing cars.)

Ordinarily, Kenneth tried not to pay too much attention to his surroundings, and liked to keep his mind from becoming idle. But, through the prism of his waking nightmares, he found the frontage of Seaside Road depressing to the point of being oppressive. Dreary brickwork and empty, boarded-up stores seemed to be punctuated solely by takeaways, betting shops, convenience stores and funeral homes.

He shuffled past all the shopfronts in the freezing air and let himself back into his flat. It was opposite Marine Hall church and, although the view out of his bedroom window was of a dirty brick wall, his proximity to such a hallowed place was a welcome comfort.

He blew on the steaming paper packet of fish and chips and hunched himself over his laptop. Some part of his rational brain knew he should really see his GP, but the thought of penetrating the firewall of harshly voiced receptionists filled him with dread; similarly, an even smaller part of his brain wondered about getting some legal advice.

What did compute with him, though, was that he genuinely couldn't see how the chain of events that had led him to this point could have resulted in his being worse off than he was before. He was a *victim*, wasn't he? And so, deep in concentration, he scoured the web, soaking up all the things he might be entitled to, all the things that might signpost him to some kind of financial, emotional or medical help.

The vacuum was caused, he knew, by the lack of information about the case. He'd been interviewed on video by a couple of tobacco-throated, ugly-looking detectives, whose questions were so penetrating that he wondered if he'd done something wrong. Was he a suspect? He'd asked them that directly; they'd just laughed. But that had been almost two weeks ago, and he'd heard nothing since. He supposed there'd be a trial at some point, and that he might be required to give evidence, but he just couldn't know. He'd even called a couple of times. The nice lady in the call centre had taken a message and assured him she'd pass it on to the senior investigating officer, but he'd heard nothing back.

An idea came to him. A decent reason for calling again generally held all kinds of appeal, and so he flicked over to one of the internet providers and generated a new email account for himself. That way, he could go into the police station on the pretext of providing some new contact information about himself.

He closed his computer, lay down in the gloom, staring at the ceiling, dreading sleep.

* * *

To his surprise, he awoke some six hours later having slept a relatively uninterrupted sleep. He wondered if it was down to the prospect of having a purpose for the day ahead.

He dressed quickly and walked off down the road to where he'd parked the Honda. He regarded it for a moment before getting in, and thought about taking the bus. Running a car didn't seem sensible with no income, but he decided today was going to be a good day, and that getting rid of the car might be a false economy, at least until he knew what the job market held in store.

He drove to the police station in Eastbourne and managed to park outside. The entrance foyer was quiet as well, and he wondered if his luck was going to run out any time soon.

He made a grand display of informing the lady on the front counter that he had a new email address, and would she mind very much passing it on to the detective in charge. There was a trial soon, you see, and he wanted to make sure the CID could contact him at all times.

The lady was polite, and took the new information; Kenneth was back in the car in less than four minutes, feeling a little deflated. He'd expected something more, albeit he wasn't quite sure what.

As he started the engine, his heart jumped.

Two police officers were leaving the police station. Kenneth recognised one as Barnes, the rude one. The second man was in uniform. Kenneth didn't recognise him. Was that an earring he was wearing?

His frustrated instinct was to run over and collar them both and demand an update, but his stomach fluttered with disappointment and self-loathing as he realised he didn't think he had the nerve.

But, then, he landed upon a better idea.

He would follow them.

* * *

Kenneth was beginning to eyeball his fuel gauge nervously when Barnes and the other officer finally turned off the motorway on the other side of the Dartford Crossing.

He wasn't quite sure why, but some feeling in the pit of his stomach told him not to follow them into the neat, tree-lined driveway. He thought he'd been pretty clever so far, taking care not to get too close to them, using other cars to sandwich between his Honda and the police's Rover wherever possible. He'd been lucky — the motorway had been thick with traffic, allowing Kenneth to stay relatively concealed, and only now did he drop right back to keep his distance. He certainly didn't think they'd have spotted him.

There was no signage, but the driveway looked like it might lead down to a stately home, or some kind of field hospital. He carried on going as they turned off, then spun the car around a little further up and pulled into a lay-by about a hundred yards beyond the driveway.

It was a main road, with nothing in his line of sight in either direction besides the driveway, which in turn was abutted by nothing other than brown fields of crop stubble littered with frost. From his vantage point he could see the treeline marking the driveway as it stretched away from him — albeit he couldn't see anything of the driveway itself, nor what it led to — and he congratulated himself on ceasing his surveillance when he had. He'd have stuck out like a sore thumb but, from here, he had a decent view of the entrance to the driveway, and the lay-by provided a discreet cover.

He settled down to wait. He had no idea how long they would be. The car rocked gently on the occasion that traffic sped by but, besides that, the only sound was distant birdsong and, he thought, the very faint rumble of the M25 in the distance.

He awoke suddenly, the winter sun and pale blue sky replaced momentarily by the basement and the smell of blood. He sat upright in the driver's seat, smacking his lips together to try to banish the very dead taste of sleep from his mouth. He should have brought a snack. Or at least some water.

He glanced in the rear-view at the sound of an engine behind him, and his stomach did a momentary somersault. When he saw the elderly driver of a motorhome get out to stretch his legs and incline his face at the sun, Kenneth relaxed a little. The driver then — for reasons unknown to Kenneth, as the vehicle looked like it would likely have been equipped with a toilet — positioned himself between the motorhome and the wide open passenger door, and urinated into the verge.

The driver zipped himself up and climbed back in. The motorhome eased past Kenneth and out onto the main road, and Kenneth felt a stab of envy as it passed him. The thing was shiny, sleek and nearly thirty feet long.

It rumbled off into the distance. Kenneth thought about chancing a wee himself, but then he saw DI Barnes's Rover suddenly appear in the mouth of the driveway. Barnes was driving. He looked left and right — and Kenneth froze, for a moment thinking Barnes had looked right at him — and then he pulled onto the road back in the direction they had come from.

When Kenneth was sure the cops had gone, he took a deep breath and pulled out onto the main road. He slowly eased the hundred yards or so down to the entrance to the driveway, and turned into it.

He kept it very slow. He had no idea what was down here.

Eventually he reached a gravel apron in front of a large, glass-fronted building. It certainly wasn't a stately home, and his first thought ran to field hospital, but the thing looked brand new and, if it wasn't out here in the countryside, could equally have passed as the headquarters of some highfalutin corporate multinational.

The apron in front of the main entrance allowed visitors to perform a full circuit in front of the building — none of this reversing-to-turn-around nonsense — and Kenneth nearly pulled a full 360 degrees intending to push the accelerator to the floor and hightail it out of there.

Instead, he whispered some encouraging motivational epithets to himself, and stuck the Honda in one of a row of otherwise empty parking bays marked "VISITORS ONLY".

He got out and headed for the entrance. The glass door slid silently open; Kenneth took a breath and stepped inside the huge foyer. A blast of heat hit him in the face.

He'd taken only a few steps when he found a uniformed security guard blocking his path.

"Help you, sir?"

"I, well . . ."

"See some ID, please?"

Kenneth pulled out his wallet and fiddled around with it, eventually producing his driving licence.

"What is happening here?" a harsh voice asked.

Kenneth looked over and saw a tall woman in what he assumed was the modern nurse's uniform marching over from a door behind the reception. She had arms like iron and she looked vexed.

"Who is he?" the nurse asked. The guard took the licence from Kenneth's still-outstretched hand and passed it over.

She took it and examined it.

"You cannot be here," she said, and walked off behind the reception desk to, Kenneth realised, take a photocopy of his driving licence.

"I need to ask you to leave, sir," the guard said, gesturing towards the door with an outstretched arm.

Kenneth didn't want that, but the silent protest screaming in his brain kept him immobile. When he didn't immediately move, the guard placed his other hand on Kenneth's shoulder, and Kenneth felt himself turning on the spot as he capitulated.

"My licence . . ." he muttered.

The nurse walked out from behind the desk and returned it to him.

"You need to leave," she said. "Now. I will be checking in with the authorities about you coming here. You should not be here."

They were interrupted by a dull banging on the glass.

Kenneth spun and, to his amazement, saw Roxy Petrescu waving at him from outside. She was smiling, and an enormous grin broke out across his own face.

"What the . . ." the guard said to the nurse, who looked even more vexed than before.

Roxy walked to the entrance door and joined them in the foyer. She was dressed in sports gear, and she made straight for Kenneth.

"Hello," she said, smiling. "Kenneth. You visit?"

The nurse looked aghast. "You *know* this man?"

Roxy started to speak in Romanian. Kenneth turned to the nurse and explained his association with Roxy.

"You're the one who helped her?" She looked surprised. "She mentioned you. You're not what I expected."

She folded her arms.

"That doesn't explain how you managed to find this place, however. This isn't somewhere you would find in the Yellow Pages."

She looked accusingly at Roxy. Kenneth picked up on the insinuation.

"Oh, no, Roxy didn't tell me where she was. I haven't spoken to her since . . . since that night."

"It wouldn't be the first time. It's the *nadir* of irony that this institution's biggest weakness is the verbosity of its own patients."

Kenneth tried to process what she was saying, but the big words muddled his brain. He frowned. She stared, still waiting for an answer.

"I followed the police," he mumbled.

She raised an eyebrow. The entrance door opened behind them and a courier in a yellow jacket with a parcel under his arm made his way to the reception desk. He hesitated when he saw the little tableau in the foyer.

"Come on," the nurse said, signing for the parcel. "Let's take this somewhere private."

She took them to a small meeting room near the lifts. Everything was brand new, Kenneth noticed, and the furniture, walls and fixtures had the smell that made him think of a nice hotel or office block. Not that he'd ever been in either.

They all — security guard included — sat around the wooden conference table. The tableau now had a degree of additional formality that Kenneth could feel pressing down on him like a fog.

"Are you going to tell the police I followed them?" Kenneth said.

"I should," the nurse said. "If for no other reason than to confirm you're not Europe's Most Wanted. Although that seems unlikely." She looked him up and down again.

"I wasn't trying to find Roxy," Kenneth said. "Roxy and me were . . ." He faltered. What were they? The correct answer was kidnapped, beaten, bound and held at gunpoint. But he couldn't bring himself to use any of those words. "Well, we're involved in the same case."

"I know." Was it Kenneth's imagination, or had her tone softened a little?

"The police haven't told me anything since it happened, so I went to the station to ask to speak to somebody," he said, a little more emboldened by what may or may not have been a chink in her exterior. "When I saw them coming out I decided to follow them. It was a split-second thing. I didn't know they were coming here."

"Look," the nurse said, "my primary concern is the safety of my patients. If you've had to resort to such drastic measures because the police aren't giving you enough information about your case, then that's your lookout. It doesn't reflect particularly well on them, I must say. And besides . . ."

Roxy raised a hand. The nurse was silenced.

"Yes, dear?" she said.

Roxy didn't speak, but pointed at Kenneth, then at her own chest, then back to Kenneth in a repeating motion.

The nurse exhaled. "Apparently Roxy wants some time with you."

She stood. The security guard did the same.

"Listen to me. You can't go around broadcasting the fact of this institution to anyone."

"I won't. I promise."

"I won't take your word for it, I'm afraid. I will need you to sign a non-disclosure agreement to that effect."

Kenneth swallowed. "Now?"

"No. I have your details. Our legal team will be in touch."

"You've got five minutes," the security guard said, and they both left.

Kenneth watched them go, then turned back to Roxy and rested his hands on the table. She smiled at him, placing both hands around one of his club-like fists. She looked so much better than when he had seen her last — her hair was clean, thick and shiny, not lank and wet as when she'd first crashed against the shop window. Her cheeks had some colour in them, as well as being a little fuller after only a few short weeks. But the most striking thing was the total absence of fear and anxiety that had encased her whole body on that fateful night.

She began to speak in Romanian — Kenneth had no idea what she was saying but, if he didn't know better, he'd swear that she was telling him that she was pleased to see him and thanking him for his efforts on the night of the rescue. (In the last minute or so Kenneth had decided in his own mind that this sounded better than "the night of the capture" or "the night of the colossal fuck-up".)

"I meant what I said," Kenneth said, unable to keep himself from speaking slowly and loudly, as if that would somehow assist her understanding. "I wasn't trying to find you. But I am glad I did."

Her brow furrowed slightly, but the smile remained.

"I suppose I sort of knew you were here, deep down. How have you been? It's an impressive place. I imagine you are being well looked after?"

She clearly recognised the intonation of the question, because she began to speak. Lord alone knew what she was saying, but it was fast, and there was a lot of it. He nodded as she spoke, hoping she wouldn't stop, both because he feared any natural break would be a good cue for the nurse and the security guard to come back, and because when she did stop, he just felt stupid.

He decided to go for broke.

"Listen, I am sorry I got you into that mess. You had been brave enough to escape that horrible place and I managed to get you back into it in no time at all. We were so lucky, no thanks to me. I was trying to be a stupid hero and I failed. I don't even know why you're being nice to me."

He felt the tremor in his voice and the sting in his eyes, and her furrowed brow relaxed into one of sympathy. She squeezed his hands tighter and he stared right back at her huge, kind, brown eyes. Suddenly, he felt as if he were falling.

The door opened. Nurse Ratched came back in.

"Okay, I'm afraid I need to draw it to a close there. Roxy is due her lunch soon, and therapy sessions this afternoon."

Kenneth wasn't quite sure why the nurse felt able to share that with him when everything else was locked down so tight, but he didn't question it. Roxy removed her hands and Kenneth's own suddenly felt cold.

Roxy stood. She looked directly at Kenneth and uttered a final, solemn sentence, which, Kenneth believed with absolute conviction, was: *Come back and see me.*

The nurse escorted Roxy away, leaving the security guard, who leaned on the doorframe with both hands on his impressive-looking utility belt. He was chewing something.

The guard indicated towards the exit with his head, and Kenneth got up to go. The guard walked with him to the main doors without a word, and shut the doors pointedly behind Kenneth.

Kenneth didn't mind, though. He wasn't even fully aware of it. As he walked to his car, his stomach did backflip after backflip, and his footsteps felt lighter than air.

CHAPTER THIRTY-ONE

Barnes watched the vapour rise up from the unmoving line of traffic and gazed enviously as a couple of savage-looking seagulls shot over the queue and away into the distance.

The road network that threaded its way in and around Eastbourne couldn't, in Barnes's view, have been a more impenetrable, circuitous grind. Simply getting out of town was ten types of nightmare, and the system seemed to have been designed in such a way to keep people from ever wanting to leave. Getting from one police station to the other — well, it would have been quicker to walk.

He gazed at the flat marshland that stretched away across the Levels and wondered if anyone had ever attempted to build a direct cut-through to the main trunk roads circling the town and beyond. It was impossible, of course — the wetlands made it so — but in some moment of existential wonderment he marvelled at how he could *see* where he wanted to be, he just couldn't get there. Those seagulls had the right idea.

The marshland spread towards the South Downs looming up on the horizon — the exact same hills had been magnified tenfold out of his living room window when he and Eve had lived in Willingdon.

He sat up a little straighter in his seat. Spontaneous associations with his late wife were not uncommon, but they were reducing in frequency. The innocuous nature of this particular reminder surprised him, though, not least because by the logic of a couple of bits of greenery reminding him of his past, then everything around Eastbourne should be a constant reminder of her — even the shocking roads.

Maybe traffic jams were the trigger, he thought. After all, it was the shocking roads that had killed her.

He shook his head. That was a long time ago now. He had to focus. He spun round at the Birchwood estate turnoff and drove a complete loop past the car showrooms and industrial workshops back onto Lottbridge Drive, figuring along the seafront might be more expedient.

As he headed towards the seafront, his eyes flicked right towards the new, sprawling housing development springing up opposite the Sovereign Centre, on the site of the old coach park. There was the real traffic problem, he thought.

He eventually got to Grove Road and parked near the Saffrons. His melancholy didn't improve when he got to the office and saw the note taped to his keyboard.

"What the bloody hell . . . ?" he said to no one, shrugging off his jacket.

He picked up the phone and called Kane.

"Boss, we've hit a snag. I might need your muscle to weigh in."

"Go on."

"Well, the prison governor has refused our request to produce Pearce."

"Is that usual?"

"First time it's ever happened to me. Refused on the grounds that 'it would be prejudicial to the prisoner's rehabilitation prospects'."

"Interesting."

"You're not wrong. Cites the prisoner as having a range of different vulnerabilities that require specialist help."

"What do you want me to do? Call the governor?"

Barnes looked down at the note. There was more scribbled on the bottom, in a kind of deranged postscript.

"No . . ." he said slowly. "There might be another way. We'll have to move quickly, though. Are you free this afternoon?"

"According to my assistant, I've got a four-hour board meeting starting at one," Kane said. "And then somebody senior in Finance wants to talk to me about budget forecasting. So, yes, I'm free."

* * *

They drove to Lewes Crown Court that afternoon. Not wanting to attract any more jibes about his Rover, Barnes booked out a pool car — a silver Hyundai with a hundred thousand miles on the clock — and let Kane drive, finding the miles of unspoiled fields between the bypass and the coast unusually compelling. He stared at the Long Man of Wilmington as they passed it, and wondered if the seventy-metre-high chalk human figure etched into the hills was trying to tell him he should take a holiday.

"So, what is the plan, exactly?" Kane asked.

"Well, we're shit out of luck with the production order," Barnes said. "But his plea and directions hearing is today. With any luck, he'll be here in person. We can try to grab him for a quick chat before he's stuffed back into the van. But we'll have to move fast. A PDH doesn't normally take very long."

Kane parked in a pay-and-display and they walked up Market Lane to the court. Kane paused for a moment outside the massive building, taking in its Doric columns and the white stone countenance.

"Wait till you see inside," Barnes muttered.

There was a short hiatus as they got past security — the distinct inference on the part of both security officers being that Kane must surely have been impersonating a police officer — and then Barnes performed a rapid series of mini-interrogations of various court staff, racing about the building to try to zero in on their quarry.

"Well, there's good news and bad news," Barnes said as he rejoined Kane on the deep red carpet outside Courtroom 1. "The good news is, he's here and hasn't been heard yet. The bad news is, it's entirely down to him whether he decides to speak to us or not."

* * *

The only sound in the room was Pearce breathing. It was like a pair of bellows rhythmically daring the two police officers to make their move. He fixed them with a gaze from under a heavy brow; with his chin pointed at the tabletop, the resultant upward gaze was like the scowl of a zombie. His pupils were tiny pinpricks, his irises impossibly pale, like pieces of silver.

His shaved head was pale white, like an eggshell, the skin stretched tight over the surface of his skull. There was a dark blue tattoo of a serpent stretching from his neck to above his ear, and a deep, ugly scar on his head; a white, puckered hairless crevasse that ran from his left temple practically all the way to his crown.

He just sat there, breathing.

Breathing.

The prison-issue grey tracksuit was small on his muscular frame, and the handcuffs forced him to clasp his hands together, making him look like he was pondering a particularly thought-provoking question.

Which, Barnes supposed, he was.

They'd been shoved into one of the advocates' consulting rooms just off the main corridor. Barnes thought he could still smell the old cigarette smoke from a lifetime ago. The Portland stone walls absorbed the muffled hubbub from the court building proper. Somewhere a clock was ticking. If not for the tension radiating off the man opposite, the atmosphere would have been practically soporific.

"Well?" Kane said after another few minutes. His voice drowned out the silence; it sounded loud in the airless room.

Pearce said nothing, but turned his head fractionally towards Kane.

"We don't have all day," Kane said.

"Shame," Pearce said, his voice sounding like a sock full of slate chips. "I do. There's a screw looking at his watch right now, waiting to ferry me back to prison. You're making him late. That suits me fine."

"Stratton," Barnes said. Pearce's body seemed to contract slightly. "Can I call you Stratton?"

Pearce shrugged.

"You know you're going away for this, right? Kidnap, false imprisonment, GBH, conspiracy to hold a person in slavery, conspiracy to facilitate travel with a view to exploitation, the full shebang."

"Am I? My lawyer said something similar. He said, 'They've got a good case.' Which you might have. But it's not about that, is it?"

"Isn't it?"

"Nobody died. Nobody suffered life-changing injuries."

"You sure about that? You kept ten people manacled in a basement behind a fake wall."

"News to me. Didn't know they were there. I was just checking in. If I plead and show a bit of remorse, I bet you five quid I get less than twelve years. That means I'll be out on licence in five. Maybe sooner if I keep my nose clean. I'll take those odds."

"You could make it two," Barnes said.

Pearce sneered. "You don't have the clout to engineer that."

"Want to bet?"

"And how, by grassing? On whom?"

"The rest of the crew. The ones we arrested at the scene. They're nobodies. Foot soldiers. Single-celled amoebas. You're a sergeant at least. Middle manager. You have a position in the food chain."

"So?"

"So, you're connected."

"Who says I'm connected? I don't know who's running the game. I just say I was working under duress — what you gonna do then?"

"What's going to go down at the sporting event, Stratton?"

Pearce said nothing.

"The sports tournament," Barnes repeated. "We know your gang are planning something, but we don't know what, where or when. Give us that. You might save a life or two."

Pearce leaned forward, cupped his chin in a pistol grip and slowly tapped his index finger on his cheek while his eyes roamed the room.

Barnes and Kane exchanged glances.

"No idea what you're talking about," Pearce said, eventually.

"Turn Queen's," Barnes said. "Give us the rest of them, give us the tournament attack, the house of cards folds and you see daylight before you're thirty-five."

"Witness protection?"

"We don't call it that, but yes. Something like that."

"You realise I'd have a contract on my sodding head for the rest of my life? Like those fuckin' losers who burn their credit cards and keep looking over their shoulder for the bailiffs. Not appealing. My way, I get out clean and settle the debt. And no one on my side thinks I've done anything other than take one for the team."

"What about your son? And his mother?" Kane said.

Barnes looked sideways at Kane. Pearce's breathing stopped. When it started again, it was silent.

"You want to see him grow up, right?" Kane said.

Pearce straightened up in his chair and worked his shoulders. Something loud popped back there.

"Boss is right," Barnes said. "It's the difference between seeing the lad while he's still a lad."

Pearce sat forward and laced his manacled hands together.

"Don't do that," he said. "Whatever I do or don't say, your job is to protect them. That doesn't change. You have no leverage. And if anything happens to them . . ."

He jabbed both his forefingers at the detectives.

". . . it's your fault."

"God forbid," Kane said.

Pearce thumped the bottoms of his fists on the solid oak table and stood up. Barnes just about managed to catch himself before he flinched.

"We're done."

"We won't be back, you know," Barnes said. "This is a once-in-a-lifetime opportunity."

Pearce pressed past them to the door. Barnes had the sense to move back slightly — Kane, however, stayed right in Pearce's fighting arc and, if Pearce had chosen to swing, Kane's jaw would have been broken in two places before he'd had any idea what was going on.

The two prison transport escorts flanking the doorway received Pearce as he opened the door. They looked pretty sharp.

Barnes turned in his seat.

"I'm curious," he said. "We kind of got you in here under false pretences. No lawyer. I owe the prison drivers a decent six–pack each. It wouldn't have worked if you hadn't agreed to see us. Why?"

Pearce fixed Barnes with his gaze. Barnes felt himself being drawn into it. Those eyes had seen violent death. Barnes just knew it.

And then, as Barnes's peripheral vision went grey and he found himself unable to concentrate on anything other than Pearce's silver eyes, a shudder took hold of his insides like a rubber band, holding him rigid to the seat and sending a feeling like sheets of water pouring through him.

And he couldn't tear his eyes away.

"I like to know what the opposition looks like," Pearce said. "And I remember faces."

* * *

"What now?" Kane asked in the car back to Eastbourne.

"Well, we've got a couple of options. We can try to bug his cell. Or we can stay true to our word and throw everything at getting him convicted. Or we can do both."

"If he doesn't talk, what are our chances of identifying the rest of the management structure?"

Barnes pondered this for a moment. They passed the enormous stone snail marking the entrance to the Cuilfail Tunnel, just as a motorbike tore up the outside of their car, the sound of its engine rifling in the confined concrete cylinder like a rocket taking off. This time, they both flinched.

"Idiot," Barnes said. "Double-whites along here, as well."

"Let's get after him."

"In this thing?"

"It's a police car. Does it not have blue lights?"

Barnes scoffed.

"Pool car? Lucky it's got four wheels. Anyway, going back to your question," Barnes said, the wall lights of the tunnel stretching over them like amber vertebrae, "I would say being able to identify the rest of the gang without someone talking is slim. There's still plenty of work to do with their phones, online footprint, financials, all that business, but it just depends on how careful they've been."

He turned to face Kane.

"I hate to say it, boss, but his point about twelve years or less is probably right. Just depends on if he pleads or holds out for a full trial."

"We should go back and see her — Roxy," Kane said, staring ahead down the road. "She may remember something else."

"I put one of my best Tier 3 interviewers on it. There may be more she remembers, but I doubt it."

"They might get something more out of her about this sporting event she talked about. Some more detail."

"They might. But that's intelligence. The interview is evidential. All focused on what's gone before, rather than what might be coming."

"Either way, he wasn't going to give it up. We should—"

"You done your personal safety training, boss?"

Kane said nothing, but looked sideways at Barnes as he drove.

"You were right in his fighting arc. He could have laid you out cold without you even having a chance to put your guard up."

"Thanks for the advice," Kane said, still staring.

"He'd have done it, too," Barnes murmured, thinking back to the slow knowledge that had awoken inside him when he'd looked into that silver gaze. "Not a moment's hesitation."

CHAPTER THIRTY-TWO

Kenneth was unable to sleep. Unable to think clearly. Unable to concentrate on anything much beyond putting one foot in front of the other. Wave after wave of unfamiliar good feelings swept through his system on an almost constant basis, his stomach in a perpetual churn of swarming butterflies.

Roxy.

He couldn't remember the last time someone had been so nice to him. So unquestioningly pleasant. So *tactile*. On the till in the petrol station there had been the odd kind word or sympathetic cluck — usually from older ladies — that stretched a fraction beyond pleasantries and simply passing the time of day, but that was it.

Kenneth knew that it would be unsavoury to some. He was old enough to be her father, and he was acutely aware that his loud voice and somewhat intense manner had caused more than a few people to cross the road, just to be on the safe side. It wasn't at all lost on him that someone — Nurse Ratched, probably, or a concerned friend — would probably be saying to her: *You shouldn't be quite so nice. So open. He'll get the wrong idea.*

To which Kenneth would say: Stuff and nonsense. First of all, he was a gentleman, thank you very much. Second,

Roxy was a grown-up, albeit admittedly a vulnerable, traumatised one. But third, and most important of all, no one else on the outside could fully appreciate what he and Roxy had been through. What they had been through *together*. Well-meaning friends and overbearing nurses based their opinions on what they had been told and invited to imagine. But they had not been there in the basement with Kenneth and Roxy. Theirs was a shared, locked-down experience. Kenneth, whether people liked it or not, had saved Roxy from the hellhole her captors had confined her to. Admittedly, the route to freedom had been rather more circuitous than he'd have liked — and the shame of putting Roxy back in danger mere hours after she'd escaped it still licked at his core, despite Roxy's unbridled forgiveness — but it was freedom nonetheless.

The reality of his day-to-day existence was exactly that: reality. Kenneth didn't trust the good feelings associated with summer weather. They were flighty and aloof. Hot sun and salt breeze and the perpetual aroma of frying and suntan lotion on a thousand different skins were as elusive as dreams, and to be treated, accordingly, with extreme caution. Grey winter days as bleak as gunmetal, when the trees were bare and the air was a constant bite — that was reality. When the weather and Kenneth's mood were indiscernible from one another — that was reality.

So, when Kenneth trudged up Seaside Road back to his flat, past the grime-smeared windows and blackened brickwork of empty shopfronts, chips of ice and brown slush sliding under his feet, his collar turned up against the wind, he felt more at home, more awake.

That's not to say he liked it. If anything, the wind was taunting him, digging under his fingernails, telling him: *What would she see in you? She's just feeling sorry for you. You wait till the trial is done. She'll stick a lawsuit up your behind for nearly getting her killed. Get real.*

After a few days of this, Kenneth had come to believe this voice, to the extent that he almost thought he'd imagined the whole encounter with Roxy.

When he turned the key in the flimsy Yale lock to his flat, he bent down to pick up the post, such as it was. There was the usual assortment of brightly coloured fast-food flyers, leaflets advertising window cleaning services and letters that looked important but were addressed to "The Occupier" or had "Marketing material enclosed" stamped on the back.

There was one that didn't fit this mould, however. It looked important. As in, genuinely important. It wasn't a bill, Kenneth was sure. The stationery was too good.

He shrugged his reusable shopping bag off his shoulder and onto the kitchen floor. He placed the letter on the melamine worktop and carefully flicked it open with a butter knife.

There was a logo of a leaf in a circle at the top of the letter, underneath which *TENDERSTEM SERVICES LTD* was written in swirling cursive. There was no street address, only a postcode.

The letter was brief.

Dear Mr Rix,

Further to your recent visit to our patient, F has confirmed she would like it very much if you would be able to visit again. Please contact reception to arrange a mutually convenient appointment.

As ever, please treat correspondence with this facility with the utmost confidentiality.

Yours sincerely,

C. Foulkes
Senior Nurse Practitioner

Kenneth carried the letter through to the front room and sat down heavily, his heart drumming in his chest. He couldn't believe it. Just as he was wondering how to re-initiate contact without looking like a total weirdo, just as his own rotten meteorological alter ego was telling him he was a loser fantasist who'd imagined the whole thing, here was unfettered proof that confirmed what he'd hoped all along.

He and Roxy were friends.

CHAPTER THIRTY-THREE

Paul Gamble would have never admitted it, but he was rather enjoying his custody posting. It certainly wasn't anywhere near as bad as he'd been expecting. Nobody asked to go to custody — they were rotated in and out in a reasonably regular carousel of complaining sergeants. There were some who, in thirty years' loyal service, had managed to swerve it, but not many. He'd heard tell of sergeants being dragged in kicking and screaming — then, once they were established, you couldn't get them out.

This, he could believe. Sure, he did more night shifts than he ever had on CID, and some nights, when there was a full moon, the screams that echoed from one end of the cell block to the other could become a little wearing. There was always the tiny possibility that somebody might die in their cell, which was a whole world of grief, but all this was offset by the fact that he had no caseload.

It sounded self-evident, but all investigations were time-bound. CCTV got wiped, witnesses forgot, victims moved house, the press lost interest. In a career spent mostly in plain clothes, Gamble knew that, if you didn't have your perp in the cells within forty-eight hours, chances were your case was ending up in the teetering, ever-growing stack of files in the out-tray marked "unsolved". This unsteady tower usually comprised somewhere between ninety and a hundred per cent of every crime that had ever come his way.

Every so often, usually on a slow news day, the *Daily Mail* would throw a wobbly about this and run a splash about the apparent rampant wave of unsolved crime sweeping the nation. This shit subsequently slid on down the hill in varying degrees, depending on who was in charge at the time, but Gamble had pretty much got used to this. In his view, the police were an easy target. The issue, as far as Gamble could make out, was not the number of crimes that the police were solving, but the fact that there was a revolving door in and out of the justice system, with a great swathe of individuals keeping the CID in gainful employment who, despite all manner of heinous antecedents, were not — and for no good reason that Gamble could see — in prison. One of Gamble's more frequent flyers had, after being plonked before a JP for fourteen breaches of a supposedly cast-iron ASBO, been sentenced to a £20 fine and an order insisting that he go and see his GP. As far as Gamble could see, this kind of thing seldom made the front pages.

So, when you had a team of five detectives, each carrying an average of fifty investigations on their caseload, it stood to reason that the balance was finely tipped. Gamble's consolation to himself was that, despite his grizzled outlook and salty, time-to-retire mentality, he still lay in bed looking at the ceiling wondering how the hell he was meant to get around to them all. He figured this meant he still cared.

But, in custody, there was no caseload, no staff to supervise, no on-call and, contrary to his preconceptions, more overtime than he could stomach. He could come to work, strap in for his nine hours, then go home again without giving it a second thought. His work mobile had become practically redundant.

But he never would have admitted it. Outwardly, he was a disgruntled detective for whom hanging up the CID autumn catalogue of cut-price BHS plain clothes in favour of a uniform was the ultimate ignominy. Outwardly, he was on a determined mission to debunk the reasons that had led to him being here in the first place, and — who knew? — maybe take a few of the fuckers down with him on the way.

His thoughts were interrupted by an angry buzzer cutting through the relative calm at the bridge. He looked up at the CCTV monitor to see a couple of traffic cops in the holding bay, flanking a man in handcuffs who was so tall Gamble couldn't see his face in the monitor. He looked relatively calm, but seeing the two traffic officers still caused Gamble's heart to sink. A career in CID didn't lend itself to a working knowledge of the Road Traffic Act.

Gamble hit the door release button and the lock to the heavy iron door clanked open. The officers escorted their quarry up to the bridge. Gamble picked up his pen and peeled off a new blank custody record sheet.

"What have we here?" he said, not looking up.

"Positive breath test," one of the officers said. "Pulled him over on King Offa Way. Just need to do EBTI."

"OK. Quick risk assessment and you can crack on," Gamble said, trying to conceal his relief. Drink-driving was a relatively straightforward one. A roadside breath test only got you into the police station, where the Evidential Breath Testing Instrument lay in wait to provide the sample that could actually be used in court. That being the case, time was of the essence.

"Listen up," Gamble said, scribbling on his record. "I'm authorising your detention for the purposes of . . ."

He finally looked up, to give the prisoner the courtesy of eye contact, and wished he hadn't.

"Hello, Sarge," the prisoner said, a broad grin breaking across his face.

"Sarge, you okay?" the arresting officer said. "Look like you've seen a ghost."

The bridge was an elevated platform used by the custody officers, and gave them — usually — a good two or three feet on the prisoners. In this case, however, the detainee was so tall that Gamble's eyes were practically level with his.

This was not what had caused Gamble's sharp intake of breath, however. Since arriving in custody, he had encountered more than a few of CID's more loyal customers, many of whom had wanted to know why Gamble had been bumped so unceremoniously back into uniform. (It was strange, Gamble thought, how so many of the criminal fraternity saw uniform as a step down.)

Gamble's recognition of this particular individual came from somewhere else, though.

The goon that had approached him outside the hospital. Not the yappy one that had done all the talking and had come to his house dressed as Royal Mail, but the huge great neck-snapper that had sat in the back seat.

He'd come to visit.

"How you been keeping, Sarge?"

Gamble swallowed. The goon's grin didn't falter.

The traffic cops looked from their prisoner to Gamble and back again, the confusion apparent on their faces. Eventually they ushered him off to the EBTI room, the goon looking back over his shoulder to offer Gamble another winning grin as he was marched off.

Gamble managed to hold it together, his mind racing. He finished the risk assessment and populated the remainder of the custody record, then got one of the custody assistants to go and process the goon after he'd finished blowing into the EBTI.

Once the fingerprints had been put into the system, a confirmed ID came up on the screen.

Vernon "Golden Wonder" Dodge, born 1972 in Willenhall. Six foot six, according to the PNC. Jesus wept. The list of prior convictions included some meaty sentences for knifepoint robbery, GBH, assault, aggravated burglary and conspiracy to kidnap. This only played to Gamble's earlier social theory that there were certain people that had no business ever being outside the four walls of a prison, and yet here we were.

Gamble scratched his head. Up until now, he'd had no idea who the knuckle-dragger was, other than a physical description. As a result of Dodge gracing his presence in the cell block, he now had a confirmed ID. In the normal run of things, this was fifteen-love to the cops.

If, however, he'd deliberately engineered the arrest to get close to Gamble, then this was a concern. Whatever outfit he was operating with, bringing yourself to the attention of the cops for some kind of minor infringement such as a traffic offence was not likely. This meant it was either a sanctioned tactic, or the guy was a bit of a loose cannon.

All of the theories intertwined like a maze in a kids' activity book, but ended up in the same final destination of Bloody Bad News.

One of the traffic officers appeared from the EBTI room, peering at a printout that resembled a till receipt.

"Well?" Gamble said. "What did he blow?"

"Thirty-two," the traffic officer said. He looked disappointed.

Gamble raised his eyebrows in query. "Career detective."

"Means he walks out of here with a flea in his ear. But he walks. No charge sheet."

Gamble swallowed.

Fifteen-all.

If the whole encounter wasn't a big fat coincidence, then he was doubly nervous. Could Dodge — his gang — have deliberately orchestrated the drinking of just enough to get pulled over and arrested, but no more than that? Was that worth the risk of Gamble knowing his name, if it meant he could put the frighteners on hope by turning up at the cell block?

Only one way to find out.

Gamble discreetly dialled the desk extension to the bridge from his mobile phone. When it rang, he snatched it up before anyone else could answer it. Not that he would normally have needed to rush — when the custody phone rang, it was usually a Mexican stand-off as to who answered it. Still, better safe than sorry.

"Custody, Sergeant Gamble. Who? Yes, he's here," Gamble said loudly into the phone, wishing he'd muted his mobile. Hearing his own voice echo back at him with a half-second delay made it difficult to concentrate. "They've just finished on the EBTI. No, it doesn't look like he'll be charged. Didn't blow high enough. He'll be out of there toot sweet. You still want a word? Okay, hang on."

Gamble placed the receiver carefully on the desk and stepped down from the bridge. He walked over to a tiny, brightly lit consulting room barely bigger than a phone booth, which was partitioned off from the main cell block by a large pane of soundproof glass. Its only features were a bench moulded to the wall and a tabletop jutting out from the wall with a desk phone on it.

Gamble stepped into the booth, picked up the phone, pressed the receiver against his chest and stuck his head out of the door.

"Phil?" he called. The traffic officer holding the EBTI printout looked over. "Your man's brief is on the phone. Can you spare him for five minutes?"

The traffic officer frowned, and Gamble felt a shiver ripple down his back.

"I'm about to kick him loose. No further action. What's he want to speak to him for?"

Gamble smiled sweetly. "Something about PACE rights applying twenty-four-seven including during bank holidays and acts of war."

The traffic officer shrugged. "I'm done with him. He's getting out scot-free in ten minutes. I'm not hanging around just so he can talk to his rep, though."

Bonus.

"Don't you worry about that," Gamble said. "You stand down. I'll kick him out."

The traffic officer brightened a little. "You sure?"

"Yep. Got to get you boys back on the roads. Save us from all those other idiots on four wheels."

The traffic officer tossed his paperwork in the bin and practically skipped back into the EBTI room to collect Vernon Dodge. He and his oppo escorted Dodge over to

Gamble in the consulting booth, removed the handcuffs, and then the pair of them broke off and into the sunset without breaking pace.

Suddenly, instinctively aware that even if he took two big strides backwards out of the consulting room into the main cell block area, it would still have been all too easy for Vernon Dodge to swing his hammer-like fists into Gamble's skull, his left and right hands went to the pepper spray and handcuffs on his belt and rested there.

Dodge noticed. The grin split his face even wider. Gamble didn't return it.

"Relax, Sarge. I'm not about to lay you out in your own domain."

"Hold up the phone to your ear," Gamble said. "At least make it look like you're talking."

Dodge held Gamble's gaze, and then slowly, pointedly, held the receiver delicately up to his face.

"What are you doing here?" Gamble said.

Dodge croaked laughter from somewhere in his throat.

"Apparently that's already a matter of record," he said, nodding towards the assorted paperwork hanging on various clipboards on the wall behind the bridge. "Seems I was a little, um, *cavalier* in my attitude towards driving while under the influence."

"And yet you will shortly be on your merry way with your licence intact."

"Just lucky, I guess." Dodge widened his eyes and shrugged.

"Is everything a piss-take with you lot?"

"I can be serious," Dodge said, the affected good humour dropping from his face. "We haven't heard from you, Sarge."

Gamble tried — and failed — to suppress a swallow. He was suddenly aware that the usual chatter of activity that tended to populate Hastings dungeons on a late shift seemed to be conspicuously absent. He'd expected the ambient noise to provide some sort of cover — screaming prisoners, belligerent legal reps, constant phone traffic, detectives bustling about the place trying to get noticed. He chanced a look over his shoulder. Nobody was paying him any attention. Just a lull in the proceedings.

"Tick tock, and all that," Dodge said.

"Last I recall, you came to me. I told you to fuck off. There's not much else to fill the sandwich."

"Did you hand the money in?" Dodge's grin was positively reptilian.

Gamble was silent.

"Didn't think so. I'd say that contract is pretty well binding now."

"There's nothing to report," Gamble said, in a hoarse whisper.

"Is that right? I haven't told you what we might be interested in yet."

Gamble looked over his shoulder again. "Maybe we should do this another time."

Dodge shook his head slowly: *no way.*

"I've gone to a lot of trouble to see you," Dodge said. "We don't like being ghosted. It's a little rude on your part. Besides, it seems your change of fortunes might make you less useful. That's a shame."

Dodge waggled his index finger up and down, indicating Gamble's newly uniformed appearance.

"A real shame."

Gamble suddenly felt cold. Even he was not pig-headed enough to realise what was being insinuated.

"Look, this actually works out better," he said.

"How do you figure that?" Dodge said. "You're not working cases any more."

"Exactly. My old job . . ."

"When you were a detective, you mean. When you had a bit of something about you."

". . . I could only look into my own cases. I start sniffing around cases that are nothing to do with me, I won't get very far before people start asking questions. In here, I run the whole gauntlet. I might get Little Johnny in for a two-quid shoplifting on Monday, then for all I know I'm booking Ronnie bloody Kray in on Tuesday. And in here, I can explain nearly everything away. In the interests of prisoner welfare."

To his own ear, Gamble sounded like he was babbling.

"You're a real glass-half-full type, aren't you? I admire that."

There was a burst of activity behind them. Gamble looked round to see four uniformed patrol cops dragging a man-mountain past the bridge. His skin was bright red and he was swinging and yelling and shaking violently. They hawked him down the corridor to the cells, and the sound faded a little.

Gamble turned back to Dodge.

"Rather him than me," Dodge grinned. "You were saying."

"I was saying: you haven't told me what it is you *want*."

Dodge's heavy brow furrowed, all faux good humour gone. He breathed steadily. *This* face, Gamble was convinced, was the last thing that a good few people had seen before they died.

"The raid at the farm. Out at Pevensey."

Gamble swallowed. He wanted to say, *That was you too?* but he choked it down.

"Can you give me any more?" he croaked.

"You don't need any more." Dodge's voice was quiet, and sounded like flint scraping against a leather strap. "You know what I'm talking about. One of ours dead. Four on remand. Operation Turnbull."

"How do you know—"

"You lot put more in the public domain than you think," Dodge said. "How is it, every time the cops speak to the press they sound like a stuttering, bumbling bunch of fucking morons? Like the Stasi, only without the wit."

"What is it you want to know?" Gamble could barely get the words out.

"Everything."

"I . . ."

"*Then* make it go away."

"What? I can't possibly . . . are you insane? How do you expect me to . . ."

Dodge stood up. Gamble half wished the lug would just snap his neck and be done with it.

"I think your Code of Practice says I should have been out of here about half an hour ago," Dodge said. "Wouldn't want to get you in trouble."

He pushed past Gamble into the main cell block area, then stopped and turned to face him.

"You mind?" he said, indicating with that heavy brow the main doors to the block, the big blue iron gate between heaven and hell.

"Exit door for detainee six, please." Gamble called to the bridge, unable to tear his eyes from Dodge's face.

There was the sound of a buzzer and a heavy metallic clank, and the door was released.

Dodge reached out and grabbed the back of Gamble's head with a hand like a steel wok. Gamble went as rigid as a man having a seizure, and then Dodge leaned in and planted a huge kiss on Gamble's cheek. There was a scraping feeling like a scourer being rubbed on his face as stubble met stubble, and the smell of cigarette ash and sweat, then Dodge guffawed, pushed his way out of the blue iron door and disappeared.

* * *

Gamble eventually managed to quell the minor clamour that arose from various people in the cell block insisting that Dodge be arrested for assaulting a police officer. He told them he would sort it, and eventually they dispersed.

He took a slow drive home after his shift finished, wondering — only briefly — about going up to the East Hill and just driving off and being done with it.

When he replayed the words he'd spoken, the words that confirmed his complicity in whatever enterprise he was now embroiled in, the shame seeped down his insides like lava rolling off a volcano, shame he didn't know he had in him.

He hadn't known who Dodge was prior to tonight. As in, he had no ID for him. Like sacrificing a pawn in a game of chess, Dodge's outfit clearly thought that putting their alpha gorilla forward to intimidate Gamble — giving up his name to the cops in the process — was a risk worth taking.

In any case, it was a small advantage to Gamble. Provided the shame and despair had dissipated enough by the morning to bump him into some kind of action, he could do something with that.

But that would have to wait until the morning.

He brought up Caroline's number on his phone. He looked at his watch. Gone midnight.

He hit "Dial", then, when it started to ring, he cancelled the call. He could bother her with this another day. Besides, what would he say to her? He'd have to tell her everything. She'd be disgusted. Beyond disgusted, in fact. She'd always known that, to be effective in this game, you'd have to keep some dubious company, but this was different. This was a cancer that would eat up your life, your home, your family — and with no chance of ever going into remission. Better she didn't know about it until he felt so pathetic that he could do nothing but confess.

Instead, he drove home, reflected on the fact that he was thankful for not owning a gun, and gobbled down some industrial-strength headache tablets with a third of a bottle of Captain Morgan.

* * *

When he awoke, Gamble felt even worse, but this did not come as a surprise. The early mornings had always been the worst. That moment, shortly after waking, when the enormity of the day ahead pressed down on him like a heavy cloud, was when he always felt like he would lose. The night before, he might have rolled home in the early hours, the sudden midnight silence in the house almost as violent as the shift itself, where he might have been called out to a child death, a stabbing or a violent rape. Usually, when he got home, he felt more or less fine, but when he woke, the kaleidoscope of crime scenes that spun around his mind threatened to cripple him.

Today was the same — worse, in fact. For those exposed to trauma on the job, there was an array of different avenues of support: occupational health, counselling, psychological screening. If, however, you found yourself on the receiving end of a bung so insidious that it had taken the enormous gorilla himself to point out that failure to report the offer of dirty cash was enough to permanently sideline his career, you'd find yourself with a distinct lack of sympathetic ears. Gamble had actually stuffed the cash into an evidence bag and put it in his sock drawer — but, as Dodge had pointed out, that omission was enough. No one knew about it, of course, but it would only take an anonymous phone call from Dodge or one of his crew to get people looking.

Still, as he kept telling himself, he had the small advantage of Dodge voluntarily giving up his own ID in order to get close to Gamble. As he'd already theorised, Dodge — or someone above him — had clearly decided seeing Gamble go pale was worth the risk, but that didn't mean Gamble wasn't going to try to make the best of it.

Gamble hauled himself out of bed. There weren't many concessions to domestic comfort in his sparsely furnished flat, with the exception of his complicated-looking espresso machine. He jabbed the button and the thing roared into life, grinding a clutch of coffee beans into a fine powder. The aroma of the freshly ground beans kick-started an endorphin or two in Gamble's brain, and he felt mildly better.

He was still buggered if he was going to sit here and stew in the silence, however, and he dressed quickly, intending to go in early. His shift didn't officially start until two that afternoon, but — unlike the CID office, where shift times were irrelevant and one's mere presence was enough to get sucked into the daily maelstrom; that is, if one was stupid enough to go in early — he was surplus to numbers in the cell block until shift handover, and could do some of his own research until he took over. Another tick for the custody posting.

He drove to work and tucked himself away in the inspector's office. There was one inspector covering both the Eastbourne and Hastings cell blocks in equal measure but, given that the Eastbourne block was everything Hastings was not in terms of space, cleanliness and general modernity, the Hastings office was seldom used.

It didn't take long to establish that the so-called carelessness on Vernon Dodge's part in revealing himself to Gamble was not even an occupational hazard as far as the enormous lump was concerned. His record was pages and pages long, with warning markers for drug supply, violence towards police, firearms and intermittent mental health problems. There was enough intelligence on the record to suggest that somebody was looking at him, but Dodge's last conviction had been four years previously — a guilty plea to assault that had seen him with a four-week custodial sentence and not a lot else.

Gamble scrutinised the report. It was interspersed with one of the episodes of mental ill health; by all accounts, Dodge's mother had locked him in his bedroom to deal with his alcohol abuse the old-fashioned way — cold turkey. Dodge had taken exception to this and his mother had been in the way when he'd finally burst out of the room. While Mum was not particularly well known in terms of a criminal history, she was nevertheless of a breed that did not talk to the police, but she made an exception on this occasion for, it seemed, her son's own good.

Gamble noted that it was a domestic situation that had actually led to the conviction. When he looked at how Dodge occupied himself in terms of a day job — drug debt enforcement, suspected gun running, obedience cultivation — he had been careful. He'd not been convicted for anything resembling organised criminal activity since he was sixteen years old and had yet been, Gamble presumed, some way off getting his stripes.

A check of Dodge's documented associates led, via a common denominator known as the Keber crime group, to another ID — Len Sterling. It was a very old custody photo, but Gamble instantly recognised Sterling's fuck-you grin. Besides this fact, it looked like the small advantage Gamble had been nursing was evaporating as he read, but the one thing that did interest him was that his erstwhile CID colleague, DC Chick Grant, seemed to feature as investigating officer on quite a few of the cases, as well as being named in a few of the intelligence reports.

He logged off the machine and sat for a moment, thinking. The office was silent apart from a small carriage clock ticking quietly on a display cabinet behind the desk. Grant was main office CID, so wouldn't normally have anything like the capacity needed to do anything proactive on mid-level knuckle-draggers. Of course, everyone would like their local detectives to be on the front foot when it came to organised criminality, but the constant churning through case files like hamsters on a wheel seldom lent itself to such targeting. The kind of attention Dodge deserved needed to be at a Force or possibly even a regional level.

He got up and stretched. He would have to ask her.

He picked up the desk phone, thought for a moment, then replaced it.

Better to do this in person.

* * *

As luck had it, Chick Grant was also on a late shift. Unlike Gamble, whose duties necessitated him being in the cell block at all times, Grant, as a detective, could come and go pretty much as she pleased in the interests of working through her caseload. Despite this, and unlike himself, Gamble figured that Grant finishing on time was optimistic indeed. This gave him time to get over to Eastbourne and intercept her.

When he got to the patrol base in Hammonds Drive, he hesitated. He was in half-blues, and the thought of walking into his old office in uniform looking like a kid in the dressing-up box was suddenly too much.

Instead, he drove circuits around the car park until he saw Grant's Mini Cooper, parked in one of the red bays marked "Operational Vehicles Only".

He shook his head. Typical.

He checked his watch. If she had a prisoner, she could be hours. If she was out at a scene, likewise. If she was just finishing up some paperwork, she might only be a few minutes.

The patrol base was a utilitarian, single-level building that, apart from the Horsey Sewer that ran behind it down to the Bridgemere allotments, was practically surrounded on all sides by industrial units and distribution centres. It had been purchased from one of the big-hitting energy companies some years previously and was seriously in need of an overhaul. Gamble could, in theory, have mooched around the sides of the building and peered in at the windows to see what Grant was up to, but he eventually decided that, even in uniform, that was going to attract some attention. Not only that, but it was bloody cold. In the end he reclined the seat in his car and waited for her to come out to the Mini.

She appeared about half an hour later, jacket on, bag over shoulder, and walked to the car. The Mini's hazards did a quick double flash as she approached and unlocked it, and he was out and over to her before she could drive off.

She looked up in alarm as he approached, and he eased off his stride a bit. The car park was not particularly well lit, just picking up the residual wash from the arc lights on the street and the pallet warehouse next door, and she didn't immediately recognise him.

"Chick. It's me, Paul."

She squinted. "Jesus, Paul. I was about to lamp you."

"Got five minutes?"

"Something wrong with the phone?"

"There is, actually."

She looked suspicious.

"It's about Vernon Dodge."

"Who?"

"He's a suspect in one of your case files."

"If we're talking shop, can I at least book back on and claim the overs?"

"Do whatever you need to."

She frowned in the gloom. "Want to come back into the office?"

"No. We can talk in your car, if you like. Or mine."

She eyed him. "No. Mine. Get in, then."

Gamble got in the passenger seat and eyeballed the Darth Vader air freshener stuck to the dashboard, which, he surmised, based on the faint smell of cigarettes and the less faint smell of perfume, was no longer emitting anything useful.

Grant got in beside him. The leather creaked. She looked uncomfortable.

"Okay, this is weirder than talking outside. What's with all the cloak and dagger? Can't we go to the pub or something?"

"This won't take long. Vernon Dodge."

"Not ringing any bells."

Gamble raised his eyebrows, instantly suspicious. Was she really going to play dumb?

"You remember how I had fifty jobs on my caseload?" she said, as if reading his mind. "Well, it didn't get any better after you left."

"I didn't *leave*. I was *moved*."

She lit a cigarette and cracked the window.

"You mind?"

"It's your car."

There was a moment's silence.

"New guy's a dick," she said, expelling smoke.

"I'll take that as a compliment."

"They've put an acting in. Don't know him. He's from off Division. He actually said to me: 'I don't do unsolved crime. Either we charge, or the victim signs to say it didn't happen and we no-crime it.' He actually said that. And he's *acting*."

"Sounds like he's been Shaw'd."

"Good and proper."

"Well, Vernon Dodge is a suspect for one of your fifty."

"More like seventy now."

"Whatever. He was in the cell block yesterday."

"As in, arrested?"

"Yes."

She hit the dashboard. A flake of ash tumbled into the footwell.

"For fuck's *sake*. And no one thought to tell me?"

Gamble felt himself flush, and was momentarily thankful for the gloom. For most detectives, a prisoner in the hand was worth an awful lot of elbow grease. Failing to check what else your prisoner might be of interest for — and to whom — was a fairly basic error for an arresting officer. *Not to mention a custody officer*, he thought.

"What was he in for?" she asked.

"Drink-drive. Blew under and got chucked out."

She expelled smoke. "And?"

"And he's one of your suspects. I just wanted to know about the job."

"You'll have to give me a bit more than that."

A couple of uniformed cops ambled out of the patrol base and took up position in the arc of Grant's headlights. They lit cigarettes and chatted in low tones. One of them cast a bored look towards Grant's car.

"Come on," she said, starting the engine. "Let's go for a drive."

They headed out onto Lottbridge Drove and Grant kept to a steady pace just inside the speed limit, the overhead lights rhythmically blipping over the car. Brightly lit car showrooms and huge factory outlets lined the dark road, bringing images of Americanised consumer boulevards to Gamble's mind; then they were past them, and there was nothing but the marshland of the Levels on one side and the black expanse of the golf course on the other.

"From what I read, it's a bit of an overinflated kidnap. Happened a few weeks ago. Street user owes mid-range dealer a few hundred quid, so our friend Mr Dodge is appointed to extract the debt."

"Oh, *that* one," Grant said, turning off towards the town.

"Finally," Gamble said. "Anyway, Vernon takes the poor unfortunate on a bit of a guided tour of the area before dumping him at a petrol station outside Gatwick. Our victim has a couple of black eyes but is otherwise okay. The journey was peppered with several threats and an ultimatum for delivering the money — twenty-four hours — and at one point the barrel of a gun was shown to him."

"Yes, I remember it now."

"What happened? Did he live to tell the tale?"

"What happened is, the suspect was almost deliberately conspicuous. He drove chummy to practically every public place en route. The CCTV trawl took me fucking days."

For no good reason that Gamble could see, Grant stuck the Mini half on the kerb at the apex of Whitley Bridge, and got out to peer at the railway track.

"I sometimes stop here to look at the trains," she admitted, as if sensing Gamble's bewilderment.

Gamble joined her on the bridge wall, and gazed out at the oddly inviting lights of the main railway terminus in the distance. Below them, the soot-coated walls separating the tracks themselves from the tired-looking overhanging residences either side were deluged with colourful graffiti. A line of rolling stock stood silent and still in a siding lined with massive vertical roller brushes, awaiting a morning jet wash before heading off to wherever.

Gamble found himself quietly hopeful that the trains were all she contemplated when she came up here.

"What happened to the job?" Gamble said.

"That's the funny thing. Our victim is — bizarrely — still onside. You know what they're like — all piss and vinegar in the first ten minutes, wanting the perp's head on a spike. Then you try and pin the little shits down for a statement and it's like trying to catch a baby rabbit on crack. Only not as cute," she added.

"He going the distance?" Gamble said.

"So far. I eventually got his statement, and he assured me that it was all true, that he would turn up in court and even look half-presentable."

"And was it? True, I mean."

"Well, after much expense, the CCTV jumble now forms a coherent narrative and, yes, it does seem to corroborate most of the story. Senor Dodge must not have banked on him actually talking to the cops."

A blinding flash lit up the underside of the bridge. For a moment Gamble thought it was lightning, then there was the crunch of metal rolling on metal as the evening train to Ashford ground its way into the terminus. Eastbourne, strictly speaking, wasn't the end of the line, but to connect to Hastings and beyond necessitated rolling all the way into the V-shaped terminus, and then back out again to continue your journey like a puppet on a string.

"Why do you think he did?" Gamble asked.

"Well, CICA were only going to cough up if he cooperated with the investigation."

"Two shiners wouldn't get you much in the way of compo."

"True."

"Fear, maybe? Did Dodge come to collect?"

"He did. And chummy paid up. About nine hundred quid."

"How did he manage that?"

"Well, that's my only other rationale for why he is so keen to cooperate. To come by that kind of money in less than a day, he must have gone on a spree. Burgling, robbing, shoplifting, you name it. With the clock ticking he wouldn't have been able to invest too much effort in covering his tracks, so he probably figured he'd get caught. This was a pre-emptive strike. You get to make yourself look good by supporting an investigation, you get — maybe — enough police attention to stop the heavies coming back through the door, and, if you're really lucky, you tell a jury you only went nicking because you were under duress."

"Where is he now?"

"The victim? Spaced out in his hovel of a bedsit, I expect."

"Know what that sounds like to me?"

"What?"

"Operation Blackwater. The house fire that killed Kevin Bridger."

Grant shrugged. "Neanderthal enforcers in donkey jackets terrorising street users is not a new enterprise, Paul."

"You'd better check he's still alive."

Grant eyeballed him, then flicked her cigarette. "Was that all you wanted? What's your interest?"

"Just curious," he shrugged.

"Bull*shit*."

"I told you: he was in the cell block. I was running him against any active investigations and saw your name. Thought I'd come say hi."

"You didn't tell me while he was still somewhere that was of use to me, though, did you? Like a cell?"

Gamble looked at her. He didn't think she was buying it.

"You involved in the other job?" he said.

"What 'other job'?"

"The one out in Pevensey. Op Turnbull. The slave farm."

"Oh, that. That looks like a good one. No. Major Crime have pretty much got that locked down. They hoovered up a bunch of DCs to help them out. I wasn't one of them, though. Your man Dodge named in that one, too?"

Not in the way you're thinking, Gamble thought. He suddenly, desperately wanted to confess everything to Grant, but he managed to swallow it back down. Once that particular genie was out of the bottle, it wasn't ever going back in.

"What's happening with your thing?" she said.

He prompted her with his eyebrows.

"You know, your case. As in, *your* case. The whole dumping-the-new-superintendent-on-his-arse case."

He grimaced.

"Sorry," she said.

"Not your fault," he said grimly, after a moment. "Hurry up and wait. They've served papers. Hearing will be in six months or so. Case to answer for gross misconduct."

"Ah, shit, I'm sorry," she said.

He drummed his fingers on the bridge's cool brickwork and strained to listen to a PA announcement from the terminus in the distance.

"You think they're linked?" he said, eventually, as casually as he could manage. "The slave farm and Kevin?"

She stared at him. "I didn't. Now I do. What makes you say that?"

Because he wants me to make it go away. Wants me to shut down the whole investigation. As if I could do that.

She fixed on him for a moment. He could feel that his eyes were wide.

"Nothing," he said.

"What I mean is, you've mentioned both cases in the space of a minute. Why those two, if you didn't think they were linked?"

He didn't answer. His heart was racing in his chest.

"Do you think Kevin Bridger was somehow involved in the slave farm?"

He shrugged.

She stared.

He could see her thinking, could see the muscles in her jaw flexing as she ground her teeth together.

She took a step closer to him. "Paul . . . are you okay?"

"What do you mean?"

"I mean: you could have just come into the office to see me, but you chose to hang around by my car and wait for me to finish up."

"I didn't fancy venturing back into my old office wearing a uniform for the first time in twenty years. It's kind of ignominious, don't you think?"

"Any more ignominious than skulking around in the car park in the freezing cold looking like a stalker? You weren't *demoted*. I already said: there are these useful contraptions called phones."

"Funny."

"And then you pump me for information on my cases, but when I ask you why, you give me some flannel about just being curious."

"I don't know . . ."

"Paul, I may not be the best bloody detective on the Division, but you're not even *trying* to cover your tracks. A hamster in a suit of armour could spot you a mile off. You're up to something. I just don't know what."

He didn't answer.

"I'm not trying to catch you out, Paul. I just hope you haven't got yourself into something you can't get out of."

A wave of goosebumps swept over his shoulders.

She walked back over to the Mini and opened the driver's door.

"You coming, or what?" she said. Gamble hadn't moved.

"I . . . I think I'll go for a walk," he said, trying not think about the Mini's warm interior.

"Suit yourself," she said, then she started the engine and headed down off the bridge to Cavendish Place and the sea.

Gamble followed the direction of Grant's car, trudging down the hill to where Cavendish Place crossed with Ashford Road. He stopped for a moment at the crossroads, the street bathed in yellow light, the traffic lights silently flitting from red to amber to green, controlling invisible traffic.

He thought about a slow walk to the sea and back along the prom to his car. Clear his head a bit. But, as he realised he was five minutes from Kevin Bridger's flat, he doubled back onto Ashford Square at the foot of the bridge and walked parallel to the silent black expanse of the railway lines converging on the Eastbourne terminus — a good half an acre of sidings, scattered hardcore and green-and-yellow timber signal boxes that harked back to some forgotten year when London's Victorian elite descended on the seaside.

He cut behind the dark concrete shell of the Junction Road multistorey, and emerged next to Kwik-Fit and outside Kevin Bridger's flat.

It hadn't been touched. It was still a stinking, gutted black concrete shell, with sorry strands of frayed scene tape fluttering in the cold night air.

They walked into your house, set you on fire, and off they went again. A useless street user who was in debt to somebody his whole miserable life, and he was cauterised like an open wound.

Gamble eyed the gutter where he had pushed Kane over, and for just half a second thought that maybe he should just apologise and be done with it. All manner of sins can be washed away if you just front up, he thought.

He looked up at the burned-out shell. Dodge, the big meathead, had — intentionally or otherwise — confirmed to Gamble that, one way or another, Kevin Bridger's death and the slave farm outside Bexhill were connected, suggesting Dodge — or rather, his seniors — had some kind of hand in both.

Did Kevin know about the slave farm? Was he going to talk? Was he part of it? Is that why they silenced him? The DI — Barnes — would know. He worked in intelligence — and Kevin Bridger was an informant. He'd certainly know more than Gamble, who seemed to no longer pull any kind of access that counted.

The bare bones of the investigation reports — MO, victim details, suspect descriptions — were available on the records system for, technically, anyone with a good reason to look. Gamble didn't really have a good reason, but that hadn't stopped him sniffing around.

His browsing hadn't got him into the minutiae of the policy decisions, however. A couple of times he'd tried to reinstall himself into the Gold Group meetings for Op Blackwater, but had found himself pushing against a firmly closed door. The secretaries coordinating the meetings had put up a sturdy firewall, and weren't taken in by any of his guff. They were terribly sorry, they said, but they'd checked with the chairs of the respective meetings, and Mr Gamble's attendance was not required, thank you very much.

He heard voices behind him, and turned to see a couple of taxi drivers in the rank talking in low tones. One of them eyeballed Gamble, and he suddenly felt self-conscious.

He binned the idea of walking back to his car. It was bloody cold and his feet hurt, and so instead he walked up to Grove Road station, hoping to cadge a lift from a patrol car on a tea stop.

Quite without warning, the events of the previous forty-eight hours spun across his mind in a ticker-tape banner of career-ending headlines, causing a surging in his gullet. He threw up beside the steps outside the police station, wondering momentarily if the morning shift would put it down to some inebriated reveller or wandering street drinker, and eventually straightened up, panting.

He wiped his mouth with his sleeve and steadied himself on the solid Georgian walls. Keber had sent their heaviest heavy into the lions' den — Hastings custody — with an ultimatum for Gamble. In so doing they'd obviously considered that the fact of Dodge being identified, together with confirming — to Gamble, anyway — the link between Kevin Bridger's death and the slave farm, as being worth the effort.

This, whichever way you sliced it, wasn't good. There were any number of possible extrapolations one could draw from this particular tactic, but the most obvious one was screaming silently in Gamble's head.

Keber were ramping up.

Big time.

CHAPTER THIRTY-FOUR

Kenley fed the fish and left the house, so engrossed in his phone that he barely noticed Natalie pulling onto her driveway at the same time.

"Off somewhere?" she asked, locking the Punto.

Kenley jumped.

"Hey," he managed. "Yes, just off out."

Her eyes gleamed in the gloom.

"Just a couple of jars with the boys. Nothing exciting," he added, finally seeming to notice that she'd just got home. "You're back late."

She pulled a bottle of wine out of her bag.

"I've had a hell of a shift. Want to give the boys a rain check?"

Something pulled at Kenley's insides, and he found himself imagining what a gun barrel might taste like.

"I . . . I can't. Not tonight. Well, I say that — chances are we'll talk football and get-rich-quick schemes while contemplating the lot of the post–Gen X single man. I might only be an hour or two."

She shrugged, and gave him a smile.

"I'm not waiting up."

And then she was gone.

Kenley drove so slowly to the storage unit that he was over-taken by a couple of doddering Hondas, one of whom articulated their impatience with a blast of the horn, while the other pulled alongside and peered at him, presumably to check he wasn't having a heart attack at the wheel. Kenley barely noticed. It was as if he were attached to an invisible elastic band that grew tighter and tighter the further away he got from her house.

On the one hand, he knew he'd already blown it. Natalie knew his story about work was bullshit — she was a detective, for Christ's sake — and she wasn't going to give a career liar anything other than a swift boot to the kerb. But despite this, he desperately wanted to tell her everything. If he came clean now, they might have a chance. If he did, how-ever, there wasn't any permutation of possible consequences that didn't involve him being suspended by his ankles above an industrial paper shredder. The only storyline that had a vaguely decent outcome for them as a prospective couple was one where they spent their lives traversing the globe, trying to keep one step ahead of the Keber gang, whose intolerance for disloyalty spawned a particular brand of bloodlust. Any fool notion that this might be a romantic prospect was already dead in the water by virtue of her job, and her kid.

He felt sick as he pulled up to the barrier. His one sliver of consolation was that, he knew, the physiological reaction that glossy dating magazines might have called infatuation was fleeting. Once the chemicals in his system started to become a little less acrobatic, he might be able to make some rational decisions. Head not heart, and all that stuff. *Just ride it out for now*, he thought. *Ride it out*.

The padlock had already been removed, and so Kenley pushed the barrier carefully upwards. Sterling, Blue Ray and Golden Wonder were standing in a huddle by one of the load-ing bays. There was a dim sodium lamp above their heads, catching the sheets of drizzle as it blew through the weak beam.

"It's all right, we don't mind waiting," Sterling said. A clever comment passed through Kenley's mind, but he let it go. It vaguely occurred to him that he was the only one that

Head Office had thought to position relatively local to the hives — the house, the cover, it all played to him being a man of the town so he could keep an eye on operations. Pearce had been in the same boat. There was a logic to it, of course, but it was clearly risky. The others could waltz off into the sunset; Kenley, not so much.

This hadn't really occurred to him before, and he put it down to the gaps in his cover being exposed by his association with Natalie. A relationship with the enemy was not part of the plan.

As Kenley joined the group, they all shuffled further into the loading bay to get out of the cold. Sterling rolled the shutters down; Kenley grimaced at the sound of grinding metal. There was a small folding table by the wall. A single mobile phone lay on its surface.

"Head Office on speaker," Sterling said, nodding towards the phone.

Kenley stared grimly at the device.

"Evening," he muttered.

"Glad you could make it," the distorted robotic voice said. "I hope we haven't disturbed your evening too much."

Kenley rolled his eyes. One of the apes tittered.

"Have you all got diplomas in sarcasm overnight, or something?" Kenley said, trying not to sound too defensive.

For a moment there was nothing but the sound of the drizzle gradually turning into proper rain. It was collecting in a faulty gutter somewhere above them and running off in gushes into a puddle on the concrete. It sounded like a fat man taking a huge piss.

All eyes turned to Kenley.

"What?"

"You not chairing, boss?" Sterling said. "That's, er, what the terms of reference usually say."

"Ordinarily, yes. But ordinarily we wouldn't have Head Office as a fly-on-the-wall."

"Head Office is here because you've taken your eye off the ball," the phone said.

Kenley tried not to swallow. This wasn't good.

"Too many fine young things catching your attention," the phone continued. "We've called this meeting to consider a vote of no-confidence. So, in a way, it is good you are late."

Kenley was grateful for the dark, the rain, the shadows. He began to mentally calculate the number of steps back to his car and tried to estimate whether he could make it before one of the apes caught him and snapped his femur.

He steeled himself. Better to take it like a man. Better to retain some dignity on the way out. Not like Kevin Bridger, soiling himself and ready to give up his own mother if it meant he could save his own skin.

But it wasn't easy. The fear rose up in him, the desperate acidic urge to plead and beg for mercy surging in his gullet like vomit.

Deep breaths. Take some deep breaths.

"Well?" he managed.

"As it happens, you passed the vote. But only just," the phone said. "So, we get on with business. But consider this a . . . how do you say? A shot across the bows. Get your shit together or you'll go the same way as our little friend."

Kenley frowned. Despite the situation, Head Office had always been completely untraceable and unknowable, but they were unusually verbose tonight. No way he could make an ID, but for the first time Kenley realised English was probably not their native tongue.

He looked at the others. They didn't appear to have noticed.

"Shall we return to the agenda, then?" Kenley said, trying not to appear too relieved. "Headlines: there are two investigations in particular that I'm nervous about. We've sailed a bit too close to the sun on both. Bad news on either means our plans for a summer score will take a serious dent — and we need that to stay in the black. Give us a sitrep, Len."

"Hive prosecution is moving ahead, but slowly. If they can keep the witnesses safe, they probably think they have a good case. Pearce is their prize, though. I expect they'll be wanting him to turn Queen's."

"He'll never talk," Golden Wonder muttered.

"And if he did, who'd believe him?" Kenley said. "Man's got a dishonest streak a mile long. Besides which, let's not forget he's been in exile for the best part of five years. It would be tempting to clear that particular slate."

"He killed a cop's wife," Sterling said. "No way they'd fold that into a witness protection agreement. Besides, they have nothing on him for that. He doesn't need to bring it up."

"Mr Sterling is right," the phone said. "Proceed, Mr Sterling."

"Yes, proceed, Mr Sterling," Kenley said.

"Now who's being sarky?" Sterling said, lighting a cigarette.

"Where are we with your plant?" Kenley said. "The detective sergeant who biffed his boss on the nose?"

"Never a wise move," Sterling said, his eyes gleaming. "Besides some info about CCTV and the mother, he hasn't come across with much yet, but he will. I paid him a little home visit a while ago. Golden Wonder did the same last week. Only downside is, he's not a detective any more. He's been bumped back to uniform. The good news is that he now works the cell blocks, which he reckons will give him better access."

"How do you know he will come across?" Kenley said.

"Vernon here helped paint a picture of all the logical ways out of this."

"Did he now?" Kenley chewed the inside of his lip. "Do his windows anyway. Or torch his car."

"Consider it done, boss."

"What about the summer sporting calendar of fun? Where we at with that?"

"Looking good. It's a soft target. Family event. Cash takings onsite from hospitality and on-the-gate ticket sales. It's a six-figure score, minimum. Big names in attendance too. Day six will be the most lucrative day to go in. Semi-finals."

"Inventory? Manpower?"

"Logistics still coming together. We need kit — vehicles, tools, uniforms — and at least eight men. Ideally ten. Four to go in, two spotters, two drivers and two roaming. Not recruited them all yet. I'm not envisaging any major problems, but it would be handy for one — preferably both — of the investigations to fall flat. I might get a couple of bodies back. You want to go loud or creep?"

"Have to be loud. Too much risk otherwise. We'll need the confusion to get out."

"Understood."

"Otherwise, it sounds good. Should solve our immediate cash flow problems, at least. Bring back an update in a week, and then . . ."

"The hives are not working as effectively with Pearce in prison," the phone said, interrupting.

Kenley didn't immediately answer. The insinuation was lost on no one. He drew breath. They were testing him. Acquiescence to this point would be dangerous, a sign of weakness.

"Pearce is gone," Kenley said, slowly. "He is a casualty of war. We need to continue without him."

"Let me . . ." the phone began.

"And he would understand that," Kenley continued. "He would *expect* us to continue. The remaining hives are working fine. We need to worry less about Stratton and more about our next score. We need to up the ante."

"I'm afraid we do not share your point of view."

"Who gives a shit what you think!" The outburst surprised everyone, Kenley himself included. He thought he caught a wry look from Sterling in the gloom — *somebody's wound tight* — but he carried on regardless. "No one knows who you are. You're a bloody robotic voice on the end of a phone line, like the wizard behind the curtain. All this fear and threats and smoke and mirrors, just to keep people in line. Well, I'm calling you out. You've got no real teeth. I call good money on civil disobedience warranting no real punishment. *I'm* in charge here. And may the Lord strike me down if I'm wrong."

Kenley looked around. Sterling frowned.

"Sterling, let's get back to the investigation. Where are we with the witnesses?"

"Well, you've taken the edge off my good news, boss. All the witnesses — the drones — they've got squirrelled away in nursing homes or whatever, up and down the country. Locked down tight. Untraceable, unreachable, unidentifiable."

"All of them?"

"Yep."

"I thought you said there was good news."

Sterling beamed, and with his index finger swivelled the mobile phone so the microphone was a little closer to them. "There is, you remember, one civilian witness."

"The petrol station cashier?"

"That's him. Kenneth Rix. The one with the beard like a yellow hedgehog and a mad-eyed stare. Not to mention a belly like a kettle drum. Always seems to look like he just woke up from a nightmare about fighting a grizzly bear."

"Lovely description, Len. Get to the point, please."

Sterling beamed wider. "I've been keeping a few tabs on him and, as it turns out, despite being ten types of weirdo, he is a resourceful and canny operator. It seems, despite the secrecy around the escaper being ensconced at an undisclosed location, Kenneth was able to track her down."

"Why would he do that?"

"Not putting too fine a point on it, I think it's because he's a sly old dog."

Kenley grimaced. "Really? That's grim. How do you know he tracked her down, anyway?"

Sterling's grin looked like it might split his face. "He drove out to see her."

"He . . . what? How did he find her?"

"Well, supposition on my part, but I can only think she must have invited him. It's against their rules, but there we are. I followed him. Courier get-up."

"And?"

"And he led me straight to her."

CHAPTER THIRTY-FIVE

It was considerably easier to get to see Roxy the second time around. There was still a slight hiatus on arrival, but it was brief, and in any case Kenneth wasn't worried. He had an appointment, he was expected, he'd been *invited*, and he strolled into the main reception area with the confidence of a man who knows the lay of the land ahead.

They sat in what Kenneth supposed was a communal lounge area, which was decidedly more welcoming than the interrogation room they'd all piled into last time. This one stretched the full width of the building, which meant patients, nurses and other staff had to transit the lounge to get to other areas of the facility, but it was so large that this was not particularly disruptive. It was air-conditioned, ninety-per-cent glass, and the early afternoon sun streamed in one side of the room. Brightly coloured tables, chairs and bean bags were scattered about the laminate floor, with enough distance between each one to allow a private conversation.

Kenneth felt slightly awkward to begin with. Roxy had chosen a table by the corner and had gone off to fetch them both tea from a small, partitioned kitchen area by the doors. The lounge was practically empty, but the couple of patients that were there seemed to be interested in the fact that Roxy had a visitor. Coupled with the fact that he'd temporarily forgotten that neither of them spoke the other's language, and he — just for a moment — felt like bolting for the doors.

But as he gazed out of the window, he started to relax. The grounds were well tended, with picnic tables and arbours dotted at intervals along the white gravel paths that threaded their way around the lawns. Beyond that, the wall of vibrant green oaks, firs and willows formed a perimeter and put a natural barrier between the hospital and the rest of the outside world. It was a soul-enriching sight, and Kenneth wondered how much he could possibly benefit from staying somewhere like this.

His focus shifted, and he suddenly zeroed in on his reflection. Before leaving, he'd polished his spectacles and pulled a brush through his thick scrub of yellow hair. He'd thought about shaving the beard off, but didn't think he was quite there yet. It was a monster, no doubt about it and, really, in need of professional help. He couldn't afford a barber, however, so had to make do with some cheap scissors and conditioner.

He'd found his only tie and made a passable attempt at a single Windsor, and decided, as his reflection gazed back at him, that the effort wasn't half bad. He had even treated himself to a dab of cologne. It was possibly slightly outside its best-before date, but he had figured it was better than nothing. Lord knew it was years since he'd had cause to even think about using it.

Roxy returned with the tea and Kenneth sat up a little straighter. She sat facing into the room. Kenneth was pleased she'd done this — he never liked to have his back to anyone in a big room either, and he wondered if she'd always been like this, or if their shared experience in the basement had caused a thousand new habits to manifest.

She passed him a cup and smiled — a big expectant smile that made Kenneth want to melt. She was genuinely pleased to see him.

"Hello," she said. He raised an eyebrow in surprise. She smiled wider. "I practise."

He grinned at her.

"*Bună ziua!*" he said. "*Ce mai faci?*"

Her smile dropped. It was replaced by one of astonishment, and then she began to laugh and chatter in her native tongue. Kenneth didn't understand her — his attempts to learn some basic Romanian prior to the visit had been symbolic at best — but he got the general sense of it, and he realised he didn't need a phrase book or an interpreter on speed dial. They *understood* each other.

He knew it had been time well spent trying to do some homework on her language. He might even sign up for some proper classes, if he could afford it. His thoughts drifted briefly to the lack of employment opportunities coming his way. There would have to be something soon. He didn't want Roxy to think he didn't pay his own way.

He remembered how she had wrapped her tiny hands around his fists the last time and he found himself desperately hoping that she would do the same again.

Her face suddenly became solemn.

"*Decembrie,*" she said. "*Şase decembrie.*"

"December?" he said. "What about December?"

"*Proces,*" she said. "I am scared."

"Process? Do you mean the trial?"

She nodded.

"Oh, you mustn't be scared," he said, shuffling his chair around the circular table to get a little closer to her. "You are the bravest person I know."

She asked him a question, which he roughly took as, *What do you think will happen?*

"Well, I don't know how it is in Romania, but all the men that were at that terrible place are already in prison. They will be brought by truck to the court, and they will all stand in the dock while the lawyers make their case."

She pointed at him.

"*Ai fost?*" she said. "Before?"

"Me? Have I been to court before? Well, no. But . . ."

He paused. He didn't want to say, *But I've seen a lot of TV.*

"You will have to go into the witness box and tell them what happened. They'll ask you some questions, and then you'll be gone. It won't take long. Then the jury will deliver their verdict and the judge will send them all to prison for a very long time. Assuming, of course, that the jury doesn't find them not guilty."

She replied in a tone that suggested she wasn't filled with confidence.

"Look, I know you're scared. You'll be face to face with them, I know that. But you don't have to look at them, and they can't do anything to you. And . . . I'll be there."

He looked down at his feet. He wasn't sure that was quite right.

"I mean, I will be there. In the building. I am not sure when I will be in the courtroom," he mumbled.

He looked up.

"What have the police said?" he asked. "Pol . . . *polizei?*"

"*Poliţie,*" she corrected, then shook her head and said something he couldn't work out. He knew they'd been here, obviously, but the two meatheads in the car had probably terrified the life out of the poor woman.

An idea came to him.

"Why don't I come and get you?" he said. "I have a car. I could come and collect you and drive you to the court. That way you would be safe. You wouldn't have to go alone."

She said something he didn't understand, but which, if he didn't know better, sounded like *I don't want to go at all.*

"Roxy, I understand. I am not going to tell you that you have to go, but if you don't, these men could be back out on the street. They could be free to do this to some other poor soul."

He grimaced internally, thankful that she couldn't properly understand his rather graceless remark, and then realised that he was actually terrified of going to court as well. Having started to talk about the trial, he was finding that images of ancient oak-panelled courtrooms and purple-robed judges and whispering advocates were proving remarkably difficult to dislodge. The place would be packed, he realised — the jury, the public gallery, families of the defendants, families of the witnesses, press, police officers. At the centre of it all, in a wooden box, would be a line of society's lowest of the low, drop-dead gangsters who used guns to achieve their ends, and all those other characters in the room would be the silk-spun net keeping them at bay from the rest of decent society. The problem, he realised, was that he didn't have a remarkable amount of confidence that this so-called net would actually do its job.

Then it occurred to him, in a blast of nervous adrenaline, that his own performance in the witness box would almost certainly have a direct bearing on whether those drop-dead gangsters would walk out on a technicality or be banged up for the rest of their miserable lives.

If they did walk out, what then? They would be free to hunt him down with impunity. They would relish it. *Not to mention Roxy*, he thought, noting with shame that his instinct for self-preservation had, in his thoughts, taken momentary primacy over Roxy's own safety.

"I'm worried about the trial, Roxy. I'm very scared," he said, the heat rising in his throat at the unfamiliarity of his own naked honesty.

Her hands reached out across the table and, as he had desperately wished, took hold of his own. He looked down at his rough, ridged paw, calloused from years of stacking shelves and pushing trolleys and lifting pallets and throwing rubbish, all those incongruously honourable occupations that he somehow never managed to hold down for long enough to be able to give a straight answer to the question: *What is it you do?*

She said something that he took as *Don't worry* or *It will all be okay* or other sympathetic reassurances that had no directly translatable equivalent. It might even have been *You don't have to do it*. He felt pathetic, but he tried to tell himself they had each other, that their shared experience meant they would be able to lean on each other. He could be strong for her, but that didn't mean she couldn't be strong for him also.

He swelled his chest and felt a little better. They talked at length, the words themselves becoming increasingly irrelevant, as Kenneth realised that eye contact and intonation and inflection was all the translation he needed.

After about half an hour, when she was still holding his hands and he thought he might burst, her attention was suddenly diverted by something behind Kenneth. Her gaze shifted from his eyes to the space over his shoulder, and her brow furrowed.

Catching the puzzled look on her face, Kenneth jumped up and turned around, ready to protect her against whatever had served to cause her flawless brow to crinkle into a frown.

The doors to the lounge had opened and several terrified looking individuals started to filter in, led by a nurse and an orderly. They were clean but, physically, they appeared to have been under great strain and no amount of shampoo was going to put the light back into their dulled, scared eyes any time soon. They wore new clothes — garish tracksuits and bright white trainers — that appeared to have been hastily shoved onto worn, undernourished bodies.

The nurse held them in the centre of the room for a moment, her explanation of the surroundings accompanied by various gestures. The new additions practically cowered under her words, their nervous eyes roaming the enormous lounge as she spoke.

When the nurse had finished, she pointed at the corner of the room, where Roxy, her eyes moist, had got to her feet. She moved forwards to greet them and, as recognition slowly lit up their faces, there was a stuttering of emotion as the group reunited. They hugged, cried and clutched at each other, the group engulfing the individual, and Kenneth had to step back to avoid his toes being stepped on.

He swallowed, and attempted to smile and join in the conversation, but it was like trying to penetrate the carapace of a particularly troublesome arthropod, and he quickly had to give it up as a futile effort.

He'd been forgotten in an instant.

The nurse, who had a soft, kind face — or at least, considerably more agreeable than the last one Kenneth had encountered — appeared next to him and offered some form of explanation.

"These are the people she was locked in that horrible room with," the nurse said. "They'd been dispersed to various corners of the country — one was in some fleapit B&B, by all accounts — and Roxy has been trying quite hard to get them all back together."

"She did this?" Kenneth mumbled.

"Well, not on her own, obviously, but she was the driving force. She's quite a strong one, that one. As it happened, it wasn't particularly difficult to organise. The logic of separating them didn't really stand up, and we have the space, so . . ."

She paused. Kenneth knew he was betraying his feelings from every pore, and was probably making the nurse uncomfortable, but he couldn't help it.

As the former captives chattered in the language that was familiar to all of them, he took a couple of steps backwards, then turned and left the room, trying desperately not to run.

CHAPTER THIRTY-SIX

Sixty miles away, in a council flat somewhere between Croydon and Lambeth, several sheets of toilet paper were carefully draped over a powerful bulb in an ordinary table lamp. After only a few seconds the paper began to smoulder on top of the white-hot bulb; one then caught, and a yellow flame erupted towards the ceiling, catching more of the toilet paper as it went.

The toilet roll, unspooled across the floor as if put there by a gambolling puppy from a television advert, acted like a fuse, and the flame gobbled up the paper and raced up the living room curtains like the claws of some desperate creature scrabbling to climb out of hell.

In less than two minutes the living room was ablaze, the insistent rumble like an obscene, persistent thunder, punctuated every so often with crackles and pops. A thick blanket of choking smoke filled the room, burning the air, pressing with sooty fingers at the windows that confined it, while the rest of the room turned as black as tar.

The pathologist would later conclude that the two occupants died from smoke inhalation before they woke up, but this was of no comfort when the news was delivered to Stratton Pearce that his girlfriend and child were dead. He broke both his hands on the cell walls as he screamed like a demon, but not before he hospitalised three of the prison guards that broke the news. Eventually, a Tornado team was mobilised and he was subdued long enough for the onsite nurse to give him a needle loaded with enough sedative to put a bull to sleep.

Even that, however, took some time to take effect, and before he slid into an unconsciousness as black as the destruction left by the fire, he screamed and screamed and screamed his intention to deliver retribution to the three men he held responsible for the deaths of his beloved.

Rutherford Barnes.

Samson Kane.

Duquesne Kenley.

It would be an eye for an eye, he howled, and blood for blood.

PART THREE

CHAPTER THIRTY-SEVEN

June, 2010

Gamble woke in a sweaty snarl of sheets and twisted pyjamas. It took him a moment or two, but he swung his legs out of bed and sat up. A blast of nausea swept over him, and he grimaced as cold sweat erupted across his brow. The industrial-strength ale the night before had kept the anxiety quelled, but neither the volume consumed nor the time needed for it to leave his system had been calculated enough to swerve the hangover. He checked his watch. Ten past six for an 0700 start. He might even still be over the limit.

By the time he'd forced down breakfast and taken a coffee with him out to the car in a Thermos, he felt slightly better, but not so much that he wasn't worried about one of his Roads Policing brethren deciding to give him a tug. Either that or being ambushed by a breathalyser-wielding inspector on arrival at the cell block. Stranger things had happened.

As it happened, the journey was uneventful. He took a handover from the outgoing — and, at 0655, slightly grumpy — night turn sergeant, and settled into his seat on the bridge for a day that he intended to spend reading emails, looking forward to more of the moonshine and generally doing as little as possible.

He'd been feeding Keber snippets of nothing for weeks at a time. Enough to show willing, to keep the wolves from the station doors, but each time Dodge or Sterling — apparently tag-teaming — told him it wasn't good enough.

This didn't seem entirely reasonable to Gamble. They'd asked for some bizarre specifics — the murders and the slave farm were a standing item — but they wanted stuff on safety planning, event organising, fleet, response times, all sorts. For the most part, Gamble had obliged.

He'd kept them at bay with this for over three months, with a little bit left in the bank, and he anticipated that the Op Turnbull trial, the slave farm, must be looming. The expectation that, the next time they approached him, they would want some decent information had caused a sort of revolving door of anxiety when Gamble looked at his options:

Run.

Give them everything he had — which wasn't much, all told — and face the consequences of both his employers and, if the information was deemed below par, the attack dogs.

Confess all to PSD and hope for the activation of some kind of protective plan drawn up to look after idiot malcontents who were susceptible to being nobbled by organised criminals.

Tell Dodge and Sterling to go fuck themselves and, again, face the undoubtedly unpalatable consequences.

It wasn't much of a shortlist.

Caroline's face unexpectedly swam into his mind, and he felt a bolt of shame at what his ex-wife would make of this situation. His career had always been rather edgy, but he'd hitherto never been dirty, and to date his mulling over of the potential options had been both perfunctory and practical. If emotion was going to be a factor as well, that would just complicate matters further.

Without making a decision, he idly browsed the situations vacant on the Force intranet pages. He noted with interest that there was a vacancy or two in Professional Standards. Worth considering — that place would open up all kinds of access to information on practically every cop in the Force. It would contain a catalogue of every weak, suggestible and dishonest officer — hard currency indeed for someone of Dodge's ilk. Even Professional Standards themselves were known to have their share of persuadable rogues.

As if on cue, his desk phone rang.

"Paul? Colin Hind here."

Gamble looked left and right — there were two custody assistants in his field of vision, but both were engrossed in their respective tasks.

"Call my mobile," Gamble hissed, and hung up.

Colin Hind was a retired cop who, via the control room, had worked his way into PSD as a civilian investigator. He made Gamble look like Clark bloody Kent, frankly, and he was the one potential additional exit to his current predicament with the Keber crime gang.

The mobile rang.

"Dentist," Gamble said by way of explanation, holding up the phone as he hurried past a custody assistant. He went over to one of the interview rooms and shut the door.

"Well?" he hissed into the phone.

"I've got something," Hind said.

"On what?"

"Your boss, the new superintendent."

"About bloody time. It's been months," Gamble said. "Spit it out, then. I'm all ears."

"It took a while because there's nothing current. It's all archived. The record is on microfiche, so it's taken a wee while to get it."

"But he does have a record?" Gamble nearly leaped in the air.

"Yes. Old one. Obviously," Hind said.

"How old?"

"Twenty years, maybe?"

"What's on it?"

"Seems he was a bit handy in his youth. Couple of D&D arrests — got dragged kicking and screaming into custody and copped a resist charge as well. One for cannabis possession. He was beaten up by his father quite badly as a teenager — his uncle Jimmy came to his rescue. Dad then turned on Mum, and then both Jimmy and your super laid into him like a pair of land sharks. Arrested for GBH but it wouldn't stick — there was a good history of domestic abuse on Mum, and she swore blind in Crown Court that they were defending her and she would have been killed if he hadn't stepped in. So, the whole job got put in the bin. Dad went AWOL after that."

"If you weren't so bloody ugly, I could kiss you." Gamble was scribbling furiously.

"I don't know how useful it is. He's got no dishonesty or anything like that. Nothing around exploiting vulnerable victims. He's just got — or had — an angry streak and a quick pair of fists."

"It's fine."

"What are you going to use it for, anyway?"

"Don't you worry. I'll report it. Call it plausible deniability."

"I could lose my job for this, you know."

"You say that every time I speak to you. You'll be all right — it's not like you need the job. Pension must have covered the mortgage, eh? So, this gig must be just pocket money. Not like us poor sods that have to work for a living."

"You really make a man want to come back to help you again in the future," Hind said, and hung up.

Gamble went back to the bridge, leaned back in the chair and steepled his fingers. He mulled it over. Spent convictions and arrest information as old as that probably wouldn't flag on a standard recruit-vetting check, especially if Hind had needed to go scrabbling around for microfiche. Gamble had not long ago seen an email to all staff about the dire financial outlook for the coming decade, so it was unlikely that the purse strings extended to hiring out containers in a field somewhere to house mouldy old case files.

This, in turn, likely meant Kane was probably one of thousands of officers who had been asked to declare a squeaky-clean criminal history on their application form but had, for whatever reason, opted to keep it to themselves. Some of these got found out, but there were doubtless hundreds that had never been rumbled and continued to serve. Those that had been caught had no doubt had a little nudge from a helpful, public-spirited citizen in blue — which is precisely what Gamble intended to do now.

So, in terms of the information he now had on Kane, he had two choices; both were equally appealing.

It was just a question of who to tell first.

CHAPTER THIRTY-EIGHT

"How are you?"

DCI Marlon Choudhury slid open the top drawer of his desk, peered at the churchwarden's pipe that lay inside and closed the drawer again.

"I never know if you want me to answer that question honestly."

"I don't get a bonus if you all stay on the programme, if that's what you're asking," Choudhury said.

"Two murder investigations on my patch in less than six months. Not to mention the debacle out at Pevensey. And a constant churn of people doing terrible things to each other ever since."

"That's—"

"Why did you *want* me? What made you think I could be a cop? I used to design software and set up small businesses and run workshops with young people."

"I think you've just answered your own question."

"And a senior cop to boot. I could have gone in on the ground floor. At least then I might have had a bit of credibility, and if I didn't, I could have chalked it up to inexperience. On balance, the criminals hate me marginally less than my own officers. Never mind the patchwork of hate that I have for a family."

"Look, Samson . . . I think you need to drop the self-pity."

"I . . . what?"

"The self-pity. You need to stop feeling sorry for yourself. You don't like it, quit. It's no skin off my nose. Or stick at it and try to begin some semblance of a career. Yes, you're going to see sights no civilian could ever imagine while at the same time managing the politics that come with your being chewed out for the performance graphs going in the wrong direction."

"I can't actually believe you've just said that to me."

"You know your trouble? You came in too low. You came in humble. It's not uncommon — most lateral entry senior cops do it. They think that a constant aura of deference to the rank and file, the ones who have cut their teeth on blood-soaked streets, will earn respect. Personally, I think it's a mistake."

"So, what would you have suggested?"

"Someone in your position has two choices. Go in soft, or go in hard. On reflection, the latter might have worked for you. You know: 'I may not know policing yet, but I know how to run a business, I'm the boss, and you're going to do as you're bloody told.'"

"You think—"

"We're a disciplined hierarchy, Samson. In what other profession can you sanction someone for disobeying a lawful order? You don't think the chief exec of Tesco would love to bark at someone like that without being dragged in front of an employment tribunal?"

"I'm not sure you can do that in policing either."

"Whatever. I'm just making the point. Have at it, or ship out. It's a binary decision."

Choudhury ended the call and eyeballed his phone. His protégé was wobbling. A number of his charges took time to adjust, but Samson Kane was rather more left-field than most. He hoped his tough-love shtick hadn't been a gross underestimation of just how fragile he was.

Choudhury hauled his enormous frame out of the chair. He strode across the tarmac car park outside the gym, and had one hand on the car door handle when he heard footsteps. The office manager, Colin Hind, was running towards him.

"Marlon!" The man was out of breath. "Boss."

"Is it urgent, Colin?" Choudhury's phone rang in his pocket. He ignored it.

"Probably. Something you would want to know about, anyway." Hind rested his palms on his knees.

"I have to go to HMP Lewes — again," Choudhury said. "Four months ago, I took a formal complaint about two senior officers from a prisoner holding them personally responsible for the deaths of his partner and son in a fire. Not unreasonably, he reacted poorly to the news and, somehow, I seem to have been attached to him by a bungee cord ever since. Now, we do have a full command structure in PSD. There are inspectors and sergeants aplenty, not to mention at least a couple of ranking officers above me."

His phone rang again. He pulled it out and, not recognising the number, declined the call.

Hind nodded towards the phone as he caught his breath. "I have a feeling I know who that might be."

"No doubt I will find out in the fullness of time. Were you listening, Colin? I'm pressed for time."

"Natalie Morgan. She's a DC on East. You met her a few months ago."

"That's right — she notified us of her new beau, who came up empty on our searches. She brought in a wine glass for us, I believe."

"She did."

"And so . . ."

"Positive DNA hit."

"Took its time, but that stands to reason."

"With a match on NDNAD. Boss, this bloke is seriously bad. He looks like a key player in one of our organised crime groups. Not someone we would want our detectives fraternising with."

"When you say 'key player' . . ."

"Well, middle management at least."

Choudhury expelled air as his phone rang for a third time. He tutted and declined the call again. Nothing was ever simple, and the relentless public expectation that cops should be easily divisible between saints and sinners meant that his was a growth industry.

"Okay," he said. "Get me a profile of your man. I'll call you from the road and you can give me a pen picture."

"Will do."

"And brief her commanding officer. Is there anything to suggest that she is complicit?"

"Nothing on our files. She stuck her head above the parapet by coming to us, too. Seems unlikely she would have shown out if she was playing for both sides."

"Stranger things have happened. Disinformation. Or a double-bluff. She'll need, as a minimum, a quiet word about the company she's keeping."

Choudhury got in and started the engine; before he pulled away, he slid the window down.

"This OCG . . ."

"Keber, boss."

"If she's up for it, this could be a useful way to get someone closer to them. FIB will be very interested in that. Someone will have a flag against them. Find out who it is and let me know."

"I already called FIB. They were interested. And they said something else."

"Yes?"

"They seemed to think this bunch might be planning something."

* * *

Paul Gamble looked stupidly at his mobile phone and cursed at it. Here he was, ready to turn himself over as a Professional Standards informant, and the DCI didn't want to take his call. He understood command officers were busy, but anyone blessed with good grace would have realised that three calls on the bounce meant it was important.

He tried again, for a fourth time. This time it didn't even ring.

"Fucker's switched it off," he muttered, just before the voicemail kicked in. "DCI Choudhury. My name is DS Paul Gamble. I have to speak to you. I have some important information. Please call me back."

He stood up. How much of his life had he spent waiting for others? Reacting, being available when people needed him. How many opportunities had passed him by because he had relinquished control of any given situation to someone else? How much of his marriage passing him by was down to this simple fact?

With that in mind, he picked up the phone and called the one person he knew would answer.

"Sterling," he said, when the call was answered. "I've got something for you."

* * *

It did nothing for Gamble's already brittle nerves that Sterling acted immediately on his call. In fact, when Gamble left work, in a remarkable slice of déjà vu, he found both Sterling and a knuckle-dragger that wasn't Vernon Dodge waiting outside the gates at Hastings nick, not a hundred feet from Gamble's car.

Sterling beamed when he saw him.

"Hello, Sarge. It was lovely to hear from you. Get in the car."

A blue Vauxhall Insignia with rental company decals pulled alongside them less than five seconds later, driven by Vernon Dodge. Sterling got in the front seat, while Gamble was urged into the back with the other meathead, and they headed west along the coast towards Eastbourne.

Ordinarily, Gamble's defence mechanisms would have kicked in at this point, manifested in some armour-plated retort or other, but today he just didn't feel the need. Maybe it was because he'd resigned himself to the fact that once he opened his mouth, there was no going back. Or maybe because he felt that he had something of a trump card, the clever chops didn't need to make an appearance.

Either way, Sterling noticed.

"You're unusually quiet, Sarge. There's really no need to be nervous."

Gamble just eyeballed him. Sterling grinned at him.

As Gamble's phone began to ring in his pocket, he realised he hadn't been patted down or anything. He carefully went inside his jacket and pulled the device out.

"You mind? It will look suspicious if I don't answer."

"Fill your boots, Sarge. You're a busy man," Sterling said.

"Hello? DS Paul Gamble."

"Good afternoon, Mr Gamble. DCI Marlon Choudhury. You sound like you're driving."

"Yes, I'm . . . out on enquiries."

"What sort of case?"

"Beg your pardon?" Gamble said. He wasn't expecting to be interrogated on his small talk.

"Your enquiries. Anything interesting?"

"Oh. No. Well. A burglary series," Gamble said, thinking the old geezer maybe wasn't trying to catch him out after all. Just passing the time of day.

Maybe.

"Well, I hope your efforts bear fruit. Always good to see a detective out of the office, in any case."

"What can I do for you, DCI Choudhury?"

"I am simply returning your call, DS Gamble." Choudhury said, in a suddenly solemn tone that was almost comical.

"I have some information."

Sterling gestured with his fingers and thumb, like a duck opening and closing its beak, and Gamble flicked on the phone's loudspeaker.

"I'm listening."

"Information you'll want to hear. Confidential."

"Well, I would invite you to my office, but I myself am out on enquiries also, as it happens."

"Anything interesting?" Gamble couldn't help himself.

"Investigating complaints, as ever."

"Don't you have minions for that?"

"This one requires a delicate touch. I'm heading to HMP Lewes for the fourth time in as many months to grapple with what can only be described as some rather circuitous logic — specifically, a prisoner whose family recently died in a fire is holding the police responsible for his being unavailable to protect them. Did you want to come to my office in the morning?"

In a sudden, unexpected instant, Gamble realised that he wasn't sure he would even see the morning. It was like being deluged with a bucket of cold water.

"No . . . it can't wait."

"I am all ears."

"You need to look at Superintendent Kane."

"How so?"

"He's dirty," Gamble said, swallowing. *And he's in good company*, a voice in his head said. "Violence — GBH, domestics, resist arrest, assault police, drunk and disorderly."

Choudhury didn't immediately answer. Everyone except the driver stared at the phone in Gamble's outstretched hand. The car rumbled on, and Gamble realised that he had just played his only hand.

"How have you come by this information?" Choudhury said, slowly.

"Does it matter? The point is: he's got a criminal record. And he's managed to become a cop. What does that tell you?"

"You do know we check that when we recruit people, yes?"

"These are old. Spent convictions. He'd have had to declare them, though."

"I'll look into it," Choudhury said.

299

"Let me know, yes?" Gamble said, quickly. "Call me back."

"That isn't usually how this works," Choudhury said, and ended the call.

Gamble stared at the phone, then just about managed to drag his gaze to Sterling's.

"So, what happens now?" Sterling said. He took the phone out of Gamble's hand, switched it off and pocketed it.

"Professional Standards will go back over the recruitment process. If there's any irregularities, they'll do for him."

"Overlooking a criminal record check seems a pretty schoolboy error when you're hiring police officers."

"These are spent. He'd have had to declare them. If he hasn't, he's in serious trouble."

Sterling eyeballed him for a moment.

"That all you got?"

"This is the superintendent in charge of the whole patch. He's overseeing both the house fire and the slave farm investigations. You get rid of him, the whole thing suddenly looks shaky."

Sterling didn't speak. He didn't look convinced. Gamble swallowed again.

They rode the rest of the journey in silence. After twenty minutes or so they pulled up outside the storage unit and pulled into a loading bay. The shutters rattled down behind the car in a slow, horribly final way, and Gamble was flanked by Dodge and the other goons, Sterling leading the charge, as they filed out of the loading bay through a partition door that led into a dark, brick corridor lit by weak, sickly-yellow lamps.

Sterling led them up some metal stairs onto a gantry, and their boots reverberated around what Gamble could see was a large portion of the four-storey building with literally nothing in it, not even floors and ceilings. There was a metal skeleton stretching around the edges of the wall, with more gantries and vertical struts, forming a framework for what Gamble presumed would, at some point, become finished storage units.

At the end of the gantry was one such storage unit — the only one in this part of the building, in fact — a large metal, prefab shed about the size of a double garage. It was slightly better lit than the rest of the building, with a table and some metal folding chairs dotted about the place, and not much else.

There was a man standing by the table, engrossed in some kind of paperwork on a clipboard. He was tall, and his dark, wavy hair was edged with rust. His heavy, Iberian-looking brow was knotted into a frown of concentration.

They all filed in and stood in an awkward semi-circle around the man.

"Nice place," Gamble said, preparing to go down fighting. "Are we not doing introductions?"

"This is the boss," Sterling said. "Pretty much all you need to know. Tell him what we just heard."

The man finally looked over. Gamble considered trying to take a surreptitious picture of him, before remembering that Sterling had his phone. He would just have to try to commit the man's face to memory instead. He tried to read the papers scattered across the table, but was too far away. He thought there were maybe some schematics or something on there, next to a carelessly arranged stack of glossy, brightly coloured brochures and leaflets that appeared to be advertising Eastbourne's annual tennis tournament. Thinking he must be mistaken, he strained to look, and then gave up. What the hell, Gamble thought, even drop-dead psychos are entitled to cut loose with strawberries and cream.

In the corner of the unit, in dull shadow, were a line of large fibreglass drums. On the floor next to them was a stack of clear plastic storage boxes on wheels, and Gamble was able to make out sets of coveralls in polythene wrappers, motorcycle helmets, sledgehammers and bolt croppers.

"The superintendent leading the investigations into you is a criminal," Gamble said, when he was finally able to tear his eyes away. "I've just advised the proper authorities. His days are numbered."

The man tilted his head.

"You know this how?"

"I know it. It's good information."

301

"Do they know they are investigating us specifically? Or just that they are investigating?"

Gamble didn't answer.

"What I mean is: are any of us identified as suspects?"

"Well, I can't say Sancho Panza here getting himself brought into custody just to speak to me was a particularly bright move," Gamble said, indicating Dodge, "but otherwise, no. They're just looking."

"They get rid of him, someone else just takes his place, though, right?"

"Well, in time, yes. But that's time that could be well spent by you. Plus, there's no guarantee that the next guy will be anything like this one. Much as it pains me to say it, he does have something about him. He's still only got a few months' service, don't forget. Once he properly finds his feet he'll be like a dog with a bone."

The man chewed the inside of his cheek for a moment, then returned his attention to his paperwork.

"That all you got?"

Gamble set his feet. This was it. He wondered if it would be blunt force and then torture, or the cold steel of a blade between the ribs, or just a simple pistol to the temple.

"You're wasting my time. Have been for about three months. You've got forty-eight hours to get me something useful once and for all, or I'm afraid there's an alcove over there just about your size. It's due to be bricked up with breeze blocks in the next week or so."

"How do you know I won't report what I've seen the minute you let me out of here?" Gamble said, nodding towards the fibreglass barrels in the corner.

"How do you know that isn't exactly what I want you to do?"

He didn't look up from his clipboard. One of the goons took Gamble's upper arm in a surprisingly light grip and Gamble, shot through with nervous energy, quickly shrugged his arm free and used the elbow to mash the man's nose back into his face.

It went with a *pop*. Blood spurted out in a small explosion, and his hands flew to his face as he dropped to one knee.

"Sorry," Gamble said. "Eton mess."

Sterling looked genuinely surprised. He got between the two just as his victim recovered enough to charge at Gamble. Gamble didn't flinch, didn't move from where he was standing. This was it. *Bring it on.*

"No need for that, Sarge," Sterling said, holding up a palm to pacify the bloodlust revenge that was percolating behind his shoulder.

Dodge grabbed Gamble in a half-nelson before Gamble could react. Gamble wriggled, but the chokehold was effective, and he realised that standing very still was the only means by which he could keep breathing.

The man with the wavy hair walked over. He took off his glasses.

"I've had an idea," he said, addressing Sterling. "Much as it pains me to have to spoon-feed you, it's probably reasonable to expect Sergeant Gamble here to want some sort of direction. He can't second-guess what might be useful to us, can he?"

Sterling didn't answer, but stared at his boss.

"The witness. The civilian," the good-looking man with the wavy hair said.

"Rix."

"Yes. This one can call him off. Dissuade him from testifying." He pointed at Gamble with his chin.

"I'm not hurting anyone," Gamble said.

The good-looking man pulled an *oh please* face.

"You don't have to hurt anyone, silly. You just have to spook him. If we do it, it's intimidation; if a cop does it, it's just preparing the witness for trial."

Gamble thought about this. It seemed like a low-risk way to keep breathing.

"Good," the man said, putting his glasses back on and walking back to his paperwork. "You've got forty-eight hours."

CHAPTER THIRTY-NINE

Roxy moved her knight across the board, capturing Kenneth's rook in a move he hadn't even seen coming. He wasn't exactly a chess prodigy, but he didn't think he was any slouch, either. Roxy, however, was off the charts.

It was Kenneth's fifth or sixth visit. His bout of self-pity at the arrival of Roxy's co-slaves — *was that a word?* — and envy that the group had a shared experience he could claim to have come close to, but not totally — had disappeared when Roxy had called him at home to apologise and invite him back.

He was still on cloud nine, but they had settled into a bit of a rhythm now — they talked, played chess and, if the communal lounge was quiet, occasionally watched a film together. They were most certainly friends. He would bring books and gifts and, when it occurred to him that both her life and their friendship were almost entirely defined by the slave farm and looming trial, they started to talk about life beyond that. What would she do? Would she go home? Would she stay in England, try to make a life for herself? Would she stay at the facility until the trial, or strike out before that? In Kenneth's lay opinion, she was certainly healthy enough to be discharged, but he did acknowledge that there was a community here that gave her comfort and that, at a minimum, she must have been apprehensive about starting a new life.

He extolled Eastbourne's virtues, telling her about the sunshine coast and the well-documented benefits of sea air. He told her about how the town nestled in the green bosom of the South Downs, of the unspoiled promenade and shingle beaches, of the quaint and colourful gift shops, tea rooms and restaurants that stretched out beyond the pier and the bright colours of Carpet Garden that always seemed to make him think of being on holiday. If you're going to stay anywhere, he said, why not stay there?

He had stopped short of inviting her to stay with him. He had no expectations — indeed, no hopes at all — on that front. He was at least twenty-five years older than she, and despite the fact that outsiders would no doubt cast aspersions on his motivations, they were good friends, and that was enough for him. She trusted him, and he had no wish to jeopardise that. It wasn't like he had friends to spare.

She smiled as she put his king in check, and he smiled back. He was going to lose again, but that was fine. There was a thin strip of sun filtering through one of the oaks outside, giving her dark hair a reddish tint.

There was one secret he'd kept from her. Kenneth had done pretty well, he thought, with his attempts to learn Romanian, even though Roxy had, in turn, picked up English at double the pace. He had realised that the depth of their conversations had plateaued somewhat — or was at risk of doing so — and although the intonations and inflections said a great deal in themselves, he didn't want to miss a single thing she said. He didn't want to go home wondering what she said. He wanted to *know*. And, in some purely irrational way — because she was safe and well and healthy — he didn't want anything to happen to her and for those unknown words to remain unknown forever.

So, after his third visit, he had started turning on the voice recorder function in his mobile phone, which he secreted in a shoulder bag. He surreptitiously recorded the conversations, transcribed them at home, and then, in a slow and painstaking method of amateur translation, worked out retrospectively what she had been saying to him. On one occasion he had paid for a professional translator to transcribe it for him, largely because his first couple of efforts had made no sense whatsoever. But he was getting better. This enabled him, he reasoned, to understand what she had said, research what he might say back and prepare it in her native tongue. It enabled him to progress their conversations to a deeper and more natural level — as well as helping him learn the language.

He didn't want to tell her, because he was ashamed and embarrassed that he couldn't speak to her in as much detail as he wanted to and, of course, after he'd done it a couple of times, it was too late to bring it up without putting a sizeable dent in their burgeoning friendship.

But it was worth it.

Two more moves and his king was *finito*.

He applauded her silently and slowly, a broad smile on his face. She tilted her head slightly.

"You let me win?" she said.

He looked shocked.

"Of course not. You are too good for me."

She clapped and beamed, bouncing in her seat.

"I am good. I am the best."

Kenneth carefully tidied away the board and pieces, returning the box to a stack of games on a bookshelf, and walked Roxy back to her room.

She unlocked the door and walked in; Kenneth hesitated on the threshold, but she beckoned him in. She bounded over to the bed while he hovered near the doorway. It was the first time in four months he'd seen her bedroom.

It was more like a hotel room than a hospital room, but the head-height glass running around both the east and north walls in an "L" shape created an atrium effect that, Kenneth mused, you would find in neither. The green of the grounds filled the windows, and Kenneth found himself glad the room was not on a higher floor.

Despite Roxy's welcome, there was still a thick sense of privacy in the room. Her clothes and toiletries were scattered on a conference table, a wet towel hung on a chair, and the smell of shampoo and soap from her earlier shower was still apparent.

"I am not tidy," she said, and giggled, putting her hand to her mouth. "I call my family now."

Kenneth suddenly felt awkward, and he waved her goodbye. She crossed the room, squeezed his hand and then gave him a brief hug.

"Goodbye," she said. "Visit soon."

He returned the hug with a sort of slow disbelief, then turned and glided away down the corridor to his car like he was three feet above the ground.

This trance-like state of delirious bliss meant that, when he got to the car, he realised he'd left his bag in Roxy's room — with, he realised in horror, his still-recording mobile phone still in it.

He blustered his way back past the receptionist and took the stairs to Roxy's room. He heard her small voice murmuring on the phone call home to her family. He knocked gently, and a questioning voice said, "Yes?"

He pushed the door open. She turned away from the phone receiver to see who it was, and a look of surprise crossed her face when she saw him.

"Sorry. I forgot," he said, pointing at the chair he'd left the bag on.

She didn't smile, didn't say anything, didn't give any kind of forgiving look. She didn't look cross or annoyed by the interruption, but simply pointed at the bag, an almost blank look on her face.

Kenneth wasn't quite sure what he'd been expecting, but the tepid response from Roxy at seeing him again so soon after their meeting left him feeling suddenly quite sick and pathetic.

He scurried into the room, retrieved the bag and made for the door, half-turning to give a little wave as he went.

But she'd resumed her phone conversation before he'd even left the room.

* * *

It was a long drive home, and Kenneth tried not to allow his mind to wander. He'd found it refreshing that after his third or so visit to Roxy he'd stopped retrospectively analysing the significance of every tic, gesture and mannerism that had just passed between them, and instead had simply started going with the flow. After all, such evaluation was, he reasoned, reserved for lovesick boys, and he was clearly not that. The years he had on Roxy meant that she looked up to him — looked up to his *seniority* — and saw him as a protector, all borne out by the events in the farmhouse almost five months ago.

But today was different. When he'd gone back for the bag, Roxy clearly had not been her usual welcoming self. She'd not been expecting him, granted, but it was more than that. She'd seemed . . . uneasy, almost.

He made reasonable time, and arrived back in Eastbourne in a couple of hours. He backed the Honda into a tight space near one of the seafront B&Bs, and walked down to his flat. There was a small gaggle involved in a shouting match outside the café underneath his flat but, fortunately, they paid him no mind, and he stepped round them, slipped down the damp stone alley that his widening middle just about accommodated and climbed the fire escape to his front door.

He didn't put the kettle on, didn't even take his coat off, but instead took the phone out, connected his earphones and began the painstaking process of translating his meeting with Roxy, which involved the internet, a phrase book and a lot of rewinding and replaying. It was far from being an exact science, but he figured that he didn't need the specifics — the gist would do. The costs of the professional translator were prohibitive.

There hadn't actually been that much chat this time around. It had been rather pleasant, in fact, much of the visit having been taken up by the chess match.

After an hour or two, he had several scribbled pages in which she'd made a fair bit of small talk — his journey, the weather. She'd also asked about his family, his work and — inevitably — the trial. As she'd spoken, he'd guessed at her conversation, and he was pleased to note that a reasonable amount of the half-educated guesses he'd made at the time weren't actually that far off the mark.

He then heard shuffling and thumping as they'd walked back to her room, and pressed the earphones deep into his ears as he strained to listen, a strange thrill suddenly passing through him. He heard himself say his goodbyes, then the door clicked shut and she started speaking into the phone.

He knew he should stop, knew this was an almost unforgivable invasion of her privacy, but he couldn't help himself. He picked up the pen and frantically tried to keep up with her conversation. His brow knotted at the unfamiliar tone — the light, soft tones she employed around Kenneth had vanished. She spoke sharply, even harshly; Kenneth could tell that before he'd even started attempting to translate.

He scribbled and scribbled, pausing and rewinding, slowing down and starting again. A small part of him wondered if, maybe, she reserved her gentle kindness for him alone, simply because of what they had endured together.

As he wrote, however, consulting the phrase book and the internet on a cyclical basis, he realised it was far, far more than that.

He stood and walked to the window in a daze. He peered down at Seaside as the street lights began to flick on. Between the Territorial Army Centre and a row of takeaways, St Aubyn's Road led south, directly to Royal Parade, and he liked to think he could lay legitimate claim to a sea view from his window.

An electric buzz jolted him from the jumble in his mind. It was loud, and it took him a moment to realise it was the door to his flat — largely because he seldom had visitors. It sounded for ten seconds or so, then stopped, then began again.

He realised he didn't actually know how to work the door release mechanism in the buzzer, and so he instead shuffled down the fire escape, the buzzer still going. Whoever it was, they were insistent. Kenneth would ordinarily have been stricken with anxiety that it was a bailiff or debt collector or the landlord, but he was too preoccupied by what he had just transcribed, trying desperately to convince himself that his amateur efforts had simply been way, way off the mark. He certainly hoped to heaven that was the case, anyway.

The buzzer didn't even open the flat door, but simply the iron gate separating the alley from the street. He manoeuvred his bulk down the alley, frowning at the silhouette of the figure that drew gradually into focus.

He didn't recognise him, but the fact that the man kept his finger on the buzzer even after he'd seen Kenneth appear in the alleyway was not a good start.

He was tall and thin with a slight paunch. He had a widow's peak and a bad suit, and Kenneth had him pegged as a cop before the warrant card had even come out.

"Kenneth Rix?" the man said.

"Yes?" Kenneth said, pressing his face up to the bars to scrutinise the warrant card.

"Police. Let us in, will you?"

"What do you want?"

"It won't take long."

Kenneth opened the gate and shuffled back along the alleyway. The man followed.

"Nice place you've got," the man said as they climbed the fire escape. Kenneth wasn't really warming to this man at all.

When they got inside, the man stood in the kitchen and looked around, hands on hips.

"Detective Sergeant Paul Gamble," the man said. "Can I sit?"

Kenneth gestured to the only armchair in the place, suddenly feeling like an intruder in his own flat. The man made himself comfortable, and peered at the table with the desk lamp next to him, where the evidence of Kenneth's amateur translations was present.

"Writing a book?" Gamble said.

"No," Kenneth replied, silently kicking himself for not tidying it all away before answering the door.

"It's okay, Kenneth. You can relax. But I do have a couple of questions, if that's okay," the man called Gamble said. He laced his fingers around his knee.

Kenneth didn't say anything, but looked behind him and perched on the edge of a bar stool.

"Just you here? Wife? Kids?" Gamble said.

"Just me," Kenneth mumbled.

"I see. I catch you off out somewhere?"

"What?"

"You've got your coat on," Gamble said, nodding towards the parka.

"I just got back."

"Where from?"

"I was visiting someone."

"Sick mother? Secret girlfriend? AA sponsor?"

Kenneth didn't answer. The man was both mocking him and driving at something. He didn't really want to find out what.

"Who did you visit, Kenneth? Where did you go?"

"Just . . . a friend."

"A friend called Roxana Petrescu?"

Kenneth felt like the bottom had fallen out of his stomach. Sweat suddenly erupted all over his body, as if a malign virus had just invaded it. His eyes felt hot, and there was a dull pain in his throat. He swallowed, realising he was about a spider's leg away from bursting into tears.

Gamble shook his head.

"Kenneth, Kenneth. What were you thinking? You do know that by going to see her you've compromised one of the biggest criminal trials this county has ever seen?"

Had he? No, he hadn't really. Surely? He'd just made a friend who'd been through something similar to him.

"You're not friends, Kenneth," Gamble said, as if reading his mind. "You're *witnesses for the prosecution*. How many times have you been to see her? Four? Five? You know any defence advocate worth their fee is going to mount a very compelling and easy-to-construct argument that the two of you have been colluding? You know, getting your stories straight?"

Kenneth felt the hot wave of shame slide over him like molten lava, weighing him down, fixing him to the spot. It was all his fault. He'd felt it when the only relationship he'd ever had went belly up. Felt it when the apprenticeship fell through, his one attempt to better himself. Felt it both before and after his total nervous breakdown. And he'd felt it when the poxy petrol station convenience store had let him go. Rescuing a terrified woman was a breach of store protocol, apparently.

"On the plus side, at least the CPS can pull the plug way before you see the inside of a courtroom. Take that stress off you. I mean, what do you think it would be like, standing there alone in the witness box, facing all four defendants there in the dock. All eyes on you. Willing you to drop dead on the spot. Entertaining themselves with fantasies of seeing how much of your insides they could pull out through your navel before you finally bleed out."

Kenneth swallowed. Gamble leaned forward.

"You see, the problem with most cases is that the person complaining to the cops about their annoying neighbour, or the little shit who threatened them in the street, or the idiot who opened their car door a bit too carelessly in Tesco car park, thinks that the cops can make it all better. They think if we put the bracelets on, whisk them away, maybe in some cases even present them with a charge sheet, then all their problems will go away. They think we'll take them off the streets for good.

"But even if they do end up in court — which in most cases is at least a year after the fact — the vast majority are going to get a fine. Or a conditional discharge. Or fifty hours picking up litter. Then they're right back living next door to you, and it's as if the cops never happened."

"I don't know what you mean."

"This is just the tinpot stuff, of course — although let's not overlook the fact that the tinpot stuff is ninety per cent of what we deal with. Even the real, meaty cases, the ones with actual prison time on the end of them, don't all mean a lifetime's reprieve for the victim. A ten-year sentence is actually three by the time you've factored in guilty pleas, good behaviour and time served on licence.

"And those cases with proper, nasty, organised villains — they *know* the game. They *know* about tactical legal arguments, evidential continuity, procedural errors, last-minute changes of plea and time served. They know about nobbling jurors and paying off witnesses. It's *easy* to do, Kenneth.

"And that's for the cases that actually get home. There's a multitude of cases that walk right out of the door. They're the really insidious ones — the ones where horrible defendants, defendants everyone knows to be guilty, just skate. And then they're untouchable. Bulletproof. Bigger than the game. Bigger than the system."

An ambulance flew past with sirens wailing. Its blue strobes briefly lit up Kenneth's front room.

"What is it you—"

"Kenneth, the point I'm making is that they will get to you. They will find you, one way or another. And they won't forget. Do you really want to go through with this?"

Kenneth frowned. Something didn't make sense.

"Why . . . you sound like you are trying to talk me out of giving evidence."

Gamble shook his head.

"That's a moot point now, Kenneth. Your canoodling — or whatever — with a fragile, vulnerable, traumatised kidnap victim has put the whole case on the skids. You're not kindred spirits, Kenneth. You spent an hour or so getting threatened by some nasty bastards in a piss-soaked basement, sure, but she'd been trafficked in from Romania and held captive for months. Alone, terrified, unable to even speak the language. Your experience can hardly be called similar. There isn't a jury in the world that isn't going to think you haven't tried to get something out of it."

Gamble stood up and buttoned his jacket. He took another look at Kenneth's translation papers, then walked to the door to the fire escape.

"She got exploited by these bastards. And you exploited her all over again."

The words were like a cold wind blowing in through a smashed window.

"Okay, I'll drop it," Kenneth said, his back to Gamble.

Gamble raised his eyebrows. "I'm sorry?"

"I'll drop my statement."

The raised eyebrows became a frown. Gamble slowly turned. "You'll what?"

"I'll drop my statement," Kenneth said for a third time.

Gamble put his hands in his pockets and leaned on the doorframe. "You think . . . it's as easy as that?"

A jolt of irritation shot up through Kenneth's sternum. The man apparently wanted it all ways.

"What I mean is, we're closer to the end of the investigation than the beginning of it. Right now, the CPS, the SIO and whichever silk they want to play leading man — or leading lady — are working out a strategy for the matinee performance in the world's oldest piece of theatre: a jury trial."

Kenneth looked blank.

"You don't just get to drop your statement. You've already signed it, and it's been shoved in the case file bundle. No one ever tells you that when you sign your statement, you're signing a contract to go to court. I can practically guarantee you that if you back out now, a very grumpy circuit judge is going to order a patrol car round here to turf you out of bed and get you to the box, toot sweet. Prosecution witnesses turning up in handcuffs is never a great look for the jury, but it's better than the alternative. You're the star witness, Kenneth. Well, one of two."

Kenneth looked down at the transcribed notes on his jotter pad. He read a couple. They made him feel sick to his stomach.

"So, what do you want me to do?" he said.

"You'll have to have a wobble, that's a given. Don't just say you're backing out. Tell them you're petrified. Even better, tell them you've been intimidated."

"But I haven't been—"

Gamble waved a hand: *please*.

"At least if you come over as intimidated, it puts the ball back in their court. They'll have to at least make an effort to give you a cuddle and get you to court. Straight refusal will just put their backs up."

"And then what?"

"Then . . . well, it'll be like the biggest duvet day you've ever had. Feign illness. Fall down the stairs. Have a nervous breakdown."

Kenneth eyed Gamble. Just what did this horrible man know?

"Anything. Just make them *earn* it. Either way, you won't be giving evidence. They'll go free, of course, but you won't spend the rest of your life looking over your shoulder. Trust me, it'll be worth it."

"Okay."

"Okay?" Gamble looked positively jubilant.

"Okay. I'll do it. I'll back out."

Gamble grinned, opened his mouth to say something, and then closed it again. He looked down at the mobile phone lying on Kenneth's jotter pad.

He picked it up. "What's this?"

"My phone."

"I'm going to need to seize it as evidence."

"Evidence of what?"

"Collusion. Conferring between witnesses. Tainting the prosecution case. Perverting the course of justice. And more besides. You could be in a lot of trouble. Or, I could just make it all go away. What's on it?"

Kenneth shrugged. Ordinarily his mind would be racing in a panic over the recordings stored on the phone, but he suddenly found he didn't care. His friendship with Roxy was one huge lie. *He* had felt bad for lying to her, when all along *she* had been lying to *him*.

"This and that?"

"Evidence of calls and messages to Roxy. To the facility? Emails too, I'd wager."

"A few. You can have it."

Kenneth didn't care if he never saw the damn device again. Gamble slipped the phone into his pocket. He peered briefly at the table, but didn't seem too interested in Kenneth's scribblings. The man was plainly too ignorant.

"I'll write you a receipt. You can come to get it from the station."

"Why are you doing this?" Kenneth said, flatly.

The smile disappeared from Gamble's face.

"Why are you trying so hard to get these people off? Why don't you want them locked up?"

Gamble's expression went from neutral to bilious. "You're lucky I don't just arrest you right here and now."

Kenneth shrugged. "Do whatever you have to."

Gamble eyeballed him and scowled. If Kenneth didn't know better, he'd have said that he'd managed to needle the detective.

"Stay out of trouble," Gamble said, opening the door.

"What happens now?"

"Now?" Gamble's boots scraped on the fire escape as he turned to face Kenneth. The day was slowly falling, and a spilled egg yolk sunset was starting to filter through the chimney pots and rooftops directly behind Gamble's head.

"Now I go and speak to your 'friend'."

* * *

Gamble was as good as his word. Roxy's location was locked down tightly on the official systems — and even in his custody environment he couldn't come up with a legitimate reason for asking around to get it — but a cursory inspection of Kenneth's phone led to a confirmed location in less than an hour of poking around.

It wasn't really an address, just a name and a postcode, but it was certainly better than a poke in the eye. Gamble had been around enough domestic abuse refuges to know that the biggest risk of the location being compromised was the residents themselves.

He sat in the car, breath steaming up the windscreen, and continued his illegal interrogation of Kenneth's phone. There were no photos, videos or website history of interest — weren't modern phones clever? — but Gamble was nothing if not methodical, and it wasn't long before he found the audio files stored by the voice recording app.

He recognised Kenneth's simpering — God, how he must have soaked up that one-on-one female attention — and heard a female voice that he presumed to be Roxana. The ambient noise of voices echoing in a large room, along with the faint sound of a television and the activity of cleaners and caterers, led Gamble to work out pretty quickly that Kenneth had been recording his encounters with Roxy.

He didn't understand what she was saying but, to an astonished Gamble, it stood to reason that she was quite clearly being taped without her knowledge.

That was even better. *That* was beautiful.

He turned the key and the car stuttered into life.

After leaving Kenneth, he'd intended to update Sterling about the prosecution witnesses — one down, one to go — drink a large Captain Morgan and then drive out to see Roxana early in the morning.

The discovery of the recordings, however, put a different lens on it.

It couldn't wait.

It would have to be now.

CHAPTER FORTY

At that time of night, the light traffic meant it only took an hour to get to the Dartford Crossing, and Gamble wondered why he'd even considered going during the day.

Another ninety minutes and he turned off the motorway, followed an A-road that cut through the countryside into a whole lot of nothing, and then turned off again onto a neat, well-kept driveway lined with junior birch trees that cut between two fields in an undulating series of S-bends on an incline that led into a slight valley. He could have been heading down to a country club, or a vineyard, or a luxury hotel. The driveway was unlit, however, and Gamble felt just a stab of unease as he left the lights of the highway behind him.

Eventually the driveway opened out into a large gravel apron with parking and a turning circle. This part was lit, and as Gamble broke through the treeline he saw a large, square building that looked a bit like a private hospital. It was clearly too nice to be an NHS facility.

He turned off the engine and waited for a moment. Not quite nine o'clock. Late enough that they'd likely be down to a skeleton crew, but not so late that all the residents would be asleep.

Not that it mattered, particularly. This was an emergency.

Gamble walked across the tarmac to the main doors, noting a golf buggy parked on the flagstones outside. Through the glass, he saw a security guard behind the desk, who appeared to be engrossed in some paperwork. He wasn't asleep, wasn't munching on a Big Mac, wasn't watching football on a portable TV. He looked alert, and pretty sharp.

This was obviously not great news, but nor was it insurmountable. Gamble held his warrant card aloft; the guard saw him and came out from behind the reception desk. Gamble saw that the paperwork was a clipboard that the guard had been writing on as Gamble approached.

An intercom barked into life on the doorframe.

"Help you?"

"Police." Gamble held his warrant card up to what he presumed was a camera.

"Can I help you?"

"I need to speak to one of your residents. I'm afraid it's an emergency."

There was a second or two of crackling static, then the intercom clicked off and the guard walked to the door.

There was another buzz and a metallic clank, and the door was opened a fraction. Gamble held his warrant card up to the gap.

"My name's Paul Gamble. I'm a detective sergeant."

"Who with?" The guard was no more than twenty-five. His eyes were bright behind his glasses.

"What do you mean, 'who with?'"

"Which force are you with?"

Gamble cursed his luck. This time of night he'd expected a disinterested jobsworth but, apparently, he'd chanced upon someone actually bothered about doing his job properly. Or maybe he was just bored and glad for the distraction. He'd have to hope it was the latter.

"Met," Gamble lied, pocketing the warrant card before it could be scrutinised further. "If you need to verify my credentials my shoulder number is four-seven-six-Charlie-November, and the relevant CRIS number is—"

"That's fine. Come in."

The guard opened the door wide, and Gamble stepped in. The guard scanned the outdoors for a moment.

"Thanks," Gamble said.

"Only you?" the guard said.

"Yes. We understand the need to be discreet, especially here."

"I thought you went everywhere in pairs."

"Cutbacks," Gamble said, shrugging: *what can you do?* He nodded at the golf buggy through the glass. "Just you on tonight? A lot of ground to cover."

"You said it was an emergency?"

"Yes, it is, I'm afraid. One of your guests has, we think, been compromised. I need to get her a message, arrange for her to be protected overnight and then relocated in the morning."

The guard mulled it over. Gamble didn't think he was buying it.

"What's the name?" the guard said eventually.

"Roxana Petrescu."

The guard retreated behind the desk and began performing tasks on a computer. Gamble went up to the counter and leaned casually on it — or what he hoped was casual.

"You ever think of joining up?" Gamble said, while the guard searched the system. "You're pretty diligent. Most guys on a night shift would hurry me through so as not to miss the second half."

"There are a lot of vulnerable people here," the guard said, not looking up.

Gamble said nothing, but tried to resist the urge to drum his fingers on the counter top.

"Here we go," the guard said. "You want me to get her down?"

"No," Gamble said, nodding towards the glass. "Bit exposed. Can we go and see her?"

The guard thought about it, now plainly uncomfortable.

"I ought to call up first," he said. "She might be asleep."

"Whatever you need to do," Gamble said. "I don't think she's got much English, though."

The guard attempted it anyway. Somebody answered — Gamble presumed it was Roxy — and after a few abortive attempts to explain to her that she had a visitor, and reassure her that the time of night was neither here nor there, he told her they were coming up.

"I'm not sure she understood me," the guard said, hanging up the phone.

"She's awake, at least," Gamble said.

They took the lift up to Roxy's floor; Gamble was mildly perturbed to note that the guard didn't stay in the lift, but headed purposefully off down the corridor, intent, it seemed, on at least making introductions.

Gamble followed the guard off down the corridor, noting the general show home condition of the carpets, fixtures and fittings. It was only a fake Constable watercolour or two short of a country hotel rosette.

Fake Constable. Funny, Gamble thought to himself.

The guard stopped outside one of the bedrooms and tapped on the wood with what Gamble took as extreme deference.

"Think she'll hear that?" Gamble said.

"Time will tell," the guard said, keeping his eyes on the door.

A shaky female voice called what Gamble took to be "Come in" in an unfamiliar tongue.

The guard opened the door and remained on the threshold; Gamble appeared behind him with a big smile and a wave, and noted that Roxana Petrescu was about as far away from them as she could get. She was on the other side of the room in her dressing gown, hands clasped, her back to the window.

"Miss . . . Roxy," the guard said, in soft tones. He really would have made an excellent police officer, Gamble thought. "I'm sorry to disturb you. This gentleman is a police officer. He has to speak to you. It's urgent."

"My brother?" Roxy said, in heavily accented, almost indiscernible, but nevertheless clearly worried English.

Both the guard and Gamble frowned.

"Not exactly, miss," Gamble said, manoeuvring himself past the guard and into the room. "But it won't take long. Sorry to disturb your evening."

Roxy's evening appeared to consist of some soft music and a cup of tea. A Penguin Classic of one type or another was open on the bed; the bedside lamp was the only light in the room, giving an overall impression of someone who had been winding down and thinking about bed. All the curtains were open, and beyond the huge windows was the black, suggestive landscape of the facility's country footprint. Gamble noted a large china vase stuffed with some kind of impressive bouquet on the windowsill, and a framed soothing river vista above the bed.

Gamble stared at the guard. He may as well have said, *You can bugger off now*. This wasn't lost on the guard, who looked at Roxy.

"Do you want me to stay?"

"Come on, chum, one sweaty bloke crowding her is enough," Gamble said.

The guard ignored him, but continued to question Roxy with his eyes. Eventually she shook her head.

"I'm downstairs if you need me," he said, pointing at the phone on the bedside table, and glided away.

Once he was gone, Gamble shut the door. He didn't say anything immediately, but made a call on his mobile. He uttered a number followed by another number, and then put the phone on speaker and rested it on the tabletop as the police's twenty-four-hour interpreter service patched him through to a Romanian speaker.

"I really am sorry about the intrusion," he said. A deep voice repeated the comment in Romanian. Roxy stared dumbly at the phone. "But there's a couple of things that can't wait."

Roxy composed herself enough to point at a kettle and some mugs on a sideboard by the television.

"You want?"

"Oh, that's very kind of you. Why not?" Gamble said with a thumbs up, and Roxy busied herself while he spoke. "Listen, Roxana."

She looked briefly over her shoulder.

"First of all, your meetings with Kenneth."

She stopped what she was doing and stared at the wall, her back to him.

"They need to stop. They have caused untold damage to the prosecution case."

She slowly turned around, and stared at the vase of brightly coloured flowers. She reached out and took a petal in her hand, with a caress that Gamble imagined must have been the gentlest touch imaginable.

"Roxy, do you understand? The case may well have to be dropped. These men could be back on the streets. As a precaution, we have to get you out of here. To a new location. I can't trust that Kenneth hasn't compromised the location of this facility."

"Why do you not trust him?" she said, turning back to the kettle. Gamble noticed that there was no economy hotel arrangement of plastic kettle and tiny pots of long-life milk — this was a china pot with a glorious aroma of something like freshly ground coffee.

"I'm glad you asked," he said. "There's something else."

He produced a second phone — Kenneth's phone — rested it alongside the one on the table, and pressed play at random.

The recording was not especially good quality, and the ambient background noise of chatter echoing around a large room almost rendered it unlistenable, but then two voices could be heard.

Kenneth: *That's a good move.*

Roxy: *I learn to play in my country.*

Kenneth: *That could be checkmate. Do you want to go again?*

Gamble looked at Roxy. She turned, her hand on the pot still, her expression quizzical.

"What is this?" she asked.

Gamble stifled an almost irresistible grin and put on what he hoped was an extraordinarily sympathetic face.

"I'm afraid — for reasons best known to himself — Kenneth has been secretly recording his conversations with you. I can't speculate on why. It could be because he just wants a keepsake. It could be because he's just a bit odd. But it could also be that he is passing information back to the men that held you prisoner."

"More," she said.

Gamble obliged, speeding up the playback until there was the ambient sound of Kenneth leaving her bedroom and Roxy making her phone call home, speaking rapidly into the receiver to whoever was on the other end.

"For what it's worth, I genuinely think he forgot his bag. I don't think he meant to record you privately, only the conversations between the two of you. He certainly wouldn't have wanted to eavesdrop on a private family conversation. At least, I don't think so."

The interpreter tried to say something, but Gamble cut him off.

"Roxana, are you understanding me?"

Roxy didn't answer. Her expression was neutral as she came over to the table and began to pour the coffee. It smelled unbelievably good. Her chest rose and fell. She seemed to be taking deep breaths.

Kenneth's recording was still playing. The interpreter was rattling through the translation.

"I know this is hard to hear. I understand he has become a friend to you. But, I'm afraid, some people will do anything for the right price," Gamble said.

He stared at her. She didn't meet his eye, but continued fussing with the coffee. The pot looked heavy and full, and her tiny hand wobbled slightly as she poured. She seemed to be concentrating fiercely; her brow was knitted in a tight frown, incongruous to her delicate features.

"Roxy, I . . ." He frowned as some of the interpreter's words finally filtered through. Gamble looked down at the devices on the tabletop, confused.

"What the . . . ?" he said, picking up Kenneth's phone, as Roxy's voice continued to emanate from the speaker.

The interpreter was a sentence or two behind, but although Gamble spoke no Romanian, it didn't sound like a phone call home. In fact, he might have said it sounded like she was issuing commands . . .

In a deceptively swift move, Roxy lifted the coffee pot above her head. The sinews erupted on her arm for a second, and then she brought it down onto Gamble's head with a tremendous crash. The bone china shattered into splinters and boiling coffee sprayed everywhere — mainly over Gamble — mixing with blood as it flowed onto the floor.

Gamble didn't scream exactly; the force of the blow had blackened a good deal of the consciousness from him, but he groaned and grunted as the burning liquid ran down his scalp and over his chest.

On the second phone, the recording of Roxy was still chattering away. On the first phone, the interpreter became animated, shouting, "What is going on?" and similar. Roxy turned them both off.

She grabbed Gamble by the ankles and tried to pull him into the bathroom, but he was too heavy. His groans were starting to become louder too, as his conscious mind began to register the scalds over his head, shoulders and chest.

Roxy dealt with this by taking an iron from a cupboard and swinging it by the flex like a pendulum. After building up a bit of a head of steam, she swung the steel hammer into the side of Gamble's temple, and he was silenced.

She moved the table out of the way and tried again with the ankle; this time, she was able to gain a bit of traction. She heaved and grunted and, after a fair amount of effort, was able to drag Gamble into the bathroom.

She looked down at her forearm, where blood was seeping from a wound caused by a shard of the coffee pot. She cursed, wrapped it in a towel and picked up Kenneth's phone. She stopped the playback of the recording and made a call.

"It is me," she said, in accented but perfectly fluent English. "There is a problem. We need to meet. The usual place. We need to move on the plan immediately."

The person on the other end of the phone asked a question.

"Yes, I am coming in person."

She looked down at Gamble's still body.

"And I'm bringing a guest."

CHAPTER FORTY-ONE

Kenneth, feeling about as flat and low as he'd ever felt in his life, shuffled side on down the alley and out onto the street with his bags, which was a feat in itself. A film of grey dew coated the early morning concrete as he walked to his car, the warmth of the day ahead already starting to burn it away, and he wrestled with his trundling suitcase, which refused to move smoothly over the paving slabs that had been forced out of position by the gradually erupting roots of a number of oaks that lined the street.

In ordinary circumstances, to see yet another plain-clothes cop so soon would have caused his stomach to sink. But the heavy blanket of depression that weighed on him had numbed him of that. His whole miserable life he'd only tried to please, and had only ever ended up disappointing or, worse, evoking apathy and dismissiveness. But this was far worse. This time he hadn't gone from zero to crap, he'd gone from having something good — something amazing — to crap.

So, when he saw Detective Inspector Barnes — the one who'd been so rude to him four months previously — waiting by his car, he was verging on hostile.

DI Barnes, however, got in first.

"You," Barnes said. He was pointing. "You've been to see Roxana Petrescu, haven't you?"

"So what?"

Barnes raised his hands to the heavens and then ran them through his hair. "Oh my God, I can't believe it. You put that woman back in mortal danger the night she escaped, and now, what? You're doing everything in your power to make sure the prosecution gets thrown out as well? If I didn't know better I'd have said you were in cahoots with this bloody gang."

For a moment, it seemed like quite a good gig; doing your day job, but with the added kudos of being undercover for some badass gangsters.

"You don't have to tell me off as well," Kenneth said. "I've already dropped my statement. I'm not going to testify."

Barnes's eyes widened. "You . . . what?" He took a step closer, and for a moment Kenneth thought he was going to actually slap him. "You don't get to back out now."

"But I thought you just said—"

"I didn't say drop your statement. I came to say: stop visiting witnesses, particularly the really vulnerable ones, and that, if we're upfront about the whole thing, then we might just salvage it. But I need to know everything: when you visited, how often, what you talked about, the lot. Hang on . . . as well?"

"What?"

"You said 'as well'?"

"Yes?"

"What do you mean by that? Someone else has told you off?"

"Yes. Last night. The other detective."

"Who? Kane? The one with the piercings?"

"No, not him. Weirdo, he is. No, the skinny one with the bad skin. Wears yellow shirts and brown suits."

Barnes looked at the pavement. "Gamble? Paul Gamble?"

"Yes, that's him."

"He was here?"

"Yes. Last night."

"What did he want?"

Kenneth made a mildly satisfying show of exasperation. "To tell me to drop my statement. He took my phone."

"He *what?*"

"As evidence. He told me off like you are now, and then he went."

Barnes stared at Kenneth, then his eyes dropped to Kenneth's bags. Two holdalls and a second-hand suitcase, to be precise. "Are you going somewhere?"

"Yes," he mumbled.

"Well, where?"

"I don't know yet. Just . . . away. This has not been a good experience for me, detective."

Barnes seemed to think on this for a moment, then he fished out what cash he had on him and pressed it into Kenneth's hand.

"Find a hotel. Call or text me when you know where. Don't tell *anyone* else where you're going. I need to get you somewhere safe."

Kenneth felt a cold feeling in his throat. He didn't like the sound of that.

"Do you think I'm in danger? I said I wouldn't testify. Why would I still be in danger?"

"Don't overthink it. Listen, did DS Gamble say anything else? About where he was going with your phone?"

"Well, like I said, he told me off for talking about the case, then I think he said he was going to go and see Roxy to tell her the same thing."

Barnes was off and running. Kenneth called after him not to trip on the uneven flagstones, but he was gone.

* * *

Kane ended the call and slipped his mobile back into his pocket. He tapped the point of his shoe on the floor as if keeping time with a particularly frenetic jitterbug, his lips pursed, his eyes fixed on a corner of the office ceiling.

Someone like Barnes would have said something like, *Something doesn't smell right*, a notion that fascinated Kane. Everything had to be watertight when you got to a court-room, but it was the smell that got you looking in a particular direction. Suspicion was a powerful dragnet — if a clumsy one: *I've done nothing wrong* was at the root of many a police complaint — and it was drumming its fingers on his insides.

It was the call that didn't smell right. Roxana Petrescu's nurse, Corinne — who, amazingly, seemed to have warmed to him — had taken his call, and told him that Roxy, along with the nine fellow slaves she'd fought be brought closer to her, had been transferred to another facility. Kane had asked why she — why *they* — had been moved; Corinne became anxious and described two Home Office officials and a team of supposed clinicians descending on the facility and whisking Roxy and the others away from under her nose. Corinne had demanded to know where they were being taken, but had been fobbed off. After they'd gone, she'd made numerous calls to her bosses and the central government oversight depart-ment, but had got nowhere. A pregnant silence on the phone had followed, and Corinne must have realised that she had just told a senior police officer that ten highly vulnerable and at-risk trafficking victims and prosecution witnesses were, well . . . nobody at that moment knew exactly where they were.

Kane signed the resignation letter that had been staring up at him from his desktop all morning and then carefully slid it into the top drawer of his desk. As a minimum, he wanted to sleep on it. He also had the most peculiar sense that it was not possible for him to resign now, that he would have to see this case through to its conclusion.

There were other cases, of course, but none that would normally warrant the depth of involvement of a superinten-dent. He'd been asked for resources and overtime approvals and surveillance authorities and custody extensions, but he wasn't as involved as he was with this one.

As baptisms of fire went, it had been an especially hot one, irrespective of the fact that he'd come along for the ride purely to learn the ropes; anyone else in his position probably wouldn't have done much more than read the case file, if that. But he'd seen the look in the eye of the woman living next door to Kevin Bridger, and, in four months, hadn't been able to shift it from his mind.

His phone rang. *RUTHERFORD B* appeared on the screen.

"Barnes," Kane said.

"Samson . . . boss," Barnes said. He sounded out of breath. "I think Paul Gamble might just have done our legs. Again."

"What's he done now?"

"He paid a little visit to Kenneth Rix last night. Managed to spook him into not testifying. Rix said he thinks he was on his way to see Roxy."

"How would he know how to find her?"

"I've no idea, but I've a horrible feeling she's been compromised."

"She's been moved."

"What?"

"I just called the facility. Spoke to the nursing manager, Corinne. Roxy's been transferred somewhere else. Along with the other nine witnesses. She didn't know where."

"They *moved* her? Without telling us?"

Kane heard a car door open and close, an engine turn and catch, and then Barnes's voice came tinnily through the loudspeaker.

"It doesn't sound like Corinne had much of a say in the matter," Kane said.

"That would have been an impressive encounter to watch."

"I don't think she was there. This happened late at night. Corinne's tried to find out who sanctioned the transfer, but has got nowhere."

"That doesn't sound right at all. Did she mention Gamble's visit?"

"No."

"Call me pessimistic, boss, but until I clap eyes on the pair of them I'd be inclined to call them both missing."

"I think I agree. In fact, the image I'm struggling to dislodge from my brain is one of our slave farmers all dressed up as nurses and civil servants, kidnapping Roxy from under Corinne's nose."

"That's good enough for me. They're missing. I'd better head up there and speak to her."

Kane was silent. He frowned.

"Boss, are you there? I said I'm heading up to the facility."

Kane didn't answer. Someone had shouted from the golf course outside. He tilted his head. It was not an especially troubling shout, but something was off.

"Sir? Hello? Samson? Are you there?"

Kane put the phone down on the table, Barnes still chattering through the speaker.

Then he realised. It wasn't the shout, but the fact that he could hear it at all.

He moved to the window and pushed it open, staring out onto the neatly tended grounds and the allotments beyond the perimeter fence.

Something was different.

Then he realised.

He picked the phone up off the desktop.

"Barnes . . . the leaf-blowers."

"What? What do you mean, leaf blowers? What are you talking about?"

"The line of leaf blowers in hi-vis orange jackets that have been outside my window for three months straight."

"What about them?"

"They're not here. They've gone."

CHAPTER FORTY-TWO

For a very brief moment, as he woke, Paul Gamble thought he had the mother of all hangovers. The side of his head felt like the top of a timpani drum and his mouth was like a scouring pad. A wave of nausea curled up inside him, but he realised it wasn't a hangover when he was filled with the urge to grab his pounding head, but couldn't, because his hands were bound.

He started to come round properly, and felt cold, damp concrete against his cheek. His clothes were wet and there was a raw, chafing feeling at his wrists where what felt like thin cord rope had been used to tie them. There was something hard on his face that seemed to crack when he flexed his jaw, and he guessed it was probably more than a bit of dried blood. All of this was superseded, however, by pain like sheet lightning on his shoulders and chest. It felt like someone was pressing down on his skin with an iron built into an all-over body wrap, and then he remembered he'd been scalded by the boiling coffee in Roxy's room.

He was in a sort of forced kneeling position, with something hard pushing him forwards, and he realised he'd been lashed to some kind of wooden chair, with his face, neck and chest pressing into the ground. Somewhere above him, he could hear water dripping slowly and steadily into an empty echo chamber.

All in all, he decided he preferred unconsciousness.

He sensed other people nearby, and groaned loudly. Footsteps approached him, sounding as if they were walking through puddles; a hand grabbed the back of the chair, and he was hoisted back up into a sitting position, which relieved some of the pressure on his chest.

He sucked in air, and tried to make some sense of his surroundings. It was dark, that was a given, but that wasn't just his eyes. The room was massive, with no walls or doors visible in the gloom. He couldn't see any ceiling, but on the opposite wall a grid of vertical windows with segmented arches rose up in front of him. They were at least twenty feet high, suggesting to Gamble it was a hall of some kind; either that or the floors were long gone. The massive windows featured only a few intact panes, the majority having been smashed at some point in the past, and they let in a pale yellow light from what Gamble presumed was either an insipid evening or very early morning.

There was a low rumble of groaning metal and the sound of snapping electricity, and a bright light flashed briefly on and off through the windows. Gamble frowned as he recognised the unmistakable sound of a train trundling slowly past, and realised with surprise that he knew where he was. The Bedfordwell depot was a long-abandoned engine house and listed building, one that Gamble had been called to on more than a few occasions in his brief uniformed career to chase away the yobs. It sat under the Whitley Road bridge, about a kilometre north of the mainline rail terminus, and had all too briefly been a nineteenth-century pumping station and boiler house. It was nestled between the Tutts Barn allotments and the functional trappings of industry on the other side of the railway line — storage warehouses, factory units and car repair workshops.

Gamble swallowed. It was an irritatingly effective place to hide in plain sight. The nearest residential street could only have been about a hundred metres away, but there was no easy way to get onto the site by car, and the way the site dropped away from the road onto an open spread of hardcore wasteland meant that nobody ever really looked unless the local little shits were tearing the place up again.

He continued his deep breaths, trying not to throw up and wondering if this would be the last place he would ever see the inside of. A low feeling of dread enveloped him from the feet up. With some reluctance, he dropped his gaze to what he knew he would see.

At least four figures in the gloom, one of whom appeared to be a child. They stood in a silent row, silhouetted against the feeble light from outside, all except the child appearing to wear a giant white reflective costume in the shape of the letter H. Gamble thought the tableau would have made a pretty moody Pink Floyd album cover.

"Lights," the child said in accented English, and clapped.

A row of generator-powered arc lights fired up with a *clunk*. Gamble screwed his eyes shut as pain flashed through his head, akin, he thought, to steak knives flying through his brain.

This time he *was* sick. He pitched forwards, instinctively not wanting to get it down himself, overbalanced, and ended up face first on the concrete again. He tasted acid and grit as the contents of his stomach oozed out over the damp ground, and he thought: *this is how people choke on their own vomit*. Amazing. They wouldn't even be able to prove homicide.

Somebody hauled him up again, and, bizarrely, he felt a little better. The figures slowly — very slowly — came into focus, and he realised that the giant white "H" costumes were actually the reflective strips of orange hi-vis vests, and that the child was not a child.

Roxana Petrescu.

She was standing between three — no, four — other men. Nobody had said anything of consequence yet, but it was clear she was under no duress. In fact, from the body language alone it was apparent that she was in charge. The good-looking prick with the wavy hair from the storage unit stood next to her, still engrossed in his bloody clipboard.

Gamble didn't try to rationalise that he was unlikely to die here, that killing a cop was a massive risk to take, and that he would be just fine. Kidnap, false imprisonment and GBH of a cop — a bent cop, no less — were just as bad, and that didn't seem to have given them pause at all.

He tried to step outside himself, tried to imagine how stories of his death would resonate among cops and criminals alike. He imagined Sterling and his cronies toasting each other with stale bitter in some off-grid drinking pit, and murmuring, *Fair play to the copper, took it like a man, he did.* Tried to imagine some senior officer telling Caroline he died bravely, that he didn't go down bitching.

However, this internal eulogising was fairly heavily drowned out by fear, dread, and a sudden urge to beg and plead for his life that was practically as impossible to resist as vomiting, all prompted by the thought that the pain he was currently in would be nothing compared to the fireball that would mark his passing.

Don't show it, he thought, trying to give himself a coach-at-half-time pep talk. *Don't give the bastards the satisfaction.*

"Roxana Petrescu," he croaked. "What the fuck?"

She didn't smile.

"Your information is no good to us," she said. Her voice was half an octave deeper than he'd heard before, and sounded as if it were coated in steel. "Superintendent Kane."

"What do you mean?" he said. "He's the man responsible for having all eyes on you."

"He is still in post."

"It won't be long, trust me."

"There is no guarantee."

"I *gave* you a string of arrests and criminal associations from back in the day. More than enough for his police career to be cut down. Someone else will replace him, sure, but at a minimum you get a head start."

Roxy held up Gamble's phone.

"We do not share your optimism."

She pressed a button, and Marlon Choudhury's recorded voice echoed out of the speaker.

"*Mr Gamble, forgive me for missing your call, and thank you for the information. However, all of the historic, ah, indiscretions allegedly committed by Superintendent Kane were fully disclosed on his appointment, and given due consideration when he was being vetted. I'm afraid you're not telling us anything we don't already know. Perhaps you'd like to call me back to discuss further.*"

The message ended. Gamble swallowed.

"It's bullshit," he said. "He was arrested for drunk and disorderly. Assaulting his father. Arson, for Christ's sake."

"None of these resulted in a conviction," Roxy said. "The assault on his father was in the defence of his mother, a point the jury accepted. The arson investigation never resulted in charges. He was fined and released for drunk and disorderly. He is of no interest whatsoever to your Professional Standards detective."

"But it was a show of good faith, no? I can't promise everything I turn up is going to hit the jackpot for you, but at least I'm playing. You need to give me some more time. Some more specifics. Speculate to accumulate. Or something."

"After four unproductive months, you were generously given forty-eight hours, by Mr Kenley here, to provide something useful. That time has passed."

"Yes . . . yes, but what do you *gain* from offing me? Does it not make good business sense to see what else I can unearth? You kill a cop — even an unpopular one — that's a whole lot of attention on you."

Roxy folded her arms, like he'd asked a stupid question. Vernon Dodge moved off to the side. A few seconds later, Gamble was aware of him standing right behind him, and his heart started to thud inside his chest. He took deep breaths, trying to keep himself under control. *This could be it, old son,* he thought.

"At least tell me what the story is here," Gamble said, trying to buy himself time. "You're, what, the boss?"

"Head Office herself," Kenley muttered.

"So, what are you saying?" Gamble said. "You broke out in the middle of the night and ran across a field when you were running things all along?"

"Trust is very important in my line of work, Mr Gamble," Roxy said, shooting Kenley a sideways look. "Like any large organisation, we need to run drills for when things go wrong. I need to see how my people operate under pressure. I need to see how they deal with crises. I need to see how they withstand the pressure of the law. And I need to test their loyalty."

Gamble thought he saw Kenley swallow.

"You could have got out at any time," Gamble said.

"As it happens, I couldn't. I was not in a position to do anything other than play the role. I had no means to end the exercise."

"Undercover boss? Bit elaborate, isn't it?" Gamble said. "For a site inspection, you could have just got a taxi."

"Loyalty has no price, Mr Gamble. Nor does trust. If you cannot be certain your own people are not plotting against you, you do not deserve to lead."

"Yeah, but, I mean: crapping in a bucket for six weeks?"

Roxy's eyes narrowed.

"I was a young child during the uprising. Under Ceaușescu. My mother hid me in a cellar when the tanks came. They ripped my house apart. I do not fear hardship."

"Fair enough," Gamble said.

"I am skilful, resourceful and can influence men. Even if I were shipped in a barrel to Doftana I would still rise to become leader."

"Maybe I should take a leaf out of your book. I could have made DCI."

"As the principal victim, I also had the benefit of seeing the case from the inside. The lead police were obliged to share details of the investigation with me that the accused would never normally get to see."

"I see. That's pretty clever," Gamble admitted. "I'm afraid, though, that your ship might be a little looser than you think. I know about your operations. I know more than you think I know." Gamble hawked and spat, then leaned his body forwards and grinned. "I know, for example, you are planning to hit the tennis."

Roxy frowned at him.

"Every summer, Eastbourne hosts the tennis. Down at the Devonshire Park. Big names descend on the seaside in the sun and get themselves warmed up for Wimbledon. Security isn't particularly tight — family day out, see — but a half-sensible operation could net you six figures in cash, minimum. It's a clever scheme, all told."

"You . . . you think we are going to rob a tennis tournament?"

Gamble swallowed. "I've seen what I need to see. I've seen enough. And for all you know I've already fed this back and you're under surveillance right now."

Roxy's expression was momentarily impassive, and then she permitted herself a bark of laughter. *Oh, that's not good,* Gamble thought.

"Mr Gamble, police officers are suggestible. They take the information they are presented with at face value. It is simply a case of controlling that information. What, when and to whom it is made available. And to know that the same information is being taken sufficiently seriously."

Gamble's eyes widened, and he nodded towards the hi-vis jackets.

"So, the orange-suited Village People? You've been keeping the cops under surveillance?"

He shook his head. Even he had to admit he was impressed.

"And you wanted them to think you were planning to hit the tennis tournament."

Roxy waved a hand as if to say, *It was nothing.*

Kenley looked up sharply. He looked, Gamble thought, a little agitated.

"So, what's the real plan?" Gamble said, eyeballing Kenley. He knew on the one hand that, if he were given the answer, he almost certainly wouldn't be leaving this building alive; on the other, he sensed Kenley's disquiet and had to at least try to use it to his advantage.

"Operations have yet to resume full productivity since I was freed. One of my captains was found at the scene. That was not part of the plan. This is what happens when one conducts an overt site inspection by taxi."

Gamble frowned, missing the rejoinder. "Who? Stratton Pearce?"

"His greatest strength is, regrettably, his biggest weakness. There is a need to limit the consequences of this."

"What do you mean?"

"Mr Pearce is . . . is a . . ."

"Loose cannon?" Kenley offered.

Roxy eyeballed him again. "Yes, I think this is the phrase. His being detained was reckless. All those years spent in exile, and he is captured during the one day he decided to show his face."

"Why . . . why was he in exile?"

Roxy frowned. "He was responsible for the death of a police officer's wife. The same police officer investigating both the hive and the death of Kevin Bridger. He had been evading capture. He did not listen to advice."

She looked at Kenley.

"Barnes? Rutherford Barnes?" Gamble shuffled forwards as best as he could. He was fascinated by the story, even though some part of his brain was telling him that there was no way they were going to let him walk out of here with this information.

"These are business decisions, Mr Gamble. I nevertheless need Stratton Pearce out of custody. I need him to think carefully about whether and when he decides to open his mouth. And I need him to run operations."

Gamble wasn't sure, but he thought he saw the man named Kenley roll his eyes.

"So, what? You're going to break him out?"

"We're what?" Kenley said sharply.

Gamble looked up. Kenley had fixed Roxy with a stare that gleamed in the darkness.

"What do you mean: we're breaking him out? What about the fucking tennis? That's half a goldmine, and a low-risk one at that. Well, low-ish."

"After a recent run of poor behaviour in prison, Mr Pearce is being transferred to HMP Belmarsh."

"Bad behaviour?" Gamble swallowed.

"Mr Pearce reacted badly to the deaths of his girlfriend and child in a fire, and continues to be difficult."

"That was you?" Kenley again, his voice rasping. He was fixed to the spot, staring at Roxy like he wanted to put a .22 round into her brain.

Roxy turned to him. "*You've got no real teeth*," she said in a low hiss.

Kenley's jaw dropped.

"This has worked to our advantage," she said, turning back to Gamble. "He is being moved during the tennis tournament. It is too good an opportunity to miss."

"And so, while all the manpower is looking towards Centre Court, you're going to be going in the opposite direction," Gamble murmured.

Roxy held up a small grey block that Gamble recognised as Kenneth Rix's mobile phone. She pressed a button and her own tinny voice began to chatter commands in the gloom.

"That's you out in the cold, then," Kenley said, sounding tired.

Roxy moved towards Gamble, as if to meet him in the middle of a dancefloor covered by half an inch of stagnant water.

"Not at all," she said, staring at Gamble but addressing Kenley. "This plays very nicely indeed. It is our final play to nudge the police in the wrong direction."

She stepped back. One of the Village People stepped forwards, a jiffy bag in his meaty hand. She took it from him, and dropped Kenneth's phone into it.

"If the police were in any doubt about the tennis being genuine information, this will remove that doubt."

"You only talked about the tennis on the recording," Gamble said, hanging his head. "You didn't mention Pearce at all."

This is it, Gamble thought. *Come on*, he said to himself. *Go out with a bang. On your terms.*

"It's funny," he said. "I've had some pretty low moments in recent years. The few occasions where I did actually think seriously about driving off Beachy Head or dangling myself out of the loft hatch, it was the fact that my ex-wife wouldn't get a payout that stopped me."

Roxy frowned, not appearing to understand.

"Suicide nullifies the life policy," Gamble said, wheezing with laughter as he figured that, at this stage, anything to keep her wondering couldn't be a bad thing. "But I guess by coming to you, I finally did the right thing."

He craned his head up, stretching his neck. As famous last words went, they weren't particularly memorable, but at least he wasn't pleading like a wuss.

Roxy stepped forwards.

She nodded. Gamble didn't feel the blade, but he was aware of the sudden warm feeling gushing down his front as his neck was opened up. It was painless, almost imperceptible, but he went almost instantly into shock. He began to jerk and thrash as panic gripped him, and he toppled forwards again, his warm blood pouring out of the gash in his throat until his body was as cold as the concrete floor.

CHAPTER FORTY-THREE

Barnes turned the key in the lock. With a bit of persuasion, the heavy wooden door popped open. A stink of stale air and damp rushed out of the darkness and out onto the breeze.

He shone a torch into the entrance chamber, and then stepped inside.

"Facilities are going to have a fit," Barnes said. "Not to mention Health and Safety."

"They'll have to live with it," Kane said. "If we aren't safe in a bloody police station, we need to get creative."

One of seventy-four defensive forts built on the south coast in the nineteenth century, Tower Seventy-Three — as it was also known — sat at the crown of the Wish Tower Slopes, with an oblong glass deck bolted onto its southern face that had been a popular café and sun lounge for most of the latter part of the twentieth century. The café had been in decline for some years and now, largely mothballed, it provided a decent location for Kane and Barnes to set up shop.

Barnes found a light switch and a feeble umbrella of yellow light was cast around the circumference of the Wish Tower's coursed brickwork. In the vault below their feet was four feet of standing water, and the main chamber was stacked with junk — plasterboard partitions, decorator's ladders, metal frames.

Kane climbed a garishly painted spiral staircase to the upper level, and, once on the mezzanine, rested his hands on an equally garish railing.

"Cheers the place up a bit," he said.

"It was a puppet museum for most of the nineties," Barnes said. "Council just use it as a storeroom now."

Kane passed through a multicoloured stone archway onto a further set of steps that led to the roof and Barnes joined him outside atop the gunning emplacement. They climbed onto a raised stone sill on the parapet wall and found themselves with a 360-degree panorama of the seafront. The glacis wall of the moat surrounding the tower led on to the Wish Tower Slopes, which dropped away to the promenade and the life-boat museum. Beyond that, Wilmington Square led down to Devonshire Park, where the grandstand peeked tantalisingly over the Brutalist roof of the Congress Theatre, while the ever-watchful South Downs rose up on the horizon in a curtain of green.

"Cracking view," Barnes said.

"What happened at the facility?" Kane said, turning to him.

"It's as we suspected. A group of six put on a convincing display of wanting to officially transfer Roxy and her co-hostages, waved court orders and the like about, and made some implicit threats when the night guard tried to apply a bit of due diligence."

"What did Corinne say?" Kane said.

Barnes shrugged. "A combination of shame and unfettered anger. She wasn't there when they descended to take Roxy, but, even so, she feels like she's been had over. Needless to say, the ears of every Home Office department from here to Gibraltar are ringing."

"No leads?"

"Nothing. CCTV was disabled. No ANPR cameras in a decent radius. No scene evidence. The night guard and the duty nurse are looking at some pictures, but I'm not optimistic."

"I wouldn't have fancied being in their shoes when they fronted up to her."

They re-entered the circular tower and found what appeared to be a suitable point to set up shop — the former officer's quarters, directly above the powder store. Kane shoved a brightly coloured shelving unit out onto the mezzanine, and the pair of them spent half an hour clearing out the contents.

* * *

To their eternal credit, the Facilities team moved heaven and earth to set Kane up with a makeshift operations room. Barnes wasn't sure if it was the weight of the crown on Kane's shoulder that got it done, the reputational ramifications of having been under observations by a criminal group — it didn't quite qualify as hostile reconnaissance, but it was close enough — or the fact that he'd just asked them nicely. In any case, Kane had been determined to make the point that they were on a war footing as a result of being compromised.

Not that it had been a particularly easy fight to win. Remote networks, electrics and other utilities had caused some headaches — why couldn't he just use a police station? — but the elevated location, proximity to the tennis club and the fact that it didn't look like anything much from the outside meant it was a winner for Kane, and he had dug his heels in on the basis that he'd been under surveillance for the best part of four months.

Nevertheless, within twenty-four hours they had heat, power, light and basic comforts. The small team already earmarked for policing the event were hastily relocated and installed alongside banks of monitors and radio equipment.

Barnes had watched from the sidelines as the Division's finance director had slowly torn her hair out, scrabbling around to make sure that the costs had been appropriately distributed among the various agencies involved. The ACC had been slightly more sanguine — unbelievably — apparently telling Kane: "It's your budget. You'd just better not be over-spent come year-end."

The June sun was like a warm blanket, and from the elevated vantage point of the CCTV, Barnes watched as tiny figures strolled along the promenade. Damp wooden groynes, encrusted with limpets, reached through the shingle into the sea like outstretched fingers, and brightly coloured bunting stretched between the Victorian gas lamps along King Edward's Parade.

Kane appeared at Barnes's shoulder.

"I just can't see it," Barnes said.

"We've done enough," Kane said. "No one's going to be eavesdropping in here."

"But what if we're wrong? What if they're going after something else altogether? This is an awful lot of effort when we're only really guessing at the real target."

Kane reached behind him and picked up a jiffy bag off the tabletop. He handed it to Barnes.

"What's this?"

"Orderlies delivered it yesterday. Just as I was packing up the office."

Barnes looked at the envelope. *SUPERINTENDENT KANE — EYES ONLY* was written on the front in black marker pen.

Barnes frowned. There was no postmark, return address or postage on the envelope. "Where did this come from?"

Kane shrugged. "It was in my docket."

Barnes upended the jiffy bag onto the tabletop.

An exhibit bag containing an old mobile phone fell out. There was a note wrapped around it, and a separate sheaf of papers with block-printed typeface. Through instinct as much as anything, Barnes pulled on a pair of blue latex gloves.

He unwrapped the note from the exhibit bag. He scanned it and frowned.

"It's from Paul Gamble," he said.

He read aloud.

SUPERINTENDENT KANE,

THIS IS KENNETH RIX'S PHONE. I BELIEVE IT MAY ASSIST YOUR ENQUIRIES. THE VOICE RECORDING DATED 2 JUNE 2010, 47 MINUTES LONG, WILL BE OF INTEREST.

YOU MAY WISH TO VERIFY THE RECORDING WITH AN INTERPRETER, BUT I CAN CONFIRM THE TRANSCRIPT IS ACCURATE.

GOOD LUCK.

PAUL GAMBLE

"Doesn't sound like the kind of thing Paul Gamble would send," Barnes said, frowning. "Unless he's had a touch of the seconds."

"Play it," Kane said.

Barnes played the recording as instructed, his expression growing in astonishment as he followed along with the transcript.

The sound was muffled, but Roxana Petrescu's voice was unmistakable, if bolder and stronger than they were used to.

> *Where are we with the police . . . ?*
> *I'm starting to wonder about your loyalty . . .*
> *I will make sure they hear the message . . .*
> *The tennis tournament plan will go ahead, under Donkey Kong's command . . .*

There was the sound of a door knock on the recording, and someone entered the room. Kane heard Kenneth's voice, and Roxy's tone became more conversational.

Barnes stopped the recording.

"She doesn't sound much like a kidnap victim," Barnes said, quietly. "Who's Donkey Kong?"

Kane shook his head.

"Not a clue."

CHAPTER FORTY-FOUR

Kenley raced around the house, shoving belongings into a holdall. It was a careless, rushed packing exercise, bordering on panicked. Essentials only — clothes, money, passport, nine-mil with two clips. Phone, credit cards, laptop — anything with a footprint — would have to stay behind.

He ran some clippers over his head, lopping off the dark, rust-edged curls and taking his hair down to a severe zero-grade cut, and pulled on a grey hoody. He touched the tattoo on his scalp, then covered his head with a baseball cap.

What an idiot he'd been. The whole plan to take out an international sporting event had sounded ridiculously off brand when Head Office — or Roxy, or whoever — had first mooted it. Now it was clear — it was a smokescreen. Classic disinformation. Head Office's personal appearance suggested they clearly didn't believe Kenley had the wit to run Keber, and so, while they had the cops looking the other way, they were going to break out Stratton bloody Pearce.

Raging, bilious, vengeful Stratton Pearce. An already violent and short-tempered individual, the loss of his girl-friend and son had left him positively unhinged, and conventional wisdom said he held Kenley responsible — a fact Head Office clearly wanted to cultivate.

There was a thud and *shushing* noise from above him. He jumped back, pressing himself against the wall in case an enormous hand was about to punch through the roof and grab him.

He waited. Nothing else happened, and so he resumed his frantic activity. He thudded down the stairs, intending to take the car, dump it in an underground car park and then use public transport to get him to the nearest port. If he could make mainland Europe before nightfall — or before the hammer came down, whichever was sooner — he might, *might* have a chance.

He carefully dropped some food into the aquarium, grabbed a bottle of water and flung open the front door.

Natalie stood there.

Her jaw and folded arms sparked anger, but her eyes read heartbreak.

"Going somewhere?" she said, barely able to part her teeth.

His arms dropped to his sides. "Natalie, I . . ."

"You lying bastard," she said, shaking her head. "NHS project officer? How stupid must I be? What kind of *detective*?"

Kenley tilted his head, just about suppressing the instinct to confess all.

"What . . . have you been told?" he said. "What is it you think I am?"

"I checked you out," she said.

Kenley frowned. "Can you do that?"

"Don't be stupid," she said. "It was official. New relationships trigger re-vetting. They run a check to see if your new partner is a wrong 'un. Apparently, you are."

The words *new partner* had the crushing finality of perhaps the biggest opportunity Kenley had felt he'd ever let slip through his fingers.

"Did . . . did they say why?"

"They didn't give me your inside leg measurement, but it was DEFCON Three when your name came up, clearly. If the head of Professional Standards tells you to choose between your next-door neighbour and your career, you know it's not a speeding fine."

"What . . . what did they . . ."

"I'm asking you!" she said. "Why don't you tell me the truth before I shitcan you? At least do me the courtesy of that."

"I can't tell you. It's for your own good." He put down his bag and tried to take her hand. She stepped backwards.

"I let you into my life," she said. "I let you into *Max's* life. I must want my bloody head examined."

The street was quiet. In the distance there was the dim sound of lorries reversing and the clank of machinery from the harbour's latest construction site, and the ever-present screech of seagulls.

The sound of tyres rumbling slowly over the tarmac added to the mix, and a dark grey Vauxhall saloon pulled up at the end of the driveway, crunching on the grit and dust swept to the kerb by the machinery.

Kenley took his eyes from Natalie when the car arrived; she obviously saw this and turned to look also. Sterling and Golden Wonder got out and leaned against the car. Even to the most forgiving of eyes, it was impossible for the tableau to look like anything but bad news. Sterling's customary grin was absent, which didn't bode well either.

Kenley stepped forward again. This time, she didn't move. He took one hand in hers, placed the other around the back of her neck and pressed his mouth to her ear. Her hair was warm, and smelled of something sweet.

"I'm sorry, okay? For everything. Not everything was a lie, though. Not everything. I couldn't tell you. You'd be in danger."

Her body started to shake.

"Listen, when I go, I need you to look after my fish. Can you feed them?" He released her and held her gaze. "There's instructions in the aquarium, okay?"

She nodded. He walked down the driveway.

"The reluctant ruler," Sterling said, opening the rear kerbside door, still not smiling. He nodded at the holdall. "Going somewhere?"

Kenley frowned, and pushed the holdall into Sterling's chest.

"You should think about something similar. This could go one of a number of ways," he replied. "Chuck it in the boot for us."

Sterling held his boss's stare for a moment, and then obliged. Kenley got in the back.

"You all match fit, then?" Sterling said as he got in beside Kenley.

Golden Wonder put the car in gear. Kenley stared out of the window as they moved off.

Natalie hadn't moved. She was still facing Kenley's empty house, her back to the road, her arms wrapped around her shoulders.

Kenley forced himself to turn his head away.

"We'd better go make this crime scene look less like a crime scene," he said. "Is it just us?"

"The three amigos," Sterling said.

"Freeman, Hardy and Willis, more like. Where's our people?" Kenley said.

Sterling frowned. "You know where they are. It's just us. The rest of them have got a big day ahead. They've already headed out with the boss . . ."

Even Sterling, with his sociopathic tendencies, must have realised what he'd said. Kenley turned slowly to him, his eyes narrow. Sterling swallowed.

"I'm the fucking boss," Kenley said quietly. "Call them. Get them back here."

"What?"

"You heard me. Pick up the phone and summon them here. As many as you can."

"That isn't the—"

"Sterling, I swear to God, if you make me ask you again, we will be stuffing *your* body in a plastic barrel."

Kenley felt Golden Wonder eyeball him in the rear-view. The knots flexed in Sterling's jaw. He didn't blink.

"What are you doing, Kenley?"

"Change of plan."

CHAPTER FORTY-FIVE

On the morning of the third day of the Eastbourne International tennis tournament, things started to warm up. The crowds fattened up, the bigger names began to appear on Centre Court, and the sun rose over the Channel in a hazy skin, wisps of mist curling upwards as the warmth started to eat into the vapour. Trains pulling into the main terminus disgorged streams of passengers in a kaleidoscope of colours; they reached the street and dispersed, mainly on foot, up through Little Chelsea towards Devonshire Park using a network of road closures demarcated with Heras fencing.

Barnes and Kane stood in their bespoke command suite in the centre of the Wish Tower.

"Weather's staying good," Kane remarked. "Footfall has been high."

"That's why they have it in June," Barnes said. "Get people warmed up for Wimbledon."

"I had half-hoped that this ash cloud over Iceland might have kept the numbers down a bit, but it seems to have all but cleared up," Kane said.

"I hope there's nothing symbolic in our choice of location," Barnes said. "The Martello Towers and Redoubt fortress were meant to be a stone defence against invasion."

"I kind of like it. 'Redoubt.' Strong. Solid. Resolute in defence," Kane said.

"I think if you trace back the origins of the word, it actually means 'retreat'," Barnes said.

Kane didn't have an answer for that one.

Arms folded, Kane stared grimly at the bank of screens in front of him, which was a networked grid of all the police CCTV cameras in the town on a live feed from the operators' mainframe. Neither he nor Barnes had moved much since the tournament began.

"Well, we know they're not going to blow up Devonshire Park," Kane said. "We've searched and sealed it to the nth degree."

"BTP have got the station," Barnes said. "They've got explo dogs, search, spotters — and it's their daily bread. You've got the possibility of a stealth attack on the people moving through the town, or even the queues, but it's a steady throughput of people. Limited crowd density, limited opportunity for maximum casualties."

"Which leaves the event itself. The grandstand."

"We've got double the yellow jackets. Double the road closures. Air support. Sniffer dogs. Rifles on the roof. Concrete barriers. Any car not local to the area is getting towed out and blown up. And that's *outside* the main footprint."

Kane rubbed his chin. The tactical options even extended to the sea, with coastguard marine patrols providing a southern flank in the relatively unlikely event that the attack came from the water.

"I still don't see it," he said. "These guys are not martyrs. They're in it for the money."

"Maybe one of them will wig out and let rip with a blunderbuss, like that taxi driver."

"Taxi driver?"

"The guy up in Cumbria. Less than a month ago. Maybe one of his crew is at the end of his tether."

Kane looked down at the monitor showing the feed from the helicopter. The streams of people, bright colours smudged against the grey tarmac, were slowly beginning to thicken as they made their way towards Devonshire Park.

"I just don't see it," Kane said again.

* * *

Kenley looked at his watch while Golden Wonder finished up in the depot. He started the engine, resisting the urge to lean over the seat and bang the horn. Daylight had well and truly arrived but, this early on a Saturday, nobody was likely to be looking down at the depot, and there didn't seem to be a good reason to change that.

That didn't make him any less tense, however. His right leg jiggled uncontrollably as he looked from his watch to the depot and back again.

"*Come on come on come on . . .*" he muttered to himself.

Head Office — Roxy, whatever her name was — would be comfortably back to wherever she was headed now. She would run point on breaking Pearce out — because she didn't trust *him* to do it — then disappear back into whatever bloody parallel-universe wormhole she came from. She had taken Blue Ray and all their other manpower off with her; Sterling had been sent off with his marching orders to remobilise their troops, leaving Kenley and Golden Wonder to clean up Gamble's body.

In the interests of expediency, the corpse had been stripped of clothing and jewellery and stuffed into one of the — latterly, extremely handy — plastic barrels. Sterling bagged and incinerated the clothing while Golden Wonder made a reasonable effort of hosing down the not inconsiderable amount of blood. It was no better than ensuring anyone peeking in the window wouldn't do a double-take, but that was all. Get a swarm of SOCOs over the place and they'd very quickly work out what had happened and to whom. Kenley was paranoid about invisible specks of blood spattered all over his trainers.

He just had to hope that the call he'd told Sterling to make had worked. They had enough people, enough of a network to redeploy who he'd asked for and put some fresh eyes in behind him to still man the breakout operation. The important thing was to get as many of them back down here with him as he could. Make them think Plan A was still an actual plan.

And when he went down, take as many of the fuckers down with him as possible.

Golden Wonder finally appeared in the driver's seat "They find him, they'll think I'm some kind of serial killer nutcase."

Kenley didn't answer. They drove out of the depot and onto the seafront, then back out onto the perimeter roads that flanked the township, a patchwork of industrial units, factories and retail warehouses threading through it.

The new RVP was an empty car showroom opposite a series of warehouses just by the Golden Jubilee Way, a long, straight flyover rising over the Hydneye Lakes that took you hard, fast and north out of town — whether it had just closed or was about to open, Kenley wasn't sure. He also wasn't sure if they had any kind of lease on the place or whether they were just squatting. It was a shell for the crash-and-burn plan, so maybe it didn't matter.

As they walked into the glass-fronted showroom, Kenley thought he could detect new car smell, and decided he leaned more towards the just-vacated theory. Times were tough, he reasoned, and it seemed that taking a fall might, after all, be the most sensible play in the game. Everything would freeze until the day he came out.

They traversed the empty showroom, the pile soaking up their footsteps, and Kenley wondered if maybe he could start up something like this when he got out, if there would be something waiting for him. He'd still be young. Maybe it could be something honest.

Yeah, right.

He pushed open the door of a corner partition office that, he presumed, used to be a sales manager's office. Blue Ray and Sterling stood there, along with four others.

Better than nothing.

"What are we doing here, Kenley?" Sterling said.

"You sweep this place?" Kenley said.

"It's clean," Sterling said. "Has been for months. What are we doing here?"

"Plan isn't going to wash. We need to make it look real."

"The dead sergeant stuffed into a barrel isn't real enough for you?" Sterling said.

"Look, we need to make enough noise to keep the cops looking the other way, otherwise it isn't going to play. Pearce needs to get enough clear air between the sweat box and wherever the hell he's headed to go and stay gone. That won't happen if they don't treat it as the real thing, or as near to the real thing as dammit."

Sterling took a step forward. "Kenley, you're talking about hooning into a public event in broad daylight in a couple of four-by-fours. That's the 'T' word. They'll shoot first and not give a flying tit about whether it's the real deal or not until much later, if at all. For all I know, that's enough to *call* it terrorism — whether you mean it or not is a moot point."

Kenley squared up to him. "You're not scared are you, Len?"

Sterling ground his jaw.

"If it makes you feel any better, Head Office signed off on this. You don't want to hear it from me, give her a call."

Kenley pulled out his mobile phone and held it out to Sterling, whose eyes flicked from Kenley to the device and back again.

"We don't do this, we're dead anyway," Kenley said. "Pearce doesn't get safely away, we're all dead. Now, can you do your part?"

"Know what I think? I think you don't *want* him out. I think you want him in prison," Sterling said.

Kenley wiggled the phone, then put it back in his pocket. "Just be sure to put your hands up when you get out of the car. Let's mount up."

He turned on his heel and walked out.

* * *

The crowds widened out as the day got warmer, but Kane had barely moved, scanning the screens without blinking for almost two hours. In the end Barnes's leg began to seize up, and he pulled up an ancient office chair, stretching out his leg on the desk next to Kane with a grimace.

Kane finally tore his gaze away to look at Barnes. "Bad leg?"

"Car crash. Few years back. Gives me jip every once in a while."

"Must make the fitness test tough," Kane said.

"It's nothing. Wait till they mandate it."

"Line of duty?"

Barnes eyeballed him for a second.

"Not exactly." He went back to staring at the monitors. "You realise that this is a seven-day tournament, yes? You're going to need to take a break at some point."

Kane looked back at the screens.

"If something's going to happen," Barnes continued, "chances are it will be more towards the end of the week than the beginning."

Kane didn't answer. He'd looked perturbed when Barnes had briefed him that the visiting players were distributed among the seafront hotels, and even more so when he found out that only the top seeds had bodyguards, despite the top seeds being the only ones that could stay in hotel rooms whose daily rate reached triple figures. It had got worse when he'd found out that the number of visiting dignitaries could reach double figures, but that those with their own protection wouldn't get anywhere close to that.

Eventually, Barnes decided on a brief break, and he carefully stretched himself upright.

"I'll be back in ten," he said, moving past a decorator's scaffold to the door. "You want anything?"

Kane just grunted.

Barnes opened the door — and almost walked into DC Natalie Morgan.

She was standing there, red-eyed and shaking, her hands pressed into her breast.

"Good grief, you gave me a fright," Barnes said. He tilted his head. "I know you. DC Morgan, yes? Natalie? Child Protection?"

"Can I come in?" she said.

Barnes frowned.

"How the hell did you know to find us here?"

"Marlon Choudhury," she said, simply, and that was enough for Barnes. The circle of knowledge of their clandestine command centre was tight, but Marlon was in it, and Barnes trusted him with his life.

He opened the door wide. Kane turned as she entered. She stood in the middle of the room, moving from one man's gaze to another; after a moment or two, Barnes pushed the office chair towards her.

"What is it?" Kane said. "Are you okay?"

"I need to tell you something," she said, and uncurled her hands to reveal an evidence bag with a single piece of paper inside, which she thrust towards Barnes.

"What's this?" he said, looking from the paper to Natalie and back again. His eyes widened as he read what was on the paper, then passed it to Kane.

"What is it?" Kane asked.

"We need to clear those crowds, boss. As in, now."

* * *

Kenley drove, Golden Wonder next to him. On the back of the truck were Blue Ray and some other primate Kenley didn't know. Riding in close convoy in a ten-year-old Jeep Cherokee were Sterling and whichever musketeers he'd brought with him. Two others had been left at the showroom, cop-bait for when the doors were kicked in.

They were grim-faced, and Kenley knew that the last dregs of his influence had been used in securing their willingness to accompany him — actually, if not for the fact of forward motion, he felt fairly sure their obedience would have already evaporated during the short journey. He still wasn't completely convinced one of them wasn't going to stick a Sabatier in the back of his neck as he drove.

The tennis didn't result in quite the same complete shutdown as the air show or the fireworks, and the weekday traffic was steady, if not particularly heavy. The journey was smooth until they neared the coast, heading around the industrial network of Highfield Link and Lottbridge Drove and south towards the Sovereign Centre, where the traffic began to slow with dozens of motorists descending on the seafront for a stroll in the sun — and, if they were lucky, a glimpse of the odd tennis megastar.

Kenley's mobile phone buzzed in his jacket. He pulled it out and handed it to Golden Wonder.

"See who that is."

Golden Wonder flipped open the phone.

"Head Office," he said. "They're on schedule for Pearce."

"How long?"

"Ten minutes. No more than fifteen."

Kenley grimaced. He was behind schedule. What the hell was Natalie playing at? He'd practically drawn her a map.

He pressed the accelerator and, gradually, the sound of the revving engine became incongruous to the idling, ambient traffic noise as it bimbled around the town.

* * *

Kane called the control room, barking at them to raise Event Silver, while Barnes tried to debrief Natalie, who was having a difficult time staying composed.

"Tell me again what happened," Barnes said. "You've been in a relationship with this guy?"

"He . . . he's my next-door neighbour," she said, through hitched, shallow breaths. "We . . . I confronted him after PSD told me to steer clear of him. Some horrible thugs collected him in a car, and he gave me that. Or rather, hid it in his fish tank."

"Why has he *given* you this?" Barnes said. "He's putting himself smack bang in the middle of an attack plot. He's signing his own life sentence. Or worse."

She shook her head and her eyes glistened. "He . . . I think he was trying to protect me."

Barnes stared again at the note in the exhibit bag, somewhere between disbelief and incredulity.

"What's his name?" Barnes said, spinning around to the desk, a pen between his teeth.

"Kenley. Duquesne Kenley." She spelled it for him, and he bashed it into a keyboard.

"DK. Donkey Kong," Kane said.

"Got a picture?"

Natalie looked a little embarrassed, but held up her phone to show a picture of her and the man called Kenley grinning for the camera.

"You two were getting on, huh?" Barnes said, then he frowned, and peered at the phone more closely.

He returned to the keyboard and started bringing up images uploaded to the case files for Op Blackwater and Op Cavalier.

A grainy CCTV image in one.

A grey sketch likeness in profile in the other — jaw, cheekbone and thick curls caught in the wash from a streetlight.

Barnes lined them up and compared them with Natalie's photo — and inhaled sharply.

"Can I see?" she said. Barnes moved aside, watching her closely.

"That's him," she said. She looked at Barnes. "What is he a suspect for?"

"Double murder," he said, softly.

Her eyes filled with tears. Barnes looked down at the sheet of paper in the exhibit bag, and then back to the screen. Four clicks and he had a list of Kenley's documented associates.

"They're breaking him out. Today," Barnes muttered, tapping the glass.

"Who?" Kane said, placing his hand momentarily over the receiver.

Barnes turned.

"Stratton Pearce," he said, in a quiet voice. "They're breaking the prick out. He's being transferred to Belmarsh today."

Kane frowned. "Where?"

"That we don't know. Somewhere between Lewes and Belmarsh, I guess. Not a long journey."

"What are you saying? The attack is a smokescreen?"

Barnes stood and edged towards the monitors — just as the desktop radio set burst into life.

"Hotel-900, permission." There was urgency in the voice of the police helicopter operator.

"Go ahead, nine hundred," the controller responded.

"Be advised, you have two vehicles travelling at high speed along Royal Parade from the east towards the event footprint. Motives unclear. Recommending immediate evac."

"Barnes, get the prison governor on the phone. We need the itinerary of the transport. I'll call . . . Barnes? Are you okay? You look a little grey."

Barnes had sat back down heavily.

"He's the one," Barnes said, staring at the piece of paper in his hand, his knuckles white as he gripped the edges of the sheet. "It's here. *In exile for killing a cop's wife.* Pearce. I knew it was him when we met him. I just knew it. He's the one that killed her."

* * *

Kenley gripped the wheel as he pushed the accelerator to the floor. He was already ten miles an hour above the speed limit, which, on a normal day, was a difficult thing to achieve. The parade was lined on both sides by rows of parked cars.

He pressed harder, his adrenaline flooding through his system as his peripheral senses got lost in the face of the increasing speed. He heard car horns and screeching brakes and the thump-and-tinkle of collisions happening all around him as drivers took evasive action. The sound of the parked cars whipping past him sounded like the *whup-whup-whup* of a helicopter's rotor blades.

The engine roared louder, the pitch rising. People were starting to scream and move out of the way, the sound only partly distinguishable from the screech of the seagulls. Kenley fought the urge to shut his eyes, wrestling with the umbrella of peripheral senses being left behind in the wake of his increasing speed. He knew he should check to see if Sterling was still behind him, still matching his speed, but he felt pressed into the seat, like he weighed a thousand pounds.

He overtook a car idling at a zebra crossing by the Metropole Court, narrowly avoiding a couple clutching rum raisin ice cream cones from Fusciardi's parlour. The needle reached thirty-five . . . thirty-seven . . . thirty-nine . . .

He reached the pier, where the road inclined up and widened into a sprawling apron for coaches and emergency service vehicles. He offsided the Royal Sussex Memorial, a large dirty bronze statue of William Cavendish keeping a careful eye on the pier mouth.

The road narrowed again, and the car lost momentum as Kenley scraped alongside the bright blue iron railing separating the road from the vivid beds of Carpet Garden in a flash of sparks and grinding metal. A woman shrieked, and Kenley suddenly heard the thudding blades of a helicopter somewhere above him. He punched his way through the traffic lights at the mouth of Terminus Road and onto King Edward's Parade.

Forty-one miles per hour . . . forty-two . . . forty-five . . .

He swerved around a VW camper van reversing out from a parking bay onto the parade. He felt the back end of the truck fishtailing, but he worked the accelerator and it held its course.

The tournament road closures were up ahead. He was half a mile from the turning into Wilmington Square — five seconds further inland and he'd be on top of the event itself.

The road ahead was suddenly, strangely empty. He didn't know if this was happenstance, or if his activity had caused the evacuation of the seafront's regular footfall, either enforced or otherwise.

He zeroed in on the Wish Tower Slopes, immediately opposite Wilmington Square. The lawned mound inclined upwards to the Wish Tower itself, the moated fortress at the top of the hill. There was a network of neatly kept paths traversing the slopes, and a row of park benches lining the perimeter of the Wish Tower's moat wall. All seemed to be empty.

That would be his run-off. He would pick up speed as he dropped down onto the paved standing in front of the lifeboat museum, but he had made the largely unscientific calculation that the grass and the steep incline would arrest most of his momentum. And if it didn't, there was a bloody solid stone fort at the top of the hill.

He'd done enough. He was travelling at nearly seventy now.

He veered towards the drop-off, the engine howling, trying not to wrench it too hard for fear of flipping it. There was nobody at the foot of the slopes. He braced himself for the sudden lurch down towards the promenade, and prepared to relinquish control.

But then he was aware, just about, of a dark presence filling the right-hand side of his peripheral vision like a sudden raincloud — and then, a split-second later, a huge impact that smashed into the side of the car.

Then there was darkness, and silence.

* * *

There was a light rain falling. Barnes stood on the damp promenade, arms folded, and surveyed the wreckage inside the scene.

A square of blue cordon tape extended from the lower promenade railings up to the street and back around the lifeboat museum, and down past the hatched area that had once served as a launch slipway. Patrol vehicles flanked the cordon and a helicopter hovered ahead — Hotel-900 or Sky News, Barnes didn't know. He didn't look up. Traffic cars were positioned around the square, augmented by a forensic collision investigator who was measuring various points around the impact site.

The four-by-four was on its roof, wedged up against a row of spearmint-green beach huts. Glass had been vomited out across the concrete, with bits of bumper and bodywork ripped off and scattered across the ground, and a dark patch of some unidentified fluid leading from the point of impact to the fifty yards or so to where it had come to rest.

The second car in the convoy, a Vauxhall of some sort, had carried on going after the impact and headed up King Edward's Parade. It was found a short time later in a lay-by on the Beachy Head Road, completely burnt out.

By all accounts, there had been at least three people in the jeep. One was dead in the back seat. One had been flung out at the point of impact and was now lying in a crumpled heap on the concrete, covered by a shroud of thick black plastic.

One had been found about half a mile further east, having apparently decided to cut his losses somewhere around the pier.

The driver was the only survivor. Fire and paramedics had begun a painstakingly slow process to extract him from the mangled wreckage and get him onto a board.

Eventually he was hoisted up and onto a gurney, decorated with various accoutrements including an oxygen mask. He was wheeled carefully to the back of the ambulance.

Barnes walked slowly over and shouldered his way between two paramedics as they fussed over the casualty.

He stared down. The guy was groaning, his eyes open, roving around the sky.

"Hey," Barnes whispered, leaning forward, his arms still folded. "Hey, you."

The eyes continued to dart around like spotlights. Eventually they fixed on Barnes.

"Duquesne Kenley, as I live and breathe. You don't look like a terrorist."

"I wasn't . . . I wasn't going to . . ." he said, then grimaced in pain.

"A little risky, no?"

Kenley continued to grimace. "Did . . . did you . . ." The pain cut through the rest of his sentence.

Barnes gave a slight, almost imperceptible shake of the head. "We were too late. He's in the wind."

Kenley screwed his eyes shut — from the pain or the noise, Barnes wasn't sure.

"We put assets to it, but the bloody red tape slowed us down. Nothing like crossing a county border to add hours to your lead time. They rolled up on the intercept just as the 999 calls started coming in. Found a G4S sweat box on its side with one of the cargo missing. Seems they were jacked when they stopped for some fake roadworks. Those orange jackets again. Clever."

Kenley groaned.

"You're in trouble now, I guess? With Stratton Pearce in the wind?"

Kenley eyeballed him.

"I thought this —" Barnes waved a hand at the mess behind them — "was meant to be a parlour trick. A diversion. I didn't think you were actually going to go through with it."

"Nobody's . . . nobody's dead."

Barnes looked over at the pile of black plastic, and then back at Kenley. Kenley held his gaze.

"That's what you were trying to do? Take out members of your own gang? Or redivert just enough of them down here so the breakout couldn't possibly be successful?"

Despite the mask and the blood and the pain, Kenley managed to give Barnes a look that suggested he'd asked a stupid question.

Barnes reciprocated, and held up the exhibit bag with the piece of paper in it.

"Didn't work, did it? And you've just put him in the frame for killing a cop's wife."

He leaned over the gurney.

"*My* wife."

Kenley didn't speak.

"Where have they taken Pearce? Where?"

Kenley held Barnes's gaze.

"Is that why you killed Kevin Bridger?"

"Who?" Kenley managed, in a hiss.

"Where's Paul Gamble? Where's his body? Where's Brian Rose, the taxi driver that happened to be in the wrong place at the wrong time? Where's Roxana *Petrescu*?"

Something somewhere started to bleep urgently.

"I don't understand. You don't want to talk to me, but you gave yourself up. You told DC Morgan everything. Why?"

Kenley's eyes rolled up into his head, and the movements of the paramedics became urgent.

"Enough interrogation," one said. "We need to go."

Barnes looked at her, about to retort, but then recognised her as Tamsin, the same paramedic that had treated Kenneth Rix outside the slave farm all those months ago. Half a smile crossed his face; she held his eyes for a moment, then they shoved the gurney up into the ambulance.

Barnes stepped back from the activity and beckoned over a couple of uniformed constables.

"Get in there with him. Write down anything he says. And keep your wits about you — he's *persona non grata* with some very unpleasant people. I'll send a couple of DCs down to you asap."

"Yes, boss," one said, and they hopped up inside.

"Cosy," Tamsin said, as her oppo scrambled through to the cab and started the engine.

"Don't let him die, eh?" Barnes said.

Tamsin pulled the door shut, meeting Barnes's gaze again as she did so. Then the lights flared, the sirens howled, and they pulled out onto King Edward's Parade.

Barnes watched it go — suddenly thinking that his planned week in the Lake District might be altogether healthier should someone like Tamsin want to tag along — then walked over to the other ambulance. Kenneth Rix was — yet again — sitting on a similar gurney with a blanket around his shoulders, holding a bloodied compress to his face and generally looking even more forlorn than he usually did.

"I have the strangest feeling of déjà vu, Kenneth," Barnes said, pointing at the compress. "Mind telling me exactly what's gone down here?"

"You don't like me much, do you?"

"That doesn't really come into my job a whole lot."

Barnes looked back at the mashed-in front end of Kenneth's sorry-looking Honda. The forensic collision investigator was peering at it and making notes.

"How's your head?"

"My face hurts."

"You're lucky to be in one piece. What happened?"

"I don't really feel like answering any questions right now."

Kenneth looked at the ground. Barnes moved a little closer and bent down so their eyes were level.

"Did you know this was going down? Were you trying to stop him? Were you on *patrol*, Kenneth?"

Kenneth just shrugged.

Barnes straightened up. "Fair enough. But whether you just happened to pull out of the junction into the path of a speeding truck, or whether you drove at it deliberately to knock it off course . . . well, that assumes an awful lot more knowledge on your part than I gave you credit for."

Kenneth looked at him. Barnes jerked a thumb at the collision investigator.

"From their point of view, it's a triple fatal. I can't promise they're not going to put the handcuffs on you. But he was driving like a moron and, personally, I think the explanation that you were trying to stop him might actually be more in your favour. A Give Way sign is a Give Way sign, after all."

"Front seat," Kenneth said.

Barnes frowned at him.

"Front seat of my car," Kenneth said.

Barnes placed a hand on Kenneth's shoulder momentarily. The older man stared at him, then Barnes turned and walked back towards the Wish Tower. The collision investigator straightened up as he passed.

"Anything in the Honda?" Barnes said.

The collision investigator shrugged.

"Mainly junk. Camping gear in the back. Some paperwork in the front passenger footwell. Haven't looked at it yet."

Barnes peered into the car. The impact had pushed the bulkhead back into the interior of the car like an elephant sitting on the bonnet, but Barnes was still able to hook out a sheaf of dirty papers with his pen.

With gloved fingers he flicked through it. The handwriting was untidy, but the attention to detail was pretty tight. It appeared to be a transcript, and, by all accounts, one that itemised the inner workings of the Keber group's plans.

Barnes looked over at Kenneth, then back at the papers, and then shook his head, impressed. He and Kenneth had lots of catching up to do yet.

"Deliberate act?" he said. "CID want primacy?"

Barnes shrugged.

"Don't think so. Just a silly joyrider. His mates paid the price. No other casualties except Honda man. Think it's staying with you guys."

Barnes slid the paperwork into an evidence bag, then headed down to the promenade and leaned on the railings. He gazed out at the Channel, the horizon indiscernible in the evening haze, and thought about a long walk.

He looked back up the incline. Kenneth was still sitting on the gurney looking sorry for himself, but now he was flanked by two white-hatted traffic officers. One of them pulled out handcuffs. Barnes turned back to the sea.

He couldn't walk down towards the pier along the prom — there was a whacking great crime scene in the way — and so, after a while, he walked east around the monstrous glass-fronted Wish Tower café overhanging the promenade, in the direction of Holywell, the Sugar Loaf and Beachy Head, the June sun warm in the late afternoon.

There was a kiosk further along the promenade, and Barnes suddenly felt possessed by a need to buy a newspaper and a coffee. Maybe a croissant.

He tucked the paper under his arm and doubled back up the zig-zag ramp to the south-west face of the Wish Tower, marvelling at how one could walk around a corner made of stone and find people jogging, cycling, walking their dogs — blissfully unaware of the carnage not a hundred yards further up the promenade.

The dank stone of the Wish Tower was cool after the heat of sun, blood and engines still burning from the crime scene below. He walked up the multicoloured spiral staircase and found Kane still muttering into a phone.

Barnes sat down with the newspaper, pushing one of the coffee cups across the dusty worktop to Kane.

"You really joined up at a rum time, boss," Barnes said, unfolding the newspaper. "Cash-wise, the service is going to well and truly have the rug pulled from under it in the next six months or so. 'Squeeze' doesn't even come close to it."

"What will happen?" Kane said, looking up momentarily from the receiver.

Barnes shrugged.

"Redundancies, recruitment freeze, selling off the family china. Anything else is just nibbling around the edges. The difficulty comes when the bosses — and I include you in that, I'm afraid — give you the line about there being 'no loss to services' and somehow keep a straight face. Mind you, the new coalition government want to dissolve police authorities altogether and install commissioners. Maybe they'll have all the answers."

Kane hung up the phone.

"Well?" Barnes said, putting down the newspaper.

"Looks like the actual intercept happened on Kent's ground," Kane said. "Just outside Dartford. But the Mets are supporting with resources. Fake roadworks. Stolen low-loader T-boned the prison van onto its side, and the workmen broke him out. Dragged him off on foot, then made off in an ambulance. *That* was found torched in an industrial estate outside Ebbsfleet."

"So they went east," Barnes murmured. "How many in total?"

"Best guess, between four and six. One of them may have been female."

They exchanged glances.

"Witnesses?" Barnes asked.

"Well, they had the presence of mind to hit the van when the light was green. A queue of traffic at the roadworks, but most of them just wanted to hurry through before it went red. No CCTV. Nothing overlooking the estate where they switched up the ambo."

"Scene?"

"Nothing to speak of, or so I'm told. Maybe a footprint. Some impact damage from the low loader, but CSI says that won't tell you much."

"Of course it won't. Something that bold, in broad daylight, they planned it to leave nothing behind. They've got the money and resources to lie low off grid, maybe even to get over to Europe. It's going to be intelligence-led from hereon in. Let's hope someone wants to tell us something."

"What about down there?" Kane said, pointing through the barred window at the seafront below.

"By the sounds of it, it was all for nothing."

"What do you mean?"

Barnes held up the exhibit bag.

"The plot was disinformation from the off. But disinformation only. It was never meant to get as close to being as real as it got this afternoon. Kenley was trying to pull enough resources to it so the breakout plan would fail."

"Why?"

"He doesn't want Stratton Pearce at liberty any more than you or I do."

"Didn't work, though, did it?"

"Apparently not. And Roxana Petrescu won't be found if she doesn't want to be. According to this, her breakout was one big contingency drill — a means of testing her crew's loyalties and competence under pressure. Not only that, but she's very successfully spent several months manoeuvring herself into a position whereby she's been receiving a regular newsfeed from the investigators about the case against her crew."

Kane was silent for a moment.

"That's quite clever," he said eventually.

"Indeed," Barnes said. "In terms of how it's being investigated, I've already agreed with RPU that it's a couple of idiot joyriders showing off on the seafront. No mention of organised crime. Certainly not terrorism. When ACC Glover phones you wanting to know what's going on, I suggest you tell him the same. And the media."

"Fair enough."

"Where's Natalie Morgan?"

"I sent her home. Asked a colleague to come pick her up."

"Let's hope she goes straight there."

"What does our case actually look like, Barnes?"

"From the slave farm: one dead, four on remand — three now, with Pearce's escape. From today: two dead, four in custody, two arrested at an empty car showroom down on Highfield Link, and Duquesne Kenley in the hospital."

"You seem quite relaxed about that."

Barnes shrugged.

"As a case goes, it's better than I was expecting. We've broken even, I'd say."

"With a dead taxi driver, a dead informant and Stratton Pearce in the wind, along with Roxy Petrescu, the boss apparent. And a missing DS," Kane added.

"Paul Gamble is dead. We're just waiting for his body to turn up."

"Can you be so sure?"

Barnes didn't answer. Kane started shutting down machines and unplugging the equipment. Barnes placed a hand on his forearm.

"What are you doing, boss?"

"Shutting down the command centre before the rats chew through the cables."

"I'd be inclined to leave it."

"Oh?"

"Well, as you say, there's still at least six of them out there. Four we don't know, two we do — one of whom is Stratton Pearce. I'm only just getting started on trying to find him."

He sat down and opened the paper again.

"We've got a hell of a lot of work to do."

EPILOGUE

After three weeks in hospital, Duquesne "Duke" Kenley was finally discharged. The cost of the policing operation to place him under armed guard around the clock — both to keep him in custody and for his own protection — had caused more than a few sleepless nights in the various echelons of finance management.

Nobody came. No threats to his life. Not even a suggestion of hostile reconnaissance.

Natalie Morgan had visited twice. Barnes knew she had. She had tried — not very hard — to dress it up as an official visit. Barnes let it slide, and persuaded Marlon Choudhury to do the same. Choudhury had triangulated this decision with Kane, while simultaneously trying to persuade his mentee to shred his resignation letter.

Kenley was brought to Eastbourne custody centre, a purpose-built block at the end of the Hammonds Drive industrial estate, flanked by food wholesalers, industrial units and motor repair workshops — ten minutes' walk from the main patrol centre, a fact Barnes had never been able to understand. Beyond the rear of the building the land stretched out towards the Levels, the Lottbridge golf course and beyond. It was a tempting vista for anyone even briefly considering slipping free of their custodians as they sat in the hangars waiting for the metal shutters to come down and the detention corridor to be opened.

It was a weekday morning. The overnighters had been packed off to court, and the cell block was quiet. The custody sergeant, Stu Nippers, greeted the handcuffed Kenley and the four Local Support Team officers that flanked him like old friends. Like he'd been expecting them — which, of course, he had been.

The custody sergeant went through the risk assessment, detention reasons and other administration, before sending Kenley off to one of the side rooms to be processed, where he was photographed and had his fingerprints and DNA taken by one of the custody assistants.

When they reconvened at the bridge, an elevated platform housed within a large, whitewashed atrium that acted as the nerve centre of the cell block, Nippers nodded at one of the LST officers to remove Kenley's handcuffs, and then frowned at the paperwork in front of him.

"What did you say your name was?" he asked.

"Duquesne Kenley," Kenley answered in a monotone.

"Quite a few aliases coming up on your file print now we've done your dibs and dabs," Nippers said. "Including: Henry Swift, Michael Quayle, Duquesne Kenley, Chris Peake, Neil Devine, plus a few more."

Nippers shuffled the papers and eyeballed Kenley over his glasses.

"Says here your file name is Blackwater, though. Ben Blackwater."

"That's me, I guess."

"Anything else you want to tell me?" Nippers said.

"Yeah," Kenley replied, looking at his feet. "I'm ready to talk."

THE END

THE JOFFE BOOKS STORY

We began in 2014 when Jasper agreed to publish his mum's much-rejected romance novel and it became a bestseller.

Since then we've grown into the largest independent publisher in the UK. We're extremely proud to publish some of the very best writers in the world, including Joy Ellis, Faith Martin, Caro Ramsay, Helen Forrester, Simon Brett and Robert Goddard. Everyone at Joffe Books loves reading and we never forget that it all begins with the magic of an author telling a story.

We are proud to publish talented first-time authors, as well as established writers whose books we love introducing to a new generation of readers.

We have been shortlisted for Independent Publisher of the Year at the British Book Awards three times, in 2020, 2021 and 2022, and for the Diversity and Inclusivity Award at the Independent Publishing Awards in 2022.

We built this company with your help, and we love to hear from you, so please email us about absolutely anything bookish at feedback@joffebooks.com

If you want to receive free books every Friday and hear about all our new releases, join our mailing list: www.joffebooks.com/contact

And when you tell your friends about us, just remember: it's pronounced Joffe as in coffee or toffee!

9 781804 058732